DREAM
&
PRETENSE

The Ramseys
"A Lover's Dream" & "A Lover's Pretense"

Includes Short Story "Lover's Muse: An Interlude"

BY
ALTONYA
WASHINGTON

DREAM & PRETENSE: THE RAMSEYS
Copyright 2014 By AlTonya Washington

ISBN: 9780989145589

Cover By Carrie Enders
Cover Artwork From Istockphoto.com
Printed In The USA By CreateSpace LLC

This book is dedicated to the best fans in the world:
The Romance Readers!

A
LOVER'S
DREAM
The Ramseys Book I

A LOVER'S DREAM

~PROLOGUE~

Savannah, Georgia 1989

Quest Ramsey's gray stare darkened to black as it often did whenever he suffered a bout of frustration. That night, a hotel room door was at the root of his foul mood. He muttered a sharp curse and tried again to push open the door that stubbornly refused to give. Following a few firm nudges from his shoulder, the door opened just a crack. Quest's mouth twisted into a grimace then. Given the circumstances, a hotel room door that would not open most often meant there was either a drunken body or a couple of lovers passed out before it.

Quest rolled his eyes and braced his shoulder next to the mahogany door once again. Using a bit more of his considerable strength, he was able to force the door open a tad wider. The obstruction, whatever it was, moved aside just slightly and Quest managed to angle his six-foot plus frame inside the room.

It didn't take long to solve the mystery of the blocked door. A tall, potted fern tree had been knocked to the floor, creating the impediment. Another curse passed Quest's lips when he noticed the tree's cracked porcelain planter and the dirt spilling from it. The white, furry carpeting was now thoroughly black and marked by shoe prints of the numerous party guests.

Moving on, Quest continued his inspection of the room. Aside from the broken planter and spilled dirt, there seemed to be no other cause for alarm. The spacious eleventh-floor suite of the Forman Hotel was littered with plastic cups, beer bottles and soiled ashtrays- the usual. Food wrappers filled the wastebaskets and cluttered around the base. Quest's long lashes fluttered in relief as his inspection turned up no signs of holes in the walls or light fixtures that were torn from their places.

"Better than usual," Quest noted sourly, acknowledging the fact that the 'usual' usually consisted of far worse and far more costly mishaps. In truth, a party given by Quaysar Ramsey most often resulted in an unfortunate hotel staff member preparing for months of renovating.

"Where the hell is that fool?" Quest inquired of the empty room, his deep-set gaze scanning the area for any sign of his brother. The place appeared deserted: there wasn't even music playing. Still, something told Quest there was more to see.

"Damn it, Quay!" he bellowed, his expression turning fierce when he'd moved on and discovered the state of the living room. It wasn't the food ground into the floor, or even the wine-splattered and overturned sofa and armchairs that had elicited his outburst. Instead, Quest's eyes, now a bottomless black, were focused on the balcony door with the glass shattered from its panes as they barely clung to their hinges.

Quest approached the massacred doors. Shaking his head, he winced at every sound of crunching glass beneath his Adidas. Quest stood surveying the damage, unable to form even one curse or admonishment toward his brother who had gone so far as to get down on his knees while swearing to him that nothing like this would happen.

Quest wondered what the punishment would be to Quay, or to himself for that matter. After all, he'd allowed his twin to talk him into booking the hotel in his name. Their parents, Damon and

Catrina, had all but told Quay that his next screwup would result in time away from home.

Needless to say, Quest and Quaysar were more than a little fearful of what that threat would entail. Quest blinked then, bringing himself back into the present. Loud voices and what sounded like screams beckoned his attention below. Slowly, he crossed the balcony and inched forward to peer over the dented rail. *How the hell did those fools dent an iron ledge?* he wondered.

Quest wouldn't have time to ponder that little item, as his eyes and attention were now focused below. Horror and fascination emerged on his handsome dark face as he realized the cause for the raised voices and commotion below. He watched a growing crowd gather around the nude body of a woman on the sidewalk. Even from a distance, he could see the crimson pooling around her body. He knew she had come from the ledge, the ledge from the room in *his* name. Stunned by the sight and dizzy from the questions racing through his mind, he backed away from the rail.

As he turned toward the room again, his eyes began to survey the suite with fresh intensity. His feet felt as though they were attached to hundred-pound weights as he retraced his steps. Soon, he was in the master bedroom.

"Quay?" Quest called out, seeing his brother lying in the center of a massive four-poster bed. Absently, he noted his twin was naked with only a sheet barely covering his privates.

Quest didn't bother to call out to Quaysar again. He'd spotted the empty gin bottle cradled in the crook of his brother's arm and knew he had passed out. The bed gave as Quest lost what strength was left in his legs and had to sit on the ledge. Completely dazed, he stared unseeingly past the bedroom door. He could still hear the screaming.

A LOVER'S DREAM

~ONE~

Chicago, Illinois, May 2006

Driggers Morgan's kind, handsome face possessed a look of fatherly concern as he studied the lovely young woman who sat behind the desk in her study. With her legs propped on the polished oak and her dark brown face partly hidden behind a thick hardback, she seemed relaxed enough. Driggers, however, knew the young woman very well. A smile pulled at the corners of his mouth.

"Whose heart have you broken this time?" he questioned casually.

Michaela Sellars smiled, easily recognizing the intense curiosity mingled within the nonchalant tone she was accustomed to hearing in Driggers's voice. "No one's," she replied in a whimsical manner.

Driggers nodded at the singsong response and pushed his solid frame from the doorjamb. "You know I don't believe that," he said.

Mick pulled her amber gaze from the page she'd been reading and fixed the observant sixty-something man with a look of phony outrage.

Driggers tilted his head to one side as though trying to get a bead on what held her attention so reverently. "Just as I thought," he announced finally, "the Cowans. You only read that story when you're debating or trying to forget some young man," he surmised.

Mick shrugged and set the book aside. "Well, I'll have you know that I'm not trying to do either. I just happened to pick up the book, that's all."

"Mmm-hmm," Driggers rebutted, then laughed when he picked up the book to inspect it more closely. "You must be preoccupied with something, so spill it," he ordered politely while thumbing through the crisp pages.

Mick moved her legs from the desk and propped her feet on the seat of her chair. "There's nothing to it, I promise," she said, bracing her elbows on her knees and setting her chin in her palms. "I was looking for something else and I just happened across the book," she explained further.

"I see," Driggers sighed in obvious disbelief. "And I supposed the fact that you turned right to the section on Blue and Esther has no real significance?" he asked, referring to the patriarch and matriarch of the Cowan family.

Mick's lashes fluttered and she wriggled her fingers about her lovely, round face. "Blue and Esther's story is the most prophetic section of the book in my opinion."

"Prophetic, huh?" Driggers perched his still-agile frame on the edge of the desk.

"What Esther gave up to be with Blue," Mick pondered, resting her head back against the tall, lavender desk chair. "I could never choose a man over my family."

"Hmph. Spoken like a woman who's never been in love," Driggers mused.

Mick took no offense. "Spoken like a woman who's never had a family," she countered softly, her sparkling stare turning solemn.

Driggers frowned then, not caring one bit for the look on her face. "You should never feel alone. You know that."

Mick realized how her words may have sounded to the man

she'd looked upon as a father for the better part of seven years. She'd known Driggers since hiring him as her houseman. Then, he'd seemed as desperate for some semblance to family as she'd always been. Over the years, they had crafted a relationship that Mick wouldn't have traded for anything. Standing then, she rounded the desk and pulled Driggers into a hug. "I'll never feel alone as long as I have you," she whispered and pressed a kiss to his cheek.

~~~

Hard, driving rhythms from a vintage Miami Bass CD filled the air surrounding Michaela's stately fifteen-acre back lawn. The perfectly manicured landscape was dotted with twenty-one women between the ages of eighteen and twenty-one, plus one thirty-two year old. The perfectly toned ladies moved in sync to the affecting music as they rehearsed another excruciating albeit dazzling routine.

Michaela, who carried the crown as the oldest dancer on the lawn, didn't miss a step. She grooved with as much energy and sensuality as the girls who were at least ten years her junior. Of course, the fact that her skills were near perfect was no surprise. After all, she had choreographed the eye-catching routine, a routine that was at least fifteen grueling minutes in length. When it ended, everyone- with the exception of Michaela- fell to the ground in an exhausted state.

Mick stood in the center of the collapsed heap and clapped. "Outstanding, ladies!" she cheered while laughing at the girls' agonizing responses. "Oh come on, congratulate yourselves for making it through another routine!" she urged, her laughter gaining volume when the girls complained in earnest.

It was all in fun. Michaela had taken to choreographing routines for the dancers of Wiley State's marching band four years ago after being granted the opportunity to perform with the alumni band of her alma mater during one of its televised homecoming games. Since then, the twenty-member dance troupe had been criticized, raved over, drooled over for their exquisite racy numbers during the band's halftime shows.

"All right people, you know the deal! I've got ten full baths, so you better hustle if you want to be in the first group to wash off that grime!" Mick's laughter resurfaced as she watched the girls scramble to their feet in unison and race for the showers-literally.

Mick followed, strolling toward the brick patio while ruffling the riot of thick blue-black curls that framed her face like an onyx cloud. A slight frown wrinkled her brow as she focused in on a woman heading toward her. After a moment, Mick's frown cleared and she broke into a grin while waving toward her publisher.

Contessa "County" Warren shook her head while approaching her best friend and associate. Her long lashes fluttered like hummingbird wings when she rolled her eyes and cast a tired glance across her shoulder. "Why you prefer to kill yourself bouncing around with these teenyboppers when you could have a workout in a stylish gym with mature women and mature conversation is beyond me," she criticized.

Mick halted her steps and tapped one finger across her full lips. Her stirring amber gaze narrowed while the delightful mole at the corner of her mouth twitched when she smiled in concentration. "Hmm...a stylish gym, with mature women no less. Ones who can't quite decide whether to get the liposuction or Botox injection next. Yeah, County, I sure do wish I could be in on such stimulating conversations."

County waved off the sarcastic remarks as though they were annoying flies. "I still question this obsession of yours, Mick. Hell, you could've joined the dance troupe at Wiley when we were students. That's what *normal* folks did," she pointed out with a look of challenge appearing in her almond shaped deep brown eyes.

Mick nodded, conceding to the truth in the dig. "Need I remind you how improbable it was that I would've been chosen back then?"

"And need I remind *you* that you've always had that

body?" County retorted, her eyes raking Michaela's figure for emphasis. "You only needed to learn how to work it, and the best way to learn that ain't taught on the field."

"Here we go," Mick groaned, knowing they were about to embark upon Contessa's favorite subject: sex.

"Of course," County said, tilting back her head as she focused on something in the distance. "Well…I guess the field could've been used as a training ground. Goodness knows I-"

"County! Please spare me another story about your sex life. It's too damn early in the morning."

County burst into a bout of rich laughter. "Baby, it's never too early for sex. You'd know that if you were getting any," she taunted, speaking the last few words in Mick's ear as she brushed past her.

Mick took the blow, then bowed her head and prayed for patience. "Are you here just to ridicule and harass me, Count? I mean, I know it's one of the things that give you the greatest pleasure. How'd you get into my house anyway?" She ranted.

Pushing one hand into the back pocket of the flare-legged jeans that molded to the generous expanse of her derriere, County stood taking in the beautiful view of the grand lawn. "Driggers let me in. And yes, I do love to ridicule and harass you, but this morning I'm here to conduct real-life, actual business," she announced, turning to pin Mick with a haughty glare.

"Bull," Mick whispered, the sparkling quality of her gaze giving her eyes the look of some exotic tigress. Though Contessa Warren was a great success and handled her business in a diligent, almost reverent manner, the woman was not known for rising before 11:00AM- not for business anyway. "The only thing you wake up for at the crack of dawn is a quickie," Mick pointed out bluntly.

County responded with a seductive smile and a naughty wink. "I don't do quickies, love," she informed her friend, giggling when Mick pretended to gag. "I'm here so early because this was too good to wait 'til later."

Mick folded her arms across the front of the figure-forming

white bra top she wore. "So spill it," she ordered.

"I took a chance and went after something. I figured I was wasting my time, but it paid off."

Mick only shrugged.

County shook her head and began to rummage through the denim canvas bag she carried. She tugged her bottom lip between her teeth upon locating a magazine, which she thrust into Mick's hands.

Mick frowned at the page County pointed to. She scanned what looked to be an advertisement. "The Ramsey Group?" She inquired, her frown deepening when County beamed. "Am I supposed to magically know what this is about?"

County grimaced and snatched the magazine from Mick's hand. "I was in Sam's office the other day and-"

"Sam?" Mick interjected, recognizing the name of County's realtor. "You know, if he was a real friend, he'd be advising you to stop pouring so much money into these ventures."

"Well, he's not a friend, he's a realtor and he's about makin' money," County threw back before waving one hand in the air. "Look, that's not what this is about. I happened across this advertisement while I was at Sam's. This group not only sells homes-homes that start, but the way, in the low eight hundreds. *Thousands*, that is," she clarified with two winks. "They also build homes and own the property. In fact, they own several upscale communities throughout Washington State, California and the Midwest." County shrugged and perused the advertisement again. "I admit that I was at first interested in finding out about an investment. I mentioned it to Sam and we discussed the group. Let me tell you," she said, fixing Michaela with a stern look, "by the end of that discussion, I'd forgotten about investing."

Again, Mick shrugged.

County smiled. "The Ramseys are African American."

Mick's eyes trailed to the advertisement. "Never heard of 'em," she retorted though she was subtly intrigued.

County nodded and began to stroll back toward the house, grinning when Mick fell in step next to her. "They're out of

Seattle, Washington and they've become giants in the real estate business. *Silent* giants. Your cup of tea," she slanted a glance toward Mick.

It was true, Michaela admitted silently. She had made a household name for herself following her debut release, which chronicled the rise, fall and re-creation of the Shelanon family of Medora, North Dakota. The Shelanons were relatively unknown in much of the country, as well as in the black community. Mick brought the phenomenal African American clan into the public eye. The family had staked a claim and made their fortune in a state most African Americans never believed they'd set foot in. The book was a smash, and following that, Michaela had obtained unimagined popularity. As a result, many families worth having their histories recorded wanted Mick to record it.

True, she had her share of well-known families who wanted to tell their stories. Michaela, however, was more interested in digging out the stories of those who didn't make the who's who lists regularly. She gravitated more toward those families who'd obtained real success while managing to remain out of the spotlight. These were the people Mick wanted to research, and they practically clamored for the opportunity to talk with her. Of course, this wasn't surprising. Michaela Sellars was known for her ability to coax the choicest bits of information from her subjects. Her unsettling yet entrancing amber gaze drew people in to such an extent they recited their life's history without ever realizing they were being interviewed. Still, in spite of her curvaceous figure, flawless dark chocolate skin, captivating eyes, and the unruly halo of thick midnight curls, Mick had never considered herself a drop-dead beauty. She felt she was too short, too curvy. Her attributes oftentimes had her waiting too long for a man to tear his eyes away from her chest. She thought her nose was too small, as its size only emphasized the fullness of her mouth. Her completely sensual appearance encased a completely intellectual personality. When it came to her work, she attacked it in a doggish fashion. And she attacked her play in the same manner. She was a woman who enjoyed her success, due in no small part to her upbringing. She'd lived a rough life as a foster child, but managed to secure a good education and made the most of it. Michaela was the first to point out that she led a good life. She had every material possession a woman could wish for. She had everything except what she wanted most: a family of her own and all the love that accompanied it.

"So anyway, I sent a proposal to Ramsey Group's administrative director and asked for the story," County rambled on.

Mick's face reflected stunned amazement, but she knew it would've been unreasonable to expect anything less from her best friend. Contessa Warren had earned her nickname, the Count, more for being take charge in business than because it was an apt shortening of her first name. County's motto was: if they don't know you, introduce yourself.

"I sent the proposal on Wednesday, got a response the following Tuesday," she boasted, her rich brown gaze pride-filled. "I spoke with the admin director at the headquarters personally," she added.

"Now I'm suspicious," Mick muttered, hooking a thumb through one of the belt loops on the hip-hugging black shorts she sported. "How could a simple proposal generate such an interest?"

County gasped. "I do believe I'm offended," she said pouting.

Mick rolled her eyes. "This is a powerful family, Count. They've remained out of the spotlight way too long to be taken in by a proposal from a Midwest publishing firm. No matter how impressive it is," she added quickly for County's benefit.

"You shouldn't be so hard on yourself, Mick."

"Huh?"

"*You* were the proposal."

"What the hell are you talking about?" Mick demanded. Now both thumbs were hooked in the belt loops.

County shrugged. "I based the proposal only on you and your work."

"You what?"

"Oh come on, Mick," County snapped, fixing her friend

with a weary glare. "The modesty is wearing thin right about now. Your reputation precedes you. Businesspeople love stories about other businesspeople. The rags-to-riches story will always be popular. You should toot your own horn a lot more, damn it. But if you won't, then I guess I have to."

Mick folded her arms across her chest and decided it would be pointless to argue. County had always been her biggest fan, ever since she'd read Mick's first short story. County, a business major in college, always aspired to become an entrepreneur. Still, an actual business venture had eluded her. That all changed when she discovered Mick's talents. She decided to become a publisher, and a fine one at that.

"Just accept the fact that my long shot paid off. The gods want to meet you."

Mick scratched her head. "Uh, don't you mean the gods are smiling on me?"

"Uh-uh," County retorted, with a wave of her bejeweled right hand, "it was no slip of the tongue. Ramsey Group's admin director is a woman. When I asked who from the family we'd be speaking with, she said we'd be speaking with the gods themselves. Of course, I was stunned, but she assured me it was no exaggeration. The brothers were aware of the name and didn't mind hearing it used."

"The brothers?" Mick asked.

County stopped just short of the patio. "Quest and Quaysar Ramsey run the whole shebang. Jasmine Hughes, the admin director, swears the whole family is filled with incredible looking men, but those two head the real estate company. They rarely meet with *anyone* outside the business. I guess they save all that for their executive staff."

"And they're called *gods* because of all this power they've acquired?" Mick asked, though she had a feeling she already knew the answer.

"They're called gods because that's what they look like. Two chocolate dipped sexy twins."

Suddenly, Mick burst into a fit of laughter. "You are not

tellin' me this admin director was that candid with a total stranger regarding her employers?"

County shrugged. "From what she says, the vast majority of the employees would love to see a book done on their bosses. They believe the guys should be recognized for all they've done. Especially when most people believe Ramsey is run by white folks."

"Mmm, and how do the twins feel about that?"

County gave a quick toss of her heavy ponytail. "From what I gather, they don't mind it so long as *they* rake in the cash."

Mick was still eyeing her publisher with unmasked suspicion. "I don't know, County, what-"

"Wait. Just wait a minute," County urged, taking the first brick step up the patio. "Just save your questions for the meeting."

"Meeting?"

"Mmm-hmm, day after tomorrow in Seattle. It's all set."

Mick tilted her head to one side. "You accepted a meeting without knowing if I'd go along or not?"

"Oh please, you can't possibly pass up this chance," County decided, rolling her eyes toward the blue sky above before bringing them back to Mick's face. "Besides," she sighed, leaning close. "Don't you want to see what they look like?" She taunted, then turned and continued on toward the house.

~~~

That evening, Mick settled down with the file County left on the Ramseys. *No pictures*, she noted. Clearly, the entire family was camera shy- at least for the public. Of course, Mick could very well understand. Instead, the file was packed with several news articles and other material on the family. The Ramseys were the cream of the crop in Seattle, not only within the black community, but in Seattle as a whole. Mick studied the folder intently, never realizing how intrigued she was becoming. As she scowled at the clips, however, a frown began to mar her soft brow. Every article shed a favorable light on the clan. There was abundant coverage of charity events, school programs, hospital dedications, and other choice bits of information.

"Where's the dirt?" Mick whispered, leafing through the clips, certain there had to be more.

She reached for the white cordless phone on her nightstand, prepared to dial County's number. But she hesitated just as her fingers brushed the receiver. Maybe there wasn't more, she considered. Perhaps County was right, she thought. Perhaps she *was* too cynical- too suspicious of people and their motives. Maybe her upbringing had jaded her. The possibility was something she'd always tried to deny, but as she grew older, especially lately, it had begun to nag at her more and more. Mick dismissed the notion with a quick shake of her head. Her grip tightened on the receiver and she proceeded to dial County's number.

~~~

Seattle, Washington

Quaysar Ramsey's long brows drew close as the easy expression he usually wore grew fierce with frustration. "Damn it, Q, the author is coming from halfway across the country."

Quest Ramsey didn't bother to make eye contact with his brother. "Do I need to tell you how little I care or can you sense it?" he inquired calmly, while casually thumbing through the report he studied.

"Don't you even care a little that someone actually finds our family interesting enough that we merit a book?" Quaysar asked, bracing both hands against the round conference table with blatant challenge in his dark eyes.

Quest's blank look spoke volumes to Quaysar, who muttered a curse and turned away.

"Well, what are gonna tell 'em when they get here?" Quaysar asked, suddenly remembering the author would be there at ten o'clock the next morning.

Again, Quest was enthralled by the report he read. "We...we won't tell 'em a thing. You were the one who couldn't wait to get them here, so you'll be the one to tell them they came here for nothing."

"You're full of crap, you know that, right?" Quaysar raged, slipping both hands inside the deep pockets of his hunter-green trousers. "This could be good for us, you know that?"

Quest sighed, dropping the report to the table. Quaysar was still spouting arguments while his brother literally walked out on their conversation.

~~~

County mimicked the impatient tapping of one sandal-shod foot by tapping her fingers along the glossy finish of the cherry-wood front desk. "Will you stop nagging me about this?" she practically growled, flashing a stern glare to her right.

Mick, the recipient of that look, reacted with a stern glare of her own. "Hmm...I'm nagging *you* for information on a book that *you* want *me* to write? Do you see any logic in that, Count?"

County rolled her eyes to study the line of chandeliers gracing the hotel's high ceiling. "Why do I even try with you?" she sighed while signing for the room keys.

Mick rolled her eyes and took a minute to study her surroundings as well. The hotel was to die for, elegantly yet comfortably furnished. The cherry-wood paneling of the lobby simply emphasized the rich color and craftsmanship of the butter-soft leather sofas and armchairs. The establishment shrieked of exquisite tastes and accommodations. Mick silently toyed with the notion of tacking on a few more days to her stay. She deserved to treat herself to a more lengthy getaway in such a fabulous place.

"There," County announced, accepting the room keys from the desk attendant. "Now," she turned to drop the card in Mick's palm. "What?" She groaned, when she saw the pointed look on the other woman's face.

"The file."

"Damn it, Mick," County whispered, her lashes fluttering as she bowed her head, "I swear you are the most-"

"Hold it. Just stop a minute," Mick urged, raising her hand for emphasis. "Now even *you* have to admit that no family is as syrupy sweet as that file made the Ramseys out to be. Hell, even the Shelanons had skeletons in their closets."

"Boy, did they!" County acknowledged, tapping one long spiced-polished nail on her cheek as she recalled the family. "But in defense of that file, Mick, it was a *promotional* packet. I mean, you really didn't expect them to place all their dirty little secrets in there all nice and neat, did you?"

Mick folded her arms across the yellow lace-neck T-shirt she sported. "Now who's being sarcastic?"

County patted Mick's cheek. "You're growing on me."

Still, Mick was determined to hear County admit that she wasn't being suspicious or overly cynical. "Families like this always have something to hide," she insisted as they took the elevator to their respective rooms.

"Well, that's why you're the journalist, girl. Dig, dig, dig," County advised in a merry tone. "Besides, you'll have plenty of time to grill your sources tomorrow and I won't even be there to kick you under the table when you ask how many people they've murdered."

Mick stood still before the elevator as the doors closed softly behind her. "What do you mean, you won't be there?"

County was already unlocking her door. "They want to meet you alone."

"Why?"

County shrugged, heading inside the room to check that her bags had been correctly delivered. "That photo I sent must have done the job," she surmised absently.

"I don't like it," Mick decided, pushing the room door closed.

County tossed her card key to the message desk. "Neither do I," she perched her curvy frame against the edge of the sofa. "From what I hear, those two are a sight to behold. I hate like hell that I can't be there to see for myself."

"How you ever managed to get this far ahead in business with such a one-track mind, still amazes me."

County took no offense. "Me too," she admitted slyly.

"Still, I can easily get over it in a place like this. Really classy of the Ramseys to put us up in one of Seattle's finest hotels, and I'm damn well gonna enjoy."

Mick, however, wasn't so in awe, as her suspicions still ran high. "Why didn't they tell us beforehand that they only wanted to meet with me?"

"Uggh!" County bellowed, slapping both hands to her navy blue crop pants as she stood. "That's it," she said in a defeated tone and took Mick by the elbow. Promptly escorting her best friend from the room, County dismissed Mick by slamming the door in her face.

A LOVER'S DREAM

~TWO~

Mick was awakened by the ringing phone on her nightstand some fifteen minutes before her alarm was set to go off. With a grunt, she pushed a hoard of blue-black curls from her face and figured she had County to thank for the wake-up call. When she pressed the phone to her ear, she realized it was a bit more than an average wake-up call.

"Ms. Sellars?"

"Yes, thank you."

"Ms. Sellars, this is the front desk letting you know that the car has arrived and is waiting to carry you to Ramsey Group headquarters."

Mick rubbed the sleep from her eyes. "The-the car?" she stammered.

"That's correct, ma'am."

Grimacing at the concierge's polite, matter-of-fact tone, Mick sat up in bed. "I'm just waking up. The car may be waiting a while."

"That's quite alright, ma'am. It will be here when you're

ready."

Mick only nodded.

"Will there be anything else, ma'am?"

"No, no, thank you," Mick said and set the receiver back in its cradle. She flopped back to the luxurious bed and took a moment to get her bearings. A wicked smile curved her lips as she imagined how peeved County would be when she discovered 'a car' had been sent for her. "Tee hee", she sighed before rolling her eyes and leaving the bed.

~~~

Later that morning, Mick stood with her head back and her eyes wide. Her mouth formed a perfect O as she studied the unbelievable complex of Ramsey Group.

"This is the private entrance. Past those double glass doors, you'll find someone waiting to carry you up."

Mick barely nodded in response to the driver's instructions. Her hand rested limp in his palm. "Oh boy," she breathed.

Gerald, the driver, nodding in understanding. "Yes, it's quite a place," he agreed, smiling as he too surveyed the impressive outlay of the corporation.

Instead of one stark high-rise, the Ramsey Group offices were situated in separate buildings that spanned the landscape. Each building housed a different area for every sort of project. The structures covered a vast expanse of the 120-acre site. Due to the hilliness of the area, the buildings were constructed at an angle. Steel beams covered the roofing of the dark brick buildings that had an unexpected airiness due mainly to the floor-to-ceiling windows that offered a prime view of the architects, designers, and other staff who worked diligently on the next Ramsey project. Mick could imagine the golden light from the interior cascading on the green surroundings during the evening hours. Her attention was drawn to the one skyscraper that towered above the other buildings. Windows were abundant on the lower floors, but tapered off and became virtually nonexistent near the top levels. Something told her the Ramseys' offices would be there- clearly they adored their privacy.

"This is some place," Gerald was saying as he guided Mick away from the Mercedes limo and shut the door behind her. "But these people really know how to make a person feel cared for."

"Thanks Gerald," Mick said, taking a deep breath while fixing him with a sweet smile. She gave his hand a reassuring squeeze before heading toward the double doors.

Gerald's stare was lingering as he admired Mick's unconsciously provocative stride.

Mick smoothed her hands across the lilac silk suit she wore and focused on the double glass doors in front of her. Her suit, with its plunging V-neckline and row of tiny buttons along the front, was coordinated with a matching above-the-knee flippy skirt that emphasized the shapeliness of her legs. The outfit was both alluring and businesslike. She looked great, but prayed she wouldn't fall flat on her face. Literally.

Past the double doors, there stood a tall young woman with a cafe au lait complexion and huge dark eyes. She would have looked severe had it not been for the warmth in her gaze and smile.

"Ms. Sellars," she greeted, stepping forward with an outstretched hand, "so glad you could make it."

"Quite a place you have here," Mick noted, as she surveyed her surroundings with an unabashed eye.

"Indeed," the woman agreed with a chuckle. "I'm Jasmine Hughes, administrative director for Ramsey Group."

Mick nodded. "Nice to meet you."

"I apologize for the cloak-and-dagger feel to the meeting, but the guys want to keep the staff and the rest of the family out of this for the time being."

"I understand," Mick assured her, then fixed Jasmine with a sly smile. "The *guys*, don't you mean, the *gods*?"

Jasmine laughed then, her cheeks darkening a bit as she grew flushed. "I see you've been talking to your publisher."

"Mmm, and she really enjoyed your conversation."

Jasmine was shaking her head. "She really has a way of coaxing information out of people."

Mick leaned close. "Don't tell her I said so, but she's even better at it than I am."

"Well nothing I said was an exaggeration, I promise you," Jasmine said, while pushing her hands into the pockets of her lime-green pantsuit. "The guys are cool, but you'll see that for yourself."

Mick's smile disappeared.. "Uh-Jasmine?"

She turned. "Yes?"

Mick saw the expectant look in the woman's eyes and prayed she wouldn't offend her. "I don't know how much Contessa told you about my work, but I don't write entertainment pieces. I dig deep for my stories, and if the *gods* believe the other is the sort of work I do, I'm afraid they'll be very disappointed."

Jasmine didn't appear the least bit offended as she nodded in understanding. "Quiet as kept, but I'm very familiar with your work, Ms. Sellars. It's one of the reasons I was so excited about the guys speaking with you. Many are eager for the story and many are against it, and unless one person in particular changes his mind, this book may never be written."

Before Mick could question the foreboding statement, Jasmine was waving her hands in the air.

"Here we are," she announced when they approached a lone elevator. "This will take you straight up to the office," she said as Mick stepped inside the car. "Good luck," she added just before the doors closed.

Inside the walnut-paneled car, Mick closed her eyes. She was unused to feeling on edge about anything or *anyone*.

"Calm down, Mick," she told herself, "you're about to meet with the gods."

~~~

The elevator's dark pine doors opened with a quiet *swoosh* and Mick took a moment to step out. Her stylish open-toed wedge heels sank into a thick black carpet. The area was bathed in dim lighting and was only partially illuminated by the calming glow that radiated from at least four gargantuan aquariums spaced throughout the room.

The sound of the central air-conditioning combined with the aquarium's ventilators provided a soothing hum that enhanced the mellow ambience of the office.

"Hello?" she called out, her voice sounding soft and melodic in the quiet atmosphere.

There was no answer, but Mick barely noticed as she was already strolling toward the bay of miniature landscapes in one corner. There were at least four of the shellacked oak boxes that reached her waist. The models were obvious replicas of Ramsey Group constructions. Mick studied each one, growing entranced by the detail put into each display.

A gasp slipped past her mouth when she discovered a massive world map that partially filled the opposite wall. It too was lit by dim spotlights and seemed to notate every location of a Ramsey Group office, residential or commercial development, or work in progress.

Mick felt that overwhelming feeling fill her chest again. "Oh boy," she breathed.

~~~

Quaysar Ramsey smiled hearing the sharp intake of breath to his right. "Somethin' else, huh?" he noted in response to his brother's reaction. From the shadows, they quietly observed Michaela Sellars entering their domain.

"Jesus," Quest's arresting stare darkened to black as he studied the curvy petite who threatened to make his heart seize in tandem with the clench of his stomach.

"Even better than her picture and her picture was amazing..." One arm folded over his chest, the other bent to allow Quay to rest his chin to his palm as he enjoyed the view. "Care to join me now?" he prompted his twin.

Quest declined with a slow shake of his head and retreated. "Let her down easy," was all he said.

Quay grinned, clapped his brother's shoulder. "I always

do," he playfully boasted and then fixed his brother with a curious smile. "You alright, man?"

The sly query prompted Quest to jab Quay with an elbow before leaving him to meet with their guest. Quay chuckled devilishly as he set out.

~~~

"Ms. Sellars?"

Michaela whirled around when the canyon-deep voice reached her ears. She blinked, her amber stare narrowing.

"Yes?" she inquired softly, though she found no one in the vicinity.

"Sorry to keep you waiting," the voice said, though it seemed to be gaining volume as if its owner was drawing near.

"No it-it's quite alright," Mick whispered, the natural arch of her brows lifting a bit as she waited. At last, she was able to just make out a figure in the distance. The more the form gained definition, the wider her eyes became.

The man who came into view then, forced a soft sound from her throat. Her lips parted, giving her an expression of complete amazement.

"Quaysar Ramsey," he introduced while extending his hand to shake.

Mick's reaction was delayed as she was struck by the man who stood before her. She remembered rolling her eyes and regarding all the accolades about the Ramsey men as fantastic musings by sex-crazed women. Now, she could see that the label 'gods' fit this man and quite probably his brother to a tee.

Mick had never considered herself to be a short woman. She wasn't some leggy model type of course, but she did have *some* height on her. Sadly, that height seemed miniscule while she stood before this male who had to be at least six and a half feet tall. His eyes were a bottomless black, set beneath long, straight sleek brows, close-cut hair, long distinctive nose and the mouth-

Mick shook her head, commanding her attention to

business. "Sorry," she whispered, accepting his hand to shake. "Michaela Sellars," she added, then grimaced at remembering he'd already spoken her name.

Quaysar grinned and only grew more gorgeous, if that were possible. His teeth were brilliantly white and even, making the single dimple and cleft in his chin more striking.

"Yes," he acknowledged her uneasy introduction as though he was accustomed to such reactions toward him. He covered her hand with his other and gently guided her into the depths of the office. "Have a seat," he urged softly, when they approached mocha suede furnishings on the other side of the room. "Can I get you anything?" he offered.

Mick waved her hand. "I'm okay," she said, quickly taking her place on one of the armchairs instead of the extremely long sofa they flanked.

Quaysar's grin widened. His dark eyes narrowed to a playful squint as he unbuttoned his sandstone suit coat and chose the chair opposite Mick. "I suppose you've wondered why we wanted to meet with you alone?" he asked.

Mick's lashes fluttered. She glanced around the dim, majestic, and clearly masculine office for any sign of the 'we' he spoke of. Finally, she offered a conceding smile to her host. "I did wonder about that," she admitted.

Quaysar leaned forward to brace his elbows on his knees. For the first time, he seemed to lose a bit of his playfulness. "Ms. Sellars, when the issue of a book being written is presented to a family as reclusive as mine, there're bound to be mixed feelings involved," he confided, the muscle twitching in his jaw as he focused on his clasped hands. "Unfortunately, that's what we're faced with now."

Mick smiled. "I see," she acknowledged with a slow nod.

"Since I was the one who wanted to go full steam with this, I'm the one who has to break the news to you," he continued. "I'm afraid it's news you won't like," he raised his ebony gaze to her face. "Call me a coward, but there was no way I could handle disappointing two women at the same time."

Michaela almost laughed aloud, but restrained herself. "You have to say no to the book?" she supplied for him.

Quaysar grimaced and leaned back against the armchair. "When you come from a family like mine, you'll find that you have plenty of sticks in the mud. Sadly, my partner is one such stick."

Mick settled her hands in her lap and stifled the urge to smile. "Your brother," she guessed.

Quaysar nodded. "He's completely against it and without his support, this thing is dead in the water," he shrugged. "Again, I apologize."

"Please don't," Mick told him while raising her hands. "I completely understand. Your brother's just very protective of you all. A book could bring unimagined attention to your family- that attention could quickly become unwanted and harassing."

Quaysar's brows drew close and he appeared a bit taken aback by her outlook. "Shouldn't you be trying to talk me into this or at least helping me to devise a way to persuade my stick-in-the-mud brother?"

Mick was already shaking her head no. "If I had a family, I'd do everything in my power to protect their privacy too."

"*If* you had a family?" Quaysar probed softly, tilting his head at the sadness that quickly ghosted across Mick's brown, pretty face.

"I lost my parents at a young age. No brothers or sisters," she said, her tone of finality a silent message to Quaysar that he not probe any further.

Again, Quaysar leaned forward to brace his elbows on his knees. "I am sorry that we wasted your time," he said in his softest tone.

"Oh, it was no waste. I promise you. I've never visited Seattle, but I love it. Now I'll have a bit more time to explore the city."

The solemn look vanished from Quaysar's midnight stare and it was once again playful and sparkling. Blatantly, he appraised the creamy brown beauty in his presence. Like most men, he grew transfixed on her heart-shaped mouth, complete with a tiny mole in the very corner. Images of the delights that mouth could provide made his thoughts run wild.

"I at least have to have you for dinner," he decided. He sounded as though he were speaking to himself and as if he were referring to dining on something *other* than food. "I'll call your hotel and we'll set it up before you leave," he added.

Mick laughed. "I'd like that," she said, nodding as she stood from the oversized chair.

Quaysar's hand settled to the small of her back as they retraced their steps through the office. "I would've enjoyed working with you, Ms. Sellars," he told her when they stood before the elevator.

"Call me Mick," she requested, watching as he pressed a kiss to the back of her hand. "It'll make our dinner conversation less formal," she figured.

"And you can call me Quay," he permitted, squeezing her hand once before releasing it. Then he pressed the button on the wood panel and the pine doors opened.

Quay waited until the elevator began its descent before leaning back on his long legs and stroking his square jaw. "Mmm...Mick...yummy," he added and then rolled his eyes when he heard the disgusted grunt from the far corner of the room. "Don't even try it, you cannot deny any compliment to that lusciousness that just walked out of here," he challenged, watching as a large form moved in the shadows while leaving the chair behind the desk.

"And that's the only reason you even considered this book nonsense," was the reply, spoken in a deep voice that possessed a softer more unsettling quality that differed from Quaysar's.

"I agreed to this book because it'd be good for the family."

"Bull."

"Why?"

Quest Ramsey perched on the edge of the desk then. "You took one look at her photo and wanted her here for however long it'd take you to get her into bed."

"Damn," Quay retorted, pretending to be stunned in the midst of his amazement. "Man, are you forgetting how many women are in Seattle?"

"No, but as you saw fit to point out, she's quite...yummy and luscious."

Quay smiled. "And I supposed you never noticed that?"

"Oh, I noticed," Quest admitted, his eyes narrowing sharply. The deep-set gray stare darkened to black as he recalled the poised, soft-spoken beauty whose perfume still lingered in the office. "I noticed something else too. Her work," he added when Quay fixed him with a dumbfounded expression. "Did you even bother to *read* anything in that proposal her publisher sent?"

Quay folded his arms across his chest and produced a pointed look. Quest laughed, revealing the dimple that flashed in his left cheek.

"And I suppose you've never read any of her books either?" Quest asked, receiving another pointed look from his brother. "Is there anything on your nightstand besides *Playboy*, man?"

"Of course there is. *Penthouse*." Quay revealed cooly.

Quest brought one hand to his left arm and massaged the dull ache forming at the brand on his arm- a reminder of college days, the result of a frat branding party gone wrong. Now it only ached when he was frustrated. "Look Quay," he urged, moving his hand from the sleeve of the cobalt-blue shirt he wore, "the *lusciousness* you're so taken by is no fool. She's got a master's in journalism, one in English, and eight years as a crime reporter. She doesn't write fluff, no entertainment stories with more pictures than words," he carefully explained, his glare now as black as his brother's. "Don't think she's so interested in the family because she wants to tell the world what great people we are. She wants a story, she wants dirt, and the Ramseys got plenty."

Quay rolled his eyes and massaged the back of his neck. "You work my damn nerves with this suspicion of yours, Q," he almost growled.

Quest shrugged. "This suspicion of mine has kept us out of

a lot of crap. Don't forget that."

"Maybe a little trouble would shake things up a bit. Get us to face some things," Quay argued softly, perching on the edge of the desk as well.

"I will admit that I don't believe she's *only* out for dirt. Unlike you, I've read her work," Quest shared. "She's got an easy style, it's nonfiction that reads like a novel, and you can almost feel her dedication to highlight both good *and* bad details of her subjects." He grimaced then, as though he was contemplating. "There's something else too-another side that I can't quite put a label on yet. She's great at showing the love and triumphant spirit in each family she portrays. I was also impressed by the way she didn't try to persuade you to change your mind when you turned down the book."

Quay's hands met in a single clap. "There you go! Now that, at least, warrants her a little benefit of the doubt."

Quest groaned, knowing where his twin was headed next. "My position still stands," he said and left the desk.

"Well, at least we won't have to waste time talkin' business during our dinner date," Quay reasoned with a lazy shrug.

Quest's expression tightened as he strolled toward the elevator.

"Where're you goin'?" Quay called, but received no reply.

~~~

Mick was fluffing out the unruly thick dark curls across her head. She and County were scheduled to have dinner later and she was trying to decide whether to do anything different with the mop of riotous locks. The doorbell chimed and Mick took that as confirmation to let her hair alone. It'd never obey her wishes to stay pulled into an elaborate updo anyway, she thought with a disapproving snort.

Turning quickly, she shuffled toward the door. The long ears on her bunny slippers slapped the carpet as her steps quickened. She figured it was County, but looked out the peephole anyway. A quick 'oh' wisped past her lips when she glimpsed her visitor.

"Damn it," she whispered, glancing down at her attire, which consisted of a cap-sleeved tee with a pair of glittery pink lips emblazoned across her breasts. The sleep pants hugged her hips, while flattering her bottom in the most adoring manner, and were covered with hundreds of full pink lips. Then there were the bunny slippers…

"Oh what the hell, he's already seen me dressed up," she reasoned and flung open the door. Her expression was light and inviting as she prepared to greet Quaysar Ramsey. But the easy look in her amber stare turned questioning as she gazed up at the man who filled her doorway. Subconsciously, she took a step backward.

"Mr. Ramsey," she greeted, her coolness returning a bit. "I was hoping to meet you before I left town."

Now it was Quest's turn to appear confused. "You know who I am?" he asked, obvious disbelief clinging to every word.

Mick nodded, her soft smile instantly drawing his eyes to her mouth.

"How?" he probed after commanding himself not to allow the woman's X-rated lips to make him lose track of his senses.

Mick was surprised by her intuition as well, but realized that although the Ramsey twins were clearly identical, they possessed distinct differences. Especially Quest. For some reason, Mick believed she would know him anywhere, and that belief was more than a little disconcerting.

At last, she shrugged. "It's my secret," she said in a prim tone, her heart fluttering when his laughter touched her ears. *Stop it, Mick!* she demanded, feeling completely disgusted by her light-headed behavior.

"I'm sorry for keeping you in the hall, please come in," she urged with a gracious wave as she stepped aside.

Quest stood just inside the suite. Mick closed the door and waited for him to precede her to the living room, but he didn't move. Finally, she realized that he was waiting on her to precede him.

"Could I get you something or have something sent up?" Mick offered as she breezed into the living area.

Quest shook his head. "I'm good. Don't go to any trouble."

For a moment, they stood opposite one another in the room. Finally Mick nodded.

"Please have a seat," she invited.

Quest simply waved one hand toward the cushiony cream furnishings and Mick saw that he was waiting for her to do so first. She responded slowly, almost stunned that this man could actually possess the rare- in her opinion, the *extremely* rare- quality of gallantry. She watched him settle into the armchair across from her and recalled the meeting with his brother.

Quest Ramsey, she surmised, moved far differently from his twin whose movements were bold and purpose-filled. Quest wasn't slow, awkward or uncertain but smooth and relaxed. It was as though he had all the time in the world and the world was waiting on him.

In the golden light of the room, Mick could assess the package more clearly. County had called the twins chocolate-dipped, but Quest's skin gave him the appearance of having been doused in rich molasses. Even at a distance, she could tell his midnight hair was silky, but close cut so that it appeared as a mass of waves across his head. Still, it was his eyes that most captivated her. They were an uncommon hazy gray and deep-set beneath the longest, straightest brows and fringed with even longer lashes. Those were lashes unfair for any *man* to have. *A god indeed*, she admitted.

Quest sat reclined in his chair. His massive hands rested along the arms as though he was waiting patiently for her to complete her assessment. When she smiled again, he couldn't have been more stunned to feel his own heartbeat lose its steady rhythm in response.

"Michaela Sellars," she saw fit to introduce herself then and watched as he grinned and inclined his head.

"Quest Ramsey," was his soft reply.

~THREE~

"Now that we have the intros out of the way," Quest teased once the laughter had subsided between them, "I suppose you're wondering why I'm here?"

Mick shrugged a bit while sitting on the edge of the chair with her hands clasped in her lap. "Well, your brother already told me you were against having the book written. I'm sure you haven't changed your mind?" she probed.

"I haven't," Quest confirmed with a slow shake of his head. "My brother tends to act first and ask questions...well, never," he mused.

Mick smiled over the comment. "I enjoyed our talk. He really made me want to laugh."

Quest couldn't mask his surprise. "Made you want to laugh?" he parroted.

"It was so hard not to. He was trying so hard not to offend me or upset me since the book was cancelled," she shared, shaking her head as she remembered. "I could tell that he was holding back a bit from being too forward or outspoken. He must've been quite the clown in school."

Now Quest threw back his head and let loose a roar of

35

laughter. "Quay would have a fit if he knew you felt that way."

Mick's eyes narrowed a tad. "Could you, um, elaborate on why?" she asked, trying to downplay how taken she was by the sound of his voice. His amusement only made him appear more gorgeous, if that were possible.

"My brother is the consummate Casanova," Quest said, resting one hand against the cobalt-blue shirt where it lay across his abdomen. "If you'll excuse me for saying so, Ms. Sellars, the man's been racking his brain trying to think of a way to get you into bed," he confided.

Mick was stunned, but not by Quest's candor. "I don't believe it," she said, "I can't believe he was that taken by me."

Quest's easy expression faded to one of disbelief. At that point, it was his turn to assess her. Not that he'd stopped tracing and retracing her every dip and curve in his mind since she had visited his office earlier that day.

Upon first glance, he'd regarded her as being exceptionally short. Now he could tell that while she wasn't exceedingly tall, she did have a nice height. Her legs had appeared shapely and well toned as though she frequently worked out. Thanks to her T-shirt's capped sleeves, he could tell that her arms were just as well toned and a creamy brown color stretched all over her alluring figure. Seated across from her, he enjoyed the hypnotic tug of her eyes. The way they just slanted at the corner, the cooly engaging amber shade could easily be compared to that of some exotic tigress.

Once again, his gray stare settled to her mouth- a perfect rendering of the heart shape if he had ever seen one. The mole was perfectly, sensually positioned in the corner and rivaled her eyes for hypnotic power.

"I guess I'll have to watch him when we have dinner tomorrow night," Mick contemplated, having missed the set look on her guest's face.

Quest blinked. "Yeah," he acknowledged, with a slow nod, "how long with you stay in Seattle?"

Mick sighed in a refreshing tone, while leaning back to survey the elegant comfort of the suite. "I hadn't planned to stay long, but since the book is dead and this is such a lovely town, I've considered staying a while longer," she fixed him with a polite, expectant smile. "Any suggestions on where to go when I sightsee?"

"The museums, definitely," Quest replied without hesitation. "We've got tons," he boasted. "Five art museums, five cultural museums, and almost two hundred art galleries."

"Wow," she whispered, already thinking about what she'd like to see first. "I think I will make this a longer trip. Thanks for putting us up in such a lovely place."

Quest closed his eyes briefly while waving a hand. "It's nothing, but I can always arrange to lengthen your stay in the hotel," he offered.

"I have no idea how long I'll be."

Quest propped his index finger alongside his temple and traced the outline of her breasts heaving prominently against the glittering pair of lips emblazoned on her T-shirt. "I'll arrange for you to stay as long as you like," he decided in an absent tone and coolly looked away when she found him staring.

Quest discovered that without trying and without even subtly throwing herself at him- which women did so often it'd become second nature for him to spot- Michaela Sellars had him mesmerized. He didn't even want to talk, he only wanted to hear *her* talk, he only wanted to watch her as she spoke.

"I should go," he decided suddenly.

"But you just got here," Mick blurted, scooting closer to the edge of her chair. Realizing her slip, she closed her eyes and tugged her bottom lip between her teeth.

Quest smiled and shook his head, delighted by her appearance. The action had changed her features from lovely and sensual to adorable and childlike. The mix was incredible. *Go, Quest*, his conscience warned, and he agreed. It'd be a mistake to remain any longer when he'd already experienced such a powerful reaction to her.

"You look about ready to turn in," he noted, grasping for the first excuse he could find.

Mick noticed her clothing and rolled her eyes. "I was about to get ready for dinner with my publisher," she explained.

"Well then," he conceded, waving his hand as though the decision was solidified.

Mick watched him sitting across from her with his fingers tapping against the cream fabric of his trousers. Slowly, she rose from her chair and her lips parted in surprise when he followed suit. Obviously he'd been waiting for her to stand. Gorgeous and gallant, she observed silently. *Don't let him see you drool, Mick!* Clearing her throat, she clapped her hands to her sides. "You never got to the point of your visit," she reminded him.

By then, Quest had closed what distance remained between them. Mick could feel her lashes fluttering as a shiver kissed her bare arms in response to the sexy, midnight giant who stood so very close.

"I only wanted to apologize for wasting your time," he said, his eyes appearing a darker shade of gray as they studied every inch of her face. "I have a lot of people in my family who never stop to consider consequences. I'm sorry you got caught up in it."

"It's okay," Mick whispered, knowing she was watching him as though he were the cherry atop a sinfully rich sundae. Sadly, she was helpless to do anything to stop herself.

Quest stared down at her a few moments longer before urging her to accompany him to the door.

"Good night," he said, his hand poised on the brass knob. He smiled, hearing the hushed quality of her voice when she returned the sentiment.

Mick watched him step out into the hall. Instead of closing the door, she studied him as he strolled to the elevator bay. As though sensing her eyes on him, Quest turned once the doors opened. He flashed her one last smile- an incredible smile. Michaela's hand was resting against her thigh. She wriggled her fingers in some sort of awkward wave before disappearing back into her room.

~~~

County closed her eyes as she popped another succulent shrimp into her mouth. "Mmm...I've always heard Seattle had the best seafood, but there's nothing like tasting it for yourself," she raved, this time helping herself to another spoonful of fish chowder.

"Mmm-hmm, it *is* somethin' else."

"I mean, I definitely plan to take a hearty doggie bag back to my room," County decided.

Mick stirred her clam chowder with an idle hand. Clearly, her thoughts were miles away from the evening's meal at the hotel restaurant where they dined.

"Isn't the chowder rich?...Mick?" County called, still focused on her food. Finally, the silence from the opposite end of the table grabbed her attention. She didn't waste time calling out to her friend again. County was more interested in observing then. She and Mick had been eating for almost a half hour. In that time, Mick hadn't uttered a single sarcastic or cynical remark. She barely tasted her food and spent much of the time staring off into the distance.

Finally, County pushed her plate aside and perched her hands along the edge of the table. "Alright, spill it," she ordered.

Mick blinked out of her daze and fixed County with a slight frown.

"Don't even," County urged with a brief hand wave. "I've been waiting- *very* patiently, I'm proud to say- for you to tell me about your meeting with the twins. Now, is your quiet, soft-spoken, and completely uncharacteristic demeanor a result of that meeting?"

Mick set her spoon aside and groaned in response.

"Damn Mick," County whined, "you haven't even told me what they look like- just that they declined the book. At least give me *one* warm and fuzzy tidbit to take with me so I won't feel the trip was a *total* waste."

Mick's expression remained solemn for a moment longer and then she softened. "They looked like dreams," she confided eventually. Surprise registered on County's face, but she ignored it.

"They're well deserving of being called gods."

County leaned back against her seat, rubbing her hands across the satiny sleeves of her coral V-neck hoodie and listened.

"They're exactly identical- like bookends," Mick stared into the distance as though she were envisioning them then. "But when you look closer, you can see little differences in their physical appearance. *Distinct* differences everywhere else."

"Oh really?" County drawled, thoroughly intrigued by the emerging new aspect to her friend's demeanor.

"Their eye colors are different," Mick described while tugging at the three-quarter sleeve of the tan boatneck top she wore. "Quest's eyes are this cool shade of gray that seems to darken at time. When he looks at you, it's like he's put all his attention on you. Like what you're saying is the most important thing in the world to him. His cologne is fantastic. I can't place what it is, but it smells incredible and he's got this deep dimple in his left cheek…"

County was trying to keep her smile from growing wide. Clearly, her cynical best friend had been more impressed by Quest Ramsey. *And the poor thing doesn't even realize it!* County mused.

"And he's such a gentleman. So gallant."

Now County was floored. *Gallant?* she repeated in her head, while folding her arms across her chest. She didn't think Mick even had that word in her vocabulary when it came to describing a man. Especially not a man she'd just met.

"Sweetie, I have to admit this is surprising talk coming from you," she admitted once Mick's description of the twins had ended. "That must've been *some* meeting."

Mick shrugged and reached for her spoon. "Actually, I only met Quest when he came to my hotel room. He wasn't at the meeting," she revealed coolly.

County's mouth fell open. "Your hotel room?"

"Mmm-hmm."

"Mick!" County raged and slammed her palms to the table. "You selfish wench."

"What?" Mick whined, nervously recrossing her jean-clad

legs beneath the table.

"You couldn't come get me from my room, I guess?"

Mick smiled and shook her head. "I was just as surprised to see him and he didn't even stay that long. I don't even think it was fifteen minutes."

County heard the disappointment in Mick's voice and she could see it in her eyes. "He didn't stay long, but he had quite an effect on you."

"Stop, I know what you're getting at and it was nothing like that," Mick insisted. "Quest Ramsey could easily make an impression on any woman," she predicted.

"But no man's ever made such an *impression* on you so quickly."

Mick waved off County's observation. "Forget it."

"Oh well," County sighed, leaning forward to resume her eating. "At least I'll have your warm, fuzzy memories to take back when we leave."

Mick pressed her lips together and prepared herself. "Um, actually I've decided to stay a little longer. Quest already offered to extend my stay."

"Indefinitely?" County blurted, shaking her head when Mick shrugged her confirmation. "Damn, I should've sent *my* photo instead."

"He was only trying to be kind, County." Mick reasoned, giving a quick toss of her tousled curls. "I mean, it wasn't like he was trying to stay in my room any longer than necessary or anything."

"Still Mick, for him to offer that, *you* must've made quite an impression of your own," County decided.

Mick laughed softly. "Well I guess that's definitely true of Quaysar. He asked me out to dinner," she said, peeking through the fringe of her lashes to judge her publisher's reaction.

"Damn," County grunted, stabbing a scallop with her fork when she heard Mick laughing. After a moment, she couldn't resist joining in.

The remainder of the dinner continued with a lively

conversation about the Ramsey brothers.

~~~

After dinner, Mick and County made plans to sightsee the next day. After saying their goodnights in the lobby, Mick headed for the front desk.

"Good evening, ma'am," the concierge greeted.

"Good evening, I'd like to find out about extending my stay. The name is Michaela Sellars, room nineteen-thirty."

The tall, middle-aged man was already entering the information into his desktop. "Sellars...ah! Yes ma'am, that's already been arranged."

"It has?" Mick questioned, her brows connecting in a frown. "I don't understand."

"Yes ma'am, Mr. Ramsey lengthened your stay when he visited earlier."

"He did?" she asked in a dumbfounded tone, barely taking note of the concierge's curt nod. "He must've stopped by before he left."

"Oh no ma'am, he took care of it on his way in. Mr. Ramsey does much business here at the Sorenson. He greeted me here at the front desk himself when he arrived."

Mick blinked and slowly backed away from the majestic cherry-wood desk. "Thank you," she told the man and headed for the elevators.

On her way to the nineteenth floor, Mick thought about Quest Ramsey more sternly. Aside from the quiet charm and gallantry he exuded, he'd done little else to show any further interest- unlike his brother. Though Quaysar was no less gorgeous than his twin, he hadn't ignited that 'something' the way Quest had. What was that *something*? Mick asked herself. And how could she of all people be so impressed, *infatuated* by a man she'd only met with for fifteen minutes?

***

The next morning, Quest rapped on the door of his

brother's private office nestled within the depths of their top-floor dwelling. "Be sure to call and cancel out with Michaela this morning," he told Quaysar, smiling coolly when the man looked up in confusion.

"I hadn't planned to cancel out on her Q," Quay countered.

Quest's gray eyes narrowed. "But you will," he commanded softly and then flashed his brother a wink and left the room.

A grin spread across Quay's face as he reclined in his office chair. Then, he bolted up and went after his brother.

"Q?" he called, spotting Quest on his way down the hall. "What's up, man?" he asked, when his brother turned. "What is this?" he added, though his black stare was narrowed as though he already had a good idea. "Q?" he called again when his twin was about to walk away.

Finally, Quest turned and waited.

"What's up?" Quay probed, tilting his head just slightly while spreading his hands.

Quest pushed both hands into his sandalwood trousers and grimaced. "She's sweet and you're…up to no good. Leave her alone."

"You went to see her, didn't you?" Quay realized, stepping a bit closer. Quest didn't reply, but his silence was confirmation enough for Quay. "Hmph," he gestured fixing his brother with a sly look. He'd always considered Quest far more selective than he when it came to choosing a woman.

Quaysar was pleased with looks, body and all that was physical. Quest looked for more. Usually, he found little to sustain his interest past three or four sexual encounters. Quay constantly criticized his brother for being too picky, but in his heart he knew Quest wanted more than a bed warmer. He wanted a woman who could accept him for who he was- a man who loved intensely, be he a multi-millionaire sought after mogul or not. Moreover, he needed a woman who could understand the lengths he would go to in protecting those he loved.

"Alright Q, you gotta come clean now and tell me why

you're makin' me cancel out on her."

Quest rolled his eyes. "Just do it, Quay."

"Uh-uh," Quaysar argued, shaking his head as he pressed a hand to the lapel of his pin-striped suit coat. "You're tellin' me to skip a date with a very sweet, very luscious lady. You gotta give me a reason here, man."

Quest fixed his brother with a look that Quaysar knew all too well. Satisfied that he had his answer, Quay shrugged and decided to drop it. Obviously, his twin was smitten. Getting him to admit that would be a chore within itself.

"So where're you off to?" Quay asked, deciding to take a break from his inquisition.

If possible, Quest's expression turned even darker. "I'm off to see the elders."

"Yuck."

"Mmm…"

"What about?"

Quest shook his head and continued on toward the elevators. "I'm about to find out."

~~~

The younger generation of the family ran the majority of the business dealings spanning the Ramsey empire. Though rather unfitting, they'd titled their predecessors the elders. The group consisted of Quest's and Quaysar's parents: Damon and Catrina Ramsey, Marcus and Josephine Ramsey, Westin and Briselle Ramsey and Houston and Daphne Ramsey. When Quest stepped into the posh white and gold conference room of the downtown office, he found only two of the elders waiting.

"Uncle Hous, Aunt Daphe," he greeted slowly.

The couple responded with barely a nod, and since Quest hadn't been exactly looking forward to the meeting, he decided not to waste time with further niceties.

"Why am I here?" he asked.

Houston pretended not to notice his nephew's curtness and idly removed a nonexistent string from the cuff of his cream suit coat. "We heard about the book offer. We also heard that you and Quay turned it down."

Quest's broad shoulders rose in a smooth shrug beneath his olive-green shirt. "We felt it was for the best."

"Hmph, we're sure you did." Houston's tone was blatantly smug. "We, however, felt that the book was a fine idea and we'd have liked more of a say in the final decision."

"I see," Quest responded softly, clearly not surprised that his uncle disagreed. "So you're eager to have the family business pried into?" he challenged in the softly sarcastic tone that never failed to sit the Elders on edge. "It may surprise and disturb you to know that Quay is also in favor of the book. I'll tell him like I told you, Michaela Sellars does not write fluff. She's a hard investigative journalist and she digs until she gets to the bottom of the story. *Every* story."

"You say Quaysar is in favor of the book?" Daphne Ramsey asked then, a slight frown marring the cafe au lait skin of her brow. When Quest nodded, her frown deepened. "That's surprising considering…"

"Considering?" Quest prompted.

"*Considering* the fact that you, Quaysar and the rest of my brothers's children have done nothing for the Ramsey reputation but run it into the ground," Houston finished.

Quest's jaw clenched, triggering the taut muscle there. "Is this why you called me here? To waste my time?"

Houston dismissed the dangerous raspiness of his nephew's voice. "You people left a mess down in Georgia and trailed it all the way up here to Seattle."

"See ya," Quest said, leaving the conference room as coolly as he'd entered.

Houston sat fuming, his deep-set brown eyes rage-filled. When the door closed behind Quest, he reached for the phone on the edge of the table.

"Find Michaela Sellars," he told the person on the other end of the line.

A LOVER'S DREAM

~FOUR~

Michaela and Contessa enjoyed a hearty breakfast the next morning. They'd planned to make a day of sightseeing. Unfortunately, the conditions were rather overcast, giving County the perfect reason to cut the walking tour down to just under thirty minutes. They'd barely spanned three blocks beyond the hotel. The two debated a bit, but County finally won out, telling Mick they'd meet back at the hotel for lunch.

Mick really didn't mind the change in plans as it gave her more of an opportunity to enjoy the sights of the city. She'd wanted to tour Seattle's cultural venues and found herself at the Bellvue Art Museum an hour after she and County parted ways.

"The artist's work is sure to be more abundant in the coming months."

Mick blinked, hearing the soft deep voice close behind. Turning away from the exquisite piece she studied, she was stunned to see who had spoken.

"Seeing as how he's from Washington State and all."

Mick smiled. "Hi Quest."

He seemed taken aback when she said his name. "How do you do that?" he whispered.

Mick made a phony show of innocence, though her eyes brightened in a knowing manner. "Do what?"

"Recognize me so easily," he clarified promptly.

"It's *my* secret," she replied just as quickly. "What are you doing here?" she asked.

Quest watched her a moment longer before shaking his head. "I love coming to the museums. Especially after an aggravating day."

Mick's amber gaze narrowed as she studied him closely. The tiny muscle working frantically along his jaw was tough to ignore. "What happened?" she probed quietly.

"Don't ever go into business with family, Michaela," he sighed, shoving his hands deep inside his gray trouser pockets.

Mick's smile was bittersweet. "I don't think I'll ever have to worry about that."

Quest closed his eyes and bowed his head. "I'm sorry," he whispered, the grimace triggering the dimple in his left cheek. "I'm sorry about what happened to your family."

"My family?" Mick parrotted, tilting her head to one side. "How did you-"

"Quay and I share the same office space. I overheard what you told him," he admitted, folding his arms across the front of the olive-green shirt that hung outside his trousers.

Mick didn't know what to make of the revelation. *Why didn't you come out?* she wanted to ask. Something told her he wouldn't be ready with an answer.

Quest, however, had judged her reaction perfectly. He knew she wanted to question his absence during the meeting. "You'd probably give anything to go through that kind of headache," he said, hoping to lighten the mood.

The summation did draw a grin from Mick. "Well...I wouldn't say that," she groaned playfully while smoothing her hands across her curve-hugging black yoga pants. "So I take it, it's pretty difficult belonging to such a huge family?" she asked, smiling when he fell in step beside her.

"Does the phrase 'the twelfth level of hell' mean anything

to you?" Quest muttered, shaking his head when Mick burst into laughter.

"Come on, you're exaggerating. It can't be *that* bad?" she argued.

Quest massaged the back of his neck where his hairline tapered off. "Hmph, it shouldn't be that bad, but it is. Just last week we were only on level ten."

Mick cast a nervous glance across her shoulder when the last remark roused a roar of laughter from her throat. Quest's attempt at brutal honesty had succeeded in thoroughly amusing her.

"I don't know whether to be impressed or concerned by my ability to make you laugh so hard."

Mick pressed one hand to her chest and closed her eyes briefly. "I swear I don't view you as a clown."

"Thank God," Quest breathed, his haunting gray stare holding traces of relief.

"Still," Mick considered as she toyed with the satin-trimmed row of buttons along the bodice of her pink polo tee, "it's interesting to find you so humorous when you first struck me as so serious."

Quest's serious side reasserted itself then."Tell me about your family," the request was soft.

Mick, who rarely spoke about her family, or lack thereof, felt no hesitation then. A part of her wanted to share her story-her secrets-with this man.

"I do miss all the craziness of family and all the drama. I miss not even having cousins to spar with."

Quest didn't like the sadness in her light eyes. He wanted to reach out and smooth back the heavy black curls that fell into her face when her head bowed.

"Cousins," he groaned, deciding to redirect the conversation, "the twentieth level of hell," he complained amidst Michaela's laughter.

The couple continued to stroll the museum's long corridors and grand rooms. Of course, they hardly noticed all the lovely pieces because their conversation was so enjoyable. Michaela wanted to swoon whenever Quest's hand curved beneath her elbow to move her from the path of some tourist or museum employee.

"Is not having a family why you busy yourself with the books?" he asked when they stood before a centuries-old bronzed statue.

"Oh I promise you I'm not a workaholic. I know how to have fun," she was quick to assure him.

"I have no doubt," Quest replied, his long lashes shielding his gaze as it raked her alluring frame. The black yoga pants hugged and emphasized her bottom adoringly. *Down, Quest*, he ordered himself.

"I grew up hard and it made me cynical," she admitted, studying the artwork with an idle gaze, "but growing up underprivileged also instilled a desire to enjoy my success to the fullest and I do that every chance I get."

A curious light brightened Quest's handsome molasses features. "How so?" he inquired.

"Well I love to play beach volleyball," she shared, grinning when she spied the surprise on his face. "I love to fish. In fact, there's a resort I visit on Rhode Island whenever I have to go to New York."

"Hmm, volleyball-"

"*Beach* volleyball."

"And fishing. I'm impressed, Michaela."

"Mmm," she used her most prim tone. "Then there's rollerblading, dog racing, car racing-"

"Whoa, whoa, you're not telling me you actually like to watch car races?"

"No, I'm telling you I like to race cars."

"Get out."

Mick threw back her head and laughed. "I hope you don't expect me to believe that *you* don't have a wild streak somewhere in there?" she taunted.

Quest shrugged, a hint of playfulness coming to his gray-black stare. "I prefer racing motorcycles and I take part in the

Seahawks spring training every chance I get."

Mick felt that went without saying. She appreciated the definition of his torso, and by observing alone, she could tell it was a wall of unyielding muscle. *Down, Mick,* she ordered herself. "So you like football?" she asked in a hasty tone, hoping to draw her attention away from his physique.

"Love it," Quest confirmed.

Mick nodded. "It's a great game."

Quest grinned. "Your looks would make a man think you like anything besides car racing and football."

"My looks?"

"Pretty." *Beautiful*, he really wanted to say, "Delicate," he added.

Mick couldn't deny the warmth spreading throughout her body. She had never considered herself pretty, let alone delicate.

"Have you eaten?" Quest asked when they'd walked a bit farther in silence.

Mick's eyes filled with regret as her lunch date with County came to mind. "I have a date with my publisher in another hour," she told him.

He nodded and then focused his eyes toward the floor as though he were debating. Mick could see the muscle working in his jaw again. She had no idea how intently she watched him, praying he would ask her to change her plans.

Finally, he looked up. "Would ice cream ruin your appetite?" he asked.

~~~

"So you visit the museum when you want to escape the office. What happened today?" Mick asked, recalling that they'd veered onto the subject of her family when she inquired earlier.

"I had a bad meeting with the Elders as usual," he shared absently, as they enjoyed ice cream in the museum cafe.

"The Elders?" Mick inquired, her spoon poised in a cup of cookies and cream.

"The grown folks in the family," Quest clarified, "our parents, aunts, uncles. My uncle Houston and aunt Daphne are the only two I had the joy of meeting with today."

"Ah and judging from your mood, I take it you don't get along so well with them?"

Quest rolled his eyes. "No one gets along with them."

"Yuck," Mick retorted, making a face.

Quest ate another spoonful of his butter pecan ice cream and shook his head. "While Quay and I and our cousins were out hoopin', hollerin' and raisin' hell, their kids were excelling in piano, mathematics, and science."

Mick propped her chin in her palm and listened.

"Dena and Taurus always did everything right. Making the honor roll- straight As, no less," he emphasized with an authoritative glare, "joining the chess club, playing polo. You name it."

"They sound fascinating," Mick said, turning back to her ice cream.

Quest's expression was grim. "Hmph, fascinating. Yeah, if it was boring as hell in everyone else's opinion, you best believe Houston and his crew had to do it."

"So your meeting was just another in a long line of aggravations?" Mick guessed, before spooning a heap of cookies and cream into her mouth.

"You said it."

"And so you escape to the museum?" Mick asked in a whimsical manner.

Quest winced. "Pitiful, huh?"

"Kind of," Mick confessed softly, joining in when he laughed. "So did your aunt and uncle want to see you just to pick a fight or what?" she questioned nonchalantly, dipping into her ice cream again.

Quest's magnificent features tenses visibly, and Mick looked up in time to witness the reaction.

"Sorry," she whispered, believing she'd delved too far into personal business.

Quest waved his hand. "No reason for you to be. Those two just get to me. Always have."

Mick could see his extraordinary gray stare darken to ebony and realized the effect took place whenever he was stressed. She hadn't much time to mull over the discovery. Tiny chimes rendering Stevie Wonder's "Ribbon In The Sky" sounded and she reached for her cellphone.

"It's Mick."

"Where the hell are you?!"

"Hello. How are you?" Mick drawled in a polite airy manner.

"What?" County retorted, her voice still bellowing.

Mick remained cool, hoping Quest couldn't hear County on the other end. "What can I do for you?"

"What's wrong with you?" County demanded from the other end. "Did you forget we're having lunch?"

Mick uttered a fake lengthy laugh. "We're not supposed to meet for almost another hour," she sang.

"I don't care. I'm hungry now!"

Mick kept the phony smile plastered to her lips. "Alright, I'll be there shortly," she promised and quickly clicked off the phone. She glanced up to find Quest grinning broadly at what he'd overheard.

"Sorry," she whispered, rolling her eyes. "My publisher is a beast," a solemn smile came to her face. "I should go," she told him, hating having to do so. Odds were, they wouldn't be running into one another during the few remaining days of her stay.

"Can you find your way back okay?" he asked, standing once she rose from her seat.

"Yeah, I'll be fine," she assured him softly. Her amber stare lingered on his fantastic dark face coolly appraising every angle.

"Thanks for joining me," Quest said, glancing back at the booth they'd shared.

Mick shrugged. "I enjoyed it a lot," she said. Her eyes drifted around the elaborately designed museum. "This was so much fun. The museum is definitely not a place just to come to when you're feeling frustrated," she advised quietly, then nodded and moved past him.

Quest turned to watch her leave. He pushed one hand into his trouser pocket while massaging his jaw with the other. His eyes narrowed then. Ice cream in a tiny shop of a museum and she enjoyed it. If the successful author was anything, she was not predictable.

~~~

"Well why didn't you tell me you were with Quest?" County was asking once they'd ordered lunch at one of the hotel's three restaurants. "And why are you giving *me* the evil eye?" she demanded, watching her friend with a haughty stare.

Finally Mick shook her head, sending a slew of blue-black curls into her face. "It was probably for the best that we were interrupted. I think the conversation was getting a little too intense."

"Really?" County's brown eyes took on that familiar light that said details were necessary.

Mick took the hint and settled back in her chair. "I don't think he appreciated my probing so much about his family."

County flipped a lock of her thick hair across her shoulder. "Well, the book's dead, so what the hell?"

"Still...I mean, I can understand him being reluctant to talk with me about them," Mick admitted.

County's mouth curled into a knowing smirk. "Nah, there's more going on there. I'm sure of it."

Mick laughed and nodded. "Mmm-hmm, I was waiting for you to start reading too much into all of this." She leaned forward, the glint in her eyes a clear warning. "Listen to me, County, there is nothing-*nothing* going on here. He was stressed. I was there. He confided a bit. It got uncomfortable and that was it."

"Well since the book isn't going to happen, what's the harm in getting to know each other a little better?" County coolly reasoned.

"I can't answer that," Mick countered, hoping County wouldn't read more into that as well.

"You have such a sad view of romance," County remarked, pretending to be interested in removing a string from her low-slung black crop pants.

Michaela groaned. "County...come on. Romance?"

"Possibly."

"Just the thought of it makes me want to cringe. Romance. Love. They have an aftertaste I just can't stomach. All the newness that has you so foolish and giddy with excitement eventually fades and the true light of the person always shines through."

County traced a light pattern in the peach tablecloth. "So you just want happiness all the time, no aggravations."

"And we both know how unrealistic that is, don't we?"

County leaned back in her chair as well and finally pinned Mick with an airy look. "You know, you try to come across as so hard-assed and cynical, but you're the biggest dreamer- the biggest romantic."

"I allow you to believe that," Mick replied with a flip wave.

"One day you'll admit it to yourself," County predicted.

"You know," Mick said, fixing County with an unwavering look, "this may sound like a cliche', but my work is enough for me. It gives me satisfaction, notice, money...and it hasn't let me down yet."

"Mmm...and does it make your toes curl and your heart flutter when it looks at you?"

Mick had no reply.

~~~

After lunch with County, Mick returned to her hotel suite to be greeted by the sound of a ringing phone. A low groan rose deep in her throat as she pulled the receiver from its cradle.

"Michaela Sellars," she greeted.

"Mick!"

"Quaysar?" Mick returned, frowning slightly in surprise.

"Damn, how in the hell do you do that? I should be

flattered that you recognize my voice so quickly."

Mick laughed at the man's never ending supply of self-confidence. Amidst the lightness of the mood, however, she could sense something wasn't quite right.

"Is there a problem?" she asked eventually.

Quay was silent on the other end and Mick thought she could hear him grinding his teeth.

"I have to cancel our dinner date."

Mick smiled. "I see."

"Damn it. I really hate this. I really wanted us to go out."

"It's alright Quay. I understand, really."

"Can I make this up to you?"

Mick shook her head. "There's no need. I assure you. This great hotel I'm in is make-up enough, trust me."

"You're a great lady, Mick Sellars."

"And don't you forget it," she ordered, pointing her index finger toward the floor. "Just look me up if you're ever in Chicago."

"Count on it."

"Good night, Quay," she said and then set down the phone. Closing her eyes, she inhaled deeply and rubbed her hands across her face and through her hair. She ambled across the softly lit living room and flopped into one of the cushioned armchairs.

"What a day," she moaned to the empty room, kicking off her white Reeboks and rubbing her feet. Again, she closed her eyes to savor the treat to her aching toes. *So much walking*, she recalled from the day. Of course, she knew she'd do it all over again if it promised a chance to spend time with Quest Ramsey.

"Damn it, Mick," she hissed, becoming angry with herself for behaving like a fool. *Just because the man is charming, interesting, intelligent, smells great, acts like a gentleman, looks like a god...*

"Stop it, Mick!" she bolted from the chair to make a beeline for the bar cart in the corner of the room. She splashed a bit of the forbidden juice into the cooler and heartily imbibed. After two tangy glasses of vodka and OJ, she was quite at ease.

The relaxation ended a second or two later when the phone rang. Mick pressed her hands to her ears briefly before turning herself in the direction of the message desk.

"Yes," her greeting was lazy.

"Michaela?"

"Mmm, hi Quest," she recognized the man's voice when it filtered through the line.

Quest didn't bother to ask how she knew it was him. He only knew that he liked it. He liked it very much. He shook his head, remembering the purpose of his call. "Do you have plans for dinner?" he asked her.

Mick laughed and leaned against the desk. "Well, I thought I did, but your brother just canceled out on me."

"I'm sorry to hear that," he lied, "but it must've been something really important to make him do that. I know how much he was looking forward to, um, seeing you."

"Mmm…"

"So will you settle for second best?"

Mick's lashes fluttered as she gazed up at the ceiling. "Well, since *second best* just cancelled out on me, I'd love to have dinner with you. If you're asking."

Quest leaned back against the leather headrest in his truck where he'd placed the call. "I'm definitely asking," he confirmed, loving the low husky sound of her voice drifting from his cell. "Be ready by seven," he requested.

"I will," Mick closed her eyes when the connection ended and praised herself for not fumbling the two words. She set down the phone and then squeezed her hands tight and twirled right where she stood.

"Hold it!" she commanded, raising one hand as though she were about to testify. "Michaela Sellars does *not* twirl in place because a man asked her out. Besides…all that twirling makes one dizzy," she acknowledged with a haughty sniff before trudging away from the desk toward the sofa. Her fingers traveled to the buttons along the bodice of her pink tee and she had every intention of removing the top. Sadly, she had only managed to finish unbuttoning the shirt when her eyelids grew heavy and she fell face first into the sofa cushions.

~~~

Michaela opened one eye. "Ow," she groaned, feeling a fierce pain pulse to life there. Her agony wasn't eased a bit when the insistent ring of the doorbell pierced the silence. Slowly, she pushed herself into a sitting position while smoothing a hoard of curls from her face. Taking a deep breath, she scooted off the sofa and headed for the door. Without looking through the privacy window, she whipped open the door and focused in on the man who filled the doorway.

After a moment or so, Mick's lashes fluttered close over her eyes. "Quest," she groaned and rested her head against the doorjamb.

The cool smile Quest wore faded, as it was replaced by a look of concern. "Are you okay?" he inquired softly.

"I'm so sorry," she tried desperately to keep her eyes open. Her legs weakened then and she would have fallen flat on her face again had it not been for Quest, who took her in his arms and carried her to the sofa.

"I don't know why I did that," she rested back against the arm of the sofa while she stared at the coffee table.

Quest's gray eyes narrowed and he turned his head toward the direction she looked. A knowing smile crossed his mouth when he glimpsed the cooler with remnants of OJ in the bottom. "Hmm...orange juice and...vodka, I take it?"

Mick closed her eyes. "Mmm..." she confirmed.

"One?"

"Two."

He chuckled, sparking the dimple in his left cheek. In an absent manner, he tugged the curls away from her chocolate face that was relaxed in drowsiness. "Can't hold your liquor, hmm?"

"Can't hold *any*," Mick massaged her temples before sliding both hands through her curls. "It puts me completely out of it and I say things-*crazy* things-before I fall asleep. So excuse me if

I make a fool of myself. After Quay's call, I just wanted to relax. I'd only planned on one drink but…" she grunted. "Oh Quest, I'm sorry."

"Hey, hey, shh…" he leaned forward to pat her knee. "You should get some sleep."

"No, I don't want to miss our dinner date," she pouted, folding her arms across her chest. "I was really looking forward to it."

"Don't worry about that," Quest ordered, moving to pull her into his arms again. "Right now I'm taking you to bed."

Mick's eyelids grew heavy and she smiled, moaning the first thing that came to mind. "It's so sad that you're saying that to me because I'm about to pass out."

Quest knew she was out of it and chuckled as he lifted her close. Mick's eyes closed, her head falling to one side as she lost consciousness. Quest simply held her for a time, staring down into her face. His intense gray stare caressed every nuance. Her features were relaxed and trusting as her head rested against his tan linen shirt. Quest faced an acknowledgement and it stunned him. In the day and a half that he'd known her, he'd become hooked and it was just that simple. Yes, she was lovely, luscious and completely alluring, but she was also the sort of woman who intrigued him. He presumed there were things in her past- unpleasant things- that had formed her into the woman he assumed she was: no-nonsense, focused and dedicated. He'd give anything to hear *her* story and believed he'd give more to keep her with him.

Quest shook his head as though to clear it. The depth of his feelings came as a total shock. After all, as he'd acknowledged, he'd only known her a day and a half- if that. This couldn't be more than physical attraction, could it?

Mick stirred a bit, grimacing as she snuggled her head against his chest in search of a more comfortable position. Quest ceased his contemplating and carried her up the short staircase to the bedroom suite. After laying her down, he debated upon whether he should relieve her of the snug pink tee and form fitting pants. He decided against it, knowing he'd never make it out of the room if he saw any more of her body. He tugged an afghan from the foot of the bed and covered her prone form.

"Quest?" Mick croaked, feeling him moving away.

"I'll be here when you wake up," he promised watching her closely for only a second longer before he left the room.

~~~

Mick shuffled from the bedroom two hours later, following the sounds of the TV that led her back into the living room. She walked in and took a seat on the sofa before Quest had the chance to stand.

"How do you feel?" he asked, after shutting off the television.

Mick produced a weary, yet serene smile. "Not like I'm about to pass out," she told him.

"Good," he chuckled the word.

Mick's look turned apologetic as she opened her mouth to put that expression into words.

Quest raised his hand before she could utter a word. "I don't want to hear the word 'sorry' again."

"But your entire evening's been shot to hell."

"I wouldn't say that."

Clearly, she didn't believe him. "You could've stayed at home and watched television," she pointed out.

"True," Quest conceded with a nod. "But I couldn't look around and find a woman strolling into my living room, could I?"

"I don't know," Mick sighed, shrugging lazily as her brows rose a notch higher. "From what I've heard, you have no problems in that area."

"From what you've heard?"

"Mmm-hmm, your staff- the women especially- have nothing but the sweetest things to say about their boss," she said in a teasing tone.

Quest's smile sparked his dimple. "What sort of things?" he inquired while leaning forward to clasp his hands together.

Mick couldn't help but laugh over his curiosity. "I won't

betray confidences except to say that they're all a little in love with you."

Laughing softly, Quest looked down and appeared every bit the shy little boy. "I swear to you I've never slept with any of them."

"Mmm...and does that go for your other half?"

"Ha! *I've* never slept with any of them," Quest emphasized, knowing his brother's sexual escapades were legend. He cleared his throat once the laughter quieted a bit. "We should order," he suggested.

Mick's spirits sank when she saw him reaching for one of the restaurant menus. "Room service," she lamented.

Quest ignored her tone. "Here. You order," he decided and passed her the card.

Mick sat fidgeting with the menu. Her eyes were riveted on Quest. *You should leave tomorrow on that plane with County*, a voice warned and she silently agreed. Quest Ramsey was too...*mmm*. She truly believed that all he had to do was snap his fingers and her panties would come tumbling down. Then she'd be done for. Both mentally drawn to him and physically dazzled.

~~~

Following a hearty Italian feast, both Quest and Michaela were patting their stomachs in satisfaction.

"It's been a while since I've had a meal at the Sorenson." Quest said.

"So you visit their restaurants during business meetings, huh?"

Quest shrugged, his eyes narrowing devilishly. "I wouldn't exactly call them *business* meetings."

Mick figured as much. "I got it," she said and then gave a long lazy stretch. "We didn't do much talking once the food arrived," she pointed out when she noticed him staring.

"No problem," he was still appreciating the stretch she'd given. "It wasn't much different from most of my dates," he confided while silently thinking of how he had no real desire to talk with most of the women he took out. They were pretty easy to peg after the first fifteen or twenty minutes- if that long.

"I'm sorry it was such a boring night," Mick whispered as though sensing his thoughts.

Quest blinked and fixed her with an intent stare. "No Michaela, I didn't mean it the way it sounded," he said, pressing one hand to his chest. "This was one of the best dates I've ever had."

"Mmm-hmm. I don't believe you, but thank you."

"I swear to you it's true," he returned, his gorgeous gray eyes fixed and unwavering. And it was true. He'd talked with Mick enough to know she could hold his interest talking about toenails let alone anything more worthy. The silence during dinner wasn't strained. It was easy and he enjoyed every minute. This date wasn't just one of the best, it was *the* best. He knew she'd really think he was full of it if he told her that.

Mick took a deep breath, tugging on her lower lip as though she were debating. "Quest? May I ask you something," she said finally.

His gaze remained fixed. "You can ask me anything."

"Um," Mick looked down in her lap and cleared her throat. "Why didn't you come out during the meeting? I mean, you were there and-why did you stay away?"

The muscle worked along the curve of his jaw when he heard her question. A question he had no answer to-not an answer he wanted to share anyway. Michaela Sellars had captivated him from the moment he saw her. He knew if he'd joined her and Quaysar during the meeting, he'd have spent the better portion of his time staring at her. He'd wanted the opportunity to do that alone without having to participate in a conversation he had no interest in.

"I don't know why I stayed back," he told her at last, running an index finger along the perfect crease in his navy trousers, "but I'd like to make it up if you'll let me."

If possible, Mick's eyes sparkled more vibrantly. "How?"

"Let me take you out?"

Mick smiled. "Again?" she teased.

"*Outside* the hotel."

"Definitely."

Satisfied, Quest nodded before fixing Mick with a look that said he should be going.

She stood and watched him follow suit. She was about to pass the sofa when his hand cupped her elbow. She turned, sighed as though she was preparing herself.

He simply tugged her close. Mick stood on her toes, her eyes focused on his heavenly mouth when he dipped his head. Her eyes grew wide and she studied his face up close before her lashes drifted shut.

Her lips parted in eager anticipation, but Quest merely applied soft kisses to her mouth in rapid succession. Each time, Mick arched closer, her lips parting further in a quiet plea for him to cease his torment.

Moments away from moaning her need, she brushed her fingers against his neck and sought to bring him closer. Quest's hands remained curved around her elbows, flexing slightly as he added more pressure to the kiss. His tongue thrust lightly- still teasingly so. Briefly, he stroked the roof of her mouth, the ridge of her teeth. A brief smile flashed on his face when he heard the helpless cry lilt from her throat. His hands moved from her arms to cup her face. His thumbs began a sensuous assault on the soft skin below her earlobes.

"Mmm…" She whimpered, when his tongue rotated around hers, caressing in the same manner as his thumbs were caressing her skin with slow sweeping circles. Her next gasp caught on another helpless cry and her legs weakened. Quest never broke the kiss and allowed her to take refuge on the arm of the sofa. He followed her down, his big hands fisted against the chair on either side of her.

Mick toyed with the buttons on his shirt, before her fingers curled weakly into the neckline. Aside from her lips, she could feel no other part of her body. She mimicked the lazy strokes of his tongue and knew she could have kissed him forever. She found herself praying as hard for the kiss to go on as she did for it to end.

Just don't let him snap his fingers. The panties will surely come tumbling down...

He kissed as though he were making love to her mouth and as though he had no intention of stopping. When he would have pulled away, Mick uttered a smothered cry of disagreement. In a spontaneous gesture, her teeth fastened to his lower lip and a jolt of power surged through her when he grunted his satisfaction.

Finally, Quest returned his hands to her arms squeezing firmly while breaking the kiss. "Tomorrow at seven?" he suggested, pressing his forehead to hers and taking deep breaths.

Mick nodded. "I'll be ready...and sober," she promised, her breathing just as strained.

Quest grinned. "Good night," he whispered applying a lingering kiss to the mole at the corner of her mouth before he walked away.

She sat there with one hand curved over her mouth. Her fingers massaged her throbbing lips as she watched him go. She realized that finally she understood what the phrase 'thoroughly kissed' meant.

The ring of the phone shattered the dream and Mick reluctantly blinked herself back to reality. Stiffly, she moved off the sofa and made her way to the message desk.

"Michaela Sellars," she greeted in her softest tone.

"Ms. Sellars, Houston Ramsey."

The curt, businesslike voice on the line quickly snapped Mick from her spell. "Mr. Ramsey," she greeted.

"Forgive the hour, Ms. Sellars. I'd planned to contact you earlier today."

"Uh no, that-that's quite alright," Mick assured him, tousling her hair as she began to pace the living room. "What can I do for you?"

"Well first, let me apologize for not meeting you when you visited the other day."

Mick nodded. "Well, it was a brief meeting. I'm afraid we won't be doing business."

"Ah, the book."

"Yes. We won't be pursuing it, I'm afraid."

"My nephew's decision. Not mine."

The clarification brought a curious frown to Mick's face. "I was under the impression that the family was against it?" she probed, settling back on an armchair as she spoke.

Houston uttered a short, bitter laugh. "No, young lady. Certain members of this family are against the book. My wife, Daphne, and I would've been completely behind the project."

"I see," Mick said.

"We want that book written, Ms. Sellars and we'd like to speak with you about it."

"That could be arranged."

"Good. Shall we say a breakfast meeting in the morning?"

Mick crossed her legs. "I'm afraid tomorrow morning won't be good for me," she said, remembering that she was seeing County off at the airport then.

"Perhaps lunch, then?" Houston suggested. "We can have a car sent to your hotel and you can meet with us at our club. We have a private dining room."

Mick raised her brows. "That sounds nice. I'll look forward to seeing you then."

"Good night, Ms. Sellars."

Mick stared at the phone once the call had ended. Leaning back in her chair, she gazed up at the ceiling. "What now?" she groaned.

A LOVER'S DREAM

~FIVE~

"Don't let this man mesmerize you so that you forget you have a home and responsibilities back in Chicago," County warned, as she and Mick shared one last hug after her flight had been called.

Mick smirked and pulled away. "You are definitely overreacting," she accused, while toying with the myriad of rings adorning County's right hand.

County rolled her eyes. "I don't think so. Damn it, I didn't even get a chance to meet even one of the twins. It's not fair," she pouted.

"Well you could always stay another few days. I know they'd arrange for you to remain at the hotel."

County's full lips twisted to one side as she seemed to consider the proposal. Then, with a flashy wave, she grimaced. "Nah, I think I'll pass. Seeing how goo-goo you are, I know I can't afford to lose my head like that."

"Hush," Mick ordered, tugging on the sleeve of County's periwinkle-blue cardigan.

"Seriously Mick," she said and stepped a bit closer. "I like what going goo-goo over a man has done for you. It's only been a few days and I've seen you looking happier than you have in a long time."

"County," Mick sighed, doubt tingeing her voice.

"That is, except when you're bouncing around with your little half-dressed girlfriends," she chastised in a tone of phony disdain.

Mick laughed and slipped one hand inside the back pocket of her jeans. "Yeah, well you can rest assured that I won't lose myself here when I know I have to get back to my little girlfriends. Not to mention Driggers."

"Hmph," County sniffed, kissing Mick's cheek before she headed toward her gate.

Mick waved, all the while ignoring the voice that told her she should be getting on that plane. "Oh, shut up," she hissed.

~~~

Quest and Quaysar were in the midst of their morning meeting. Seated at the spacious round table in the office's living area, they sat with their calendars before them while confirming dates for meetings, events and other obligations.

"I talked with Spotty and it looks like the center will be on schedule to open as planned," Quaysar mentioned, referring to their foreman for the project Spotty Crawford.

"Good," Quest mumbled, making a notation on his book.

"Yeah, that's gonna be some ribbon cutting in Cali. Those kids are gonna go crazy over a community center on the beach," Quay predicted.

Quest laughed. "They deserve it," he said, thinking about the project. Each year Ramsey Group chose a group to work with to provide housing, counseling, recreation and job placement. That year had proven to be especially rewarding as Ramsey Group completed the first community center of its kind. One that would combine recreation, shelter and education for a select group of youth. Should the endeavor be successful, the number of teens housed by the center would increase as would its state funding.

A devilish glint sparked in Quay's dark eyes as he glanced across the table toward his brother. "You know, this ribbon cutting sounds like something Mick would like to go to."

Quest didn't bother to look at his brother, though a knowing smile crossed his face. "Get off it," he ordered quietly.

"What, man?"

"Stop bein' so nosy."

Quay pressed one hand across the lapel of his navy pin-striped suit coat. "I swear that's not it. I am concerned about you though, and it's my place to make sure you're okay."

Quest couldn't help but laugh at his brother's nerve. "This is private, Quay."

"Well alright," Quay said, "but it pleases me to know Miss Michaela Sellars has earned the right to be placed in the *private* category. That tells me a lot."

"Unbelievable," Quest murmured. "Isn't there a woman somewhere who you should be trying to coax into bed?"

"No, right now we're talking about the woman *you're* trying to coax into bed."

"I won't have to coax her."

"Ahh...confidence. I like it and it also pleases me to know you're so interested in the lady."

Quest leaned back in his chair and began to toy with the stylish coral tie he wore with a tailored three-piece black suit. "Michaela is a business associate. She was here to investigate us if you recall."

"Oh, I recall," Quay nodded, "and that's exactly what has *you* so intrigued by her. She ain't here to cast her vote as your next sex partner. She's luscious *and* smart and mysterious and you is hooked, brotha," he drawled while standing from the table. "I gotta go," he said before his twin could offer a rebuttal.

Quest broodingly conceded that his brother would have the last word.

~~~

"Thank you," Michaela whispered to the escort who showed her into the Ramsey's private dining room at the Sharpe Club. The establishment was a haven for much of the commercial real estate crowd who closed the deals with the largest revenues.

"Ms. Sellars."

Mick smiled at the couple across the room. Though older, they were extremely beautiful and seemed to complement each other's flair for casually elegant attire.

Houston Ramsey stepped forward with both hands outstretched. "My wife, Daphne," he said after introducing himself to Mick.

"Thank you for agreeing to meet with us," Daphne said while shaking hands.

"Well, our conversation has me intrigued," Mick shared, smoothing her fingers across the silver buckle that secured the taupe knee-length skirt she wore. "I was under the impression that the book was a no from all the Ramseys."

Michaela missed the glance exchanged between Houston and Daphne. She was too in awe of the room to pay much attention to anything else. The dining room was designed with devastatingly beautiful bay windows that offered breathtaking views of the hazy Seattle sky on one side and a distant view of the city's skyline on the other.

"Impressive, isn't it?" Houston remarked, seeing how affected Mick appeared. "The city's realtors decided to go in on the facility several years ago. It's come a long way since then too," he boasted, stroking a sideburn as he joined Mick in watching the view. "Now the place can facilitate everything from meetings and parties to weekend stays for couples or large groups."

"You're right, it *is* impressive," Mick acknowledged while turning her back on the view. "But I'm sure you didn't call me here to discuss the history of the Sharpe Club."

Houston smiled and waved his hand toward the area where his wife relaxed. "Please, have a seat," he urged Mick. "As far as pretty much the entire Ramsey clan are concerned, a book-*no* book on the family should be written."

"Pretty much the entire Ramsey clan." Mick reiterated.

"My wife and I feel differently," Houston said, smiling down at Daphne, who nodded her agreement as he spoke. "I've always had my differences with my brothers and their sons. Those sons have done nothing but stain the Ramsey name."

Mick bristled beneath the declaration.

Houston noticed. "There are things I have little proof of, but I know a black line trails from each of their names."

Mick folded her arms over the matching taupe suit jacket. "Mr. Ramsey, forgive me for saying this, but it sounds like you have plenty of speculation. Are there any specifics?"

Again, the Ramseys exchanged glances. Then, at her husband's nod, Daphne leaned down to retrieve a folder from the cream leather satchel that matched her pumps. She handed it to Mick.

"I think a dead young woman is a bit more than speculation, don't you Ms. Sellars?" Houston challenged.

Mick didn't respond. She was too busy scanning the folder, which consisted of news clippings and a picture of a young pretty girl. One of the clippings brought a frown to Mick's face. "Suicide?" she questioned, looking up at the couple.

Houston pretended to be focused on one of his diamond cuff links. "We think a reporter of your ilk could prove that it wasn't."

Mick responded with a knowing smile and stood. "I'm not in the habit of making up lies to sell books. Mr. Ramsey, Mrs. Ramsey," she bade the couple and prepared to leave the room.

"The young woman in that photo fell to her death from a hotel room window," Houston called after Mick. He waited until her steps slows before he continued. "That room was in Quest Ramsey's name."

~~~

"The story doesn't even mention Quest's name," Mick noted later while they were dining. She had spent the better part of her time scouring a full-page article. "Most of the copy is reaction from friends, teachers and family. There's a mention of a party, but-"

"A party given by my nephew," Houston interjected. "They were all there and any one of them could've been involved in that girl's murder."

Mick set aside the folder and fixed Houston with an exasperated look. "Mr. Ramsey, I just can't understand why you'd want to open a can of worms about your family after all these years."

"Every one of those boys is spoiled rotten and has been from the minute they were born," Houston blurted, pounding his fist next to his plate of Caesar salad. "They were raised fully aware of the influence their family possessed. Knowledge of money and power is dangerous in the hands of adults, Ms. Sellars. It's deadly in the hands of children."

Mick toyed with a curl that bobbed along her ear. "You must know your nephews won't be too pleased when they hear about this. You know I'll have to get their side of the story," she forewarned.

Houston waved his hand. "Please talk to them, by all means," he urged, appearing undaunted.

Mick tapped her fingers along the edge of the table. "I understand the two of you have children?" she inquired, not wanting to consider all parents were so cold and vindictive toward others who were basically children beneath them.

A proud smile brightened Houston's handsome chiseled face. "We have two. A daughter, Dena and a son, Taurus. Both are exceptional people, beautiful inside and out."

Mick smiled and nodded. "Thank you both for a lovely meal," she said as she stood. "I'll be in touch."

***

Mick opened her door to Quest just a few minutes before seven o'clock that evening.

"Hello," his mesmerizing gray stare slowly assessed the gorgeous aqua colored V-neck dress she wore.

Mick took a deep breath, trying to hide her smile when Quest quickly looked away from her heaving bosom. "Hi," she whispered, looking askew when she heard her voice tremble. Her gaze lowered when Quest leaned down to kiss the corner of her mouth. His lips lingered against the mole there. When he pulled back, he could see the intensity in her eyes as she watched him.

"What's the matter?" he asked, concern already filtering his eyes.

Mick shook her head and smiled. "I'm just waiting on you to compliment my sober state," she teased.

Quest chuckled. "Very nice," he said reaching for the chiffon coat she held. "We better get a move on," he suggested, knowing he was seconds away from forgetting going out for the evening.

~~~

Michaela's observant qualities were in high gear that evening. She covertly studied Quest's every movement and mannerism for any sign that he was the sort that could be involved in a girl's death-er, murder. She didn't find it surprising that his every action was consistent.

In spite of her thoroughly suspicious nature, Mick simply didn't believe certain things could be completely disguised. The way he held onto her hand until she was secure in the passenger seat of his Navigator, telling her to be sure the belt was securely locked and then checking to see that it was. He teased with the valets at the restaurant-all young black men whom he tipped even though they hadn't even parked his car. He kept his hand at her waist and introduced her to everyone he spoke to.

The restaurant Quest chose for their dinner came complete with a beautiful view of the Puget Sound. Mick was quiet for a very long time as she sat enchanted by the view.

"Sorry," she whispered to Quest when she glanced up to see him staring at her. "This is so beautiful, I can't find a thing to talk about."

Quest's lashes closed briefly over his eyes. "It's no

problem," he assured her.

It was true. He could never tire of watching her. The sweet chocolate face held that perfect combination of sensuality and innocence. The silky blue-black curls made him want to lose his hands in them while he kissed her.

"Hungry?" he asked, desperate to focus his attention elsewhere.

"Starving," Mick groaned, selecting one of the leather-bound menus from the table. "What's good?"

The simple question erased any hope Quest had of focusing his attention elsewhere. His gaze locked on her X-rated mouth.

"Quest?"

"Everything," he managed, "everything's very good." he said, hopelessly fixated on her full soft lips.

"Let's see," Mick breathed, opening the menu. "Ooooh, you're right. It'll take me all night to decide."

Quest only smiled and leaned back in his chair in order to watch her more comfortably. By the time the waiter approached, she had at least decided on drinks. The young Hispanic waiter barely wrote down the order, his eyes were so focused on Mick. Quest didn't like it, but he surely couldn't blame the guy. For good measure-and agitation- he asked the young man to repeat the selection.

Mick laughed when they were alone. "So you're one of those, huh?"

Quest shook his head once in confusion.

"One of those difficult diners who send their dish back five times because of the smallest imperfections."

Quest tugged on the lapel of his mocha suit jacket. "I'm not like that and it wasn't about that. The guy was just staring at you so hard."

Mick studied the water past the window. "Are you the jealous type?" she asked in a sly manner.

"Never had any reason to be."

"I'm sure."

"I don't think I am. Besides, I couldn't fault the guy."

"Why?"

Quest grinned at her bewilderment and casually studied his own menu. "You'd have to be seeing yourself through a man's eye to understand that, Michaela."

Mick's breath caught in her throat over the obvious compliment.

Quest heard her reaction. "You have no idea what I mean?"

Mick looked down at the table. "I've never had time to worry about my looks."

"Well, when you look like this what's there to worry over?!" Quest bellowed playfully.

Mick laughed to cover her embarrassment and was thankful when the waiter returned with their drinks. The last thing she needed this night was to let Quest Ramsey charm her into another mind-numbing kiss or something more delicious. Houston's Ramsey's certainty that one or more of his nephews had played a part in a possible murder bothered Mick more than she cared to admit. Her curiosity was piqued as highly as her determination to prove Quest had nothing to do with it.

Once the waiter left with their dinner orders, Mick pulled the straw from her peach daquiri and settled back to enjoy her drink. "Thank you for dinner, Quest. You Ramseys sure know how to treat people right."

A muscle flexed in Quest's jaw. "So I've heard," he muttered. "So tell me how you became a writer," he requested.

Mick looked out over the candlelit dining room. "By way of investigative reporting."

"Yeah, I've read a few of your articles from the file your publisher sent," he shared.

"Mmm-hmm, I could really throw myself into that job. I guess I had the personality for it."

"Why'd you quit?" Quest took a sip of his Hennessey.

Mick's expression tightened at the memory. "I quit when my editor drained the last of my ability to cooperate with his stupid editorial *suggestions* by asking me to sensationalize my story on three homeless kids who lost their shelter to fire."

"How'd he expect you to do that with such a story?"

"That's what I asked him," Mick replied flatly. "And it was either quit or jump across the desk and strangle him when he told me to put a spin on it that the kids were helped by the system, put into a fabulous home, blah, blah, blah."

Quest appeared even more confused. "Seems it would've been more sensational to show the kids as they truly were."

"According to my former editor, we'd done too many *downer* stories on the subject. Readers needed to see that the system did work, sometimes."

"Hmph," Quest grunted, rubbing his fingers across his wavy hair. "Sounds like someone was paying for a little positive press."

"Indeed," Mick confirmed with a finger pointed in his direction. "The publisher had friends who were complaining about all the flack the city council and social service offices were getting from the public over such cases."

Quest took another sip of his drink. "So what'd you do?"

Mick shrugged. "Told him to take his job and shove it, covered the story freelance and sold it *my* way to another paper. Then I followed up with a book that brought needed exposure to certain corrupt officials and a wave of support to those kids."

"What happened?" Quest was thoroughly engrossed by the story.

"They're living with a loving adoptive family. The two oldest are preparing for college next year and the youngest is working on her reelection campaign for the student council."

Quest threw back his head and laughed. Michaela likened the sound to a hearty, good-natured roar and she couldn't help but laugh as well.

"That was my first book," she told him.

"Ah, so you haven't always covered us high-profile types, huh?"

"Nah, all that just sort of happened. I was always far more interested in the lesser knowns," she confessed, smoothing her hands across her bare arms. "The ones who really don't have anyone to root for or fight for them."

"Like you?"

"I guess," her brows rose slightly as she considered her response, "Of course, not having anyone to root or fight for me made me fight for myself and it made me stronger and I'm glad."

Quest believed her. Still, rooting and fighting for herself were things he didn't like to think about her doing-not alone, anyway. "I guess you think us high-profile types are pretty pathetic?" he asked, hoping to lighten the mood.

"Actually, it's pretty sad, but refreshingly realistic too."

"How?"

"To see people with so much, be so rocked by the conflicts within their own families. Most people think the rich are problem free."

"Hmph," Quest drained what was left of his drink then.

"Why *hmph*?" Mick queried.

Quest only shook his head.

"Hey," she called softly, leaning forward to knock on the polished cherry-wood table they shared. "I've just told you a lot more than I tell most people. You can feel free to reciprocate. It won't end up in a book, I assure you."

Leaning forward, Quest clasped his hands on the table. "My family is strong and close knit. Sometimes *too* close knit. We love each other a lot, so sometimes it's hard to see that in protecting one another we may be doing more harm than good."

Mick shook her head. "Protecting one another from what?"

Quest shrugged. "Everybody else."

"Strangers?"

"Yeah, them too."

~~~

After dinner, Quest took Mick back to her hotel. Both realized the evening was best ended after the meal. The drive back into the city was easy and silent. When they stepped back into her suite, Quest checked the rooms, which only further endeared him to Mick.

"Thanks," she said once he returned to the living room.

Quest merely nodded, closing the distance between them in a few long strides. He reached for her hand and stood there toying with her fingers while his head was bowed.

Mick studied him closely, loving the flawless dark of his skin and the long sleek line of his brows. She knew if he kissed her then, she would seriously consider letting him stay the night. It was far too soon for that. Besides, she couldn't let the evening end without telling him what she had learned.

"Quest," she whispered, covering his hand with her other while tugging him toward the sofa.

Quest's soft expression turned hard when he noticed the look on her face. "What?" he probed, curving his hand around her neck and using his thumb to nudge her chin. "Tell me," he urged, when she reluctantly met his gaze.

"I had a meeting with your uncle and aunt today." She felt his hand weaken around her neck.

"Houston and Daphne."

Mick closed her eyes and nodded.

"What did they tell you?"

The question triggered Mick's curiosity. "They told me about a young woman and her suicide," she continued slowly.

Quest's hand left Mick's neck to settle in his lap. Then, he grimaced and began to massage the horseshoe brand on his left arm. "They want the book."

"Very much."

"Will you do it?"

"I don't know," Mick confided slowly, her gaze faltering. She didn't notice Quest's gaze narrowing as he stood.

"The story appeals to all the reasons why I became a writer," she continued, "I just don't know."

"Why don't you know?" He stated his inquiry slowly, turning to face her.

Mick trailed her fingers along the V-neck of her dress. "I get the feeling that it's about revenge for Houston. He's certain the girl's death was foul play, told me he could prove that it was." She shrugged and shook her head. "I didn't like the vibe I got from him."

"Yeah, Uncle Hous sets a lot of people on edge," Quest agreed, massaging his jaw as he grinned. "He's always held a special dislike for me and Quay. I never got why," he said, his eyes focusing somewhere in the distance as he spoke. "Besides, the girl was his daughter's best friend."

Mick was silent as she absorbed the information.

"I better go," Quest decided, leaning down to pull Mick up from the sofa. "You've got a lot to think about, so I'll leave you to it."

Mick tried to mask her disappointment. She wanted him to stay. Sadly, she realized nothing could be salvaged from the evening after it had taken such a downturn. Silently, she saw Quest to the door and tried not to appear too skeptical when he told her he'd call.

***

Daphne Ramsey added more cream to her coffee and propped her chin in her palm. "Do you think Ms. Sellars will take the job?" she asked, watching the dark liquid turn a creamy shade of beige.

"She has firm principles," Houston noted, crossing his long legs at the ankles while enjoying the violin concerto that filled the private dining room. "I sensed that about her and this is the sort of story she'd thrive on. I don't think she'll be able to resist the power of it."

Just then, the Ramsey's houseman Tony Flores, was opening the front door. "Good evening, son," he greeted the young man outside.

"Hey T," Quest replied, obviously in no mood for small talk. "They in?"

"Yes, they're taking dessert in the private dining room," Tony informed Quest slowly. He seemed to sense the edginess of the younger man's mood, but felt no need to question him. He nodded and stepped aside. Had he known how on edge Quest was, he might have reconsidered.

Quest was on his way to the dining room located on the back corner of the stately Mediterranean-styled home. Without bothering to knock, he headed right past the brass trimmed glass doors.

Houston's brown eyes widened briefly at the sight of his nephew, yet he masked the look quickly. "Quest," he greeted casually.

"Evening Uncle House, Aunt Daph."

Houston and Daphne nodded simultaneously in response.

"Pretty late, isn't it Quest?" Houston noted, brushing a crumb from his red dinner jacket.

"Well I would've preferred to meet you both for lunch, but from what I hear you were tied up today around that time."

Houston couldn't resist catching his wife's eye.

Quest noticed. "Yeah, she told me," he confirmed.

Clearly, Houston was disconcerted. Though Michaela Sellars had said she would talk with the twins, he thought she'd simply been using that to determine how serious he was to have the story written. He was usually quite good at judging people, and he had completely misjudged her.

"She's not as predictable as you thought, huh?"

Houston's expression seemed hard as granite. "It's late, Quest."

"The book is dead, Houston. Accept it."

"Accept it?!" Houston blared.

"Sweetie," Daphne called in a hushed tone when her husband bolted from the chair. She was thoroughly ignored.

"Who the hell do you think you're talkin' to, boy? In spite of what you and your twin believe, Quest and Quaysar do *not* run this family."

"I agree," Quest stated simply, easing one hand inside the pocket of his mocha trousers, "but those who do run it-your own brothers and sisters, Houston-they feel the same as I do."

"Please," Houston spat, with a flip wave of his hand. "This mess has been covered up for too long. You, your brother and all your spoiled, egotistical cousins have only piled one stain after another on this family. It's time for it to end."

Quest was already heading toward the dining room door. "Leave this alone, Houston and stay away from Michaela Sellars."

"She's a smart woman. Determined too, and she has a craving to see justice done, I believe," Houston predicted, folding his arms across his chest. "She'll uncover the messes you all have done your best to cover all these years."

"I said stay away from her!" Quest roared, the full bass of his voice vibrating in the silence when he turned. His eyes had darkened to pitch-black. He whipped open the dining room door with such force, the glass panes vibrated and threatened to shatter.

Tony was sprinting down the hall in response to Quest's roar. Everyone watched in silence as the angry young man stormed from the house.

~SIX~

"Thank you," Mick told the front desk clerk while trying to hide her disappointment . She'd stopped to inquire of any messages being left for her. There were none. Of course, she felt she'd already known there wouldn't be. After all, she'd been faithfully checking her cell and the answering service to her room. Still, she wanted to be sure.

What for girl? What you're hoping for was over before it began.

Mick tried to deny that she was *hoping* for anything. It was simply a matter of manners. If a person said he was going to call, then he should. Besides, Quest Ramsey had struck her as the type of man who knew how to mind his manners.

Sure, but he's also a man, Mick acknowledged. *And a man*

who says he'll call almost always doesn't.

Mick shook her head and swallowed past the lump in her throat. Who was she kidding? Her job, her honesty and her strength had always been her downfall when a relationship was the issue. As for dating companions, she was usually extremely busy. Moreover, she hated what she'd labeled love's aftertaste- when the newness wore off and the true light of the person shone through.*That* was what she hated most. Perhaps County was right, maybe she did want all the happiness and none of the drama. Naive? Yes, but she felt drama was a waste of time. Would it be a waste of time if he were truly the right man? Mick had no answer to that.

It was best to quit while she was ahead, she decided with a nod. She didn't know Quest Ramsey nearly well enough to know if he was the right man or not. After the other night, she should just leave well enough alone.

But he's so gorgeous, Mick and he kisses like a dream and kisses like that could only promise more naughty delights elsewhere.

"Stop it," Mick hissed to the voice inside her head. She was so disoriented that her path to the dining room was about to be redirected to the bar. Bad idea, but Mick felt a tiny drink was in order.

"Miss?" the host called, having spotted her from his podium. "Could I be of assistance?" he asked, noticing Mick's confused state.

Mick put her most refreshing smile in place. "Yes," she said, smoothing both hands across the waistband of her casual flare-legged pants. "I'd like a table," she decided.

"No problem, ma'am," the maitre d' replied with a smile as he selected a menu from some place beneath the host's podium. "If you'd just follow-"

"Hold off on that, man."

Mick felt a hand settle to her waist just as she turned to see who had interrupted the maitre d'. Quaysar Ramsey smiled down at her, then winked.

"The lady will dine with me," he coolly decided.

The maitre d' nodded. "Right this way, miss. Mr. Ramsey," he added with a genuine smile.

"You're known here, I see," Mick said as she and Quaysar followed behind.

Quay shrugged. "Everywhere," he said.

"What are you doing here, Quay?" Mick asked once they'd shared a laugh.

"Just wrapped up a meeting over drinks in the bar," he explained, pulling her elbow with a light squeeze. "I was on my way out when I saw you."

"Well shouldn't you be getting back to the office?" Mick questioned.

"I've always heard you should never drink on an empty stomach."

Mick rolled her eyes up at him. "Uh, excuse me, but haven't you already done that?"

Quaysar pretended to be worried. "Damn, you're right," he whispered, pressing one hand to his abdomen. "I'd better eat somethin' quick then. Move, woman!" he ordered in a brisk, playful tone that sent Mick into peals of laughter.

Quaysar continued to tease and laugh boisterously as he escorted Mick. They stopped at the booth that was always reserved for members of Ramsey Group. Of course, Quay's infectious laughter and bellowing voice drew every female's eye. Some were polite enough to look away when they noticed the woman at his side. Others weren't so gracious. They stared at the man with blatant, helpless desire filling their gazes. Even those with dates practically drooled when Quay approached various tables to shake hands with the men he knew.

Michaela was in heaven as she watched Quay making his rounds from her seat at the booth. He was so good-natured, she thought. She honestly couldn't see him brooding over anything. Probably because he was single, which drove home the fact that she should keep her status the same.

"This is great," Quay was saying when he returned to the

booth and took a seat, "us meeting like this since our dinner date was cancelled."

"Mmm yes, and I don't believe you gave me an actual reason as to why you had to cancel?" Mick inquired, her tone laced with playful suspicion.

Quay shrugged. "Because Q told me to."

Mick went cold, and the fact had nothing to do with the white double-strapped tank top she wore. "What did you say?" she whispered when she finally found her voice.

Quay grinned. "He told me to," he repeated, his right dimple appearing while his dark eyes crinkled adorably.

"Why?"

"Why do you think?"

Mick shook her head slowly as though she were trying to form a response in her mind. At last, she looked up at Quaysar. A befuddled expression marred her lovely face.

Quay chuckled and leaned back on his side of the booth. "Mick, you're beautiful. You gotta know that. That face," he said as though he couldn't believe what he was seeing, "that hair...and that mouth. Hell, you make a man stop dead in his tracks, girl. My brother ain't no different."

Mick was still silent, her thoughts going back to Quest Ramsey's knee-weakening kisses.

"Course I've been known to only judge by what's on the outside- the face, the body, just the package," Quay admitted. "But with Quest, he sees that and more. He'd never admit it, but a twin can sense those things," he shared proudly.

Mick pressed her lips together and then raised her brows in doubt. "I think whatever he was feeling is probably over and done with now," she confided, although she'd loved hearing everything Quay said.

"Over and done with?" he asked.

"We haven't spoken in days," she told him. "He said he'd call. You know what that usually means."

Quay uttered a muffled curse. "What's that fool broodin' over now?"

Mick's nails grazed the gooseflesh covering her arms. "I had a meeting with your aunt Daphne and uncle Houston. They wanted to discuss the book. I told Quest about it. He asked if I'd write it. I couldn't tell him yes or no."

Quay brushed his thumb across the curve of his lower lip. "So Hous is for the book?"

"Yes, very much."

"Damn, that old man hasn't let go of all that after all these years."

"Quay?" Mick called, confused by the statement.

Quaysar grunted and jerked out of the suit coat covering his muscular torso. "A girl- Sera Black. She died many years ago, we were all on our way out of high school. She died at a party we threw. Houston always blamed us. Sera was best friends with his daughter."

"Dena?" Mick supplied, remembering what Quest had told her about his uncle's children.

Quay appeared somewhat preoccupied then, but soon shook his head to clear whatever had gotten him distracted.

"What if I invited you to a great jazz club?" he proposed, smoothly changing subjects.

Mick grinned while shaking her head. "And here I thought Chicago had the best jazz clubs in the world."

"Ah, but this jazz club is *more* than a club."

"*More* than a club," Mick set her elbows to the table. "In what way?"

"Well, aside from our house band, we've got the deejays who relieve them between sets."

Mick's brows rose. "Deejays *and* a jazz band? Well, that *is* more."

Quay shrugged, obviously pleased. "Yeah, the guys are real impressive. They spin old-school R-and-B and hip-hop. It sets the dance floor on fire and people say Double Q is the best place to go and work up an appetite before dinner or work off the calories afterward."

"Double Q?" Mick inquired of the name.

"Quest is my partner. A silent partner," Quay shared with a roll of his eyes. "*Too* silent for me."

"Mmm, you want him more involved."

"Exactly."

Mick fixed him with a doubtful look."Your brother doesn't seem to be the club type," she noted.

"He's not," Quay acknowledged firmly with clear disapproval gleaming in his dark eyes. "The fool's more interested in stuffy business meetings. And, for you, that's a good thing."

Mick sat straighter. "For me?"

"Hell yeah, now you can come out and have fun and not have to worry about running into my stick-in-the-mud brother."

"It does sound like fun," Mick admitted, thinking how long it'd been since she'd had the chance to work up a dancing sweat.

"Well come on then," Quay urged, leaning back in his chair and propping his index finger alongside his temple.

"I think I'll take you up on it," Mick decided, smacking her hands to her thighs.

"Hot damn," Quay said and waved in their waiter's direction. "Let's get some drinks over here, man."

It was Mick's turn to wave then. "Uh, I can't."

Quaysar appeared crestfallen, but only for a second. "Well, I can," he decided, winking when she burst into laughter.

Mick's high spirits continued throughout lunch. Quay definitely had a comedic gene and he loved to show it off. For a while, Mick enjoyed herself and completely forgot what had her feeling so down.

* * *

"Yes ma'am, there *is* something for you," the concierge announced when Mick returned to the desk following her lunch with Quay.

Her spirits lifted a notch or two only to sink again when she saw that it was a package instead of a message. Yes, she thought, Quest's 'I'll call you' meant what it always meant whenever a man said it.

"Stop it," Mick ordered herself in a soft hissing tone. She

was determined to focus on having fun. Hell, she'd been in Seattle almost a week and she hadn't danced once.

Mick tapped her fingers along the side of the package and thought about her past week. In one week, she'd become so attached to Quest Ramsey. It wasn't normal-especially for her. She was too smart, too on top of her game, she noted and smoothed one hand across her fitted red flared pants. *I'll be damned if I let myself fall hard and fast for a man. Any man.*

~~~

Quest kept his back turned, deciding to maintain his position while the conversation took place outside his assistant's door. The men chatting away were discussing his brother's latest conquest, whom they'd seen him with during lunch earlier that day.

"She was a sight to behold," one man noted.

"Chocolate and curvy," another added.

"Can Quaysar Ramsey pick 'em or can he pick 'em?" Still another man added his opinion.

Quest didn't care too much for the comments, which grew more graphic as the discussion continued. He decided not to join them, which was just as well since the conversation ended shortly. Quest finished the note he was leaving with the documents. He was walking out of the office when Quay stepped past the glass doors.

"What's up Q?"

"'Sup?" Quest returned. "Have a good lunch?" he asked, meeting Quay in the middle of the corridor.

"Did I?" Quay continued with a sly grin. "I closed the Nichols deal and I had lunch with Mick."

Quest's expression tightened, the muscle in his jaw performing its most wicked dance. "I thought I told you to stay away from her."

Teasing remarks formed and died on Quay's tongue. He could see that his twin was in no mood to be further agitated. "Calm down, Q," he urged softly.

"I told you to stay away from her Quay," Quest said

simply, his gray stare already an unsettling onyx.

Quay felt his own temper beginning to simmer. "Stay away from her? I guess that goes for you as well?"

Quest blinked. "What the hell are you talkin' about?"

"Promising to call and not doing it. What's up? She's obviously interested and-"

"Don't do that."

Quay shrugged. "What?"

"Don't make her out to be someone who just wants to sleep with me."

Quay closed his eyes and took a deep breath. "I didn't mean it that way," he swore pressing one hand across his stylish cobalt and silver tie. "I'd never talk about Mick that way. It's obvious she's got strong emotions where you're concerned. I could see it on her face when I mentioned your name. And *before* you ask me, I was only talking about you when I mentioned you being part owner in the club."

Quest put a bit of space between himself and his twin.

"I invited her to the club tonight."

Quest's anger resurfaced. "What?" he whispered.

"And since you're not tossing your hat in the ring, there should be no complaints over the invite, right? Good." He said, when his brother just glared. "See ya," he called and strode toward the elevator.

Quest waited for the doors to close behind Quay before he moved. Grimacing, he took a seat on the edge of Jasmine's desk and massaged his jaw. Silently, he criticized himself for not calling for the past two days. She didn't deserve that. Especially not when she'd been so honest in telling him about his uncle's meeting-something she wasn't obligated to do.

But when you asked if she would write the book, she couldn't tell you she wouldn't. He realized that no matter how infatuated he was with her, he had to protect his family. *Protect Quay.* He believed Michaela Sellars had everything he'd been praying he'd find in all the women who had filtered in and out of his life and his bed. Lovely and sweet, she had all the assets a man

87

craved to maintain physical satisfaction indefinitely. More than that, he was in awe of the way her mind worked. She was inquisitive, slow to judge, slow to believe, and firm in her arguments. In the short time he had known her, he'd discovered that she was more than outward lusciousness. Michaela was inner strength and he wasn't ready to let her go.

Still, there was his family- a family with too many secrets- and, as Houston Ramsey loved to say, theirs was a family with too many stains to cover. Michaela Sellars was a writer- a writer body and soul. She put everything into her stories and she dug until everything was uncovered. There was no way she couldn't be intrigued by a family like the Ramseys. He could understand that. What set him on edge was that she would become just as intrigued by their secrets.

~~~

Double Q was all that Quaysar touted and more, Michaela thought after giving her name to the dapper gentleman at the club's entrance. Clearly, he was the person who decided the fate of scores of club hoppers who were eager to enter the establishment's hallowed sanctum.

Mick was escorted inside by a tall, beautiful Asian man who took her to a secluded table that offered a perfect view of every spot on the club's lower and middle level. She was tapping her sandal-shod foot to a seductive classic when Quay found her.

"What do you think?" he asked, while pressing a kiss to her cheek when he bent low to whisper against her ear.

"This place is incredible!" She raved, smoothing her hands across the strapless peach paisley dress she wore with the provocative sandals. The four-inch heels with macrame ankle ties accentuated her shapely legs and were perfect dancing shoes.

"Javi, a Courvoisier for me and, Mick?" Quay probed, waiting for her drink request.

"A pina colada, virgin," she replied, coolly shrugging when Quay shook his head. "Quay, this place," she continued to marvel once the waiter was off to fill their orders, "sort of a cruel joke to have the place encased in glass to torture those who can't make it past your judges out front."

Quay laughed. "Yeah, Vic and the boys are pretty selective, but it's because of them that Double Q is on that prized list of black-owned clubs that have zero percentage for violence."

"Impressive," Mick said, beginning to move in her seat when the band broke into a vintage Luther Vandross tune. "I especially like all the gorgeous escorts," she teased.

Quay responded with a devilish wink. "I take credit for all this greatness. You know, most of my staff think you're my latest conquest," he said as though it were nothing surprising.

Mick was more than surprised. She was downright stunned and it showed.

"Well damn," Quay snapped, pretending to take offense, "I mean, I know I'm not Denzel, but jeez," he muttered, tugging on the cuffs of the cream silk shirt that enhanced his flawless molasses skin.

Laughing then, Mick couldn't even respond to the absurd statement. Quay continued to talk until someone tapped his shoulder and he excused himself to go check on some things before the floors were changed for dancing. Mick waved him off and enjoyed the club a bit more. Small round tables skirted the floor/stage where the band performed. Luxurious booths fringed the outer walls of the club. The upper level had its own private dance floor and was lined with more booths, each lit by soft electric candles. Once her creamy pina colada had arrived, Mick was in a state of sheer bliss.

"You lovely people will now be entertained by DJ Maurice G while we take our break. Enjoy."

The announcement by the group's lead vocalist was followed by a round of applause. Within five minutes, the club had changed scenes from a dim, elegant jazz haven to an up-tempo dance hall. The fourth or fifth song, a vintage Barry White piece, had Mick out of her seat instantly. Of course, there were several men on hand to apply for the chance to be her dance partner. Their hopes were dashed, unfortunately, when Quay returned and announced that the first dance was his.

On the floor, Michaela and Quaysar bumped and grinded with the best of them. Mick was in her element and savored the fact that her partner was no slouch on the dance floor. In fact, Quay matched her move for move; they had the best time and it showed. Mick's laughter filled the air several times. Other couples even left the floor to make room for the energetic couple. A round of applause filled the club as Barry White's "My Everything" faded into another classic groove and the couple left the floor.

"Now your staff will *definitely* think we're sleeping together!" Mick teased boisterously, her laughter catching on a cry of surprise when she found Quest at the table.

"Michaela," he stood and greeted her in his usually intense, softly seductive manner. Of course, he fixed his brother with a quick harsh glare.

"Q, this is a surprise, man!" Quay said, pretending not to notice his brother's agitation. "This is great, you can keep Mick company while she takes a breather and I go check on the band. Five minutes, girl. Then it's back out on the floor," he squeezed her elbow before he sprinted off.

Mick sent Quest a quick look and waited for him to hold her chair. He didn't get the opportunity.

"Allow me," a voice called close to her ear and made Mick glance back.

"Taurus Ramsey," the man introduced himself.

Mick finally found her voice and just managed to speak her name.

Taurus responded with a slow double-dimpled smile. "I know," he said, undoing the buttons on his mocha suit coat as he sat next to her.

Mick couldn't deny how taken she was by the smooth Casanova-like god. The Ramsey male was the exact opposite of the molasses dark Quest and Quay possessed. He was definitely handsome though. His features were very fair, from the amber stare to the crop of thick, wavy locks in an unexpected shade of light brown.

Quest felt his jaw muscle working feverishly as he watched his cousin mesmerize Michaela with his very soft voice. That voice was known for holding most women in a captivated state. More than once, it'd been said that Taurus Ramsey could talk a woman into or out of anything- especially her clothes.

Quest cleared his throat to muffle the grunt of disapproval erupting from his throat. He certainly didn't care for the set look on Mick's face as she took in his cousin's comments about her previous books.

"The Shelanons enjoyed quite a windfall when Grace Shelanon stumbled onto that mine shaft under her greenhouse," Quest said, half smiling when Taurus slanted a look in his direction.

"You may want to check your facts, Q, Grace Shelanon made that discovery in her garden not her greenhouse. And I believe what she found were gems. The shaft was discovered a little ways off."

Quest knew that, but decided to test his cousin's knowledge of Mick's work. He should have known the man would be prepared with a quick and accurate response.

"Now Mick," Taurus said then, returning his attention to the lady at his side. "I've been talking your head off for the past ten minutes."

"Amen," Quest muttered, folding his arms over the light sable shirt he wore.

"And I'd really prefer knowing about you," Taurus continued, smoothly ignoring his cousin. "Why don't we dance a little and continue our conversation?"

Mick's lashes fluttered and she fixed Taurus with an apologetic smile. "That sounds fantastic, but your cousin Quay wore me out a little while ago. I think I'd better be thinking about getting back to my hotel," she decided.

Taurus was already standing to assist her.

"Mick you ready for another twirl?" Quay was saying as he returned to the table.

"No and I was just telling Taurus I really should get going," she said, clasping her hands together when Quaysar looked disappointed. "I had the best time though," she said, hoping to soothe his feelings.

"No problem," Quay said, already wedging himself between Mick and Taurus. "I'll just go grab my wallet and keys from behind the bar and-"

"Forget it Quay, I'll take her."

Mick, Taurus and Quaysar all turned to look at Quest who had spoken.

"Sounds good, man," Quay replied, quite pleased that his brother was finally stepping up to stake his claim.

Mick was more curious about Quest's actions. Days had passed without him calling and now he was going to take her home in his car where they would be alone. *Easy, Mick.*

"Well I guess that's it," Quay turned to take Mick in his arms. "You're the best dance partner I've ever had," he complimented and then topped it off with a lingering kiss on her cheek. He smiled at her surprised gasp, but backed away when he felt the fine hair bristling along the nape of his neck. The signal was a warning that his twin was staring his way and that he was not pleased. "Good night," he told her, "Q," he called and tugged his cousin away from the table.

"Nice meeting you, Mick!" Taurus called.

"Nice meeting you!" Mick replied, standing on her toes to wave as he and Quay disappeared into the heavy crowd. Alone with Quest, she smoothed her hands over the curve-hugging frock and tried to ignore the chill that kissed her bare arms.

Quest said nothing and only waved his hand in a gesture that she precede him toward the nearest exit. They were silent. The club doors closed behind them and soon they were strolling in the parking lot. Quest studied Mick as she studied the exquisite Seattle skyline in the distance.

When they reached his foreboding navy blue Navigator parked in the distance, Quest trailed a lone finger across her elbow.

Mick blinked and decided to ignore the caress. Impossible, once Quest's hand curved about her arm.

"I'm sorry I lied to you," he said, once they'd stopped near the passenger side of his truck.

Mick chewed her bottom lip and then turned to face him.

"I told you I'd call. I didn't," he continued.

Shrugging, Mick tried to brush off the statement. "If there's one thing every woman knows about a man it's that if he says he'll call once something even remotely dramatic occurs, she can be sure that he won't."

Quest felt himself wince at her words and bowed his head lest she see his eyes turn a darker shade of gray. Never did he think he'd meet a woman more cynical or sarcastic that he was. Deciding to brush that from his mind, Quest moved past her to open the passenger door of the SUV. He ushered her inside and then checked the seat belt to make sure the fastening was secure. He was about to close the door, when he hesitated. "I pride myself on not saying things I don't mean. I *am* sorry," he told her.

Mick shook her head, sending a riot of dark curls swinging. "It's forgotten," she whispered, looking down at her hands clasped in her lap.

~~~

The trip back to the Sorenson was silent yet tension-filled. Thankfully, the suave croonings of Joe in the background made the trip bearable. Mick gave an inward cry of joy when they turned into the hotel's parking deck. She had hoped Quest would drop her off at the front. But, of course, that wasn't his style. He'd see her to her room, check the place thoroughly and *then* he would leave.

And he did just that, Michaela speculated as she listened to him opening and closing doors at the back of her suite. She turned toward the message desk when she heard him nearing the front again.

Just go and don't say anything, she pleaded silently while fiddling with the edge of the stationary pad that rested squarely on the center of the desk.

Quest granted part of her request. He didn't say a word, but he didn't just go.

One index finger trailing downward between her shoulder blades was Mick's undoing. Her head sloped forward, her eyes closed and her lips parted in response. When she turned, she was in his arms. Quest held her in an unbreakable grasp, bonding her to his toned, unyielding frame. Mick believed her ribs were bruising, but they were no more bruised than her lips which he suckled and kissed in an onslaught of desire that had been restrained for too long. Mick met his fire with one of her own, moaning while his tongue thrust deeper into the sweet darkness of her mouth.

Her helpless sounds of delight further stimulated Quest's driving need. He held her pinned between his chest and the message desk for more than a few minutes. His free hand roamed the line from her upper thigh to her hip before curving over the generous swell of her bottom. He tugged her even higher against his chest then and grunted satisfactorily when her shapely legs locked around his waist.

The maddening kiss continued as he carried her to the sofa. The dress she wore had teased him wickedly ever since he'd found her bouncing around with his twin on the dancefloor of their club. The little piece of nothing had him conjuring all sorts of shamefully erotic things he wanted to do with her. Now, his perfect teeth tugged at the paisley-print fabric until the rise of her breasts were only partially revealed. Quest took his time lavishing the delicious chocolate swells with wet open-mouthed kisses.

Hearing Mick gasping his name, he knew he had to see her. Really see her. Powerful fingers curved into the straight bodice and tugged until she was bared to his smoky gray stare. Mick had the strength to do very little and her hands rested weakly against his broad shoulders. Her plump, glorious breasts beckoned his mouth and he delighted in the satiny darkness igniting his desire to a heated pitch. His lips, teeth and tongue manipulated the firm nipples in a relentless fashion. His fingers offered stimulating consolation when he left one to favor the other.Michaela arched her back sharply, wanting him to bestow attention to every inch of her skin. Quest growled deep in his throat as his tongue swirled around one of the marbled peaks. He was so in tune to her reaction, he could feel it stiffen more in response to his actions.

Mick's gasps intermingled with breathless cries and sultry moans. Her curvaceous form wiggled fiercely beneath his unyielding one. She wanted all he had to give.

But Quest would not submit to the demands raging within his mind and body. He rested his handsome dark face between her heaving breasts and prayed for the strength to leave without taking her the way he wanted.

When he raised his head to look at her, Mick was stunned by the darkness of his gaze. "Quest?" she whispered, curling her fingers around the buttons lining his shirt.

"Don't ever dance with Quay again," he commanded softly.

Michaela blinked once before a slow curious smile began to tug at her mouth. "Why not?" she whispered, searching his eyes with her hypnotic stare.

"Because I don't like it," he admitted. "And it could get him hurt," he added.

Mick nodded slowly. "Ahh...so this is for his own protection?"

Quest could no longer hold out against smiling. "Exactly," he confirmed.

"I see," she shivered, thoroughly amused. "Does that go for your cousin Taurus too?"

"Goes for all the men in my family," he clarified without hesitation.

Then, slowly he moved. Mick watched him backing away from her with the grace of a big cat who was done with its prey. He was unreal, she thought. He was every fantasy she'd never considered herself wanton enough to have.

"Good night," he whispered when he stood and looked down at her.

Mick didn't try to cover her nudity. In his eyes she saw raw desire and something more. Never had she felt more beautiful. When the door closed behind him, her lashes fluttered closed. She squeezed her legs together and moaned.

~SEVEN~

Michaela sauntered from bed the next morning feeling as though she'd been deliciously ravished and it had only been a bit of foreplay. A bit? She wondered about that. The way Quest Ramsey made her feel last night...she doubted foreplay was an adequate description. It was however, a foreshadowing of things to come. Things she *hoped* would come. Things? Sexual satisfaction or something more? Mick closed her eyes and shook her head, feeling as though she were drowning in her own thoughts. She and Quest had simply acted on the attraction existing between them-that was all.

Sounds good, Mick. That should get you through the next two hours.

She swung her legs from the bed, but remained seated on the edge deciding on her next move. Call County? Mick knew the woman was probably at her wits end wondering what was going on in Seattle. Driggers had grilled her to no end when she called him the previous afternoon, and Mick knew her demanding publisher would be no different. Besides, Mick had already planned to leave after one week. Now she wasn't sure. She believed she wanted to stay longer. Like an avalanche, her curiosity about Quest Ramsey was growing rapidly. She wanted to know everything about him and not for any book. Massaging her eyes then, she silently scolded herself for falling head over heels for a man she'd known little over a week. This was not the way Mick Sellars behaved.

The phone rang then and she welcomed the interruption. Reaching across the bedside table, she pulled the burgundy cordless from its cradle. "Yes?" She greeted softly.

"Ms. Sellars? Good morning. This is Dion, the host at Sorenson Cafe."

"Yes, good morning," Mick replied, recognizing the name of one of the hotel's restaurants.

Dion cleared his throat. "Ms. Sellars, will you be dining downstairs this morning?"

The question caught Mick by surprise. "Well-I-I hadn't really thought about it."

"Well ma'am, your attendance *is* desired."

"Why?"

"Just a little thank-you breakfast. Something special we've just started. For our guests that have been staying with us a while."

"I see," Mick whispered.

"So may we expect you?"

Finally, Mick shrugged. "Why not? Yes, I'll be there."

When the call ended, Mick leaned back against the huge cushiony pillows lining the headboard and studied the ceiling. Then she was glancing around the elaborate room and her light stare fell upon the package the front desk concierge had handed her the day before.

Forcing herself from bed, Mick ambled over to the lounge chair where she'd tossed the package. Ripping into the wrapping, she found a leather-bound book. The front cover was engraved with what looked to be an etching of a school and cursive writing of the words *Remans Golden Bears 1989.* Obviously a yearbook, she quickly surmised.

Written in bold script inside the front cover were the words: *Georgia, p.118.* Mick turned to the page of class pictures and saw that one row had been circled with a red pen. There were the identifying names at the end of the row, but Mick already knew at least three of the students. She recognized Quest, Quaysar and Taurus, brushing her fingers across their photos and acknowledging they'd been drop-dead gorgeous even then.

The entire row was marked however and Mick reluctantly moved her gaze past Quest's photo to the other young men on the row. Fernando, Moses and Yohan Ramsey. Mick could only shake her head, for no one could dispute that the Ramseys were a devastating brood. Mick's attention wavered from the six sinfully handsome teens to the scribbling at the bottom of the page: *143* was all it said. Figuring it to be another page number, Mick turned and found only one photo highlighted. It was the picture of a young girl with a shy brown gaze and a happy laugh. Mick recognized her instantly- Sera Black.

Mick frowned, studying the young woman's picture longer than she realized. She took another look at the photos of the six cousins. In her mind she could hear Houston Ramsey. *That young woman fell to her death from a hotel room window. The room was in Quest Ramsey's name.*

"Fool," Mick hissed, slamming the book shut. Still, she couldn't resist going downstairs to look through the photos and news clippings on the death. She scoured the material as though she expected some answer to magically leap out at her. At last, she snapped out of her trance and decided it was time to get dressed for breakfast.

***

The Sorenson boasted restaurants with some of the best cuisine Seattle had to offer. Sorenson Cafe was one of those places. Located on the lower level of the hotel, the area was an elegant, cozy hideaway that offered its guests a more mellow atmosphere instead of the rushed craziness of most breakfast spots.

Mick arrived, appearing somewhat uncertain as her amber eyes scanned her surroundings. The dining room was practically deserted with the exception of the staff. She glanced at her watch.

"Ms. Sellars."

Mick turned to find a short, balding man rushing toward her.

"Dion, ma'am," he introduced in a voice that matched the pleasant smile he wore.

"Am I in the right place?" Mick asked, smiling when Dion chuckled.

"You most certainly are and we thank you for joining us this morning. Right this way," Dion urged.

A resigned smile in place, Mick smoothed her hands across her flare-legged khaki chinos and followed the little man into the cafe. She stopped in her tracks after walking a short distance. Her heart leaped to her throat when she saw Quest across the room speaking with one of the waiters.

"This way, Ms. Sellars," the host urged, taking a second to look back at her.

Mick complied, though her steps were a bit less confident.

Quest turned to see her approaching. His mesmerizing gray stare lowered to rake her slender yet curvy form several times. The white, asymmetrical halter she wore outlined her full breasts adoringly while drawing attention to her flawless chocolate skin.

The host nodded toward Quest and then left him and Mick alone. She opened her mouth to speak, but failed.

"I forgot to ask if you'd like to get together for breakfast this morning," Quest said as though reading her thoughts.

"Breakfast?" Mick parrotted, looking around at the beautiful dimmed atmosphere. "Place looks deserted," she noted.

Quest grinned, sparking the gorgeous left dimple. "Not closed, just opened for two at the moment."

"Two?" Mick questioned, hating the feeling of total confusion surging through her. Suddenly, realization dawned and her eyes narrowed. "Tell me you didn't have this place shut down just for us?"

Quest shrugged, his gray eyes holding an expectant light. "Why not? We're worth it, aren't we?"

"Obviously *you* are."

Quest stood back and wondered about this cool beauty who seemed totally oblivious of her power. "Don't tell me a man has never shut down a restaurant for you?"

Mick was speechless, unable to form a cohesive comeback as she studied his face. "Um...no, no I can't say I recall any man ever doing this," she finally replied, pretending to be in deep concentration.

Quest made a *tsking* sound while folding his arms across the slate-blue shirt that hung out over the sagging dark denims her wore with black Gortex boots.

"Well, it's past time that one did," he decided finally and cupped her elbow to lead her to the round table that had been prepared.

Mick settled into one of the deep cushioned black armchairs he held for her. Her lashes fluttered minutely when she felt his fingers in her hair.

Quest couldn't resist the touch. Michaela was becoming more than a woman to him. She was a light- a light he desperately needed and wanted in his life. He had known more than his share of sensual women, beautiful women and sweet women. Michaela was the first woman he'd met who had the perfect proportion of each quality and then there was that mind of hers...

"Thank you," she whispered looking up at him.

Quest moved his hand from her curls reluctantly and took his place at the table.

They studied their menus in silence for a moment before Mick uttered a short laugh and set hers aside. "I'm sorry, but this *is* a bit over the top. Don't you think?"

Quest propped his chin against a fist and regarded the expectant look on her face. His eyes locked on her heavenly mouth and again he allowed himself to envision the delights it was capable of offering.

"Quest?"

"I'm sorry," he whispered, shaking his head. "'Over the top', you were saying?"

"*Very* over the top."

"So you really don't think you're worth this?"

Mick leaned back in her chair. "I'd like to think I am, but-"

"You'd like to *think* you are?" he whispered in disbelief.

Mick rolled her eyes while waving her hand in the air. "Don't sit there and think I have *any* self esteem problems. I don't. But you've only known me a little over a week, and this isn't the sort of thing you do for a woman you've only known a week."

"It is when you want to know her longer than that," he countered, "it is when she lives in Chicago and you live in Seattle. It is when you know she'll be leaving soon and you very much want her to stay."

Mick had no chance to reply, for the waiter had arrived to take their orders. She realized she wouldn't have known what to say anyway.

* * *

Later, Mick and Quest enjoyed an easy silence over a spread of golden brown, expertly seasoned salmon croquettes, cinnamon toast, hash browns, and fruit.

"You don't like to see food go to waste, I see," Quest teased, taking note of the way she wholeheartedly indulged in her breakfast.

Mick nodded. "This is true, but I also know you had to spend a pretty penny here today, so I figure you might as well get your money's worth."

"Hmph, well that all depends."

"On?"

"How long I can convince you to stay."

Mick cleared her throat, her fork pausing over hash browns. The man had no qualms about speaking his mind, she'd give him that.

"Well I *am* a working girl," she slyly reminded him and savored another bite of the browns. "Besides, I read the Ramseys own at least three jets. You can always visit Chicago," she suggested softly.

"True," Quest acknowledged with a nod. "But here in

Seattle my brother and my cousin are my only competition so far. In Chicago, I may find myself standing in line for your time."

Mick almost burst into an hysterical fit of laughter. "Standing in line behind who? Oh! Other men, you mean? Ha! No, no I'm afraid you won't find a line."

"That I don't believe."

"Believe it."

Quest didn't press further. Her words more than pleased him. "So what are your plans for the rest of the day?" he asked.

Mick shrugged. "I hadn't thought about it."

"Would you like to see what I do for a living?"

Mick took a sip of raspberry juice. "I thought I already had?"

Quest shook his head. "You saw a building. Ramsey Group is successful because Quay and I are hands-on. We hardly spend more than thirty percent of our time inside the office."

"Impressive."

"Necessary," Quest corrected. "The real estate division is not part of the family's main holdings as you might've thought. In college, Quay and I wanted to revitalize one of the group's poorest performing companies. The realty company was formed by Houston but it floundered partly because he'd focused his attention elsewhere. He was all too happy to let it go when we asked for it." A wicked grin further darkened his incredible features. "Besides, my father bought it from him for more than it was worth. No one was more surprised than Uncle Hous when the company turned a significant profit."

Which would explain why there's no love lost between Houston and his nephews, Mick thought.

"So? What do you say? You up for it?" Quest challenged.

Mick clapped her hands. "Let's go."

~~~

Quest and Mick spent the remainder of the day in his Ford truck. They seemed to travel from one end of Seattle to another.

He was right, Mick thought. She hadn't really seen what he

did for a living. In truth, her idea of a real estate developer was a person in a big office, behind a big desk on a big phone making it happen while he delegated the more menial duties to his subordinates.

The Ramseys were anything but. They were truly hands on. They did everything from meeting one on one with the architects and construction workers to dropping in on the donut and deli shops to ensure that the goodies kept flowing steadily to the workers. Mick was more than impressed; she was astonished by the company's attention to the little things.

"Last stop," Quest announced, while turning the truck down a rock-laden dirt road. "Forgive me for boring you to death today," he added, flashing her a quick apologetic glance.

"Please," Mick retorted with a flip wave. "This was anything but boring. I've seen more of Seattle today than I ever could've taking some old tour. You really run an exciting business Quest." He didn't appear too convinced. "Mmm-hmm, well on to the next round of excitement. Feast your eyes."

Mick looked past the streaky windows to an expanse of property beneath the sunny skies. The outlay of the land was a seemingly unending mass of dirt and small patches of grass. The only thing that had been 'put down' on the property were the wooden stakes with their red ties at the top and the miles of string that seemed to connect them.

Quest left the truck and then went to escort Mick out. It was then that she noticed an old black pickup in the distance. The driver's side door opened and a man stepped out,.

"J.C.!" Quest called, grinning when the man returned the wave. "Careful," he whispered, his attention instantly riveted back to Mick. "Watch your step," he advised, keeping an arm about her waist as they began to trek across the uneven landscape.

"What's goin' on?" Quest greeted the man once the distance was closed between them. After shaking hands he turned back to Mick. "Michaela Sellars, this is Ramsey's top construction chief, Jason Calloway, J.C., this is Michaela Sellars visiting from Chicago."

Jason whistled. "Chicago," he noted with an impressed nod. "Good to meet you, ma'am."

"Same here," Mick replied, smiling as his callused hand closed over hers in a shake.

"What do you think, Quest?" J.C. asked.

Quest's gray eyes narrowed when he squinted against the sun to get a better look at the land. "Incredible. It's everything you said it was."

While J.C. and Quest talked, Mick glanced around. Her expression was skeptical as she decided they were clearly seeing more of the property than she was.

Quest noticed the look on her face and felt the need to explain. "Michaela, this is the site for our next development," he said and pointed to the sign they stood next to.

Mick was surprised she hadn't seen it before and took a closer look at what would be the completed project. "Hmm, nice," she uttered after a moment or two.

The men exchanged glances.

"That's it?" Quest asked softly.

Mick's amber gaze was blank. "That's what?"

Quest bowed his head while massaging his jaw. "Well, I know it's just a sign, but this place is going to be one of our most ambitious housing endeavors. You just don't seem very impressed," he added, without realizing how much he wanted her to be.

"Oh Quest, I'm sorry," Mick said and laid her palm flat against his chest. "The homes look like they'll be exquisite-*beyond* exquisite. It- it's the yards that put them to shame."

"The yards?" Both men sounded off in unison.

Mick trailed one hand through her curls as they whipped against the wind. "I've seen these high-end high-income developments before, and for the most part one thing is both consistent and disappointing-the yards."

"Go on, Ms. Sellars," J.C. urged, interest clear on his tanned face.

"Well, all the yards just appear so small. They make the

homes seem like giants crouching for space on the same hill. Sure, many of these developments boast private parks, but it should be considered that some parents may prefer having their kids play closer to home. You guys should take that into account, that this *is* a Ramsey Group project. It should boast spacious yards in addition to spacious homes."

Quest and J.C. stroked their jaws simultaneously. Their eyes surveyed the land with renewed understanding.

"Sorry for speaking so frankly, I'm sure whatever you guys decide will be great," Mick said hoping to assuage their egos.

"Ms. Sellars, please don't apologize. Your honesty is more than appreciated, believe me," J.C. assured her.

"Michaela, honestly you've not only given us a new direction to take our project, you've given us a terrific selling point to exploit." Quest added.

"I can't believe we didn't discuss this before. We should set up a meeting with Stanton and his group right away," J.C. suggested, referring to their architect. "We could definitely use a troubleshooter like you on our team, Ms. Sellars," he added, smiling down at Mick before he looked over to Quest. "When does she start?"

Quest's laughter was easy. "She's mine," he responded simply.

Mick wondered if she was the only one who heard the underlying message in that remark.

~~~

The day wrapped up at the Cigar Bar, an establishment frequented by the area's most powerful professionals. Men and women alike flocked to the dark, stern watering hole that harbored a surprisingly relaxed mood with its hand-rolled cigars, top-notch whiskeys and liquors, light menu, and very own pianist.

"Mmm...so this is where the deals are made," Mick noted, inhaling the intoxicating aroma of leather and cigar smoke.

"Made or broken," Quest teased, nodding toward those he recognized. "It's best to dangle this treat before the client *after* the papers are signed," he added and graced Mick with a sly wink.

"Mr. Ramsey!" the bartender called when Mick and Quest approached. "And Mr. Ramsey's beautiful companion," he added.

Quest grinned. "Ralph, this is Michaela Sellars."

"Beautiful," Ralph continued to compliment.

"Pleasure to meet you," Mick said, enjoying the man's adoration.

"We're going to eat here at the bar, Ralph," Quest said as he ushered Mick into one of the high-backed maple-wood stools skirting the bar. "What'll you have, Michaela?"

"Hmm?" she responded absently, her eyes feasting on the portraits of all the well-known celebrities from Hollywood's Golden Era. Each portrait featured a different actor or actress puffing on a cigar.

"Michaela?"

"Oh! Um, I'll let you order," she responded hastily.

"What sort of cigar do you want?"

The question almost rendered Mick speechless. Quest asked the question in the same manner he would had he been inquiring if she liked her steak well done. She managed to contain her amusement enough to address his question.

"Quest, I'm afraid you're with a woman who is completely out of her element here. I'm not afraid to admit that. I honestly wouldn't know what to do with the damn thing," she confided, staring skeptically at the small menu of cigars he held.

Quest only nodded while his deep set gaze scanned the book. "You up for a lesson?" he challenged.

"No," Mick sang, "I'm not about to let you waste a bundle on an expensive cigar that I'd only mess up."

"Ralph," Quest called, waving in the barkeep's direction, "bring me two Royal Jamaicas. The lady will have a Robusto and I'll take a Ten Downing Street."

"Yessir," Ralph replied and quickly obliged the order.

"Alright," Quest announced once he'd used a brass cutter to clip the end of the longer cigar. He took it between his thumb and index finger. "You light the end like so," he demonstrated, puffing intermittently, "and you're all set," he added, motioning for Mick to take the cigar he held.

"No way," she refused flatly.

"Come on.

"*No* way."

"I hate to smoke alone," he said then, fixing her with his most disappointed expression.

Mick was thankful he hadn't requested anything more involved. That expression could make her give in to anything. Of that, she was sure. She took the cigar and put forth a valiant first try. Sadly, she only succeeded in a bout of coughs and sputters.

Quest leaned forward to pat her back, chuckling as he did so.

"I can do this," Mick decided, bracing herself for another puff. After a few unsuccessful attempts, she managed to take a long drag from the cigar that had to be at least ten inches long.

"Mmm…" she murmured, offering a little smile. She found the taste and smell to be quite intoxicating.

Quest was intoxicated as well. He was entranced by the sight of her, not quite believing how alluring and arousing was the sight of a woman with a mouth like hers puffing on the end of a cigar. He'd driven around town all day with her trying to keep him mind off how good she looked and smelled. The majority of his thoughts revolved around how very much he wanted to carry her off some place and make love to her until she couldn't walk. Now, he'd brought her there and she was succeeding in arousing him to an even higher level. *Down, Quest,* he warned.

Mick noticed his intense stare. "Sorry," she whispered, believing she'd been hogging his cigar.

"You're fine," he said and reached for the other cigar. "Are you ready for your own?"

"Yaay," Mick said.

"Don't make this a habit," he warned softly.

"I promise I won't," she lowered her eyes in a demure fashion when he began to laugh.

~~~

"I'm sorry for putting down the project before," Mick said later when they were dining. "I've been known to be pretty opinionated," she explained when he looked over at her.

"What are you talking about?" Quest set aside his knife and fork. "Your opinion was very valued. We're real big on constructive criticism at Ramsey. You've got a job there if you ever decide to leave the writing business."

"Mmm, is this another ploy to get me to stay, Mr. Ramsey?" she teased, watching him slice off another morsel of his ribeye.

"Is it working?" he asked.

"No comment," Mick decided with a chuckle. "I must admit though, this place is incredible. *Seattle* is incredible. I'd definitely like to visit a lot more."

"Glad to hear it," Quest said, amidst savoring the tender beef. "I really want you to consider coming back."

"Well I'm not gone yet," Mick made her point lightly.

She had no idea how serious he'd been in his statement, Quest realized. He didn't like her use of the word 'yet' and it showed.

Mick glanced over at him and caught the tightness of his expression before he could mask it. She decided to let silence settle for the duration of the meal.

***

When Quest returned Mick to her hotel suite that evening, he went through his ritual of checking the room. As usual, Mick waited by the message desk near the front door.

"Lunch tomorrow? If you're free?" he asked when he joined her out front.

She rolled her eyes. "Quest no," she said, groaning when she saw the hurt flash in his misty gray eyes. "You've taken up enough time with me today. You *do* have a business to run, you know?"

"One has nothing to do with the other," he argued, folding his arms across the slate-blue of his shirt.

"So why'd you insist on showing me every aspect of it today?" she challenged.

"Because I'm trying like hell to impress you."

"I was impressed way before today," Mick admitted and then looked away as though she'd said too much.

"Lunch tomorrow?" he asked again softly.

"I'll be ready," her response was just as soft.

Unfolding her arms, Quest stepped closer. His hand curved loosely beneath her chin while his mouth slanted across hers. Mick parted her lips eagerly, moaning seconds before his tongue began to caress her own. What could have been a sweet good-night kiss quickly became something heated and intense. Soft moans rose in Quest's throat as his tongue delved deeper into her mouth. He was lost in a sea of unsatisfied and constantly building desire.

Mick stood on her toes and kissed him with wild abandon. She squeezed her eyes tightly shut and wished he'd never stop thrusting and curving his tongue around hers. Quest's hands tightened upon her waist as though he were struggling to keep them there. He lost that battle and soon his thumbs were brushing her nipples outlined against the smooth cotton fabric of the asymmetrical shirt she wore. Mick tried to gasp his name, but she couldn't breathe beneath the kiss and she didn't care. When she felt Quest moving back, she frowned and curled her fingers more tightly into his shirt.

"Michaela," he whispered, breaking the kiss to speak against the corner of her mouth. "Baby wait."

The soft urging in his voice told Mick that the magical day had truly reached its end. She refused to look up at him while stepping out of his embrace. She turned her back toward him, leaning into the kiss he placed at her temple before he left.

~~~

"That's what *you* think

Mick rolled her eyes in response to County's rebuttal to her announcement that the Ramsey book was dead in the water. "As far as I'm concerned, it is," she retorted.

"Well, the last time I checked, Contessa House had *my* name on the sign," County challenged tersely. "You won't feel betrayed by us continuing our research and putting another author on it, will you?"

Again, Mick's lashes fluttered in the midst of another eye-roll. "Betrayed, hell. You probably already have another author in mind."

"You know me so well," County sighed over the phone. "Seriously, Mick, I *really* want you on this. A book like this has the makings of millions- dollars *and* awards."

"I know," Mick fully agreed, but silently admitted she'd choose Quest Ramsey over a tell-all *any* day.

"So have you made a decision about L.A. or are you gonna disappoint me on that too?"

Mick was slapping her palm to her forehead as she approached the hotel restaurant where she was to meet Quest for lunch. "The literary conference?"

"Mmm hmm…"

"Next week, right?"

"Mmm hmm…"

Mick groaned. "Oh County-"

"Damn it Mick! This man has got you floating in the clouds."

"Yeah...yeah he does," Mick didn't bother to lie. Her amber eyes sparkled when she saw him already seated in the restaurant. His head was tilted and his eyes were narrowed as he concentrated on the menu he held. Mick felt completely removed from her body as she studied him- admiring the presence he made without doing a thing. He raised his head and his gaze shifted to hers. Mick smothered a gasp and barely managed a wave.

"Mick!"

"Sorry-sorry, County, I- um-"

"Forget it. I'll have a fine time at those boring lectures and an even better time all alone in my room for the week."

Mick fiddled with the hem of the thin-strapped copper swing tee she wore and smiled. "You must think I'm a fool to believe you'll be all *alone* anywhere. Especially your hotel room."

County sucked her teeth. "On that note, I'll say good-bye."

"I'll call if anything changes."

"Which it won't."

"County…"

While Michaela debated with her best friend, Quest watched from across the dining room. His sleek brows drew close and his head bowed again when his heart refused to cease its frantic beating. Lord, he felt like a kid overjoyed because the girl he liked had just walked into the cafeteria. Sure, she was a luscious beauty but he'd been a fan of her work long before he ever met her. Putting such a face (and body) to such a sharp mind held him in a captive state and he wanted to remain there forever. She affected every last male hormone he possessed. He felt almost desperate to lose his fingers in those gorgeous curls of hers and take her body until only exhaustion forced him to stop.

Last night he'd almost scared himself by the intensity of how much he wanted her. If he hadn't left they would've gone too far, too fast. It was the reason he'd suggested they meet in a crowded restaurant that day. The more people, the better. Michaela Sellars was too sexy and sweet and alluring and intelligent and even still there was so much more that intrigued him.

"Hi Quest," Mick greeted when the host escorted her to the table. Her voice was surprisingly airy since she could barely look into his probing gray stare when he stood.

"I got it, Graham," Quest told the host, already holding Mick's chair.

She cleared her throat and reached for her own menu. "Have you ordered?" she asked.

Quest reclaimed his seat and grimaced. "No, no, I haven't. There's something I wanted to ask you."

Curious about his tone, Mick leaned back and watched him. He was clearly on edge about something judging from the repetitive manner in which he tugged on the cuffs of his camel-colored suit coat and the white shirt beneath. "What's wrong?" she inquired softly.

"Ramsey's unveiling a new project next week. I'd like you to go with me."

Mick blinked, certain there was more to it. She decided against asking 'that's it?' seeing how unnerved he appeared. "I'd like that," she told him in a careful tone.

He grimaced again and the deep left dimple flashed. "It's in California. Malibu," he clarified, sounding as though he were waiting for her to decline.

Nodding, Mick realized why he was on edge. "I'd *still* love to go."

"It's an overnight trip."

"That's fine, Quest."

"I mean, of course you'd have your own room," he began to explain. "I don't expect you, to um...you'd have your own room."

"Alright Quest," she assured him, enthralled by his uncharacteristic unease. "Malibu, you say? County'll be out in L.A. that week."

"Great! Tell her to come out! The more the merrier," *and a better chance of me behaving myself.*

"So what kind of project is is?" Mick asked, hoping the conversation would keep her from smiling overmuch.

Quest cleared his throat. "It's a teen center."

"In Malibu? Wow, yes I'd love to see that."

"Well, hold on before you toss out any accolades," he warned with a raised hand. "Quay and I haven't been down there as much as we'd like, so we hope the construction crew followed our instructions. It's already complete, but I want your honest opinion on it."

Mick's light eyes narrowed playfully. "Why?" She asked, leaning closer to the table. "Will you have it torn down if I don't like it?"

"I might," he replied without hesitation, without humor.

Mick had no doubt that he'd do just that. Thankfully, the waiter arrived then and their attention was directed toward lunch.

A LOVER'S DREAM

~EIGHT~

Malibu, California

"If you're still trying to impress me, trust me, you've done that and then some," Mick proclaimed a week later when they stood in the entryway to the grand, state-of-the-art Malibu Beach facility.

Quest grinned over Mick's hushed admission. He kept one arm neatly in place at her waist, while his free hand grasped her bare arm in an overtly possessive manner. "I'm impressed myself," he told her, also scanning the outstanding establishment.

Each year, Ramsey Group sought to outdo themselves with the cause for the upcoming year. Each member of the company believed the people they were helping deserved nothing but the best.

"Do you think the kids will be pleased?" he asked Mick.

"Oh I think they'll be well past pleased," she assured him, propping one hand on her hip. "Is this something you guys do often."

Quest spoke while escorting them through the sea of guests that filtered through every hall, room and staircase of the teen center. "Each year we take on a project for charity or, as we prefer to call them, causes. Last year, we constructed a complex for battered women and their children. There's even a school constructed on the grounds with a full faculty available to teach and train the mothers who want to obtain degrees or job certifications."

"That's incredible," Michaela marveled, folding her arms across the bodice of her strapless black A-lined dress. "It's so rare for a high-profile company to take interest in such issues," her eyes misted with a faraway look. "I wish there was a place like this when I was a kid in search of a home," she said, taking in the spacious rooms complete with oversized furniture, bean bags and plasma TVs.

Quest's gray stare bordered on black as he listened, not caring for the lost tone in her voice. He wanted to know more, but didn't want to intrude on unwelcomed territory. Thankfully, the moment was saved.

"Michaela Sellars!"

Mick whirled around and expressed a gleeful shriek when she saw Contessa switching toward her. The distance closed quickly between the two friends and soon they were hugging.

"Girl, thanks so much for inviting me out here. This place is incredible!"

Mick fixed her best friend with a knowing smile. "Only the place is incredible?"

County rolled her eyes. "Honey please, it goes without saying that the men are delectable."

"Hmph, yes they are," Mick turned. "Contessa Warren, I'd like you to meet Quest Ramsey. Quest, this is my publisher Contessa Warren," she introduced, eager to witness her friend's reaction.

"Ms. Warren," Quest greeted as he took County's hand in his. "It's a pleasure. I hope you'll accept my apologies for not meeting you when you visited Seattle. My brother and I were very

115

sorry we wasted your time."

"No, no, it-it was no trouble," County practically gushed, feeling gooseflesh riddle her skin beneath the sleek, midnight blue, spaghetti-strapped evening gown she wore.

"Q! Man, I see you're hoggin' all the ladies again!"

Mick smiled broadly and took just as much joy in introducing County to Quaysar Ramsey. She had never seen the woman so off-kilter. The fact that the tall, molasses-dipped twins were both gorgeous and charming to a fault held County in an even greater state of awe. Mick tried to conceal her laughter, though the knowing smile remained as she watched County interact with the magnificent twosome. When Quay took County to the bar, Mick let her giggles run free.

"Will you let me in on the joke?" Quest asked, tugging on the cuff of the black sport coat he wore with a plum shirt and matching trousers.

"Oh, it's just a treat to see my girl so speechless," Mick hugged herself. "Thank you so much for such a great night."

Quest sent her a heart-melting wink. "There's more to come. I promise you."

Before Mick could find out what *more* there was, Quest was being summoned across the room to make a few statements about the teen runaway's facility.

"Damn it," he muttered, before turning to Mick. "I'm sorry," he told her, hating to leave.

Mick was already squeezing his hand. "Go take care of your business. I'll be right here when you get back."

Something flickered in the haunting depths of Quest's eyes. Then, surprising Mick, he leaned down and pressed his forehead to hers. "I like the sound of that," he said, and then softly nudged her chin with his fist before he walked away.

Mick's lashes fluttered while she fought the urge to drag him back to her. *Down, Mick,* she ordered herself. A waiter passed just then and she eagerly took a champagne glass from his tray.

~~~

Mick nursed the champagne for the better part of twelve minutes. She hardly sipped the bubbly liquid, painfully aware of the results that would follow. She saw County heading towards her and smiled as the woman joined her on a secluded sofa. Mick watched as her best friend flopped back into the cushions and began to fan herself.

"Didn't I tell you?" County said, a look of sheer delight illuminating her face. "Didn't I tell you they were beautiful? Didn't I, Mick?"

"Yes, yes, you did," Mick confirmed, raising her champagne glass in a mock toast.

"Mmm-mmm..." County grunted, shivering a bit as she did so. "And it's every one of 'em who's gorgeous, and the twins...Mick, girl..."

Mick burst into laughter when County appeared unable to form more compliments.

"I can see why it's taking you so long to get back to Chicago. I'll bet you've bought a whole new wardrobe in anticipation of remaining indefinitely," County probed, slanting Mick a sly gaze when she turned her head against the sofa cushions.

Mick shook her head and refused to admit she'd done such a thing. "I bought a *few* new pieces, not a whole new wardrobe," she rolled the glass between her palms. "Besides, you know me well enough to know I'm not naive enough to stay halfway across the country just because a man looks good."

"Actually his looks are the last reason I think you'd stay," County shared, watching her toes wiggle along the opening of her strappy black heels. "Anyone can see that he adores you, he's obviously very attentive. In short," she sighed, "all the things you noticed about him after your first meeting, I noticed too."

"So you don't think I'm naive?" Mick's amber stare filled with doubt.

"Quest seems like a really great guy Mick, I wouldn't be at all surprised to hear you say he's the one."

Mick blinked. She had no denial or snapping comeback to

County's unexpected prediction.

"Sorry to interrupt you ladies," Quest called out to them as he returned. "Contessa, would you mind if I steal Michaela away for a little bit?"

"No problem," County waved her hand as though giving her permission. She watched the couple disappear into the crowd. "Congratulations Mick," she whispered.

~~~

Mick smiled and inhaled the fresh sea air from the beachfront. "The kids are gonna love it out here. A chance to breathe clean air instead of smog? There's nothing like it," she testified.

Quest stopped walking, his hand squeezing on her upper arm. Mick grew silent and looked in the direction he stared. A volleyball net waited in the distance. It was set in the sand as though it were nothing out of the ordinary for it to be there.

"Quest," Mick breathed, delighted by the sight. She held her sandals in one hand, the other gripping the hem of her dress as she made her way to the net.

"I've been thinking about having one put out here since you told me how much you enjoy the game," Quest said, when she stared back at him. "I figured the kids would enjoy it as much as you do. But I wanted you to be the first one to use it."

Mick was practically speechless as she trudged in the sand while moving closer to the net. "You did this because of me?" she whispered, glancing over in time to see him shrug. "Why?" she insisted on knowing.

Quest ran one hand across his soft hair. "I thought it'd make you happy," he told her as though it were that simple and smiled while he looked down at the sand beneath his loafers. "Unless you were just teasing about being familiar with the game," he chided noticing how emotional she was becoming and hoping to lighten the mood.

"You just get on the other side of that net," Mick ordered, tossing her sandals to the ground and smiling when Quest tugged

118

his bow tie free. "My serve," she called and grabbed the pristine white ball from the sand.

Quest held his own, but was very much in awe of Mick as he watched her play. She was clearly competitive, having no regard for her gown as she jumped and dived for the ball with fierce passion. When her final serve caught him by surprise, Mick shrieked in victory and fell to her knees in the sand.

"You were holding back on your skills, Mr. Ramsey," she accused, bracing herself on her elbows while looking up at him from the ground.

Quest grinned. "I didn't want you to be intimidated," he said, while dropping next to her in the sand.

"Did I look intimidated?" Mick asked, taking in huge gulps of fresh sea air as she lay on her back.

Quest's deep set eyes roamed her face. "Not a bit."

"Did you want me to be intimidated?" Mick asked, her voice falling an octave.

"I don't think it'd work for both of us to be intimidated."

Mick blinked. "*I* intimidate you?"

"Quite a bit."

"How?"

Quest leaned down, supporting his upper body on one elbow. "Because I have no idea what to make of you and that doesn't happen to me. It's *never* happened to me. Maybe that's why I never see the same woman past three or four dates."

Mick's stare widened. "Uh-oh, I think we've been on more than four dates."

Quest closed his eyes. "Yes," he confirmed with a nod.

Mick's sigh was intentionally dramatic. "So I guess you're about to dump me, huh?"

"You're still a mystery to me."

"So you'll dump me once the mystery is solved?"

"I don't see that happening," he predicted, leaning down close to her.

Mick touched her tongue to her lips tentatively as she prepared herself. "Oh," was the last word she spoke before he kissed her.

The moment was sweet beneath the stars and crashing ocean waves. If Quest was determined to solve his mystery of her, that would have been the perfect place to begin. But he ended the kiss, waiting for her to move her hand from his neck before he sat up.

"We better get back," he helped her from the ground and moved to brush the sand from her skin, hair and clothes.

Quest held Mick close during the walk back. She was glad, since she was quite certain she had no strength left in her legs.

***

Time went by in a blur. So much, that Mick didn't even realize the days-weeks that had passed. She saw Quest every day, be it for lunch, dinner or breakfast. He took her to many of the Ramsey Group sites in development and others that had been completed. There were days filled with sightseeing and everything else under the sun. Mick spoke with Driggers every day and she was both elated and mildly uneasy when he told her how much he was enjoying the fact that she'd found something else to occupy her time with besides work. Still, Michaela wished the nagging reminders of home and responsibility would leave her be. She knew if they did, she would stay in Seattle forever.

The phone rang then and Mick welcomed the interruption. Still, nothing had quite prepared her for the loud voice on the other end of the line.

"Morning County," she groaned, leaning back against the headboard to massage her eyes.

"Mmm-hmm, girl what the hell is going on? Have you decided to put down roots in Washington State, or what?"

"County-"

"I mean, you know I think Quest is a dream, and personally I wouldn't blame you for staying. Just keep me posted, alright?"

"It hasn't been that long, Count."

"The hell you say, It's going on four weeks. An entire month, Michaela Sellars. Is he *that* good in bed, love?"

Mick's laughter came in a quick, robust burst. "I wouldn't know."

"Stop lyin'. Wait a minute. Are you serious?"

"Quite."

"Well just what *is* going on out there?"

"Everything's just so unreal, County." Mick kicked back the covers and swung her legs from the bed. "I guess that's why it's taking me so long to come back. I can't remember when I've enjoyed myself so much."

"Yeah... Quest Ramsey seems like quite a man," County acknowledged. "That's why I can't believe he hasn't made a move."

"Oh, he's made several moves," Mick reached for the room service menu. "Just not *the* move," she added.

County giggled. "And you're still a-hoping." She teased.

Mick rolled her eyes. "It's not like that. I just really enjoy being with him. In spite of what you think, it *is* possible to look past all that gorgeousness."

"Hmph," County snorted, "my eyes ain't big enough to look past all that."

"Damn, you are so scandalous!" Mick accused, a rumble of laughter tickling her chest.

"And you've always known that. Now tell me about this book," County easily switched gears.

"Well...you know the book is dead," Mick was thrown by the subject change.

"And could anything make you reconsider?"

A picture of the yearbook flashed to Mick's mind, but she quickly dismissed it. "No."

"So you're just gonna let the mystery of a lifetime slip through your fingers?"

"Baby there *is* no mystery. The girl committed suicide."

"And you believe that?"

Mick tossed aside the menu. "It doesn't matter what I believe. The case is solved and closed, has been for well over a decade."

"And does this outlook have anything to do with the fact that you're falling hard and fast for one of the sexy twins?"

"No, hell no!" Mick left the bed, shoving a hand through her blue-black curls. "No man has or will ever determine anything that has to do with my business-my writing."

"I don't believe you."

"County-"

"Look just hurry up and get your butt back here. If only for a day or two. Your little playmates have already been sniffing around the office asking when you'll be back. It don't look good for me to have so many teenyboppers around," County added with an indignant sniff.

"Damn it," Mick whispered, both concerned and upset with herself for not keeping in touch with her girls. She'd been trying not to think of them as her trip lingered on. The girls depended on her so. They had since she peeked in on their troubled practice one day over two years ago. The line consisted of fifteen freshman and three very harried juniors. Mick offered tentative advice as any fan might. The girls were enthralled. Soon, Mick was not only offering advice, she was choreographing moves-moves that had catapulted the marching band's dance troupe to great heights.

"Mick? Are you listening?"

Mick massaged her eyes. "I am."

"Well?"

"Not much longer," she said while pacing the bedroom.

"You've got it real bad, girl."

Mick's chuckle held no trace of humor. "I know."

"You take care of yourself and call me in a few days, alright?"

"I promise," Mick whispered and told County she loved her before the connection ended.

Less than ten seconds later, the phone rang again.

"Hello?"

"Michaela Sellars?"

"Yes?"

"This is Johnelle Black. My daughter was Sera Black. I see

you recognize the name," Johnelle noted.

Mick's breathing had stopped on a gasp. "Mrs. Black," she spoke in a hushed almost reverent tone. "I am so sorry. What happened to Sera was terrible."

"Yes, it was," Johnelle whispered, her usually strong voice wavering just a bit. "It happened very long ago and I guess I should be past it, but it still hurts. My baby was just about to begin her life, when she-"

"Committed suicide," Mick added softly, knowing the assumption was about to be disputed.

"Homicide," Johnelle's response was decisive.

"I know this must be hard for you, Mrs. Black," Mick went on, determined not to further agitate the distressed woman, "it's just that the facts-"

"The facts?" Johnelle cut in, her voice holding no trace of anger or frustration. "Ms. Sellars, those *facts* were pieced together by certain members of the Savannah press who were influenced or should I say, bought by the Ramseys."

"If you're talking to me, then you obviously know about the book. Most of the Ramseys are against having it written. "

"Of course they are, dear, and why do you think that is?"

Silence.

"This isn't a conversation I want to have over the phone. Would you agree to meet me?" Johnelle proposed.

Mick expected herself to produce an instant refusal. *Actually, I have another exquisite day planned with a fabulously fine, fabulously gentlemanly, and fabulously sexy Ramsey,* she wanted to say.

"When and where?" Mick asked instead.

~~~

Quaysar twisted his mammoth-sized pearl gray suede chair back and forth while studying his mirror image across the round glass table, where they met for their morning meeting.

"What?" Quest asked, feeling his brother's eyes on him even as he studied the plans he held.

"So how is she?"

"Who?"

"The yummy Ms. Sellars," Quay teased in a manner that usually roused a grin from his brother.

Quest barely smirked and the narrowing of his stare told Quay that he'd spoken out of turn.

"Sorry," he apologized promptly when Quest slid a quick glare in his direction. "Damn Q, you always keep me in the loop about your latest squeezes," he complained, pressing one hand against the front of his metallic-blue crew neck shirt while pleading his case. "Now you're cutting me out when it's obvious you're growin' more and more infatuated with the woman and not even bothering to hide it."

Quest finished scouring the plans and stood. "Michaela's fine. She asks about you every time I see her."

Quay was delighted and chuckled over his brother's stern manner as he delivered the tidbit. "So?" he prompted.

"So?"

"So what's up, Q? How serious is this, man?"

"As serious as it can get," Quest shared after a pensive stare commanded his expression for several moments.

"That doesn't sound good, man," Quay said, leaving his chair then. "What's going on?"

Quest reached for the light sable brown sport coat and slipped it on over a beige shirt. "We live very different lives, Quay- in distant places. Besides, she's a writer- an investigative journalist at that."

"So?" Quay blurted, his pitch stare growing stormy at the cool shrug Quest gave. "Hell man, why should you care about that? You've got nothin' to hide."

"I gotta go," Quest said after taking a moment to consider his brother's words. A minute later, he was gone.

***

Mick and Johnelle Black decided to meet for brunch at a local bistro. The place was surprisingly quiet despite the time of day.

"The owner says they may have to consider closing during the morning hours since they're more popular with the lunch and dinner crowds," Johnelle shared as she and Mick waited for their juice orders. "They may be forced to shut down altogether since the Ramseys opened their club and serve dinner as well."

"That's right," Mick acknowledged softly, recalling that Double Q was close by. She fixed Johnelle with a half smile and an unwavering gaze. "But I'm sure this isn't what you brought me here to discuss."

Johnelle took no offense and smiled as she shook her head no. "I didn't, I asked you here to discuss my daughter," she said and produced a portfolio from the red canvas tote she carried.

Mick leaned forward to take a closer look at the pictures that spilled from the bag's zippered opening.

"She was so beautiful as a child and in high school," Johnelle said, as she focused on the picture she held. "I can almost envision what she'd look like today," she confided and then shook her head as a shudder tinged her words. "Ms. Sellars, my daughter was a determined girl who knew what she wanted from this life. She was goal oriented. She received a full scholarship to Clark. Nothing to sneeze at," Johnelle's dark eyes brimmed with motherly pride. "Full scholarships are impressive to anyone," she dropped the picture and leaned against the oak ladder-backed chair.

"Sera was so happy and confident. I believe she began to think she could do anything. Including going after and snagging one of the beautiful Ramseys."

Mick looked up from the photo she'd been studying. "Should I take that to mean that she wasn't interested in boys much?"

"Sera was interested," Johnelle said, pulling the wrapper from her straw, "but from afar. She wasn't going to let it get in the way of her studies. But-" she sighed, "the lure of the Ramsey men is hard for any woman to deny for long. Sera had begun to push herself, to use her confidence to go after what she wanted."

"And which Ramsey did she want?" Mick asked, absently stirring her straw in her juice.

Johnelle smiled. "I think she was a little in love with them all," she smoothed both hands across the coral button-down skirt she wore. "Of course, it was the twins who snagged the majority of the nods then."

"And how did the Ramseys feel about Sera?" Mick asked.

Johnelle seemed to tense, her round face losing some of its soft, haunted appearance. "I never really knew. I never had any idea how interested she was in boys, let alone the Ramseys, until after she was- I found a diary Sera kept. That's how I discovered much of it. The one I found seems to pick up in the middle of something, so I think there could be another that goes into more detail."

"Mrs. Black," Mick leaned across the table. "You know I'm not here for a story anymore. The Ramseys consider this book to be a closed issue."

"I called you here today because I want to hire you to investigate my daughter's murder."

"Mrs. Black. I'm not an investigator-"

"You're an investigative journalist," Johnelle challenged. "Use what you find and write that book on your own. Blow those sons of bitches out of the water."

"Mrs. Black-"

"They killed my baby!" she hissed, her eyes pooling with tears. "I know it wasn't suicide," she swore. "I'm not saying they all did it, but one of them is sure as hell responsible. I can't rest. I can't live without knowing what happened. My life has been a hollow shell since that night."

It was easy for Mick to see the sadness and love on the woman's face. Tears began to pressure her own eyes for release. What she wouldn't have given to know her own mother loved her that way. But she hadn't. Johnelle Black couldn't live not knowing what really happened to her child. *Her* mother had left her alone and gone to live her life elsewhere without a care for her own daughter's well-being.

"Mrs. Black-"

"If it's a question of money, I have plenty," Johnelle

informed her. "The phrase 'filthy rich' is a perfect description of me. I've felt filthy ever since I accepted that damn payoff."

"Payoff?" Mick set her jaw against her palm.

Johnelle grimaced, while adding a clear liquid from a silver flash to her glass of OJ. "They came to me, asking me not to make a scene, not to make it harder for them. 'Let Sera's memory be peaceful', they said. They even arranged and paid for the funeral," she paused to wipe her tear-streaked face. "I took the money they offered. It was dirty, but it was a comfort. I invested wisely and could repay them a hundred times if I wanted. It's allowed me to indulged in things-" she waved the flask- "in things that could dull the pain...you must think I'm trash?" she unscrewed the flask cap once more.

"I think you're a mother who loves her daughter and was robbed of a life with her." Mick closed her hand over Johnelle's before she could pour more vodka into the juice. "I'll do it," she decided smiling when Johnelle shed tears of happiness and leaned down to kiss her hand.

~~~

Quest relaxed one massive shoulder against the wall, his hands hidden inside the deep pockets of his eggplant trousers. His seductively haunting gray-black stare began a leisurely ascent past the sexy, completely feminine strappy high heels, up the incredible shapely length of toned legs and thighs. Tilting his head just a fraction, he was able to glimpse more than a few tantalizing peeks offered by the splits along each side of the figure-flattering dress. The unconsciously arousing heaves of her breasts were igniting every hormone he possessed.

"Damn it," she hissed and effectively drew his stare to her mouth.

Mick's fingers trembled as did the rest of her. Nervousness and a case of the shivers hit her body relentlessly. She didn't need to look at Quest to know that his eyes were on her. The intensity of that look was as potent as any touch.

"Damn key," she whispered, forcing a laugh to mask her

uneasiness as she tried unsuccessfully to gain entrance to her suite.

Quest continued to lean against the wall near the door. He indulged in a few more minutes of sightseeing before leaning over and pulling the card from her hand. "Maybe it's not working because it's your library card."

Mick's mouth fell open and then she closed her eyes and uttered another nervous laugh. "That explains it," she said and began to rummage in her purse again. She couldn't resist a sideways glance at Quest when his soft chuckles filled the air.

Come on, Mick, shape up. You can do this," she told herself while scouring the bag. All night she'd been consumed by her conversation with Johnelle Black and the decision she'd made to go forward with the book or rather the investigation into a young woman's death. Quest had to be told. This wasn't something she could or should wait to get into.

When? When was the right time? She'd wrestled with those questions most of the evening. Before dinner? No. They'd had a great meal, great conversation. The usual. They took in a set by the group at the club. Lovely. Now they were back at her hotel and it was time to show and prove. She located the key, then cleared her throat and unlocked the door.

"What'll you have?" Mick asked, once they were inside the room and she was heading toward the bar cart. She never completed the trip.

Quest's hands folded over her upper arms and he pulled her back next to his solid frame. His mouth found her earlobe and began a merciless assault, teasing the satiny skin there. One of his massive hands left her arm to cup her breast. The nipple, already rigid and pouting, was the lucky recipient of his affections.

Oh yes...she'd forgotten this part- the heart-stopping love scene that usually took place right there in that room. It never went further than a devastating kiss and possessive caressing. Still, it was enough to leave her writhing in ecstasy on the sofa as he pressed a brotherly kiss to her cheek and said he'd see her tomorrow before he walked out the door.

Mick turned in his arms, determined to tell him the scene

would play differently that night. She never had the chance.

Quest captured her mouth in a fantastic kiss. His tongue thrust lustily and deep as though he were thirsty for the taste of her. His eyes were tightly closed, so that a tiny furrow formed between his sleek black brows. He had the look of complete and unflinching concentration to kiss her senseless.

Mick whimpered, her hands smoothing across the incredible breadth of his shoulders. Her fingers grazed his soft, close-cut hair and she gave in to the delicious sensations the kiss roused. Her confession could wait until the scene ended, she decided.

Quest however, had something different in mind for the evening. Had Mick known that, she would surely have told him her news the moment she'd seen him that evening. His mouth was everywhere, kissing her lips, outlining the mole there with his tongue, grazing his teeth across the curve of her jaw and suckling her earlobe in a feverishly possessive manner.

He placed her on the oversized sofa and then followed her down. Mick uttered an indecipherable sound into the air as her breasts and nipples were thoroughly manipulated. The row of tiny buttons had proven to be a minute obstacle. He favored the undersides of her breasts with gentle nudges from his nose, before delving lower. His mouth dipped past one of the splits in her dress in search of what he most wanted. His nose grazed her sex clearly outlined against the lacy fabric of her white panties. Mick's lashes fluttered amidst waves of unexpected arousal.

"Wait," she gasped, a moment later, her hand tensing on his shoulders. "Oh wait," she moaned. "Mmm…" she added, when his tongue teased her through the material.

Quest's expression was arrogance pure and simple. "You're sure?" he queried, mouthing the words against the dampening center of her undergarment.

"Wait…" she tried, failing when a sob followed the word.

Quest rose above her then and pressed his mouth to her ear. "Do you want me to?" To help her decide, he smoothly inserted his middle finger just slightly inside her center.

129

"Mmm...no...no don't...don't stop...don't stop yet..." she chanted, arching up to take just a bit more of the caress. He barely rotated the digit in the wealth of moisture he discovered.

Quest suckled the diamond stud adorning her earlobe. He loved the helpless whimpers she emitted when he barely moved his finger or when his thumb stroked the extra-sensitive nub of her clit.

He ended the caress and she moaned her disappointment. When he settled himself fully against her and Mick felt the extent of his thrusting power, she forced herself to sober.

"Quest, Quest, wait, wait."

"Mick..." he sounded tortured then, hiding his handsome face in the crook of her neck.

She was just as agitated. "I don't *want* you to, but you should. I...I have something I need to say."

He raised his head to search her light eyes with his unsettling ones. "Something you need to say? Now?"

She nodded, tugging her bottom lip between her teeth. "Mmm-hmm," she confirmed and then cleared her throat. "Yes," she said firmly that time.

Quest closed his eyes and rested his forehead against the base of her throat. Michaela's lashes fluttered as she silently commanded herself not to arch or grind her hips against the delicious hardness right next to the part of her that ached most for it. To her relief, she felt the powerful erection subside as Quest took deep breaths and sought to quell his desire.

He moved away at last and leaned back against the opposite end of the sofa. Mick slowly pushed herself up, her feet resting in his lap as she watched him. After a while, Quest raised his hand, signaling for her to go on with what she wanted to say.

Mick swung her legs to the floor, smoothing her hands across her hips as she stood. "I met with Johnelle Black today," she announced when she felt there was enough space between them.

Quest's head snapped up when he heard the name, but Mick had her back turned and didn't see his reaction.

"We talked about her daughter, Sera. Her death," she went on, wringing her hands as she spoke. "She insists that it wasn't suicide, but murder. She wants me to investigate, she says she'll financially back a book or simply a look into the case. She told me about the payoff she got from your family."

Mick stopped talking then and turned to observe Quest. She didn't care for the set look on his face, the darkness of his eyes, or the way he absently massaged his left arm. She took a seat in the armchair opposite the sofa and waited.

"Will you do it?" he asked finally.

"The woman loves and misses her daughter," Mick leaned forward to brace her elbows on her knees. "You wouldn't understand what it does to someone like me to see that. You've always had the love of your parents. I don't know what that is," she settled back in the chair. "I can't turn away from a request like that."

Quest studied her for a long moment. His expression offered no clues about his thoughts.

Mick wanted to scream at him to show some sort of reaction. It was then that he told her he should go. With a nod, Mick stood and followed him to the door. Quest left without a word or a look back.

~NINE~

"I swear I didn't give anyone your contact information in Seattle," County said again as Mick grilled her by phone about the call she'd received from Johnelle Black. "I was hoping something like this would happen though. I wish I could give the person who did give her your number a big hug."

Mick flopped down into the chair before the message desk. "Huh?"

County hesitated a moment. "This should be done and you know it. *That's* why you agreed to help her."

"Quest looked like I'd just thrown a brick at his chest," Mick envisioned the look on his face before he left her suite the night before.

"Look Mick, you know I think Quest Ramsey is fantastic," County heard the dismay in her friend's voice, "but his family has a lot of secrets. Some of those secrets may be worth revealing, you know?"

Mick fidgeted with the lace hem of her nightie. "Yeah," she admitted.

"You're in love with him, aren't you?"

"County!" Mick cried, sitting straight in the chair. "Just because I'm concerned about what this news did to him doesn't mean I- I've seen him a lot and we've gotten close, but- you're impossible."

"Mmm...so that's a yes, right?"

Mick groaned, laying her forehead against the desk. "I'm so weak," she lamented.

"Girl, it's not weak to have those feelings."

"It is when they get in the way of work."

"Work? Mick look, alright? Yes, when *you* work, *I* make money. But that's not what life's all about. All that dramatic, silly, heart-pounding stuff you find so corny, so bothersome is what makes life-*love* worth having. It's what tells you you're alive, hon."

County was right. Mick knew it. After all, hadn't she been telling herself that very thing? "So you're saying I shouldn't do the book or become involved in the investigation? Just turn it down, run to Quest and confess my love before we race off into the sunset?"

"You phrased that well. Could it be you've already thought of doing that very thing?"

"When'd you become so sarcastic?" Mick asked, running a hand through her tousle of curls.

"You've rubbed off on me," County said. "And now that you've mentioned it, you don't seem *nearly* as sarcastic as usual. Could it be those sappy emotions of love are wearing away at that protective shell around your heart?"

"It may be just that," Mick admitted, none too happy over the fact. "It's all the more reason to become involved with this."

"Mick-"

"Quest Ramsey is a dream. A woman's fantasy. But dreams and fantasies fade, love grows old. Once the newness wears off the pain begins. I was new to my parents once. Then they got bored and threw me away."

"Baby? You alright?" County asked, concerned by the turn

in the conversation. She could hear Mick's shuddery breathing across the line.

Mick shook her head as though she was even surprised by her words. "County I'll let you go now. I'll call and tell you what flight," she added hastily and clicked off the cordless phone.

***

Selma Murphy's cheeks must have been burning furiously if the blush darkening her milky skin to a deep crimson, was any clue. Still, she managed to efficiently wrap the huge roast beef on rye, secure it in a bag stamped with the deli's logo and pass it to the absolutely stunning man on the other side of the long glass counter.

"Thank you, Mr. Ramsey." Selma's voice carried a hushed reverence yet its underlying laughter was richly evident.

"Now Selma...you know what I'm waiting to hear…"

"Beat it, Ramsey. No more advising my daughter to ask me for a raise!" Bueford Murphy called from the kitchen directly behind the busy counter. His voice was filled with as much laughter as Selma's.

Taurus faked a look of astonishment and raised his roast beef on rye. "When you can make a sandwich this good, you *should* be raking in the big bucks!"

"She'll be raking in the big bucks when she graduates highschool and college and goes to work for you at Ramsey!" Bueford predicted, sending a roar of laughter waving out from the busy kitchen to the equally busy front counter.

Taurus shrugged, sending Selma Murphy a playfully forlorn look. "I tried, kid. Come see me in about five years and we'll get you working for folks who'll appreciate you."

"Hey!" Bueford Murphy playfully raged.

Taurus slanted the teenager behind the counter a wink that sent her blushing and then bade her father a good afternoon before he left the counter. His intention was to leave and enjoy his lunch back at the office. That intention fled his thoughts when he spotted Michaela Sellars seated alone across the deli's airy naturally lit dining room.

"Safe to join you?" he asked, smiling when she looked up as he approached.

"It is," Mick returned the smile and waved toward one of the empty chairs at the round table where she'd enjoyed lunch while reviewing her notes.

"What are you doing here?" Mick cleared papers from the table as she questioned him.

"My usual lunch stop," Taurus shrugged sending barely a ripple through the honey-wheat vest he wore over a mushroom colored shirt. His bright entrancing gaze scanned the room. "Food's fantastic and it's close to the office, so..."

"And what is it you do for Ramsey again?" Mick worked on finishing off the last of her chips.

"I'm in legal," he unwrapped his sandwich.

Mick waved a chip in realization, "Right, right- *President* of Legal Affairs. Impressive."

Taurus shrugged sleek, light brown brows. "If impressive, means 'a crap-load of work' then I guess it is," he joined in when Mick laughed.

"Actually all the branches of the company have their own legal divisions but all of them- national as well as international report to my end."

Mick released a low whistle. "What your family has accomplished...it's fascinating."

"It is that," for the first time Taurus' expression seemed to darken, "but no big success is ever made without a lot of big secrets underneath." He forced a smile as if sensing the unwanted route his thoughts were taking."

"So what about you?" He asked her. "Why are *you* here all by your lonesome?"

Mick's expression darkened then too. "Oh I...I'm debating on whether to go see your cousin."

Taurus smiled, not looking at all surprised. "Man's a lucky dog to have you come his way."

"You don't know me, Taurus," Mick warned, her expression resigned. "Your cousin's probably *not* feeling so lucky given the fact that I'm here to chronicle some of those 'success secrets'".

"I'm willing to bet that doesn't matter to him nearly as much as you do."

"And what about you? How do *you* feel about the book?" Michaela felt comfortable enough to ask. "Something that might call attention to your family that way."

Taurus rested his hand across the as yet unwrapped sandwich. "While it's probably a necessary thing," he seemed to consider his next words, "I don't think it'd be such a *good* thing."

Mick brushed potato chip crumbs from her fingers. "It would seen that you and your dad disagree about that."

He smiled a curious smile. "My father and I disagree about a lot."

Mick was primed to start questioning the man's outlook when she saw Quest approaching the table. She ordered her lashes not to flutter, but was unable to get her heart to adhere to the same command. His face appeared a cold, beautiful mask when he inclined his head toward Taurus. His expression softened the second his eyes met hers.

"Michaela."

"I was just heading back-"

"Stay, T," Quest urged, halting Taurus moves to repack his sandwich. His gaze never left Michaela's. "You're not breaking any rules," he said and brushed Mick's arm lightly on his way past.

In spite of the light brush, Mick felt just as shattered given his soft reminder of the night he'd forbid her to dance with any other man in his family. The memory of him fondling and kissing her shamelessly while giving the order threatened to make her swoon.

"My cousin's a lucky man. And an intense one," Taurus noted once Quest had moved on.

Mick turned her head a fraction, but resisted the urge to turn in her chair and follow Quest's departure.

***

"Any coffee in the break room, Jazz?"

Jasmine Hughes smiled up at Vincent Carroll, Ramsey Group's lead attorney. "There sure is. What's wrong? Didn't get your caffeine fix this morning?" she teased.

"Nah," Vincent said with a shiver. "Just cold as hell," he complained.

"Are you feeling sick?" Jasmine asked.

"It's Quest," Vincent jerked his thumb across his shoulder. "Do you know what kind of mood he's in?"

Jasmine's lashes fluttered close. "Yeah, I got a taste of it when I got here this morning."

"He doesn't say a thing," Vincent went on, "What he *does* say is barely above a whisper. He barely nods or shakes his head, just watches you talk. It's creepy."

Jasmine nodded in perfect agreement with Vincent's assessments. She recalled feeling the same way when she had spoken with Quest earlier that morning. The man's gray stare was even more haunting and unsettling in light of his mood.

"Hey Jazz, what's up with Quest this morning?" Theo Stone from accounting asked when he approached.

"What have you heard?" Jazz asked.

"Nothing good," Theo said.

"Well you heard right."

"Morning group!"

Everyone turned when Quaysar arrived. Conversation was silenced, but only for a moment.

"Could you take this up to the office for me, Quay? It's paperwork you guys should look over before I can move forward." Theo explained.

Quay was already reaching for the file. "No problem. Did Quest leave already?" he asked.

"Unfortunately not," Vincent grumbled.

"What?"

"Quay, it's Quest. His... mood, more specifically." Jasmine said.

Quay nodded once, understanding perfectly. He'd noticed

his brother's mood during their meeting earlier that morning and believed it had everything to do with Mick. At the time, he dared not question it. In many ways, Quest's moods were far more unsettling than his own. While Quay roared his anger so that everyone was aware, Quest raged in silence. He'd barely say a word, yet his anger and frustration seethed so close to the surface they could almost be felt. Quay slapped the folder against his palm, braced himself, and headed up to the penthouse office.

~~~

"Quest?...Q? You in here, man?"

Quay received no answer when he entered the dim room. Setting the folder on one of the Gothic iron bookshelves, he stepped farther into the office. He continued to search for his twin until he found him seated in the living area. Quest gazed intently at the myriad of colorful fish frolicking in the huge extravagant tank.

"Q?" Quay called, a bit softer that time. "Damn, man, keep your foul mood at home. You got everybody edgy as hell," he snapped, hoping to rouse some reaction from the man.

Quest closed his eyes and offered a humorless half smile. Determined to ignore his brother's obvious attempts to rile him, he remained unresponsive.

"This have anything to do with Mick?" Quay asked, easing both hands into the deep pockets of his blackberry trousers.

The muscle danced furiously along Quest's jawline. He left his chair and went to prop his elbow against the tank while gazing at the fish more closely.

"Why don't you just call her?"

"Quay?"

"What?"

"Leave it."

"Then leave your mood at the crib, man. We don't need it around here. You got half the building afraid to talk to you," Quay chastised, glaring when he received a flippant wave from Quest. "What happened between the two of you?" he queried softly.

Quest turned suddenly, slanting Quay a fierce stare before

he literally brushed past him.

Quay, of course, was undaunted and simply followed his brother to the other side of the office. "You're a fool if you let her get away."

Quest had just reached his desk when he heard the words. Both hands curled into massive fists which he brought thundering down to the maple surface. Everything jumped in response. A few papers and a cup of pens splashed to the floor.

Quay stood quietly, taking in his brother's murderous expression. Silence bathed the room until the phone buzzed. "Yeah Jazz, this is Quay," he greeted using the speaker.

"Um, hey Quay is Quest there by any chance?"

"He's here J," Quay supplied when Quest remained mute.

"Michaela Sellars is here to see him."

Quay fixed Quest with a taunting look. "Send her up, Jazz," he instructed.

"You stay out of this, Quay," Quest's tone was low, dangerous.

Quay folded his hands across his chest. "Or what?" he challenged, grinning devilishly at his twin. "Seriously Q," he said, sobering a little "She's too special, I won't let you lose her."

Quest blinked, looking as though he was actually surprised that his brother noticed about Mick what he had the moment he'd met her. In minutes, the elevator chimed then and its doors opened.
~~~

Mick felt much the way she had the first day she'd stepped into the Ramsey's hallowed penthouse office. Like before, she was uncertain and curious. But with those feelings came a new sensation of being hopelessly in love. She was there to tell Quest that she was leaving. Childish as it may have been, she prayed he would ask her to stay. As much as she wanted to help Johnelle Black, she knew she'd stay if he asked her to. Aside from their fiery physical encounters, she had no idea of his feelings. Perhaps this meeting would tell her if his feelings even trickled in the same direction as hers.

"Hey girl!"

Mick uttered breathless laughter at the sound of Quay's roar before she was pulled into one of his crushing hugs.

"How you doin'? I hardly get the chance to see you with my brother keeping you locked away," Quay voiced his complaint playfully.

Mick tossed a few curls from her eyes and returned Quay's broad grin. "I'm good, and I see I don't need to wonder how *you* are."

Quay winked. "Lookin; good, huh?" he said, probing shamelessly for a compliment.

Despite her mood, Mick couldn't resist laughing. "Is Quest here?" she finally got around to asking.

"Come on," Quay instructed, dropping an arm around her shoulders as he led her deeper into the office.

Mick's shivers had nothing to do with the long, muscular arm across her shoulders or the sheer fabric of the powder-blue shirt she wore. She had never relished confrontation.

"Q, look who's here!" Quay bellowed when he brought Mick into the main office. He grinned at his twin, even as his eyes narrowed in a clear warning for his brother to remain civil.

Quest's hazy stare had already softened. He had no idea how much emotion radiated from his stunning gaze. He nodded once toward Michaela.

Quay rubbed his hands together, satisfied by the man's reaction. "Alright sweetness," he smiled down at Mick, "I'm gonna give y'all some privacy."

"Actually Quay," she called, curving her hand across his wrist, "you should hear this too," she said, risking a quick glance at Quest. "I spoke with Johnelle Black," she said.

Quay's dark gaze lost its cool appearance. Instantly, he realized why his brother was in such a foul mood.

"We talked about her daughter," Mick said, "she doesn't believe it was suicide and wants me to conduct a new investigation," she stopped and turned to Quest. "I accepted. I'll be leaving Seattle in a couple of days."

Quest went rigid, his eyes now as black as the shirt he wore. He couldn't move, though every nerve ending cried out that he do something- anything to stop her from going.

Say something! Mick pleaded in silence, knowing she was a fool. *You, say something!* she ordered herself. No! As badly as she wanted this man- wanted to be a part of his life- she would not humiliate herself more by begging him. After all, *she* was in love with him, not the other way around.

Sighing, she turned to Quay. "Thanks for being so great," she said and laughed when he pulled her into another smothering embrace.

"Don't you be a stranger," he ordered pressing a kiss into the top of her head.

"You either," Mick said, her voice a bit muffled against the fine fabric of his blackberry suit coat.

Across the top of her head, Quay fixed his twin with a disgusted stare.

"Bye," Mick whispered as she stepped back. With barely a glance in Quest's direction, she all but ran from the room.

"Fool," Quay breathed at his brother before he too left the office.

Alone, Quest stared down at his desk but a moment, before he shoved all the contents to the floor.

"Mick, wait!"

Michaela's steps halted on her way to the elevator. She whirled around, her eyes blurry with tears. On seeing the man bounding toward her, her first thought was that it was Quest. Her face clouded again when she saw it was mistaken."Quay…"

"Sorry baby," he apologized, frowning when he saw the wetness on her cheeks. "Hey," he soothed, using his thumbs to dry her tears.

The tender gesture forced another slew of tears from her eyes. The elevator doors opened then and Quay hurried her inside.

"It's alright," he continued to reassure her as she cried fervently.

"Damn it," Mick muttered, "weak," she berated herself,

wiping her eyes with the back of her hand. "Damn tears," she hissed.

"Hey, don't do this," Quay whispered, keeping his hands folded across her upper arms as he leaned down to peer directly into her eyes.

"I shouldn't have come here today," she said through her sniffles. "I knew it wouldn't make a difference, but I had to see him."

"You don't have to explain a damn thing to me. Hell, I'm glad you're doing this, Mick."

Some of the sadness left Mick's eyes as her curiosity soared. "What?" she whispered.

Quay's gaze was unwavering. "I need you to do this."

The elevator arrived on the ground floor, but Quay gave Mick a chance to prepare herself before he let the doors slide open in the lobby office.

"Jazz hold my calls. I'm taking Ms. Sellars to her car," he told the woman.

When they reached the rental Altima Mick had acquired after her third week in Seattle, Mick just stood at the driver's side door. She waited patiently, simply staring up into Quaysar's handsome face.

"The party that night was my idea," he said folding his arms across his chest while leaning against the trunk of the hunter-green car. "Quest had to get the room in his name because I had a...not so nice reputation with many of the finer hotels in town." He grinned with a shrug. "My parents were sick of it and not about to put their names to a room I'd be in charge of."

"Who was Sera there to see?" Mick asked, easing her hands into the pockets of her silver-gray crop pants.

Quay shook his head. "Probably me. She didn't have class with Quest or any of our other cousins who went to the school. At least, I don't think she did," he added quietly. "Anyway, I don't know if she even knew the other guys who were there." He looked over at Mick. "Far as I know, Sera Black was no one's 'girl'. Everybody knew her though. Pretty, smart, somethin' special. *Too* special to be played with or messed over. She wasn't easy and we Ramseys didn't like to work for our sweets back then, if you know what I mean. Still, Sera liked us for some reason. Liking me is probably what got her killed."

Mick stepped closer. "Quay-"

"Didn't you know?" he cut in, standing to fix her with a lopsided grin that held little amusement. "I'm cursed."

"Huh?"

"Ask Quest. Hell, ask anybody in my family. Every girl who ever *really* liked me, moved away, came up missing...or died."

"Quay-"

"You think I'm exaggerating? I wish I could think like that," his onyx stare softened as he reminisced. "Q is the only one who knows this, but in high school there was a girl. I had to let her go because of this crap."

Mick pressed her lips together and stepped closer to rub Quay's shoulder.

"I loved her, Mick. She was the only one. The *only* one, Mick," he stressed, fixing her with a stern look. "That was in high school. Do you know how many women I've known since then? None of 'em ever came close to her."

"So you invited Sera to the party?" Mick asked, hoping to shift the conversation away from the woman who still haunted Quaysar Ramsey's dreams.

Quay cleared his throat. "Only the guys were *invited*," he clarified, smoothing a hand across his close-cut waves. "There was an open invitation for *all* the girls- as many as we could fit into that room."

"Would've been easy for her to go unnoticed then," Mick pointed out.

Quay curved a fist into his palm. "I wouldn't know. Drunk as I was."

"You don't remember anything?"

"Not a damn thing, besides what I just told you and after I woke up."

"Where were you?"

"In the hotel room. In bed, butt-ass naked," he shook his head, staring off as though he was envisioning the scene. "Q was sitting at the foot of the bed, he was the only one there, he-he looked like he was in a daze or somethin'. I started to call to him and then I heard the screaming. I never asked Q what he was doin' there just sittin' spaced out like that, and he never asked why I was naked in bed and passed out while a naked girl was splattered on the sidewalk below our room."

Mick propped both hands on her hips. "What do you think happened?"

"I don't know!" he snapped, leaning back against the car. "But I've been too scared for too long, Mick. I need answers. The only reason this thing was covered up is that Q was involved. My parents never asked him to explain it. They just did what they had to do to make it go away. But I know Q, it's *me* I'm concerned about."

"You think you-"

Quay was shaking his head helplessly. "The Ramseys got a lot of secrets, Mick. Second generation out did the elders royally, I think. Quest's always been there tryin' to protect us fools. I just pray none of this involves him."

"So do I," Mick whispered.

***

Catrina Ramsey had always taken pride in the fact that she never interfered with her sons' private affairs. By doing so, she'd received the greatest reward. They came to her with their worries willingly without her ever having to ask. She basked in knowing her boys held her opinion in such high regard.

But now, one of her boys was keeping her out of the loop. Catrina realized she was indeed like every other mother on earth: nosy and proud of it!

When the elevator doors opened to the penthouse office at Ramsey Group, Catrina walked in with the grace of a queen. "Quest? Quaysar?" she called.

Her voice was soft- so soft that people often wondered how the tall, molasses-toned beauty with such fragile looks had managed to rear two rambunctious boys at once. Catrina, however, was patient to a fault. That soft voice she possessed held an underlying firmness that warned her twins and every other man she knew to stand and take notice.

The elevator doors closed with a soft thud while Catrina stepped slowly through the dim office. She found comfort in the mellow atmosphere of her surroundings while natural motherly concern told her the boys should work in better lighting.

"Quaysar? Quest?" she tried again. Again, she received silence as her answer. Sighing her disappointment, she debated on leaving.

"Price for admission is a kiss."

Catrina turned, hearing the voice sound from the depths of the room. Propping both hands on her slender hips, she grinned. "That's a price I don't mind paying." She laughed seeing Quest emerging from the shadows. They shared a hug and Catrina paid her price by smacking a kiss to her elder twin's jawbone.

Quest, like his brother, always enjoyed visits from his mother. If it was true that laughter was the best medicine, Catrina Ramsey had a storage tank full of the stuff. That day however, she wasn't there for comic relief as she quickly informed her son when he questioned her visit.

"I've noticed you've been down lately," she slipped her hand through the crook of Quest's arm.

He laughed shortly and bowed his head. "How could you tell that when we've hardly seen each other over the last few weeks?"

"And I don't like being shut out," Catrina argued, with a quick toss of her head. The move sent clipped silver-gray locks bouncing around her beautiful face.

Quest ran a hand across the back of his neck. "Ma-"
"Who is she?"

The soft question caught Quest off guard and he hesitated. Catrina noticed and her mahogany brown eyes widened expectantly.

"Aren't you sick of hearing about our women problems?" Quest inquired, folding his arms across his navy short-sleeved crew neck shirt.

Catrina's expression was serenity personified. "I never tire of it, because those problems are always so interesting," she was unable to contain her laughter then.

"So happy we can amuse you."

"Oh baby," Catrina soothed, stepping closer to pat his chest. "I just know something's different. True, we haven't seen much of each other lately, but when we have, I've noticed something about you that concerns me."

Quest looked down into his mother's upturned face. At first, his misty gray gaze revealed nothing, but slowly his resolve began to crumble. "It's very confusing, Ma," he admitted with a shake of his head. "I've never met anyone like Mick."

Catrina eased one hand into a side pocket in her cream flair-legged pants. "Mick? Sounds spunky," she noted with a sly smile.

"Short for Michaela. Michaela Sellars," he explained.

"What a beautiful name," Catrina went to perch on the back of a sofa. "Sounds sort of familiar."

"She was here to write that book we all said no to," Quest stretched out on the sofa as well. "She agreed not to write it, but she's spoken with Johnelle Black and the woman's convinced her to at least get on board with a new investigation into Sera's death."

"I see," Catrina sighed, a part of her praying this new investigation would actually be a good thing. "So where do things stand between the two of you now?"

"Nowhere," Quest frowned as he recalled the scene in his office two days ago. "She's left Seattle."

"And you just let her go?" Catrina snapped suddenly, turning to glare at her son from her perch on the sofa.

Quest watched his mother with a look of total exasperation. "Ma, didn't you just hear what I told you? She's going to dig up all that old mess."

"Maybe she will," Catrina predicted with a shrug. "But I don't think that's why you didn't stop her from leaving."

Something flickered in Quest's deep set eyes and he looked away. "Ma, I admit it. I don't have a clue what to do. I sure as the devil don't know what to say to her."

"How about I love you?"

"Love?"

"Don't you?"

The simple question sent realization rolling in like a tidal wave. Quest pressed the heels of his hands to his eyes. "Ma, I'm in trouble," he groaned.

"And I'm so happy for you!" Catrina laughed.

"I don't even know what to make of my own feelings much less hers," he pushed himself up on the sofa, "she's so closed off sometimes. She gets this faraway look in her eyes and I know there's a lot of pain fueling that look."

"Is it from a past love?" Catrina asked.

Quest shook his head slowly. "I can't say. How in the world did she get under my skin so fast? I don't really know a thing about her."

'   Catrina leaned over to pat his cheek. "Maybe it's time you found out."

Again, Quest's expression clouded. "The way things happened before...it's probably too late. She's so damn tough. I don't know."

"Are you afraid she won't be completely open with you?"

"I honestly don't know, Ma," Quest said, so frustrated he bolted from the sofa. "I can't even begin to figure her out. I think if she answered every last question, I'd lay out for her, I'd still be starved to know more."

The firm admission only increased Catrina's delight. She couldn't believe he was so uneasy over this woman, when he'd known so many. Yes, she thought, her baby was definitely in love.

***

Savannah, Georgia

Michaela arrived in the city on a mission. She was there to meet with Jamilla Stokes and Harriet Forman, former classmates of the Ramseys and Sera Black. When Mick left the airport, however, she was stunned having never visited the beautiful Southern city. Evidence of its rich culture was everywhere. Mick spent her time strolling the quaint shops, enjoying lunch at a Creole cafe, and taking in the myriad of sights. She told herself not to get caught up in the beauty of another city, remembering what had just happened.

She knew of course, that she was safe on that count. She'd never have to worry over losing her heart to another man. Quest Ramsey, she believed, had effectively spoiled her for any other and she hadn't even slept with him...yet.

Would there be a *yet*? she wondered. Not if her career had anything to say about it. She recalled the scene in his office where she'd prayed for him to stop her from leaving. But then what? Would she *really* have been able to give up the investigation had he asked? Did she love him that much or was it plain old sexual frustration for a molasses dark god with the broadest shoulders and the most entrancing eyes, whose every manner and movement practically shrieked the promise of erotic fulfilment?

"Mmm," Mick grunted with a quick shake of her head. She warned herself how easily thoughts of Quest could send her into a fit of sensual delight.

"Taxi!" she called to a passing car.

~~~

Jamilla Stokes was a middle school principal/guidance counselor/school nurse/janitor. She had her finger on the pulse of almost every aspect of Littleton Secondary School. When Mick arrived, she was certain the woman would have little or no time to speak with her. She was mistaken.

No sooner had the front desk receptionist announced Mick than Jamilla waltzed out into the main office to greet her. In the next moment, she was chastising two boys, putting a band-aid on the arm of another, and delegating a cleaning chore to one of the hall monitors.

"You're amazing," Mick watched in astonishment as the woman performed the tasks with ease.

"And after hearing complaints all day, compliments are like music to my years," Jamilla hugged herself as she and Mick strolled to her office. "I should've followed my head and gone into politics, but I followed my heart instead and became a teacher," she confessed.

"Well, being a principal gives you the opportunity to dabble in both, doesn't it?" Mick probed.

"You know, I've never thought of it like that," Jamilla said, a brighter gleam appearing in her dark brown eyes.

"I suppose this all correlates to your high school days on the student council."

Jamilla threw her head back and laughed. "Lord, I haven't thought about that in years," she said, folding her arms across the money-green blazer of her pantsuit.

Mick smoothed her black, pleated skirt beneath her as she took a seat in one of the chairs before Jamilla's desk. "If I've done my homework correctly, Sera Black was your treasurer."

"She was a damn good one too," Jamilla swore, the expression on her honey-toned face a cross between sadness and pride. "She proved a lot of people wrong. Especially since no one thought she could handle the job."

Mick recrossed her legs. "And why was that?"

Jamilla's gaze drifted off into the distance. "Sera was so sweet, not really timid but she had a soft heart and she wore it right on her sleeve."

"Mmm," Mick nodded. "Those sorts of people are often liked, usually misunderstood and quite frequently taken advantage of."

Jamilla grinned. "You're so right. But Sera didn't think like that. She trusted everyone."

"Including the Ramseys."

"The Ramseys," Jamilla repeated, rolling her eyes to the

ceiling in a dreamy manner. "They were the finest. I wonder if they're still that gorgeous?"

"Trust me, they are," Mick confirmed. "At least the twins and their cousin Taurus are. I haven't met the others," she added.

"Hmph, the twins," A soft smile captured Jamilla's lips. "They conquered so easily and could betray a girl so smoothly, she never knew she was being made a fool of. They always got what they wanted, when they wanted it and how they wanted it."

"And they wanted Sera?" Mick leaned forward a bit on the cushioned chair.

Jamilla shrugged and went to rearrange the potted plants lining the sill behind her desk. "I honestly don't know. I don't think Sera had any female friends she felt close enough to confide in."

"Could she have been interested in any of the cousins?" Mick left the chair.

"My guess is that she was interested in one of the twins. She practically swooned when either one was in the room. All us girls did," Jamilla admitted.

"And you say the other cousins are just as gorgeous," Mick probed, grinning slyly when a devilish sparkle appeared in Jamilla's eyes.

"Oh honey, yes! But with them...the danger they exuded was so blatant. They were outright bad boys and if you wanted to keep your panties on and your virginity intact, you stayed away from them." Jamilla slapped her hands to her sides and perched on the windowsill. "With Quest and Quaysar, you couldn't see the danger until you got too close and then it was too late. They had you and you were an all too willing captive."

Mick's eyes narrowed. "You sound like you're speaking from experience."

Jamilla shook her head. "Simply relaying the experiences of others. I've always been a bad girl and I went right to the baddest."

"Which was?"

"Fernando Ramsey. The only cousin who'd done time in

juvenile hall."

Mick blinked. Clearly the Ramseys did carry secrets and consisted of some pretty dangerous characters. She couldn't help but wonder what secrets Quest may have harbored. The thought brought her back to Sera Black.

"Johnelle Black doesn't believe it was suicide," she told Jamilla.

"Hmph," the woman grunted. "No Michaela, Sera didn't commit suicide. She was raped before she was tossed out that window."

~TEN~

Because they were Ramseys, Jamilla Stokes said when Mick had asked why and how something so terrible could happen to Sera Black and no one be brought to justice or, at the very least, investigated.

After all, this was the South, Mick pointed out. The Ramseys were still black, and didn't the good southern law-abiding mindset demand that any opportunity to toss a black man behind bars be taken advantage of? Jamilla's response was simple and Mick grimaced that she'd allowed herself to be so senseless as to not come up with the answer on her own.

"They're rich-obscenely rich, have been for years. What you call *old money*," Jamilla had stated simply and coolly.

Of course in Savannah that meant everything. High society cotillions, luncheons...no one was going to touch the Ramsey youth. Their parents may have given them a good talking-to, maybe something a tad harsher, but no handcuffs or jail time. Jamilla made a point to mention that even the juvenile delinquent

Fernando Ramsey had often received little more than a slap on the wrist. Sadly, Fernando committed one of his *indiscretions* during an election year. The voters were getting testy about teen criminals going unpunished. As a result, the DA begged Fernando's father to help him set an example. With at least the appearance of the Ramseys being treated like everyone else, the DA secured a victory in the election. Unfortunately, there never seemed to be enough to force Fernando to straighten his act and his next offense resulted in a bit of jail time.

Mick looked up from rereading her notes in time to see Harriett Forman approaching her in the hotel lobby.

"Ms. Sellars, forgive my being late. It's been one of those days."

"No problem," Mick assured the petite thirty-three year old who was also a former high school classmate of the Ramseys. "It's a pleasure to be speaking with you," she added.

"You wanted to talk about Sera?" Harriett asked, her close-set brown eyes dimming with slight sadness. "You know this is where the, um, accident occurred?" she took a moment to look around the elegant interior of her family's hotel.

Mick followed suit, taking in the airy gracefulness of the Forman. "It's a lovely place," she complimented, taking in the historic murals, tall windows and high ceilings.

Harriett sighed, her expression clouding her round face. "Yeah, Ramsey money has made a lot of dreams come true in this town.."

"So you were paid off?" Mick watched Harriett nod.

"They told my father they'd give him a five-star hotel if he kept his mouth shut. They made good on their promise and he made good on his."

Mick pulled her notebook from the burgundy Coach tote she carried. "Do you know everyone who came to the party?" she asked, her pen poised to write.

"Yeah, pretty much all the guys. The cousins and a few of their friends. There weren't many guys there," Harriett folded her arms across the square bodice of her periwinkle-blue dress. "They intentionally let the girls outnumber them. There were only a few boys I'd never seen before."

Mick also produced a packet from her tote. She'd given a similar one to Jamilla Stokes at the close of their meeting. "These are photos and news articles that covered the story. If you'd just go through them a few times, let me know if anything sparks more memories."

Harriet smiled, already peering into the ten-by-thirteen tan envelope. "No problem. I hope your investigation will finally give us some answers."

"So do I Harriet. So do I," Mick said.

***

"Q?"

Quest focused on his brother and fixed him with an irritated look. "What?"

"What do you think?"

"About what?"

"About what I asked you."

"You didn't ask me anything."

Quaysar groaned, the muscle working feverishly along his jaw. He'd tried to give his brother space, knowing he missed Michaela. But this quiet, closed-off demeanor of his had even worn thin on Quay's easygoing persona.

"You know you're being a stubborn, brooding jackass," he blurted, his gaze unwavering when Quest's eyes snapped to his face. "You're letting a great lady, not to mention a sexy, as hell dimepiece slip right through your fingers. And everybody always called you the smart one," he added with a soft snort.

A second later, Quest rose from the chair and turned the round table upside down between him and his twin.

Quay only raised a brow. "Finally a reaction."

Quest's chest heaved and he closed his eyes for a moment to give his temper a chance to cool. Finally, he looked down on Quay who was still seated. "Leave this alone," he breathed, "I've asked you before and I don't want to take this out on you, but you know I would and I'd damn well enjoy it."

Quay acknowledged the threat, knowing his brother would show no hesitation in carrying it out. Still undaunted, he stood and was about to walk past Quest when he leaned close instead. "You love her," he said near Quest's ear. "I can see it when her name is mentioned and every time you're in a room with her. You can barely concentrate, you can't focus on another damn thing besides her. Go after her, hmm? Before you go completely out of your mind."

Quay moved on, leaving Quest to stand there. After a second or three, Quest's shoulders slumped as though the anger and tension were leaving him.

"And offer her what?" he asked in the softest tone and then turned to meet his twin's dark stare. "And offer her what, Quay?" he spread his hands in a helpless manner. "A family with so many secrets, that-"

"Damn Q, when are you gonna get it?" Quay snapped, "it's time to think about *you* for a minute. You been the protector too long and it's time for the rest of us to face our deeds and deal with 'em. *You* deal with findin' some happiness, man. You deserve it."

Quest massaged the back of his neck. "She may not talk to me," he admitted feeling heated, even beneath the short-sleeved gray linen shirt he wore. "I damn well couldn't blame her."

Quay grinned, instantly igniting his deep right dimple. "Damn, does Mick know how much power she has over your ass? You're Quest Ramsey. You know how to persuade all the ladies."

Quest returned his brother's grin. "I've never persuaded a woman like her."

Quay closed the distance between them. "That's because you're not only attracted to Mick, you love her. You're a lucky man to have found that and you'd be a stone idiot to let it go without a fight."

Quest watched his brother closely, considering his sage advice. Remaining true to form, Quay shed his serious demeanor and erupted in a roar of infectious laughter. Quest joined in, pulling his brother into a tight hug.

~~~

Quest experienced momentary optimism following his talk with Quay. Sadly, it slowly evaporated when he'd called Mick's home only to be told she wasn't there and hadn't returned after leaving Seattle. Michaela Sellars had been slowly driving him insane and it terrified him. Of all the women he'd known, she had somehow slipped past the walls guarding the part of his heart he'd deemed inaccessible. He hadn't even realized she was so deeply implanted into his heart- into his *being*- until he was without her.

***

Chicago, Illinois

Quest parked the rented Expedition and tightened his hands over the steering wheel. After a week's worth of calls to Michaela's home, he'd decided on a more personal visit. Besides, he'd been curious about the man answering her phone. He'd introduced himself as Driggers Morgan when they spoke and had promptly identified himself as Ms. Sellars houseman. House-*man* was the part that had Quest curious and on edge.

~~~

Quest took a moment to size up Driggers Morgan when he finally found the nerve to knock on the front door. The man was probably in his late fifties, but didn't look a day over forty. Quest realized that he was more content with *his* version of what Driggers would look like.

"Is Michaela Sellars here?" Quest asked, acknowledging that he was there for more important matters.

Driggers fixed Quest with a cursory glance before offering a response. "I'm so very sorry, sir, but the lady isn't here just now."

Quest studied the man just as closely and then shook his head and turned away. "You're telling me the truth," he murmured.

"Excuse me, sir?"

"I'm sorry," Quest apologized with a wave. "I thought if I asked in person, I'd know whether I was being lied to. I see that's not the case," he cleared his throat and tugged on the sleeve of his light-weight Seahawks sweatshirt. "Can you tell me when she's expected back?"

Driggers offered a sympathetic smile. "But for the occasional call to tell me she's fine, she hasn't said when she'll return."

Quest smothered a groan of disappointment by smoothing a hand across his face.

Driggers stepped closer. "Are you the Mr. Ramsey I've been speaking with this past week?"

"Guilty," Quest admitted with a sheepish grin.

Driggers laughed and then reached out to shake hands. "Come inside for a drink, son," he urged.

Quest hung back. "I probably shouldn't."

"Micky told me about meeting with a Seattle family named Ramsey. I assume you're one of them."

"Yeah," Quest confirmed, not appearing too proud of the fact.

Driggers stroked his jaw. "*The* one?"

Quest tilted his head. "Sir?"

Driggers waved off the sly probe and stepped away from the tall oak doors. "Come inside, son," he smiled when Quest complied.

Quest surveyed his surroundings, having already approved of the beautiful three-story Spanish styled home. Inside, it was just as lovely and shrieked comfort and warmth in spite of its open make-up.

"What's your business, Mr. Ramsey?" Driggers asked on his way to the built-in bar located in the sunken living room.

"Real estate," Quest called, reading the bookshelves lining the opposite wall.

Driggers selected two glasses and a bottle of Hennessey. "Pay well?" he asked.

Quest grinned. "We do alright."

"I'd say better than alright if my Micky wants to write a book about you."

"Yeah," Quest sounded less jovial then.

"She told me how that turned out."

Quest accepted the glass Driggers handed him. "In big families it's hard to get everyone to agree on what's best."

Driggers nodded. "I can understand that."

Quest studied his drink and couldn't resist a soft laugh.

"What's that?" Driggers' politely inquired.

"She can't hold her drink, but she's got Hennessey in the house," Quest laughed again softly.

"That's my Micky, intent on making a home. Wants everyone to be comfortable when they visit." Driggers explained, laughing softly then too.

"How long have you been with her?" Quest took a sip of the dark drink.

"Years," Driggers sighed, looking off as though he was trying to calculate the exact time in his mind. "That girl," he chuckled, "she didn't care what anyone had to say. She wanted a houseman and that was that."

Quest grinned while shaking his head. "Sounds like her," he stared into the glass then as though he could see Mick's face amidst the sparkling ice and rich liquid.

"I suspect your visit is about something other than business?" Driggers pried again, taking a sip from his glass and motioning for Quest to have a seat.

"It is," he admitted without hesitation and settled back against the cream suede sofa. "I was stubborn, keeping quiet about how I felt about her. I should've told her how much I wanted her to stay. I won't miss the opportunity again," he swore, sealing the statement with another swig of the liquor.

Driggers was intrigued by the young man with the deep voice- a strong voice. He was sure that was just what his Micky needed-what she'd need *after* he left... She deserved the best and yes, he thought this man seated to his right was just that.

"I'll keep you posted," Driggers promised, knocking his

glass against the arm of the sofa. "You'll know the minute she returns."

Quest's appreciation was reflected in his gray eyes.

~~~

Mick returned home just a few days later. She raced out of the cab like a little girl, flinging herself against Driggers' hard chest and smiling when she heard his playful grunt.

"I missed you so," she whispered, burying her face against the side of Drigger's neck and inhaling the spicy scent of the tobacco he used in his pipe.

"I thought I'd enjoy all that quiet. I hated it," Driggers admitted, his arms tightening around her small frame. He pulled away and brushed his hand across her brow, easily detecting the weariness on her lovely milk chocolate face.

"I'm so tired, Driggs," she said, knowing there was no need to put on airs of strength.

"How was Georgia?" Driggers asked, smoothing a curl from her cheek.

Mick smiled, sadness mingling with the weariness in her eyes. "This is a painful situation. Johnelle Black needs answers. I don't know how she's survived this long without them. I have to help her," she said, her lashes fluttering against unshed tears.

"I know," was all Driggers said.

The simple acknowledgement made Mick all the more happy to be home. Driggers promised a freshly made bed, hot tea, and her favorite pastry waiting inside. Mick eagerly allowed herself to be led to relaxation.

By the next day, she was back to her old self and in need of a workout. She contacted the girls, who practically screamed the phone to pieces at the news of her return. They had two months before the season began and they had a lot of rehearsing to do if their most ambitious routine yet was to be all it could be. Mick discovered that the girls had not grown lazy during her absence. They'd been practicing hard and it showed. Mick decided to keep her instructor's cap off that day and enjoy the dance.

***

As promised, Driggers kept Quest informed and was leading him into the house the following afternoon. Mick and the girls had gotten a late start that warm July day, but were in the throes of the routine by the time Quest had arrived. Driggers was full of mischief and had the unexpected guest wait in the den. The room just happened to offer the perfect view of the immaculate back lawn where the rehearsals were held. Driggers knew Mick would kill him for letting anyone-especially another man- gawk at the group. But, Driggers thought, well...he was an *old* man and he could get away with it.

"Have a seat, son and try to stay calm," Driggers advised, smirking when the younger man fixed him with a confused smile.

It wasn't long before Quest's ears caught the sound of hard bass under voices rapping out a popular old school single. He was thankful Driggers had suggested he sit, or his legs would surely have given out beneath him at the sight that greeted his eyes. The vision of the twenty-one beauties on the lawn, all moving in erotic sync to the music, was enough to make any man stare in awe. While they were all luscious, Quest's eyes were riveted on the most luscious of all. He'd known she had curves-he'd felt them....seeing them so deliciously encased in hip-hugging camouflage boy shorts with a matching tank top and her thick black curls haphazardly twisted in a camouflage bandana, drove the fact home. The sight of her enflamed his hormones so quickly, his shaft lengthened, swelled and hardened to an almost uncomfortable state. He whispered a curse just as Driggers returned to the room with a chilled mug of beer.

"Thought you might needed this," Driggers set the mug on the glass table flanking the armchair.

"What is this?" Quest barely breathed, nodding toward the backyard.

"Mick took the girls under her wing a few years ago. Dancers for the band at her college alma mater. I think she needs them now just as much as they need her," he slapped Quest's

160

shoulder. "Enjoy the show."

~~~

And Quest did just that. Erotic was a nice beginning to describe the routine that promised to have every man who saw it in the same state that he was. A smile crossed his handsome face as he thought of his brother. Quay would surely kick himself for knowing he'd missed such a treat.

Quest's intense gray-black stare was riveted on Michaela as he followed her every move. At times, he went as far as to tilt his head to enjoy every twist of her limber, curvaceous figure. When the routine ended, he had managed to quell his raging hormones so that he'd be presentable when the rush of women filled the room.

"Good work, ladies! Good work!" Mick congratulated the troupe as they headed toward the house. "I'm happy to see you haven't let all my hard work go to waste!"

The girls filed into the den, but slowed just after stepping past the sliding glass doors. It took Mick a moment to realize the group had stopped moving altogether.

"Hello!" she called, her steps hindered by the motionless bodies. "Hello?" she called again, squeezing between the girls. "What are y'all doin'?" she noticed all heads turned toward the far right corner of the big room.

The girls' eyes were focused on the beautiful molasses-dipped male who stood there. When Mick saw the cause of all the stunned gazes, she too was mesmerized.

"Ladies," Quest greeted softly. His eyes moved to rest on Michaela. Slowly, they raked her body as though he were stripping away each garment as he went.

The girls glanced at Mick, envying her power over the tall god who watched her so intently.

Mick slowly regained her senses and nodded toward the doorway leading out of the den. "Showers," she instructed softly. "Showers. Now." she managed only minimal firmness in her voice then.

When the last girl left the room, Quest closed the distance

between himself and Mick. His mouth came crashing down on hers, his arms enveloping her in an unbreakable hold. Mick moaned against the powerful thrusts of his tongue, but matched it with a fire of her own. She arched and angled her neck, frantically kissing him as she reached for a remote on the oak shelves. One click activated the panel, which slid in place across the doorway, bathing the room in privacy.

Quest lifted her effortlessly against his tall, muscular frame and carried her to the futon in the farthest corner of the room. He stood there for a moment, savoring the deep hot lunges of her tongue as she kissed him as if she were starved for his taste. He angled a foot beneath the edge of the futon and pulled it into a flat position. Gently, he placed Mick on the olive-green cushioned liner.

Soft moans and ragged groans filled the room as Quest made quick work of Mick's clothing. He had her nude in minutes. She was in heaven, her sighs and moans of encouragement giving him permission to do with her as he pleased. His handsome face was shielded by the lush mounds of her breasts as his tongue trailed the chocolate orbs before his teeth grazed the nipples and then soothed them with his lips.

Mick felt powerless to do anything other than curve more of her body closer to his mouth. Her arms lay weakly above her head, when his tongue outlined one nipple before sucking it madly. Not to ignore the other, he squeezed it between thumb and forefinger molesting it into a throbbing bud.

Mick thought she'd lose her mind in a whirlwind of sensation. Quest's mouth was everywhere: tonguing her belly-button, lavishing her thighs with moist kisses while his mouth nudged the light smattering of black curls at the joining of her legs.

Then, unbelievably the kisses just stopped. Quest rested his head on her hip and inhaled deeply. Mick thought that it reminded her of that night- the night when things went haywire...

At last, he raised his head and covered her nude form with his fully clothed one. "I can't take you this way," he said.

"Yes you can," she blurted, small fists curled against the

front of his white T-shirt. Her body was set aflame by his touch- a flame only he could extinguish.

"I can't," Quest squeezed his eyes shut to take his mind off how good she felt beneath him. "Not with a house full of people, on a futon in your den." He pushed the curls from her forehead and kissed the tip of her nose. "It's tempting and an encounter I intend to fulfill one day. But not the first day, not the first time."

Torn between her desire for him and her appreciation for his concern, she rolled her eyes and steeled herself from begging him to reconsider.

"I want you to get dressed," he whispered, brushing his thumb across the curve of her cheek. "I'm taking you somewhere else."

"Why?" she blurted again. She had to know. "Why are you doing this? Why does it matter to you where or how?"

Quest grinned his captivating left-dimpled smile. He appraised her expressive, incredible eyes and that mouth...the curls that framed her face so sweetly… he adored everything about her. Bringing his lips within a hairsbreadth of hers he whispered, "It matters because I love you."

A LOVER'S DREAM

~ELEVEN~

Mick had ordered her legs to pick up the pace earlier when she headed upstairs to pack for the impromptu getaway. But her legs felt like syrup- all warm and oozy. She was in a dream, a lover's dream and never wanted to awaken.

He's not your lover yet, girl, a voice had said. Still, he loved her. He'd said it clearly and she had remained speechless. But he didn't seem to mind. Now her brows tugged close and she bit down on her lip debating the concern that had suddenly surfaced. Slowly, she turned to face him across the gear console of the Expedition.

"Tell me," Quest said, knowing she was watching him with a question in her eyes.

Mick's gaze faltered upon hesitation. She cleared her throat and pushed unease from her voice. "Are you doing this because of the investigation? do you want me to reconsider?"

"Investigation, book, radio broadcast, Internet or TV movie. I don't care," he replied flatly, his gray stare never veering from the road. "This doesn't have a thing to do with that. You can ask me whatever you like," he said when she started to turn away. "I'll tell you whatever you want to know."

Mick pressed her lips together and nodded.

Quest reclined a bit more in the driver's seat. "But I'll tell you later," he said, "much, much later."

~~~

When they arrived at a cabin located right on the river, Mick was again stunned. *Close your mouth, girl*, she told herself. She didn't wait for Quest to open her door, but eased out of the SUV as though her feet were about to touch sacred ground.

The cabin was a rustic masterpiece surrounded by towering pines and spruce trees. The river it sat next to mingled with the sound of trickling water with birdsong and the gentle sway of leaves and tree limbs against a cool breeze.

"Quest," she breathed, her amber gaze sparkling as she surveyed the scene. "When did you plan this?"

Quest grinned, reaching into the rear of the vehicle to collect their bags. "I wanted you to think I just snapped my fingers and all of this fell into place."

Mick pushed one hand into the back pocket of her jeans. "I guess it wasn't like that, huh?" she teased.

"The cabin's mine. I usually stay here when I have business in Chicago for an extended period of time. I've got my own *houseman* who stops by to check on things," he shared, shutting the rear door on the storage compartment. "The place is always ready for a sudden visit."

"Mmm, convenient," Mick tugged on the lemon, white and blue-striped crew sweater she wore. "It must come in handy with all the women you woo," she noted softly and walked on ahead having no idea how her tease had affected Quest. She stood on the massive porch toying with the cropped hem of her top while waiting for him to unlock the door.

Surprising her, Quest took her by the arm and turned her back against the door. "I've never brought anyone here. *Anyone*

Michaela. No family and no other woman."

Mick could only nod, thoroughly off kilter by the serious tone of his voice and the intensity in the gray of his eyes. She waited, her back still against the door as he unlocked it and pushed it open. She backed into the magnificent dwelling. Her nostrils instantly flared in response to the crisp, masculine scent of spice and wood. She watched Quest relieve himself of their luggage, which he'd carried in all at once. Slowly, her gaze shifted to assess her environment.

The masculine presence of the two-story cabin was real and heady. Everything was oversized and comfortably. The dwelling was crafted for relaxation and Mick couldn't help but feel a bit like a maiden in the lair of a seductive pirate. She almost burst into laughter and turned to Quest again.

Any words she would have uttered were silenced as his mouth lowered to slant across hers. She moaned when his tongue took swift possession, thrusting powerfully before softly stroking the roof of her mouth and ridge of her teeth with subtle mastery. Of course, the same starving quality of his kiss was sweetly noticed when he lifted her against him and carried her up the stairway that was covered by a carpet bearing distinct Native American markings.

Mick heard another door open and realized she was in the bedroom. *Pirate's lair indeed*, she thought when Quest let her ease down the length of his body. The room seemed to be fashioned around the bed. And what a bed it was- a round sea of black satin linens littered with round burgundy pillows. Rich maple casing constructed the surrounding headboard which housed small speakers and electric candlelights all around.

"Quest-"

"Shh," he urged, his perfect teeth nipping at the silky line of her jaw.

"But I have to tell you-"

"Later," he dipped his thumb into her belly button left exposed by the cropped hem of her top.

Mick gasped when he rotated the tip of his thumb there in

the same manner his tongue was encircling her earlobe. She succumbed to the expertise he possessed.

Quest loved her with his hands first, peeling away her top, slipping her out of the lacy bra a second later. His mouth captured hers in a kiss that was the perfect mixture of sweetness and desire. He unfastened and tugged the jeans past her hips and over the full curve of her bottom, dropping to his knees as he removed them with her socks and sneakers.

He literally kissed her out of her panties, his sensuous lips trailing the lacy fabric of the garment. The tip of his tongue disappeared intermittently beneath, tracing the skin there briefly before his teeth tugged the panties down. Mick could do little else than gasp and grasp his shoulders for support until he rose and carried her to the center of his magnificent bed where he pleasured her all over again.

Michaela enjoyed every moment, but soon her hands greedily sought to feel the devastating hardness lying beneath the softness of his sweatpants. Quest didn't want to lose his clothes just then. He knew if he felt her silken chocolate form against his bare skin 'going slow' would be a hollow intention.

"Quest please," she whispered, shaking her head against the pillows.

"I will," he promised with a soft chuckle. His fingers began to tease her shamelessly. He suckled her earlobe while fondling her breasts, taking turns manipulating the nipples into firm jewels. Low moans rose from his throat as he lost himself in the feel of her skin responding to his touch.

Mick arched against him, uttering a cry of disagreement when his fingers moved on past her breasts, dipping once more into her belly button before immersing themselves in the silky black curls dusting her womanhood. He massaged the velvety petals there with his thumb, his middle finger smoothly delving ever so lightly inside the waiting pool of creamy moisture.

Quest was so in tune to her every reaction that he felt her tense when he touched her there. "Relax," he whispered while brushing a sweet kiss across her cheek.

"Quest-" she panted, just before his mouth swooped down to capture hers again.

Mick gave up trying to communicate verbally and lost herself in the pleasure of his touch. She kissed him shamelessly, then found his neck and jaw to be the most delectable targets for the nips she applied there.

He could barely stand the exquisite torture she so gently provided. To pacify himself, he settled his fully clothed form between her thighs and began to grind himself against the welcoming center of her body still wet from his earlier attention and her own need.

Michaela cried out at the power raging beneath the front of his sweats. "Quest-" she tried to speak again and again he silenced her. He placed her arms up near her head, holding them there while lowering his mouth to feast on her breasts once more.

Tiny, indecipherable sounds fluttered past her lips, so incredible was the sensation of his mouth against her breasts. His lips outlined the rigid nipples before repeating the gesture with his tongue. He paid the same attention to every other part of her body, burying his handsome face between her thighs as his tongue delved into the lush core of her body. He thrust hungrily, his massive hands curved beneath her derriere to hold her in place. Mick felt completely weakened as the unspeakable pleasure overwhelmed her and her thighs quivered uncontrollably. When Quest drove his tongue deep inside her, the inner walls of her sex contracted fiercely.

A low chuckle swelled inside his chest when he felt her reaction. He knew she was more than ready to take him. He broke the intimate kiss and rose above her, watching the lovely picture she made writhing on his bed in the midst of her second orgasm. He stripped the T-shirt from his back and went to work on the rest of his clothes. At last, he was gloriously nude.

Michaela marveled in his dark beauty, splaying her hands across the chiseled expanse of his chest. The rigid muscles of his arms and abdomen were both extraordinary and sensual in appearance. She moved lower until her fingers grazed his arousal.

Her hands cupped the steel power that had ground against her only moments before. Her lashes fluttered as she realized the extent of the breathtaking length and girth of the organ. It was impossible to close her hand around it. Biting her lower lip, she swallowed.

"Quest-"

He silenced her this time with his index finger, slipping it past her lips to massage her tongue. Mick responded with all the zeal of a woman gone wild with desire as she suckled his finger. Quest alternated with his finger and tongue inside her mouth while he reached for protection from a tiny drawer inside the maple casing surrounding the bed. In moments, he had it in place and settled himself against her core once more before plunging forward.

A tiny shriek escaped Michaela's lips and Quest went completely still, but for his head snapping up. He fixed her with an incredulous look.

"Christ Mick...Why...Why didn't you tell me?" he whispered, placing his weight on his forearms, hoping not to apply any more pressure to her bruised maidenhead.

She gasped. "I tried," she said, feeling as if she were being ripped apart in the midst of an erotic massage.

Quest's deep-set eyes, once darkened with passion were then wrought with uncertainty. "I don't want to hurt you."

Mick managed a saucy smile. "From what I understand, it can't be helped. Just do it."

Wasting no more time with words, Quest curved his hands around her thighs to move them far away from his hips. He buried his face in her neck and plundered past the barrier of delicate tissue. Mick's agonizing cry faded on a low moan as the pain disappeared to gradually be replaced by the most fascinating sensation as he took her with a deft ease. That sensation spoke to her hips, invoking them to move in an age-old rhythm that drew sounds of fulfillment from both her and Quest.

Mick could do little more than lie there in ecstasy, her fingers toying in her hair as her hips arched and rotated against Quest's. He claimed her slowly, with a provocative expertise that forced satisfied sighs and gasps past Michaela's throat. Her intimate walls were stretched and sensually bruised amidst the incomparable sensation roused by his deep, deliberate strokes. The low grunts and whimpers he uttered gave her a confidence she never knew existed. He shielded his face within the hollow beneath her arm and inhaled the softly sweet scent there as he increased the speed of his thrusts. Their moans gained volume as they arrived simultaneously on a cloud of satisfaction.

~~~

"Are you hurt?"

Mick frowned a little, confused by the question as she lay on Quest's chest and was lulled by the steadiness of his heartbeat. She had already forgotten the pain associated with the loss of her virginity.

"Michaela? Did I hurt you?" he persisted.

She blinked, at last understanding. "I'm fine. I'm *more* than fine," she assured him and pressed a kiss to the middle of his chest.

"Why didn't you tell me?" he asked again, massaging her shoulder blades. "After all the times we almost-"

Mick looked down at him from her position atop his chest. "I guess I was one hundred percent sure that it would happen this time," she shrugged.

Quest shook his head, disbelief filled his eyes as he studied every inch of her face. "How?" he whispered. "How could you still be a virgin?" he kissed her nose when she appeared wounded by a question. "Babe I saw that routine out in your yard, not to mention the way you react to me. You're walking sexuality and I just can't believe you've never been touched."

"Please don't tell County," her lashes fluttered. "I've done a good job of keeping it from her all these years."

"Your secret's safe," Quest's gaze narrowed with sudden slyness. "And you wanted to be taken on your den floor," he teased.

She giggled, slapping at his shoulder. "Well for your information I have been touched before."

"But you gave one of the most important things about yourself to me," he pointed out, all playfulness leaving his gorgeous face. "Why?"

She kissed his mouth. "Because you love me and I believe you."

Quest's stare faltered momentarily. He steeled himself against commenting that she had yet to return the sentiment. But he could accept that- for the moment. Burying one hand into her curls and cupping her chin with the other, he looked directly into her light eyes. "I hope you know what you've done Michaela Sellars, because you're never getting rid of me," he swore and pulled her into a branding kiss.

~~~

Mick ambled downstairs much later that evening. Night had triumphed over dusk hours ago and now the entire lower level of the cabin was bathed in candlelight. Delicious aromas in the air beckoned her toward the kitchen where she found Quest working diligently.

"Mmm...it smells good in here," she complimented, hugging herself as she inhaled deeply.

Quest ceased whatever he was doing at the counter the instant he heard her voice. Mick's eyes widened as he headed toward her. His big hands spanned her waist before cupping her hips and lifting her high against his chest. The long, possessive kiss that followed curled her toes. She wrapped her legs high around his waist, while he carried her to the countertop. She moaned, cradling his face in her hands as they savored the sweetness of the kiss they shared.

Quest sat her gently atop the counter and quickly pulled her out of the peach sleep shirt she wore. His hands smoothed across her skin, worshipping the satiny feel and flawless chocolate tone of her skin. Mick massaged and grazed her nails across his bare muscular back. When he cupped and fondled her breasts, she threw back her head and moaned.

"Quest..." she sighed, arching closer to his mouth when he

171

began to suckle one nipple and then the other. Her hands fell away from his body to brace behind her on the counter. She was eager to let him have his way and wished he'd do more than torture her with the long, slow strokes of his tongue gliding across her extra sensitive skin.

"You need to eat," he decided abruptly ending the kisses and leaving her under the spell of his touch.

Grudgingly, Mick obeyed and let him pull her off the countertop. She fixed her shirt and took her place at the beautiful round cherry-wood dining room table in the corner of the spacious room.

"This is so beautiful," she whispered, taking in the fantastic scene of moonlight shining upon the lake. The tall windows lining the dining area provided an unforgettable view. "How long have you had this?"

Quest took a moment to stare out into the night. "Yeah, it is incredible. I loved it the first time I saw it six years ago. It's calm, peaceful, away from the hubbub of the city," he graced her with a sexy smile across his shoulder. "Please don't tell Quay I have it," he joined in when Mick laughed out loud. After a moment, however, his expression turned dim. "The room was in my name. The room where Sera Black...I'm sure you know that," his eyes remained fixed on tossing the Caesar salad he'd prepared to accompany the butter sauteed shrimp with fresh veggies on a bed of rice.

Mick watched him from the table. She remained silent and let him have his say.

"I had to register the room in my name because Quay had been banned from doing so by most of the nicer hotels in the city. Behavior problems," he added, shaking his head as he spoke. "Anyway, I only stayed fifteen or twenty minutes before I went down to the hotel restaurant for a drink. I must've stayed there longer than I thought because when I got back to the room, everyone was gone."

"I checked out the place," he turned to retrieve the dressing chilling in the refrigerator. "It was a mess, but I was happy to see no damage at least. That was before I walked into the living room and saw the broken balcony doors," he stopped talking for a moment and leaned against the counter. "I looked over the edge and saw Sera bleeding and naked on the concrete eleven floors down." He shook his head, rubbing both hands across his silky waves. "I was in a daze. Obviously, she fell from our room. I stumbled backward wanting to get as far inside as possible. I made it to the bedroom," he sighed, folding his arms across his chest. "Sat down on the edge of the bed, that's where I found Quay-naked and passed out too," Quest's eyes darkened to onyx as he stared off into the distance. "I don't know what happened before I got there. When Quay woke up and looked at me, I went cold."

"Why?"

The simply inquiry sent Quest's eyes flying to her face. "I *don't* know what happened. All I know is it's enough to put him away for a long time."

Mick blinked and scooted forward in her seat. "You think...Quay did it?"

"I don't know!" he snapped, slamming his fist against his palm before he winced. "I'm sorry," he grated, reaching out to caress her cheek and smiling when she kissed the back of his hand. "Baby, I've never told this to anyone- not even Quay."

"He thinks you did something," Mick breathed as though she were speaking to herself.

Quest leaned close. "What?"

"He's been afraid to ask you about that night for the same reason. He believes you tried to protect him."

"Protect him from what?"

Mick fixed him with a pointed look. "He was naked and passed out in bed. Sera was naked and dead on the sidewalk directly below your room. She'd been raped. He thinks you could've...to keep her quiet, to keep him safe."

Quest appeared as though he were in a daze. "Quay didn't do it..."

Mick shrugged. "He can't remember half as much as you. He asked me to continue investigating as well."

"Who would have done this? Sera was a sweet girl," Quest whispered, his gray eyes even more solemn as he thought about his murdered classmate.

"It'll be almost impossible to find them since all the evidence is now missing because-"

"My parents covered it up. 'Made it go away' was what they said they'd do," Quest recalled, massaging his hand across suddenly tired eyes. "I'd never been in any trouble like this and they weren't about to let this touch me."

"Quay's going crazy not knowing," Mick said, smoothing her hands across his arms as a wave of sadness enveloped her. "I have to do my best to get him some answers," she vowed, leaning back in her chair as Quest went to get dinner to the table.

When he resumed his place, he reached for Mick's hand and smothered it within both of his. "My brother's very lucky to have you in his life," he said.

"And I'm lucky to have *you* in *my* life," she leaned forward to request a kiss that he was all too willing to give.

The simple action quickly turned into something more erotic. Thankfully, Quest's cooler head prevailed and he ordered her to eat.

~TWELVE~

"Oh, that's not today, is it?"

Quest appeared disappointed when he heard Mick's groaning complaint. "I told you I wanted to take you out on the lake today," he said, glancing at the fishing poles he held.

"Oh Quest, I can't even move," she whined, snuggling deeper into bed. "I ache all over."

The disappointment left Quest's handsome face and was replaced by concern. "Have I been hurting you?" he asked, taking a few uncertain steps closer to the bed. "I could do that easily and not even be aware of it. I'm um, pretty, um-"

"Huge?" Mick suggested, fixing him with innocent eyes. "Or should I say well endowed?" she rephrased softly.

Quest's face would have flushed beet red were his complexion lighter. "Please tell me, Michaela. If I'm too rough or if it's...too much, tell me, alright?" he urged.

Mick sat up and reached for his hand. "It's never too much," she said, pressing her cheek against his palm. "This ache is a delicious ache that can be a bit cumbersome if I try to get out of bed and go fishing, that's all," she told him. Her legs and a few other things were thoroughly weakened by all the *activities* they'd enjoyed over the last several days.

"Wait here," Quest said as he set the gear against the wall in the room's entryway.

Mick happily complied. She waited until Quest left the room before allowing herself to drift off into a light doze. When she opened her eyes again, she saw that Quest had doffed his sagging dark jeans and olive-green T-shirt and now stood nude before her. Before she could utter one compliment in response to his glorious form, he pulled her from the bed and carried her to the adjoining master bathroom.

A tub of bubbly water waited, smelling inviting and looking heavenly. Michaela gasped, thanking Quest for the sweet gesture by kissing his jaw. Gently, he placed her in the foamy water before settling in behind her. Mick turned in the water, slipping her arms about his neck to thank him with a more thorough kiss.

Quest's hands were everywhere, kneading the sore muscles at the small of her back, weighing her breasts in his wide palms. He kissed her long and slow, his tongue stroking the roof of her mouth with the same sensuous swirls his thumbs applied to her nipples.

Despite the telltale ache in her lower regions, Mick hungered for him and moved to straddle his lap. Quest groaned, he wanted her more every time he had her. Somehow, this time, he found the will to resist. Pressing a kiss to the end of her nose when she watched him disappointedly, he turned her away from him. "I don't want any excuses tonight," he whispered close to her cheek.
~~~

"I can't believe you've never shared this place with your family," Mick noted, stretching her bare legs out against the lounge.

"What for?" Quest focused on the scene of the sparkling lake before the trees in the distance that afternoon.

Mick watched him in disbelief. "Look at this," she ordered, waving her hand toward the beauty they enjoyed from their spots on the deck. "It'd be an incredible place for family reunions, birthday parties, barbeques…"

By the time Mick was done with her events list, Quest sat watching her as if she'd gone mad. "Michaela, that is something I'd *never* consider. My family is a disaster waiting to happen," he admitted, pressing one hand to the front of his burgundy T-shirt as though confirming the sincerity of his words. "I'm not exaggerating here. Disaster can and always does strike whenever we all get together."

Mick waved her hand. "But that's forgivable where family is concerned?"

"Hmph, that's because you've never been around us," he explained, leaning back against the lounge while crossing his legs at the ankles. "There's always someone arguing over money or insurance or who got richer, who cheated who and with who and who did what fifty years ago. I could go on."

"Spare me," Mick tiredly urged, tugging on the hem of her gray and baby-blue tank top.

"So you don't believe me?" he asked, looking over at her. "Alright," he turned to face her across the small wooden table between their lounges, "let me just start by telling you about my cousins. I've got one who's a bounty hunter and was so low he once courted the woman of the man he was trying to capture just to get the guy out of hiding. One who's intentionally gone after the lovers of his enemies just to stick it to 'em and prove who's the more powerful adversary. One who's done time, one who's made his fortune from all the senators and governors he carries in his pocket and then there's my brother who has a temper so foul it's actually frightened people to the point of not wanting to leave their homes."

Mick propped her chin against her palm. "And just where do you fit into this collage of rough riders? Are you telling me you haven't been so terrible?"

Quest's expression darkened like the gray in his eyes. "I've probably been the worst of all," he admitted, looking down at his hands clenching and unclenching. "I've intimidated, used muscle to get my way, unnerved people sometimes without merit-by showing them that silence can be just as potent as a loud temper. I've ruined quite a few engagements, but none of that holds a candle to helping conceal certain things my brother and cousins have done. In doing that, I may have contributed just as much in preventing them from having a better shot at being better than what they were."

Mick offered no words of wisdom, knowing Quest needed to vent. She felt it was something he'd rarely, if ever, allowed himself to do. In spite of all the luxuries at his fingertips, she could see the horrors as well. A life of privilege could be as destructive as one of poverty, she guessed. Still, for the chance at having a family of her own, she would gladly have chosen his life over hers.

~~~

Quest carried Mick right back to bed following a late supper that evening. Her arms were linked around his neck in much the same fashion that her shapely legs were locked around his back. They kissed slowly- deeply savoring every thrust and caress of their tongues. Soft moans filled the air and added more sensuality to the darkened scene.

Quest kicked the bedroom door shut and Mick broke the kiss. She gave a start, seeing the transformation the room had undergone.

"So this is what you were doing when you left the dining room for fifteen minutes," she said, taking in the sea of candles that cast their wild flickering shadows across the walls.

"Surprised?" he queried while lowering her to the center of the stunning bed.

Mick could offer no response, she was so in awe of him. Lying there, she watched him shed the T-shirt he wore, leaving him clothed in a pair of black cotton sleep pants. Her fingers flexed, eager to graze the solid molasses wall of his chest.

Quest joined her on the bed, intending to massage every

part of her body- first with his hands and then with his mouth. His fingers penetrated the supple line of her leg, traveling onward until he cradled a small foot in his hand.

Mick arched and moaned, feeling his fingers provide a soothing massage to her toes before he suckled them one by one. Her eyes opened to thin slits and she watched him, looking even more darkly gorgeous as he focused on pleasing her. His fingertips began to play along the sleek line of her calf, stopping to tease the soft flesh behind her knee. Soon, his lips were charting the same trail. Slowly, he brought himself closer until he was smothering her bare, silken form. They shared another deep kiss, only the faint snap of flickering firelight mingling with their whispered words of desire.

Mick's moans of disappointment transcended into sighs of pleasure when Quest broke the kiss to glide his mouth across her neck. She leaned into the sweet treat, unconsciously holding her breath when he tongued the base of her throat and curve of her breasts. At last, he was fulfilling her with the most intimate kiss. His tongue delved deeply inside her as his hands cupped her bottom to settle her more snuggly against his mouth.

Mick could scarcely breathe, especially once he added the touch of his fingers. She gasped his name softly yet uncontrollably as wave upon erotic wave engulfed her. Quest pleasured her shamelessly as though her breathless cries were fueling his desire to do so. His fingers manipulated her firm nipples with intermittent squeezes and strokes, and he groaned every time his tongue delved deeper inside the fragrant warmth of her femininity. He satisfied her with one orgasm after another- each more powerful than the last. Mick was as limp as a wilted flower when he was done, yet her surprise was obvious when he pressed a gentle kiss to her temple and ordered her to sleep.

"What about you?" she whispered, feeling his unsated arousal nudging her thigh.

He smiled and kissed her mouth that time. "I'm fine," he said and pulled her into a spooning embrace. "That was for you."

Mick blinked, completely shocked by him. Shaking her

head in disbelief, she tugged his hand from where it lay next to her hip and kissed his palm. she would never love another man as she loved him.

~~~

The rest of the week passed in much the same manner. Mick never realized there were so many ways a man and woman could love each other. She found that physical pleasure was so much sweeter when the real emotions of love and respect were there. And she did love him, knowing he'd been waiting to hear her say the words. She feared if she did, the magic would end. Something would sour.

"Tell me about Driggers," Quest asked one evening they danced in the den while waiting for his quiche to finish baking.

Mick laughed, fiddling with the tassels on his Howard sweatshirt. "You tell me. What'd you think when you found out I had a houseman?"

"I thought his voice was too deep," Quest answered without hesitation, linking his fingers at the small of her back. "I had to see him for myself."

"And when you did?"

Quest rolled his eyes. "I didn't care if he *was* fifty-something. The man's too ripped for his age."

"Try *sixty*-something and yeah, he is a handsome devil," Mick sighed, her amber eyes sparkling as though she was envisioning Driggers then.

"No family?" Quest asked.

"They died one night in a fire," Mick's expression clouded. "Kerosene heater malfunctioned. I'd been looking for someone and when he interviewed for the position, I asked about his family. He told me that story and he had my heart. Over the years, I've loved him more every day. He's like the father I never had the chance to know."

Quest stroked her back, left bare by the cut of her blue and green striped sundress. "What happened to him?"

Mick blinked and shook the curls from her face. "He died

shortly after I was born. At least that's what she told me."

"She?"

"My mother," Mick grimaced when she uttered the word. "I really believe she never knew *who* he was."

Quest heard the pain in her voice and knew she was only pretending to be unaffected by it. "Where is she now?"

Mick shrugged. "I don't know. She left when I was eight. I remember that day so clear," she looked as though she couldn't quite believe it. "I cried so hard. My mother never told me she loved me, but the day she left I told her. I childishly believed those three words held some power that would change things. They didn't. She didn't even act like she heard me even though I yelled it at the top of my lungs." Her hands tightened reflexively across Quest's forearms.

"Did she leave you with friends?" he asked.

Mick's lips curved into a dark smile. "That would've been *too* loving. Instead, she left me in a rat-infested apartment where I spent a week before a concerned teacher came looking for me."

Quest had stopped swaying to the music long ago. Now he pulled her to sit with him on the sofa. Mick continued to talk about her foster homes, foster fathers who were more interested in sleeping in her room than their own. She was always fighting to stay ahead of their games. Fighting and winning, but fighting just the same.

Quest felt his jaw muscle tightening with murderous rage. He let go of Mick's hands, afraid that he would crush them out of the anger he felt over what she'd had to endure.

Mick laughed nervously and wiped at the tears pooling her eyes. "I've been fighting to hold onto my virginity for years."

The left dimple flashed when Quest smiled. "I still find it so unreal. I hope that doesn't offend you?"

Mick shook her head. "I found it unreal myself. Lots of times," she admitted, toying with the edge of a throw pillow. "I just couldn't let go and be with a man that way if I didn't truly believe he could be with me-always."

Quest nodded, understanding why she'd feel that way.

After all she'd endured- all the loss she'd experienced. "Did anyone else ever come close?" he had to ask.

Mick shrugged. "A few, but they didn't stick around long once they realized I wanted to know them better before going to the next level. Then I realized they wanted to *know* me on that basic level first before moving forward- if they ever intended to move forward," her gaze appeared distant then. "I watched my mother dish out sex like it was ice cream in hopes of keeping a man. It never worked. The men always ate and ran and I swore I'd never be used that way. Especially when the stakes could be so high. Facing that sort of reality growing up, virginity, or the loss of it, was a huge deal to me." She blinked and smoothed her hand over Quest's forearm. "*You* frightened the hell out of me," she told him, "I didn't give a damn about knowing you first. I wanted to *know* you and cursed myself because you could make me feel that way, desire-filled and only complete in your arms. You're the very first man who ever appealed to me so soon and on *every* level."

Quest leaned close and pressed his forehead to hers. "Then that's something we definitely have in common because that's exactly the way I feel about you."

Mick searched his beautiful eyes. *I love you*, she wanted to tell him. Still, she feared the beauty and everything else the word implied would fade if she spoke it.

On cue, the oven timer sounded in the distance and she was more than grateful for the interruption.

~~~

The weather was warm enough that Saturday for Mick to enjoy the delightful pool in the backyard. She sat on the edge, trailing her toes across the water.

Quest studied her from afar, loving the daring bikini she sported, but hating the faraway look on her face. Her life had been filled with pain and all he wanted now was for her to know happiness and security. After a lifetime of protecting those he was linked to by blood, he wanted nothing more than to keep this woman sheltered from the demons of her past and any that sought to threaten her future.

Mick smiled and cuddled back into Quest's warm embrace when he moved close behind her. His legs were on either side of her, his feet disappearing into the pool.

"You okay?" he asked against her hair.

Mick nodded. "Mmm-hmm, I'm fine," she spoke honestly.

"So tell me about your dancing," Quest hoped to bring her out of her doldrums.

It worked, Mick's cloudy expression cleared at once. "I literally stepped into it. I was on campus during homecoming one year and found myself in the music hall. By mistake I interrupted their practice. If you could call it that," she laughed, wiggling her toes in the water as she recalled the day.

Quest was laughing as well. "Quay would die if he knew he missed out on that performance I had the pleasure of enjoying."

Mick turned a little in his arms. "And just how much of it did you enjoy?" she asked.

"All of it. All of *you*."

Mick threw back her head and laughed. "Please! With all those younger, firmer girls bouncing around before you?"

Quest's sleek brows rose as he considered her words. "Younger, yes. Firmer that you? Not a chance," he declared.

Mick arched up to meet his kiss when he lowered his head. She cupped the back of his neck, her fingers stroking the soft close-cut hair that curled there. A delicious scene ensued in the warm sunlight and concluded in the sparkling coolness of the pool.

A LOVER'S DREAM

~THIRTEEN~

Michaela's moan of disappointment echoed in the otherwise silent bedroom. She tried to push Quest's head back beneath the covers as he emerged. She'd awakened that morning amidst sensational waves of another incredible orgasm courtesy of Quest Ramsey. Her dreams had been filled with erotic images of his potent lovemaking. Waking to find those dreams a reality made her pleasure that much more intense.

"I can top that," Quest promised with a grin, when Mick tried to silently urge him to continue the sensational massage.

Mick's eyes widened just as he kissed her and her delight returned as she suckled the taste of her body from his tongue.

Quest was settling himself, his hands curving around Mick's thighs, when the doorbell rang. Slowly, he turned his head in the direction of the bedroom door. "Damn thing's just for show," he grumbled in reference to the bell. "It'll go away," he predicted.

Mick squealed when he began to nibble at her breasts. "You have to get it. It could be an emergency."

The bell rang again and Quest uttered a savage curse before leaving the bed. Michaela giggled, watching him jerk into a pair of gray sweats. He whipped open the door before turning toward her.

"Stay," he ordered, his gaze desire filled.

Mick snuggled back into bed, feeling more content than she could ever remember being. Quest hadn't been gone five seconds when a tiny ring tone pierced the silence. She recognized the chiming of her cell phone, leaned over the side of the bed and pulled a black leather tote from beneath.

"Hello?" she answered.

"Ms. Sellars? This is Harriet Forman. The Forman Hotel?"

"Oh yes," Mick breathed, propping herself up on her elbow.

"I'm sorry to be calling you so early-"

"No please, it's fine. I assume this is about the investigation?"

"I remember something about that night. I can't believe I'd forgotten it," she said, sounding as though she were speaking to herself. "When I started looking through the file, it hit me."

"I'm listening," Mick said, already perched on the edge of the bed.

"On the night of the party, I was working the front desk at my parents' hotel. I took a break, and my curiosity led me to the eleventh floor where the party was being held. I remember feeling disappointed because things seemed so quiet and it looked like the party was over. So when I saw this guy going into the room, I was interested."

"What guy?" Mick asked.

"This guy from the news photo. I've scanned the picture and I'll email it to you. You could probably see him on your copy of the article, but I don't want there to be any mistakes about who I'm referring to."

"I appreciate that, Harriet. I haven't been near a computer in almost a week, but I'll call you as soon as I see it."

"I circled his face and drew an arrow around it also," Harriet said.

"You sound sure about this. Do you think he had something to do with what happened?"

"I don't know, Michaela," heaviness weighed on Harriet's voice. "When he opened the door, a girl was giggling and I heard him call Sera by name."

"Did you recognize him?"

"I tried to place him, but I can't. I just can't seem to remember who he is."

Mick nodded. "Harriet, you've done a great job and I'm very thankful. I promise to call when I view the email."

"Thanks Michaela."

"You take care. Good-bye."

When the connection ended, Mick tossed the phone to the bed. She clapped her hands to celebrate the break in the case and jumped up to tell Quest what she'd learned.

~~~

Quest's handsome dark face harbored a glare as he watched his uncle down a second round of Scotch.

"How'd you find me?" Quest turned to prepare his own drink.

Marcus Ramsey chuckled. "When you're a member of a family like the Ramseys, escaping reality isn't only for vacation, it's to maintain your sanity," he shared, his dark eyes gleaming with smug delight. "The specific details on how I found you are my little secrets."

"Well are you going to at least tell me what you're doin' here?" Quest didn't bother with preventing the agitation from clouding his voice.

"Why don't you tell me about this lovely young thing you've gone crazy over?"

Quest's suspicion increased ten-fold. He set the glass on the mahogany bar with such force that remnants of Scotch sloshed over the edges. "Get to it, Marc," his voice took on a deeper, more gravely undertone.

"She's a writer," Marc replied without hesitation. "If I

understood correctly, her genre revolves around powerful black families," he folded his arms across the crisp blue shirt he wore. "From what I hear, she's quite a lady and I'd have no problem with you seeing her if our family were more *normal*."

"The book is dead, Marc."

"But the investigation isn't."

Quest turned away, his jaw muscle working fiercely beneath his skin.

"This investigation has to come to an end," Marc was saying as he followed his nephew across the room.

Quest turned. "Do you realize there may be a chance that we're not even responsible for Sera's death?"

"Fool," Marc hissed, his brow furrowed to the point that it was difficult to tell where his brow ended and his bald head began. "This is about more than the death of some little fast-assed girl who was sniffin' around you and Quay! Your little girlfriend's poking around could uncover a great many things. She'd be too interested not to poke further."

"Things," Quest's misty gray eyes had darkened to pitch black. "A great many things, you say," he added, strolling the line of his cheek as he circled Marcus. "I hope you're not leaving out your own dealings. Dealings I'm sure my father knows nothing about. You always stay true to form, Marc. Always lookin' out for number one."

Marcus managed a smile. "Know this," he said, sneering and stepping closer to his nephew, "aside from my foolish brother, Houston, no one in this family wants a book, an investigation, or any knowledge of what happened at that damned party. Get rid of her, Quest...or forget us."

Quest winced. "What?"

"You heard me. No way will this family tolerate some snoop hoping for her next big story to break." Marc rested a hand on Quest's shoulder. "I don't care how good a lay she is."

A gargled sound filled the room then. Marc had barely finished his last statement when Quest's hand rose to practically smother his neck in an iron grip. Marc's eyes widened in obvious

187

shock over Quest's uncharacteristic loss of temper. His fingers pried against Quest's hand in hopes of loosening the grip.

Quest maintained his hold, until he'd escorted his uncle across the living room. He whipped open the door. "Michaela is my family, Marc." He said, pulling the man close. "The fact that you're my uncle will not stop me from half killing your ass," Quest released his hold. "Forget this address," he advised, before slamming the door un Marc's face.

Mick had listened to the angry exchange from her spot on the first floor landing. With a quiet sigh, she turned and headed back upstairs.

~~~

Lunch that afternoon was enjoyed beneath the gazebo near the river. The incredible spread of roast chicken and beef sandwiches was barely touched by the diners, however. After a while, Mick tired of pretending and set her plate aside.

"I talked to Harriet Forman this morning. The Forman Hotel?" she added for clarification.

Quest recognized the name and grimaced., "Michaela, I'm not interested in that right now," he told her in his softest voice.

Mick took no offense. She wasn't interested in the subject either. "Then let's discuss the real issue at hand," she decided, her heart lurching in dread of what she was about to say- what *had* to be said.

"This has all been lovely and I'd do anything to relive it, but I think we both know it can never happen again."

Quest looked up then, his eyes filled with unspoken questions.

"I heard you talking with your uncle this morning."

Anger returned full-fold and Quest's face tightened into a sinister mask. He pushed his plate away. "Jackass," he muttered while leaving the table.

"He was right, Quest."

"Mick-"

"Your family would never accept me," she pulled the

napkin from her jean-clad thighs and slapped it to the table. "If all the things you've told me are true, they'd always be on guard around me. And you'd always be on edge with them because of the way you feel it's affecting me. I can't have you lose touch with your family and that closeness because of me."

Quest fixed her with a suddenly helpless look. "I love you," he whispered as though it were the only thing he was certain of.

Her heart melted. "I love you too," tears pooled her eyes when he appeared shocked that she'd returned the sentiment.

A moment later, Quest was pulling her into a crushing embrace. His mouth melted with hers in a searing kiss.

"You made me see that love is real," she said when he pulled back. "Not just some word that may or may not have power. Love is action. Physical, yes, but also the act of sharing, sharing *all* your fears and truly being concerned about mine. You've shown me all that and more and I love you for it."

Quest's eyes narrowed as he brushed the curve of her cheek with the back of his hand.

"But while you're ready to turn your back on your flesh and blood for that love," she said, squeezing his hand in hers. "I'm not ready to let you do that. Family is too important."

"You're my family."

"They're your blood They've *always* been there. *Always* cared for you," she shook her head as she spoke. "I've never had that and while you may take it for granted, I *can't* and I can't be with you knowing what you're sacrificing by being with me."

Quest leaned closer, peering directly into her eyes. "Are you suggesting I let you go?" he whispered in disbelief.

"You have to."

"That's not an option."

"Quest-"

"No."

"Listen to me," she whispered, making him sit along the gazebo's vine-covered ledge. "My third book was about a family out of Oklahoma. The Cowans."

Quest rolled his eyes. "Michaela-"

"Please listen," she pounded her fists lightly against his denim shirt. "Let me say this, alright?" she waited for him to nod. "For me, the most emotional part of the story involved the patriarch and matriarch of the family- Blue and Esther Cowan. They'd overcome so many struggles to be together, raising seven children, being black during the Depression." Mick shook her head. "They had all the odds against them, but they knew they wanted a life together," she said, taking a seat next to Quest along the railing.

"She was fourteen and he was fifteen when they married. Her parents weren't as much against their youth as they were against Blue himself. Esther said they hated him passionately- he had no family, no money, no prospects, but she loved him. They were both in their eighties when Esther told me this story. She'd loved Blue all of her life, in spite of the struggles. But even with all that love, there was still a place in her heart that was filled with hatred. It was a tiny place, but a place just the same. She said she didn't hate her husband, but it was because of him that she had to choose against ever having her parents in her life."

Quest pulled a windblown curl away from Mick's cheek. "Baby what the hell does this have to do with anything?"

Mick caught his hand. "Quest, don't you see? I can't live knowing a place like that could exist in your heart for me. That's a choice no one should have to make, especially when their family loves them the way yours loves you."

Quest muttered a curse. "That's a foolish reasoning Michaela. Besides, a family with that sort of love wouldn't allow there to be a choice to begin with," his gray eyes slanted Mick a probing look as he watched her shake her head. He knew that he wouldn't convince her. She'd been through too much, years of disappointment and hurt- longing for family and love. What she couldn't understand was that unconditional love wasn't always an option in family. Because of that, it made one wonder if family was worth all the headache.

"I'm going to pack," she said softly already easing off the railing.

Quest caught her wrist before she got too far. He said nothing, simply held on to her wrist, his thumb stroking the pulse point hidden beneath the extra-long sleeve of the lavender knit top she wore. When he released her at last, Mick all but ran from the gazebo. Alone, Quest walked over to the table they'd shared. With one swift move of his arm, he swiped everything from the surface.

A LOVER'S DREAM

~FOURTEEN~

Instead of remaining home after she and Quest parted ways, Mick prepared for another trip. This time, to a private park in Newport, Rhode Island, where she often traveled to enjoy a few days of fishing, hiking or just quiet thinking time. She knew it was all a cowardly act, but she couldn't handle Driggers' questions, mostly because she had no answers. Letting go of Quest was the very last thing she ever wanted. Of course, she better than anyone was well aware that one could rarely have what one wanted.

Mick squatted near the straw basket she'd carried to the lake. Setting aside her fishing poles, she opened the basket to check her supplies. She was placing the cap back on a can of bait when she heard boots crunching upon dirt and brush in the distance. She waited, her exotic amber eyes widening just briefly when Quest came into view.

"County," Mick breathed, standing to wipe her hands across the seat of her jeans.

Quest placed his fishing gear to the ground. "She and

Driggers asked me to come out and check on you, since you won't talk to anybody else," he fixed her with a challenging stare while folding his arms across the front of his oatmeal heather polo shirt.

Mick spread her hands about her. "As you can see, I'm fine."

Quest offered no response, though he couldn't help but treat himself to the sight of her looking sexy and deliciously rugged in the faded jeans and snug-fitting navy blue and olive-green flannel shirt. Slowly, his gray stare narrowed toward the lake. "That your boat?" his mouth curved into a half smile as he surveyed the twenty-foot Bowrider in the calm lake.

"It's mine," she confirmed, her expression grim. "I was looking forward to being alone."

Quest smiled and looked down, accepting the dig. "I know, but you wouldn't want to be breaking your promise to me now, would you?"

Mick only tilted her head and watched him curiously.

"The fishing trip, we were supposed to take back at the cabin," he said, "you weren't up for it," he added softly.

Michaela blinked, feeling her cheeks burn as memories of that time filled her mind. Without another word, she collected her gear and headed for the dock, Quest followed.

The lake was calm and crystal clear with a spectacular view from any direction. Quest and Mick did not speak as they baited hooks and cast their lures. They celebrated one another's catches, but that was the only interaction they shared. Hours passed, morning turned into late afternoon. The two headed back to shore and came to an unspoken decision that Quest would follow her back to the cottage she'd rented. Inside, their unspoken communication continued. They cleaned the fish in the shed a short distance from the cottage, then took their catch inside.

Mick told Quest where he could settle in, before she headed for a shower. She pampered herself beneath the water's heavy spray and indulged in the fragrant gels and shampoos she'd packed. She would not allow herself to think of Quest and why he wouldn't at least *try* to accept that it couldn't happen between them. But, then, she already knew why. It was the same reason that she'd been so surprised and so very happy to see him that morning. It was why she was so happy to have him there now. She loved him.

Later, Mick stood at the top of the short, navy-blue carpeted stairway and inhaled. The unmistakable smells of fish and fresh vegetables filled the air. The lulling tones of classical instrumentals softly intruded into the otherwise silent atmosphere. After a moment, Mick shook herself to reality, hoping to dismiss the deja vu that washed over her as she recalled a similar scene the evening after she and Quest first made love.

He was there in the kitchen, placing the last of the golden fish on a heavy blue and white ceramic platter. Mick saw the table was set with condiments for the fish, a bottle of white wine chilled in the center of the table.

"Dig in," Quest called, seeing her standing there.

Mick offered no hesitation in obeying the request. Dinner was a silent event.

~~~

Mick dozed lightly from her spot on the armchair before the fire. After they ate, Quest had insisted on cleaning the kitchen himself. No hefty task, since he cleaned as he cooked which made the chore far less cumbersome. Now he too enjoyed the fire, relaxing on the sofa that flanked Mick's chair. His long legs extended before him as he rested his feet against the coffee table.

"You know I love you, Michaela," his deep voice was solemn.

"I know. I love you too," she managed once her heart had ceased its lurching.

Quest grimaced. "So you say."

Her head lifted. "You doubt me?"

Quest didn't take his eyes from the fire. "I don't doubt you meant to say the words. If you know *what* the words mean, is what I question."

"Quest-"

"Love doesn't run when things get rocky, Michaela," he said, still reclining on the sofa with his hands hidden in the pockets of the forest-green sweats he wore. "Love fights to stay," he continued, "it doesn't give a damn about who does or doesn't approve. If you knew what love was, you'd know that."

Mick's breathing came in shuddery gasps, her eyes pooling with tears. Quest's words had been as hurtful as a slap. Yet, reluctantly, she acknowledged that he was most likely right. Sitting up straight in her chair, she smoothed her hands across her legs left bare by the short hemline of her denim dress. "If I don't know what love is, Quest, maybe it's because I never had it in my life. Not until I was grown anyway," her words were a tad shaky as she spoke, "By then I had Driggers and County...but having no real family when I was a child- it does something to you. It deadens something inside you." She pinned him with a sharp glare then.

"But you aren't dead inside, Quest, that part of your heart was nourished by a family. Whatever they've done in the past, it isn't right to turn away from them," she said, unable to stop thoughts of her mother's rejection from entering her mind. "It isn't right," she whispered.

Quest massaged his eyes and muffled a curse when he saw how his words had upset her. Leaving the sofa, he went to kneel before her chair. "Shh," he brushed away the tears that streamed her face. "Shh," he kissed her cheeks and the tiny mole at the corner of her mouth. "I'm sorry," he whispered before burying his handsome dark face in the crook of her neck. "I'm sorry," he pulled her into a gently rocking embrace.

~~~

The next morning, Mick woke with a jerk, realizing she was secure in her bed in the cottage's upstairs suite. She squeezed her eyes closed, trying to recall whether the previous night, the bittersweet scene before the fire, had all been a dream. She rested on a very firm pillow. Upon lifting her head, she discovered that it was Quest's thigh. He was fully dressed and sat playing in her hair while he waited for her to awaken.

195

He kissed her mouth when she looked up at him. "I'll tell County and Driggers you're doing fine," he said against the top of her head.

"You're leaving?" Mick whispered, while pushing herself up to sit facing him.

Quest followed the path of his fingers toying with her curls. "Yeah, I think I should."

"You're angry," she guessed.

"Not a bit," his hand curved around her neck, squeezing reassuringly.

Mick focused on the bed linens. "You're giving up," she figured.

"Never," he swore.

"But-"

"I'm going back to Seattle. You need time to think. You can't do that with me here."

"Then why'd you come in the first place?" she pouted, hating the whine in her voice. She couldn't help it. She wanted him to stay.

Quest's entrancing gray eyes fixed on the mole at the corner of her heart-shaped mouth. "I wanted to give you more to think about it," he whispered just before his lips melded with hers.

"Mmm," the sound came out weak and tortured. Instantly, Mick moved onto his lap, snuggling the center of herself against the part of his body she wanted him to share.

Quest groaned, as affected by the closeness as she was. He kept the sheets bunched at her hips while cradling the fullness of her bottom in his wide palms. A surge of arrogance swelled within him when she cried his name upon feeling his thrusting power stiffen beneath the zipper of his jeans.

"Please stay," she begged, unashamed, her hands moving to bring him closer as they disappeared beneath the vintage Tribe Called Quest sweatshirt he wore.

He delighted himself in her body only a minute longer and then eased away. "Love, if I don't leave now, I'll never go."

Michaela declined to tell him again that she didn't want

him to leave. His mind was clearly made up.

"How long will you be here?" he retrieved his bag and jacket from the armchair near the door.

Mick shrugged, tucking the sheet beneath her arms. "Only a few days more."

"When can I see you?"

"You can see me now."

"Mick…" he warned, closing the distance between them to plant a hard kiss to his mouth. "I'll call in a few days. We'll make plans. Use this time," he encouraged.

"I will," she promised, hating him for leaving and loving him so very much for putting what she needed above what they both wanted. But she was trying to do the same, wasn't she? He had to see that nothing was worth turning his back on his family, right? Never having a real family of her own, she believed she knew better than he how very important they were. *They* were who he needed and she had to put that fact above what *she* wanted.

***

"Who are you?" Mick asked as she stared at the photo she'd downloaded from Harriet Forman's e-mailed message later that week. The knock on her office door went unanswered for quite some time before she set aside the photo. "Yeah?" she called.

Driggers stuck his head past the doorway. "How are you?" he asked.

"Fine," she flopped back on her lavender office chair. Her expression tightened when Driggers simply folded his arms across the moss-colored cotton tee he sported. "Considering I'm breaking the heart of the man I love," she admitted.

"Doesn't have to be that way," Driggers said as he stepped into the room.

"Yes it does."

Driggers shrugged. "Because?"

"Because he's talking about turning his back on his family for me!" She shoved back her office chair when she stood. "I can't let him do that."

"Are you sure that-"

"I'm positive," she used both hands to push curls out of her eyes. "It's an intense situation, an intense family, but they're all he has."

"He has you. At least he *thought* he did," Driggers' gaze was firm and unwavering.

Mick rolled her eyes. "Family's supposed to be forever, Drig. He can always find another woman to love."

Driggers' smile was slow and knowing. "I guess you'd be alright with that, huh?"

Mick shoved her hands inside the front pocket of her red, hooded sweatshirt. "I've made up my mind."

Driggers stood. "Baby, I just don't want you to wind up alone in this world," he stepped forward to pull her hands from the pockets. "You have a chance for love and a family of your own."

Mick laid her palms flat against Drigger's chest. "I'll never be alone as long as I have you."

"But I won't be here forever, love," Driggers said, taking both her hands into one of his.

The tone of the statement triggered a tiny furrow in Michaela's brow. "Is this your way of telling me you've found a better job?"

Driggers chuckled. "I love you," he pulled her close.

"I love you too," she closed her eyes to savor the hug. She pressed a loud kiss to his bearded cheek and tightened her arms about his waist.

The phone rang, intruding on the moment. Mick kept Driggers close. "Is there something you're not saying? Seriously?" she probed.

He patted her cheek. "Answer your phone."

Mick captured his hand again. "Drig, you'd tell me if something was wrong, wouldn't you?"

He kissed her forehead. "You know me. Now answer your phone," he tugged on one of her curls and left the room.

Mick stared at Driggers until the door closed behind him. Slowly, she turned to see to the phone call.

"Michaela Sellars?" a woman's voice inquired.

"This is she," Mick greeted, forcing airy politeness into her voice.

"Ms. Sellars, I'm Dena Ramsey. We didn't have a chance to meet when you visited my family in Seattle."

"Ms. Ramsey," Mick said, already intrigued. "It's nice to be speaking with you."

"My father, Houston Ramsey told me about your visit. I live in North Carolina and don't get the chance to travel out to Seattle very often," Dena explained.

Mick nodded. "I understand."

"Anyway," Dena cleared her throat, "you're investigating Sera's murder."

Mick perched on the edge of her desk. "So you don't believe it was suicide?"

"Sera was my best friend. She was an only child and I had no sisters. We were very close. She wouldn't have taken her own life. I'm willing to stake *my* life on it."

"Did she talk to you about going to the party that weekend?" Mick asked, reaching for the pad she kept next to the phone.

"Our family reunion was that week. We have one every year. It was understood she'd be my guest to all the festivities. I don't know how she wound up at the damned party."

Mick nodded while jotting down the information. "So, this party wasn't part of the reunion?"

"Please," Dena hissed, "That was Quay's idea. He wanted to start a tradition for the younger set. He organized that party for the Ramsey *men* only with a select few of their closest friends in attendance."

"How many made up this *select few*?" Mick asked.

"There were probably about fifteen guys at the party. I only know that because they left the family barbeque to go to the hotel. After all this was over, I found out that there were at least three girls to every guy in that suite."

"I see," Mick whispered, chewing her bottom lip as she

199

wrote the numbers 15 and 3 on the pad and drew a circle around each.

Dena sighed. "So, when will you be returning to Seattle?"

Mick set the pad down and began to massage the tense area that had suddenly formed at the base of her neck. She didn't want to consider such a trip in light of where things stood between she and Quest. Of course, that would be inevitable as she had investigating and research that would surely demand another visit.

"I'm not sure of my plans yet," she said finally.

"Well then, I'd like to invite you to the party we're organizing. It's time for another Ramsey reunion. It'll be a perfect occasion to put names to faces. This marks forty years of reunions. Family will be in town for weeks," Dena predicted.

"Mmm...I appreciate that, but it really is a family thing and I shouldn't intrude," Mick decided.

"Michaela, a reunion is a time for family and *friends*. You are most certainly a friend if you're trying to find out what really happened to Sera."

Mick told herself that it was quite possible that the man Harriet Forman had circled in the photograph could be there. Besides, she missed Quest so much...

"Michaela?" Dena called. "Can we count on seeing you?"

Mick nodded. "I'll be there."

~~~

Catrina Ramsey's lovely almond-brown eyes harbored concern as she watched her son staring fixedly at the pool in her backyard. She managed a brief smile when she was pulled back into a firm embrace.

"I'm worried about him, Damon."

"He'll be alright," Damon Ramsey told his wife, though he was far more interested in nibbling at the soft skin below her ear.

"He said she wouldn't make him choose between her and his family. That's what he said. That's *all* he'd say," Catrina worried. "What do you think it means?"

Damon chuckled. "It means just what he said," he favored

his wife's other ear with soft, delectable nips.

"But why would she feel he'd have to do that?"

"Whatever it is, it's between them. They'll figure it out."

Catrina rolled her eyes. "I can't stand not knowing. I hate seeing my baby this way."

Damon propped his chin against her shoulder. "He's not a baby, Trina."

"But if there's something we can do-"

"He's a grown man."

"Talk to him, Damon."

"Trina-"

"Please baby," she turned to nuzzle the base of her husband's throat. "Please," she whispered, trailing her mouth across his collarbone..

Damon's hands smoothed across the silky fabric of Catrina's azure blouse and he uttered a frustrated growl. He knew he could refuse his wife nothing when she put her persuasive powers in full gear. Muttering a low curse, he pulled away and headed out to the pool.

Catrina fixed her husband with an adoring smile. She turned back toward the window as concern clouded her face once again.

~~~

"Q," Damon Ramsey called, approaching his son.

Quest just managed a smile. "Hey Dad," he hugged the man after they shared a hearty handshake.

"Your mama's worried," Damon announced.

Quest nodded. "I'm alright."

"I figured as much, but Trina won't go for it. What else can you tell me?"

Quest debated telling his father the entire story. He didn't want another foul scene to erupt in the family's long line of upsets, but he realized he just didn't care anymore. He'd just let himself and Mick drift out of each other's lives for a third time. Helping to prevent further unrest in the family was the least of his concerns.

"Michaela overheard a conversation I had with uncle Marc."

Damon's onyx gaze narrowed with murderous intensity. "Marcus," he breathed, then rolled his eyes and turned to wave toward Catrina who still watched from the bay windows in the sunroom.

Quest continued the story once his mother joined him and his father out on the deck.

"Baby, you know we'd never put you through anything like that," Catrina swore, while Damon stood cursing his brother. "I can't speak for the rest of your father's foolish family but you know we love you and Quay regardless."

"I know Ma," Quest whispered, figuring he'd come there to his parent's home because he needed the reassurance. He graced his mother with a dimpled smile but the sadness returned to his haunting gaze. "That's not the issue though. Michaela can't stand thinking that she's the cause for tension between me and *any* member of my family."

"But baby, she can't control that," Catrina pressed her hands to the front of Quest's brownstone knit jersey. "There always has been and always will be some sort of craziness going on between one or more members of this family."

Quest rubbed a hand across the hair tapered at his nape. "I know that," he groaned, a well of frustration swelling inside his chest. "But you don't know Mick. Family or the lack thereof, has put her in some very bad places with some very bad people. I can't get her to look past it. She thinks there's nothing more important than the love of my family. *Nothing's* more important. Not even *her* love."

"To hell with this," Damon muttered, pulling keys from the pocket of his twill driftwood trousers and storming off the deck.

"They can never be friends for long," Quest noted in a wry tone.

"Please," Catrina groaned with a wave of her hand. "Marc knew better. My guess is he's somewhere now hoping to avoid your father," she smiled when Quest began to laugh. "Now tell me," she fixed him with a stern look. "Do you love this girl?"

Quest's expression was serious at once. "She has all of my heart."

The simple, genuine reply sent Catrina nodding. "Of that I have no doubt. That's why-" she sighed, digging around in the front pocket of her jeans, "I want to give you something I've been carrying around for a while now."

Quest's brows rose when he saw the small exquisitely crafted emerald ring in his mother's palm.

"This was my mother's," Catrina said, "I decided to give it to the first one of my son's who lost his heart." She rested her hand against Quest's cheek. "I know love when I see it and I've seen the change in you these last few months. Love like this can take years to craft and you found it in a surprisingly short time. Maybe it's because you finally recognized what you needed." She paused to wipe a tear from the corner of her eye. "Anyway, I know you won't let Michaela go. You simply need to formulate a new plan. This is for your future wife when you're ready to put that plan into action," she folded the ring into Quest's palm and laughed when he pulled her into a smothering hug.

Quest kissed the top of his mother's bouncy, silver-gray hair. Silently, he vowed he would have another chance with Mick and this time he'd be playing for keeps.

***

After her phone conversation with Dena Ramsey, Mick left to spend another week in Georgia. She had to see if anyone there recognized the man Harriet Forman had circled in the news photo. There were no new leads and she left Savannah feeling as though she'd completely wasted her time. Now, as she took the steps to Houston and Daphne Ramsey's glorious home, she prayed for a break, or better yet a familiar face at the family gathering.

"Michaela!" Dena Ramsey called, rushing forward with outstretched arms. "So glad you could make it," she pulled Mick into a close hug.

"Dena?" Mick inquired, hearing the woman laugh.

"I'm sorry, yes, Dena Ramsey," she introduced herself and stepped back. "My father told me to look for a lady with a head full of gorgeous black Shirley Temple curls."

Mick threw back her head to laugh. "I haven't heard that description in a long time!"

"Let's get you introduced," Dena hooked a hand through the crook of Mick's arm as they strolled the majestic foyer.

Houston's and Daphne's home was as elegant as they were. Each room seemed to have waltzed right off the pages of an interior designer's portfolio. Every room housed an elaborate chandelier, there was gorgeous carpeting throughout the house and every flower arrangement was housed in a gleaming brass pot. Classical jazz arrangements sifted through the built-in speakers in every room. Michaela couldn't believe how hospitable the group was. She'd expected them to be at least a little reserved. Sure enough, the good feelings came to an end when she was introduced to Marcus Ramsey.

"I don't think anyone here has time to be cross-examined for your investigation, Ms. Sellars," were the man's first words to Michaela.

Though she didn't have his height advantage, Mick did an exemplary job of looking down her nose at the man. "Well then, I suggest you direct your complaint toward your niece here. She was the one who invited me."

Marc blinked as though surprised by her frigid comeback. He recovered quickly and fixed Dena with the same disdainful look. "Your father would have a fit if he knew she was here."

"I doubt that," Dena wore a cold smile. "Especially since he was the one who told me how to find Michaela and seemed quite pleased when I talked about asking her to come out," she hugged her thin frame and rocked a bit to the music coloring the background.

"What's he thinking?" Marcus breathed as though speaking to himself. His attention quickly redirected itself to Michaela. "You shouldn't be here. I think you know that. I'm sure you'll understand if I ask you to leave."

"That's enough, Marc."

The small group turned toward the tall, dark man who had spoken. He stopped right next to Mick an extended his hand.

"Hello Michaela, I'm Damon Ramsey, Quest's father," he covered her hand in both of his.

Mick blinked, words failing her as she studied Damon. It was clear to see where his sons had acquired their sinful good looks. "So nice to meet you," she managed finally.

Damon patted her hand. "I hope you'll accept my apologies for my brother."

Mick acknowledged Marcus with barely a glance. "I've handled far worse, I can assure you."

"Ha!" Damon bellowed, revealing a striking double-dimpled grin. "I see why my son loves you so. We'll speak more later," he leaned close to plant a kiss to her forehead. The warmth of his expression vanished however, when he turned to his brother. "We need to speak. Right now."

Mick was intrigued by the exchange, wishing she could be a fly on the wall. Marc was clearly reluctant to follow his brother and she could tell it wouldn't be a pretty scene. Before her thoughts could get too far ahead, she caught sight of Quest across the room. Her heart flew to her throat and her tummy did all sorts of crazy flips while her knees turned to water. She commanded them to continue to support her.

She loved his man! Fierce emotion filled her amber stare as she watched him laugh and mingle across the room. A chestnut sport coat molded to the incredible breadth of his shoulders while matching trousers accentuated the length of his strong legs. Quest Ramsey had become her world and she had scarcely realized that his presence in her life was so very important. Where he was concerned, she was selfish-undeniably so. She yearned for the love he offered. Every day she dreamed of the happiness she could find with him. So what if his family had a problem with it. So what? He was hers. He held every bit of her heart as completely as she held every bit of his. Family be damned.

~~~

Damon maintained his cool even after he closed the den door behind himself and his older brother. "I've been waiting to talk to you for weeks. You been avoiding me?" he approached the man on easy steps.

Marcus merely pursed his lips and pushed his hands into the pockets of his pin-striped slacks.

Damon positioned his index finger a few inches in front of the man's nose. "Approach my son or the woman he loves with this crap of yours once more, Marc, and I'll take great pleasure in making you sorry."

Marcus tried to remain composed, but his lips trembled. "Threats, Damon?"

"Damn right."

"You got some nerve," Marcus seethed, maintaining his stance. "Do you understand how dangerous it would be to have someone nosing around our family affairs?"

"Marc, if someone *had* nosed around our family affairs a long time ago, maybe the family would be in a far better state of mind than it is now."

Marcus rubbed a hand across his bald head and chuckled. "Damon, please. Don't you stand there and act like we're different people. You've done the same thing to protect your sons. Have you forgotten how far you went during the ugliness of Sera Black's death? Not to mention all those strange happenings before? Quay's girlfriends always seemed to come up missing- all except Sera of course. You never *really* questioned him about all that, did you?" Marcus asked, his deep-set gaze sparkling with devilish curiosity. "Maybe you never wanted to know," he shrugged. "As you say, no need to live in fear of the past."

Damon shook his head, while fiddling with his gray and tan silk tie. "I won't deny that I've done things to protect my kids and I'd probably do them again, but none of this has anything to do with Michaela Sellars."

"She's a writer."

"And he loves her, so deal with it."

"*You* deal with it," Marcus snapped. "She won't be *my* daughter-in-law."

Damon's fist clenched and he realized he could easily have snapped his brother's neck. "And how shabbily you treated your daughter-in-law," he cooly reminded Marcus. "Melina and Yohan might still be together to this day."

"You shut your mouth, Damon."

"What Marc? Do you intend to run off everyone who expresses an interest in your sons if they pose a threat to you?"

"If they pose a threat to the family? Yes."

"And what threat did Melina pose?" Damon frowned when he glimpsed the never before seen look of sheer terror in his brother's dark eyes. "Man, can't you get past whatever has happened in the past? It's over. Good or bad, it's in the past and we can't live in fear of it forever. That's not living at all."

Marcus muttered a curse and fixed his younger brother with a scornful glare. "You've always been so absorbed in Catrina and those boys that you never focused on what the rest of the family was going through."

"Jackass," Damon sneered, both hands now clenched into fists. "I guess you forgot all the times, all the nastiness I covered for y'all? I won't allow my boys to live like that. You should want better for your sons as well."

Marcus shook his head then. The anger left his face and was replaced by an expression resembling regret. Sometimes the past and present intermingle, Mon. It hasn't been as easy for some of us to push it aside as it's been for you."

Damon frowned at the strange melancholy in his brother's voice. Marcus said nothing more and simply raised his hands to indicate his readiness to leave. Damon stepped aside and watched him go.

~~~

"Ms. Sellars?"

Mick heard the soft voice behind her and turned. Standing there was a lovely woman with sparkling brown eyes and bouncing silver-gray tresses.

"I'm Catrina Ramsey, Quest's mother."

"Oh!" Mick gave a start, immediately extending her hand to shake. "So nice to meet you."

"I have to say the same. You're lovely," Catrina complimented, instant approval filling her eyes. "I can see why he's so far gone over you."

Mick blinked and looked down at the pale pink flip skirt suit she wore. "Thank you," her words were hushed.

Catrina was tickled, realizing that Michaela had no idea how lovely she was. "Welcome to the family," she said and kissed her cheek.

"Excuse me?" Mick whispered, clearly dumbfounded.

"Honey, first let me apologize for my brother-in-law's actions. Marcus speaks for no one else in this family. Actually we're all quite relieved. We were worried that Quest was doomed to never find a woman who made him want to surrender his heart. Obviously Quaysar's happy flitting from one relationship to the next, but I prayed at least one of my sons would have a real family."

"But he has a real family," Mick pointed out though she'd already made up her mind to take hold of what she wanted.

Catrina grimaced and smoothed her hands across the slitted sleeves of her heather-gray V-neck dress. "His *own* family, sweetie," she clarified. "With a wife he adores and loves to no end. I think that would be you."

Michaela frowned, surprised to feel moisture pooling her eyes. "I didn't want to come between you all. I love him and need him, but I never wanted him to lose you."

"Oh honey," Catrina huffed, "we're his family. We're not going anywhere. We've been through some rough times and we're still together. Nothing can change that. Nothing he could say or do could ever make that happen. Well...not unless he told us he was going to let you get away."

Laughter erupted between the two women and Catrina pulled Mick into a tight squeeze. Across Catrina's shoulder, Mick saw something that made her gasp. She masked it with a brief cough when Catrina pulled away to look at her.

"I'm surprised to see Quay," Mick said.

Catrina glanced back. "I'm sure he won't be here too long. My youngest needs a woman to hold on to and is probably on his way to meet one now."

"I'm gonna go speak," Mick decided.

"Alright, sweetie," Catrina leaned close to kiss her cheek. "We'll talk later."

Mick smiled and then turned back to where Quay stood. She hadn't been surprised by his presence. It was the man he stood next to. On determined steps, she made her way over to the twosome.

"Well hey!" Quay called, seeing Mick heading his way. "While my brother ain't breathin' down my neck," he grumbled while taking the liberty of hugging Mick close and kissing her cheek. Keeping her by his side, he turned to the man he stood next to. "Michaela Sellars, this is one of my closest friends. Wake Robinson."

Wake Robinson, Mick repeated the name in her mind as she shook hands with him. This was the man Harriet Forman had circled in the photo.

"Mick is my future sister-in-law," Quay explained and flinched when she slapped his shoulder. "Hey, I'm just telling the truth," he whined.

"Listen to me," Mick tugged at his silver-gray tie. "I've got a lead on the case," she announced.

"Mick," Quay breathed, his dark eyes shining with hope. He knocked his hand against Wake's arm. "Mick's a writer and she's reopened the investigation into Sera's death. You remember Sera Black, right?"

Wake's reaction was just what Mick had hoped it'd be. He blinked once and his easy expression quickly took on a glow of nervousness.

"Sera Black," he said.

"That's right. It wasn't suicide by a long shot," Mick told

him before looking to Quay. "We may even have a witness who puts another man there at the room after the party was over. According to this witness, Sera was still alive when the man walked into the room. She opened the door for him."

"Good work, Mick," Quay said, clearly elated by the report. The fact that someone else could know what happened- could possibly be responsible- filled him with true relief.

Michaela was about to comment further when her cell phone rang. "Excuse me," she told Quay and Wake, turning to answer the call.

"Mick, it's County."

"Hey girl, what's up?"

County paused a moment to clear her throat. "Honey, I need you to come home."

Mick frowned and looked around the room. "Well I'm afraid it may be a few days. I just got to Seattle and-"

"Sweetie, I really need you here now."

"Why? What's wrong?"

"Just come home," County urged, unmistakable firmness clutching her every word.

"What the hell is going on back there?" Mick snapped, her friend's vagueness only agitating her further.

"Mick one of the girls went to your house to pick up a tape or something. She went into the den and she-she found Driggers there."

"What do you mean...she *found* him?" Mick's fingers tightened around the phone.

Again, County cleared her throat. "Sweetie, Driggers...Driggers is dead. They think he passed in his sleep."

"What?" Mick whispered, her lips barely able to form the word. The sharpest pain knifed through her and she lost the strength to stand. She was still holding the phone to her ear when she fell to the floor.

"Mick?" County called through the line "Mick!"

Quay was already kneeling beside Mick as he called out for his brother. Quest had been across the room, trying to pay attention to a conversation and keep his mind and his eyes off Michaela once he'd caught sight of her. When he turned into the sound of Quay's voice and saw the scene on the other side of the room, he broke into a run to get to Mick. Questions abounded, but Quest simply pulled her into his arms and carried her out of the living room. Mick was shaking fiercely by then. Quest, thoroughly terrified, managed to keep his calm.

Quay had Mick's phone and was speaking to County, who told him about Driggers. He whispered the news into Quest's ear while they stormed the hall. Quest closed his eyes, muttering a curse while squeezing Mick even closer. When they entered the private den, he sat with her on the nearest sofa.

Just then, she snapped to. Instantly, she began to struggle against Quest. She twisted to and fro, attempting to escape his hold. Finally, she pounded her fists against his chest and shoulders.

"Let go," she grumbled, "let go Quest, Drig…" she moaned.

Quest held her fast, tightening his grip the more she struggled. He whispered soft soothing words in her ear and tried to rock her as she fought him. Eventually, her attempts at pounding his body eased and slowly the fight left her.

"That's it, that's it, babe," Quest kissed her temple and cheek. Over the top of her head, he locked gazes with his twin. "Get one of the jets ready. We're going to Chicago."

A LOVER'S DREAM

~FIFTEEN~

Chance Driggers Morgan was laid to rest on a Tuesday in the most elaborate of services. Driggers had no family, but his friends were numerous. Quest was proud to consider himself among that group and he spared no expense to arrange for the beloved man to be put to rest in the finest.

"Hey," he found Mick in her den. No one in the procession had seen her since returning to her home following the funeral.

Mick had the heavy drapes drawn in the room- which was only lit by a single, small lamp. She didn't turn when Quest called out to her.

He said nothing more, knowing her hurt was deep and would have a long stay. Pulling her back against him, he held her in a slow rocking embrace.

"Excuse me?" A hushed voice broke into the silence sometime later.

Quest and Michaela turned to find a thin, Caucasian man standing just inside the room.

"Drake Bynum," the man approached the couple slowly. "I

was Mr. Morgan's physician."

"Physician," Mick repeated, her expression relaying her surprise.

"I'm sure he never spoke of me, Ms. Sellars," Dr. Bynum acknowledged. "He spoke of *you* so often, I feel I'd know you anywhere."

"Drig," Mick whispered, moving closer to the doctor as though she expected Driggers to step out from behind the man.

"You were like his own child. He said it all the time," Dr. Bynum mused. "He knew you'd have questions today."

"Why?" was all she could muster.

The doctor smiled. "I suppose I was like Mr. Morgan's surrogate psychologist. He talked to me about the things he could tell no one else."

"How could he have been so sick?" Mick blurted, her lower lip trembling.

Taking her hands, Dr. Bynum led Mick to a sofa and joined her there. "I was so stunned when those tests came back. I had them redone so often my lab people thought I'd gone mad."

"What was it?" Mick squeezed the doctor's hands.

"A form of colon cancer," the doctor explained. "Mr. Driggers was a man who didn't believe in seeing a doctor if there was nothing hurting."

"That was Drig," Mick agreed softly. "Why did he come to see you then?"

The doctor took a deep breath. "He found blood in the toilet. Deep down, I think he always knew something was wrong, but he was-"

"Stubborn, proud and strong- physically and mentally." Mick supplied.

"Exactly," the doctor chuckled a little before the amusement faded and was replaced by something more solemn. "The cancer had done so much damage by the time he...Chemo and other treatments may have eased the pain he'd started to feel near the end, but he said he didn't want anything to take more life out of him than the cancer already had. He didn't want you to be suspicious in any way. When you went off to research your book in...Seattle, I believe it was, he could finally put down the strong front."

Mick could barely see the doctor's face through her tears. "When I'd call and get the voicemail, I just assumed he was out and about."

Dr. Bynum patted her forearm.

"Why didn't he tell me? I could've taken care of him until…" her sobs gained volume.

"You'd lost so much in your life- those you loved. He didn't want to think about you being alone again. In truth, I think he felt guilty about it. I think it's why he tried to hold on so long."

"Until the cancer won," Mick said.

"And I believe even *that* was a decision *he* made."

Mick sniffled and rubbed the back of her hand across her cheek. "*He* decided?"'"

Dr. Bynum looked over to Quest, who stood behind Mick where she sat on the sofa. "He knew you were reluctant to tell him about everything going on in Seattle. He had his suspicions though and then he was given confirmation."

"Contessa," Mick guessed.

"After meeting Mr. Ramsey, sensing the good in him and the love he had for you, he told me he didn't worry that you would suffer alone- forever afraid to take a chance on having a real life for yourself. He felt content that you would be fine without him."

Mick expressed no comment, and after a while the doctor felt he'd left her with enough information to satisfy her questions. Giving her hands a final squeeze, he rose from the sofa and went to speak briefly with Quest. Then, he was gone.

"Michaela?" Quest whispered, when they were alone.

"How could he think I didn't need him anymore?" she asked, sobs tumbling forth.

"Hey…" Quest drew her near.

Mick accepted the closeness as her tears flowed freely. They soaked the lapel of Quest's dark suit until they were spent. Mick was so drained she rested her head on his thigh and took solace in his hand stroking her back.

***

After that day, Mick was unable to do much else. She was at first in denial, and then the shock returned. Everyone was very concerned by the quiet detached persona she displayed. County was so worried, she opted to stay with Mick for at least a week. Quest kept his distance, fearing his presence might in some way upset her further.

But when yet another week came and went, everyone's worries increased. Michaela made no move to pull herself from her disassociated state. County called Quest to intervene in any way he could. He found Mick in Driggers' room one afternoon. She was staring out the window overlooking the back lawn and barely responded when Quest called to her.

"He loved the view from up here," she said after long moments of silence.

Quest took a step toward her, his gray eyes also focused past the window.

"He was probably enjoying one of those dance rehearsals," he said, taking a chance on teasing and his heart soared when she laughed.

"He was all I had," she told him, pushing her hands into the pockets of her nylon joggers.

Quest bowed his head. "He was, but that's not true anymore...is it?" he risked a sideways glance toward her.

Slowly, Michaela met his gaze. She started to shake her head as the tears arrived. Quest drew her close, holding her as she wept.

~~~

When Mick opened her eyes, she was lying cuddled close to Quest's chest. They were on the furry dark carpeting that covered most of the bedroom floor. She yawned and blinked several times to get her bearings. At last, she focused on the glitter before her eyes. Her lips parted when she realized the effect came from a ring.

A smile tugged at her mouth and she shook her head once. "You knew he was the one, didn't you Drig?" she asked and could have sworn the ring gleamed brighter in response.

"Do I have his permission to ask?"

Mick heard his voice and raised her head to look directly into Quest's unforgettable gaze. "You do," she confirmed.

Quest trailed his fingers around the curve of her dark face and cupped her chin. "Will you marry me, Michaela Sellars?"

"I will," she accepted in a tone of fierce certainty. "I will," she whispered then, her amber gaze searching his face until their lips met to seal the promise.

***

The incredible view from the balcony of Quaysar's penthouse apartment had Mick spellbound. Inside, the place was alive with conversation and laughter. Outside, she and Quest were in their own little world there on the spacious, vine-covered balcony.

Sighing her contentment, Mick rested her head back on his chest. The steady beat of his heart made her feel cozy and delighted. Quest smoothed his hands across her arms bared by the thin knotted straps of her multicolored silk dress.

Mick's lashes fluttered when she felt his hands cupping her breasts. His thumbs were barely grazing the firming nipples. "Quest…" she warned.

"When can we get out of here?" he murmured against her temple.

"For the fifteenth time, we can't leave."

"Why? No one's paying attention to us."

"This is our engagement party, man. Quay went all out for us," Mick pointed out.

Quest wasn't softened. "He'll get over it," he toyed with the zipper at the back of the dress. When Mick wiggled, he switched tactics and lowered his hands to the hemline of the curve-hugging frock.

216

"Quest…"

"What?"

"No," she brushed at his hands while pulling the hem back into place.

"Damn it," Quest turned his fiancee around to face him. "At least let me kiss you."

Laughing, Mick stood on her toes. "That I'll do," she decided she'd be safe with a simple kiss.

Of course, a *simple* kiss was far from what Quest had in mind. His tongue thrust deep and Mick eagerly met the throaty lunges with a fire of her own. Their moans mingled in the night air as desire surged in an almost intolerable wave of need.

Mick curved her fingers around the open collar of Quest's maple-brown shirt as he hoisted her against his chest. He was preparing to place her on the balcony ledge when knocking rose from somewhere behind them.

"Break it up," Quay sang, a devilish smile on his gorgeous face.

Quest's lashes fluttered close as he turned back to Michaela. "I really hate him sometimes."

Her laughter filled the air.

~~~

Quaysar's grand apartment seemed awfully small with the number of guests who'd arrived for Quest and Michaela's party. Of course, everyone came bearing gifts. The largest and most extravagant
of all came from Ramsey's construction and architectural divisions. It was to be the final gift presented that evening.

"We pride ourselves on having the best ideas, which result in the best creations," said Jason Calloway, Ramsey's construction chief. "But for our latest residential division, our best idea came from someone who isn't even on our staff. Ms. Sellars- soon to be Mrs. Ramsey," Jason rephrased when Quest cleared his throat. "I hope this is more of what you had in mind."

Several gasps and applause rose when a veil was lifted to

reveal a scale model of the next residential endeavor. Construction was set to begin that fall. Mick recognized it as the project site Quest had taken her to when he'd shown her around Seattle.

"The yards are fantastic," she commended, rousing laughter from everyone in the room.

Shortly, the group dispersed but Mick was still captivated by the model.

"You approve?"

"I approve," she nodded as Quest's arms settled about her waist. "This is beautiful. I can't believe they even took my advice into consideration."

Quest pressed a kiss to the top of her head. "Why?"

Mick flashed him a funny look. "Please, the boss's girlfriend? Hell, I wasn't even your girlfriend then."

"We don't care who the idea comes from, so long as it's good."

"And you," Mick turned in his arms, "most men don't even want their women involved in their personal business, let alone professional."

Quest leaned close and cradled her face in his palms. "Most men don't have a woman like you."

Mick squeezed his hands and smiled. "Baggage and all?"

"I like 'em thick," he teased, joining in when she laughed. "*Now* can we get out of here?" he pleaded.

"Let's go," she shook her head when her fiance' clenched his fist in triumph.

***

The following week, Michaela was surveying a familiar sight. Her look of surprise was mixed with suspicion. "What are we doing here?" she queried to her fiance in a sly tone.

Quest shrugged beneath a butter cream suede jacket. "We needed to get away and I had a good reason for wanting to get away to here."

"Ah...our honeymoon," Mick sighed, her tone laced with mock sweetness. "But uh, sweetie, I think you're backward. The honeymoon comes *after* the wedding."

"Funny," Quest fixed her with a warning glance. "Do you remember the last time we were here," he turned back to the truck's flatbed.

Michaela's eyes took on a dreamy look as she reminisced of the time spent at the secluded cabin in upstate Illinois.

Quest shook his head, knowing where her thoughts were centered the moment he saw her face. "You have a one-track mind. I wasn't talking about the good times."

The light dimmed in Mick's eyes. "Quest," she groaned, bowing her head. "That's over now, why-"

"Because I want *all* our times here to be good ones and I'd like us to deal with the bad ones the moment they happen," he said, hooking the strap of a garment bag across his shoulder. "After what happened here before, it took us a while to get back on track, remember?"

Mick nodded. "I remember," she pulled the cuffs of her cobalt-blue hoody over her hands.

Quest sent her a wink and then finished collecting their things from the truck's flatbed.

~~~

Dusk had settled and night was right on its heels by the time Mick and Quest got everything unpacked. That evening, Mick decided to show off her culinary talents. In addition to homemade sweet bread and juicy herb-roasted chicken, she prepared a recipe for a saucy vegetable rice dish. The aromas of the combined dishes filled the house with the most exquisite smells.

"I'm starved!" Quest bellowed for the fifth time since Mick announced dinner was ready.

Michaela was silent while preparing her plate. She placed it upon the intimate round table, and then sat with her arms folded across her chest. Patiently, she waited watching Quest devour his food as though he hadn't eaten in weeks.

He glanced up once from his plate, doing a double take when he noticed her stale expression. "What?" he queried.

Mick parted her lips, her surprise evident.

Quest shrugged. "What?" he repeated.

"I have been patient. *Too* patient waiting for you to get to the point of this visit," she kept her voice soft.

Quest's sleek brows tugged close above his deep-set eyes. He appeared thoroughly confused. "I thought I had gotten to the point."

"Quest!" Mick cried.

He laughed then, raising his hands defensively. "Alright," he set his knife and fork alongside the plate. "There are things we never discussed when we talked about my uncle's visit here."

"Oh, we discussed it," Mick's expression soured. "I hated every minute of it, but we discussed it."

"But there was still something left unsaid."

"Such as?"

"The people who attended that opening mixer are the best of my family. They always arrive several weeks early for the reunion."

Mick's eyes narrowed. "So? What's wrong with that?"

"What I'm trying to tell you is that you haven't met the worst people. My uncle Marc was just the tip of the iceberg," his expression grew darker with agitation. "No one can accuse the Ramseys of biting their tongues. We all speak our minds regardless of who it hurts. I can almost guarantee you'll have a nasty scene with another member of my family be it over your job or some other aspect of your background." He shook his head and settled back wearily against his chair. "I'll do my best to protect you from it, but even my best won't stop it from happening," he warned.

Michaela watched Quest closely as he spoke. She'd never heard the man ramble before, and it was fascinating. He looked so much like a little boy trying to get out all of an explanation in one breath. Slowly, she left her chair and deposited herself in his lap. Quest was still talking and, aside from bringing his hands up to cup her waist, he barely seemed to register her being there. In one smooth move, Mick cupped his jaw and kissed him.

He silenced instantly, becoming an eager participant in the

kiss that ranged from sweet, to bold, to sultry. Mick emitted tiny, soft moans as she thrust her tongue feverishly over and under his. In no time, Quest had situated her so that she was straddling his lap. He arched his neck and tilted his head to capture every nuance and angle of the kiss. The soft, helpless moans he uttered filled Mick with a sense of possessive power. When she broke the kiss, he grunted his disapproval.

"Are you afraid we won't make it?" she asked against his mouth. "That someone might come between us?"

"It happened before," Absently, he brushed his thumb against her lush lower lip.

She settled back a bit to study him closely before speaking. "Nothing and no one could ever do that again. I'm never letting you go. I'm just as much your family as they are and if I have to, I'll fight for you. No matter what."

Quest closed his eyes and pressed his forehead to hers. The muscle in his jaw performed a wicked dance as he seemed to meditate on what she'd just said. His hands roamed her thighs, left bare by the hem of the sunflower nightshirt she wore. After a while, he started to move his forehead against hers.

"I don't know what I'll do if you walk away from me again, Michaela. I don't think I could handle it."

"Hey," she called, leaning down a little to peer into his eyes when he bowed his head. "Sweetie, I'm not goin' anywhere, there's nowhere else I want to be. Please, please believe that. Don't upset yourself with this, not now."

"Do you know how much I love you?" he massaged the nape of her neck before threading his fingers through her thick curls. "I've always wanted what my parents have and I was afraid I'd never find it. Having many women has its benefits. Hollow, worthless benefits that never last."

Michaela planted herself more snuggly against Quest and cupped his face in her hands. "Baby, we're not hollow and we *will* last. As long as we don't lose sight of what's in front of us, by focusing too much on the big picture. One day at a time," she advised, kissing the end of his nose. "One day of love at a time."

Suddenly, a grin broke on Quest's dark face. "I thought you were as cynical as I was," he noted, kissing the corner of her eye.

"I *was*," Mick's lashes fluttered at the breathtaking length of him outlined beneath the loose jeans brushing her bare legs beneath the nightshirt, "but then I met this incredible man..."

"Me?" he guessed.

"Uh-huh," she giggled, gasping when his tongue thrust past her lips. Her fingers curled beneath the neckline of his white T-shirt when he stood from the table.

"Dinner later. Bed now," he decided.

***

The Ramseys, known for being reserved and aloof, pulled out all the stops for the gathering easily crowned the event of the year. All of Seattle society turned out for the wedding of Quest Fenton Ramsey and Michaela Dionee Sellars. The bride walked down the aisle preceded by twenty bridesmaids- the dancers of Wiley State University and one very proud maid of honor, Contessa Warren.

After an unforgettable rendition of Anita Baker's "Angel", the bride met the groom at the altar where they became husband and wife.

~~~

In spite of his earlier attempts to interfere, Marcus made a point of attending the wedding with his wife, Josephine. Michaela had to beg her husband and brother-in-law not to make a scene in asking the man to leave. She knew the twins would do more than *ask*. Thankfully, Marc did nothing to cast a foul element over the lovely day.

The same held true for Houston who arrived with Daphne in their usually elegant style of dress. Accompanying them were their daughter, Dena and son, Taurus who quickly had an impressive share of the women all vying for his attention.

All seemed well, but Mick couldn't help but think of Johnelle Black who declined to attend for obvious reasons.

Johnelle would never have the chance to attend her daughter's wedding. Though it would change nothing, knowing that it was Wake Robinson who had robbed her of such an experience filled Mick with a sense of accomplishment. The only thing that would please her more would be to learn that he was behind bars. If he was guilty, she intended to see to it that he paid.

Later, Quaysar fulfilled one of his duties as best man. He took his new sister-in-law for a twirl around the gleaming hardwood dance floor in the ballroom of Damon and Catrina Ramsey's splendid country estate.

"You've made my brother a very happy man," Quay glanced across the room at his twin who was being teased by two of their great-uncles. "I don't think I've ever seen him look so alive," he smiled down at her, his pitch gaze soft and lingering. "Q's a lucky man and I can't think of anyone who's more deserving."

Mick frowned a bit and patted his cheek. "You deserve the same, you know?" she smiled when doubt clouded his gorgeous molasses-toned face.

"Too many fish in the sea," his teasing persona came to life.

"I don't know," Mick sighed, shaking her head. "I have a feeling one day soon you'll be hit by some sort of thunderbolt."

"Hmph," Quay replied with an indignant huff.

"So have you talked to your friend, yet?" Mick asked, toying with the salt and pepper bow tie of his tuxedo.

"What friend?" Quay asked.

"That's right," Mick breathed, closing her eyes as she recalled they never got around to the particulars of what she'd discovered. "Harriet Forman was the one who remembered seeing the man headed into the suite with Sera that night. She identified him as Wake Robinson."

Quay's brows connected into a fierce frown. "Wake? That's not possible."

Mick shrugged. "She recognized him from some old news photos I asked her to take a look at. She seems certain that it was him."

"Jesus," Quay whispered, thinking there had to be some mistake. He was horrified that it might not be. "What do you think?"

Mick wanted very much to soothe the worries clouding Quay's face. She couldn't.

"You think he did it?"

Mick squeezed his hands. "A part of me isn't ready to believe he's completely responsible. But I can't help but remember the way he looked when I said that there was someone who could identify the man going into the hotel room with Sera. He looked like he could've dropped through the floor, Quay. He acted as though *he* was that man. I guess my next question would be, has he left town yet?"

Quay shook his head. "I've known him half my life."

"And that counts for a whole lot, but I'm coming into this with fresh eyes, sweetie. Maybe I see what you won't allow yourself to," Mick noted, knowing her words were difficult for him to hear.

Quay cleared his throat, squaring his broad shoulders as he did so. "That still doesn't mean he did it, Mick."

"I know, honey."

"His involvement here could be totally innocent."

"You're right, you're right," Mick smoothed her palm across his cheek.

"Just promise me you won't stop until you know for sure that he's guilty. Until you have no doubts."

"Come here," Mick pulled him into a hug.

Quay couldn't stop the sick feeling that wretched through him then. Various details he'd allowed himself to forget regarding his old friend were slowly forging to the surface of his memory.

"Hey, hey, break it up!" Quest ordered, having just approached his wife and brother. "You're holdin' her too close," he teased.

"Mmm hmm, and I'm about to do more than that," Quay regained a bit more of his light mood. "As the best man, I get to be the first one to kiss the bride."

Quest eased both hands into the pockets of his white tuxedo trousers. "Keep it clean. No tongues," he peered close to see that he was obeyed.

"Hell, he took all the fun out of it," Quay complained to Mick and then decided to simply bestow a gentlemanly kiss to her hand. "I wish you all the good things. Both of you," he told his brother and leaned in to kiss Quest's cheek.

"He alright?" Quest asked, watching as Quay left the ballroom.

Mick smiled. "He's gonna be," she promised.

~~~

"So you're saying your cousin is a magician?"

Taurus Ramsey's insanely gorgeous face softened with an indulgent grin. "I may've used the label once or twice to describe him."

Michaela laughed over the dig at her husband.

"Seriously though, only my cousin could meet an angel one day and have her eager as a puppy to become his forever the next." Taurus declared in a tone that brooked no argument.

"Really?" Mick made a show of pretending to gush. "Don't lie. You really think I'm an angel?" She queried, apparently taking no offence to the 'eager as a puppy dog' comparison.

"You're definitely an angel," he grinned but a solemn tinge ghosted across his face soon after. "My cousin didn't need magic to get you-not when he's such a good guy." Taurus squeezed Mick's hand where it curved about his jacket lapel. "He deserved the best and he got it."

Her eyes glistened with just a hint of moisture. "Thank you," she stood on her toes to kiss his cheek.

Taurus appreciated the gesture. Evidence of that reflected in his smile momentarily. "Speak of the devil," he said, his smile playing tug of war with a grimace.

Curious, Mick glanced back to find Quest waiting patiently in the stoic silent manner he'd perfected.

"Thanks for the dance, Mick," Taurus dutifully released his cousin's wife, stepped over to clap a hand to Quest's shoulder. "Congratulations," he said.

"Thanks, T," Quest returned and then fixed his wife with a playfully reproachful look once Taurus had moved on. "What'd I say about not dancing with any of the men in my family?"

Michaela countered with an elegant shrug. "Well he's *my* family now too, so that order carries no weight."

"Is that right?" Quest gathered his wife close, bumping her chin with the curve of his fist. "Hasn't anybody told you that a wife shouldn't sass her husband?"

She pretended to be dismayed. "Sorry I missed the lesson in Brides One-O-One. Just to make sure I um...stay in my place, I should ask if your decree pertains to Damon," she referred to Quest's father. "I mean, he's technically *my* dad now, too."

Quest couldn't hold out against the smirk that fought for purchase. "I revise the rule to no dancing with the unmarried men in my family."

"Mmm..." Mick twisted her lips into a pained smile. "That's tough- I was really looking forward to a dance with your great uncle Gregor."

Quest dissolved into laughter then. He would always love her. Her persona had been wrought by years of hardship and disappointment yet she'd triumphed. To fill her thoughts with the best in life and memories to treasure was his wish for her. And he was determined to take his wish-fulfilling seriously.

Michaela felt her heart lurch clear to her throat as she studied the striking left dimple imprinted alongside his mouth. This man was truly hers and he would always be. "So is your laughter a sign of approval for Uncle Gregor to take me for a twirl? He claims that I haven't *really* danced until I've danced with him."

Quest recovered somewhat from his laugh attack at her reference to his mother's *single* 93-year old uncle. "The rule goes *double* for Uncle Greg."

~~~

Two hours later, the reception only showed signs of gaining momentum. Mick found herself growing as restless as her husband. She was a bundle of nerves in anticipation of her honeymoon. After a quick stop in Chicago, she and Quest would be spending part of their trip in Hawaii before traveling off to Tahiti for the duration. The couple had decided to stop in Malibu as well. Mick was especially excited about the visit to the teen center. The place was consistently making local and national news. Its headlines accumulated praise for the teens it housed and also presented a challenge to the city and state officials to do more to reach out to its youth.

In spite of her anxiousness, Mick had been doing her best to appear the gracious, sociable bride. Of course this was especially difficult as she tried to thwart her husband's overtly erotic advances.

"How long before we can leave this thing?" Quest spoke close to her ear as he stood behind her.

"We have couple stuff to do," she tried to remain focused, "such as cutting this huge cake they're wheeling toward us."

"Do you know how long it's been since I've had you in a bed?" Quest spanned his hands across Mick's hips and tummy, neatly encased within the exquisite embroidery lining the classic white gown with its chiffon sleeves and full hoop skirt.

Mick giggled. "I do," she shivered when she heard a low sound rumble deep in his chest.

"Just something to tide me over until later?" he bartered, his lips fastening to her earlobe.

Mick's lashes fluttered against the warm sensation stemming from the feel of his nipping and suckling the soft flesh. "Down, Quest," she gasped when he responded by settling her back against his groin. "*All* the way down," she advised.

~~~

Quay had left the reception determined to find answers. He returned feeling worse than before he left. His worst fears were realized when Mick told him what she'd discovered. He knew it was folly, but a part of him prayed Wake would be at his condo when he went to confront him. According to the security desk, he was gone- completely moved out with no warning and no mention of a forwarding address.

"Can't be," he chanted, his attention barely on the winding road leading back to the estate. "It couldn't have been Wake. It couldn't have been him all those times before-"

A blaring horn interrupted his thoughts. Quay slammed on his brakes just as another SUV moved in direct line with his own mammoth sport utility.

A dark, statuesque beauty bolted from the driver's side of the white Navigator. "Are you blind? You had to see me going for that park," she went on, fire in her eyes as she prepared to deliver more choice words for the driver behind the tinted windows of the fierce-looking black Hummer.

Quaysar's thoughts of Wake Robinson and everything else disappeared at the sight in the line of his gaze. When he stepped outside the truck, the lovely woman's doe-shaped eyes narrowed in recognition.

"Quaysar Ramsey," she propped both hands to her hips while tapping a cream pump against the brick driveway. "I see you still can't drive worth a damn."

Quay tilted his head just slightly. "You know my name?" he watched as the breeze disarrayed the black tresses that fell past her shoulders.

"I know you," she closed a small bit of the distance between them. "And I assume from your question that you have no idea who *I* am."

"I'd like to," Quay admitted at once. His words were genuine. His dark eyes raked her in a helpless manner as though he couldn't get enough of looking at her.

Tykira Lowery rolled her eyes in the direction of the scooped bodice of the elegant rose colored dress she wore. "Still playing Casanova," she softly accused, her seductive gaze becoming humor-filled. "I shouldn't be surprised. I suppose it *is* easy to forget a woman you held captive for a week," she said, her voice softening to almost a whisper. "Park my truck," she requested, tossing him her keys before she walked off to leave Quay staring after her in total confusion.

***

Michaela tried to appease her husband with a slow, sultry dance on the crowded floor.

"I love you," he whispered against her mouth.

"I love *you*," she whispered back, her fingers smoothing across the silky waves of his hair.

Quest sighed his contentment, before raising his head to scan the room. "This is your family," he told her.

"Mmm...I love them too," she murmured, trailing her lips across his jaw.

"That's just 'cause they're all dressed up. Wait'll the morning."

Mick looked up at him then. "I love them because they made you the man you are."

Quest appeared uncertain. "And is that good or bad?"

"It's *very* good."

He smiled down at his wife and almost laughed, he was so happy and excited about the life ahead of them. Mick stood on her toes to press a sweet kiss to his mouth. That kiss turned hot and desirous within seconds.

"I want out of this party," Quest demanded then, his hands tightening on Mick's waist.

She bit her lip. "Babe-"

"We already did all the couple stuff," Quest interrupted before she could argue.

"So how do you propose we make a graceful exit, Mr. Ramsey?" she challenged, her heart somersaulting when he flashed his left-dimpled grin.

"Like this," he swept her off her feet and into his arms.

Michaela's laughter rippled out over the well-wishers who cheered and clapped as the newlyweds made their exit amidst a shower of flowers, confetti and the love of their family.

This Ends A Lover's Dream.
Now Enjoy The Never Before Released Ramsey Short Story:
Lover's Muse: An Interlude

LOVER'S MUSE: AN INTERLUDE

***

Quest Ramsey wasn't about to give his wife any chance to scold him for the dramatic departure from their wedding reception. To be on the safe side, he just kept her mouth occupied with his while taking the back stairway to the wing that housed the guest bedroom suites at his parents' home.

"Are we there yet?" Michaela murmured, her words smothered yet discernable given that she was being kissed senseless.

Nevertheless, they captured Quest's attention. "Is it too big for you?" he asked, referring to the house.

"It's fine."

"Just fine? 'Cause mine is about as big," he said, still referring to the house.

"Big is fine as long as it's satisfying." Mick returned, her thoughts having journeyed away from the house and on to someplace naughty.

Quest caught on to the vibe. "It gets better," he grinned.

They were sealed away in one of the spacious guest rooms shortly after. Quest's teasing mood had apparently waned, for his expression held no trace of amusement when he settled her back against the locked door.

"I need you to understand something. I'm never letting you go Michaela. Do you get that?"

She nodded as if dazed. "I never want you to," she sighed.

"You might, once you understand how protective I can be. It borders on possessive but gets masked by the protective part- *that* can border on obsession."

"I get it Quest. I love you for it," she swore.

"I hope so," his hazy stare had almost darkened to pitch. "I've never wanted anything as much as I want you. I keep what's mine, Michaela. I keep it very well."

She swallowed. "So show me, then."

Michaela Ramsey found her exquisite gown on the floor three minutes after her taunt. The snowy white bustier and garter beneath contrasted beautifully against her milk chocolate skin. Faint lighting spilled from the partially opened door leading to a private washroom. Just enough illumination was provided to reveal the set look to Quest's profile as his gaze trailed the length of her curvy frame encased in the devilish piece of lingerie.

"Quest…" Mick bit on her lip when he brought his eyes to her face. She could just glimpse the darkening of his stare as if fixed on her mouth. She moaned, her lashes fluttering madly when he outlined her lips with his thumb and then gave her his middle finger to suck.

She did so with relish. A low, satisfied rumble stirred from Quest's chest as he watched her pleasure the digit. Eventually, he was resuming his appraisal of her encased in the bustier and garter. She looked like a treat he was hungry to unwrap.

Mick was enraptured by the taste of him and so focused on her task of suckling his finger that a gasp of surprise and rapture erupted when his mouth latched onto her nipple still covered by the satin and lace garment. She lifted a hand, wanting to draw his head closer, but Quest prevented the move, keeping her arm secured against the door. Heat rushed her and she squirmed wanting more of his touch even as she expected anything additional would send her over the edge.

Desperately, she arched more of her breast into his mouth, moaning without shame as she sucked his finger with increased fervor. "Quest please," she urged amidst the act.

Without a care for the custom stitching of the bustier, Quest reached up to jerk it down over one full, heaving breast, bringing it into full view. Michaela sobbed when his perfect mouth smothered the bud that yearned for his attention. She rolled her head against the door practically out of her mind as sensation riddled her quivering body.

Quest emitted the most adorably tortured sounds as he took more of her into his mouth. Lazily, he rotated the tip of his tongue around the diamond-hard nipple, then repeated the move with the tip of his nose before drawing the bud in for another round of merciless tugs. He didn't return to secure her arm against the door once he bared her breast. Instead, he stoked the garter fastening and the satin panties she wore. Finding the entrance he sought, he claimed her with his middle finger and launched an assault to her moisture rich core.

Suddenly, he withdrew his finger. "Kiss me," he ordered in a gruff tone that brooked no disagreement.

Michaela complied eagerly, locking her arms about his neck and heightening the volume of her moans as she kissed him with a devastating intensity. When his handling of her sex weakened her tongue, Quest gave her a jerk.

"I said, 'kiss me'."

"Quest I-"

"Tsk, tsk, there's that sass again."

She gave a low, aroused laugh. "So punish me, then," her next gasp mingled with a sharp cry at the sound of the garter being ripped. She felt the air brushing her exposed flesh then. "Quest," his name was a faint breath when the slow ooze of her need trailed her inner thigh.

The line of pearly white moisture wasn't given much leave

to travel far. Exhibiting, fluid and effortless strength, Quest lifted her high against the door. He cradled her bottom securely, positioning the part of her that he'd claimed ownership of directly before his mouth.

Mick would've slid down the door were it not for the powerful grip in which he kept her. His tongue swept her inner thigh clean of the traces of her juices lingering there. Steadily, it moved higher until claiming her center. Instantly, Mick felt climactic tremors flood her lower half then expand its effect branching out to stab and sooth her with unequaled pleasure.

Desire maddened, she greedily clenched his tongue wanting to keep it trapped until release had its way with her. The relentless rotating and thrusting of his tongue forced her to unclenched in a desperate drive to take whatever he would give her. Her hands splayed above her head along the door and she chanted his name while rocking her hips in sultry clockwise and counter swirls that stimulated as they satisfied.

"No," she rasped, when he suddenly denied her his tongue. Her arguments died as quickly as they roused when she felt his throbbing length- thick and hard taking the place of his tongue. His mouth reclaimed her breasts, his sleek brows drew close and he growled out a curse when the nipple seemed to harden to a firm bud on his tongue. The ravenous suckling mingled between pleasure and pain, assaulting her senses while his shaft plundered and stretched her relentlessly. She wanted to fold her legs around his back, but Quest kept her thighs spread, shelved on powerful forearms still hidden beneath the crisp sleeves of his tux.

He smiled, revealing the gorgeous left dimple when he felt her intimate muscles contract fiercely then. She'd be coming all over him in another minute, he deduced. The thought of that threw his raging hormones into frenzy.

Michaela smiled as hot jets of semen doused her walls when he came. Frantically, she took him, elated over the anticipation of impending orgasm.

Quest rested his dark beautiful face against the base of her throat while shuddering out the last of his satisfaction. She was so tight, the way she fisted his shaft was so exquisitely erotic it was almost painful. It wasn't a complaint and he felt himself refueling for another claiming before he was completely spent inside the curvy chocolate nymph that possessed every bit of his heart.

Michaela was barely coming down from her orgasmic high when her eyes widened and fixed on her husband's stirring gray stare. "Quest..." she felt him transition from semi-hard back to rigid in a span of a few seconds.

"It's going to be a long night Mrs. Ramsey," he promised, grinning at the sound of his wife's laughter.

***

Chicago, Illinois~

Contessa Warren strode with purpose to the half opened door and peeked just inside. She didn't take insult to the unkempt appearance of the room nestled in the enviable corner spot along the top floor of her publishing firm Contessa House. She didn't take insult, knowing the room's occupant had a method to the madness she considered her own 'special' brand of organization.

What had County striding with purpose into the cozy cluttered office was the fact that it was occupied at all- *solely* occupied.

"I'd suggest you get back out there to that sexy piece of chocolate you call a husband," County cast an astute look toward Michaela currently seated on her knees while rifling through a box of file folders. "That is, unless you've got no qualms about putting an APB out for him later."

A smile curved Mick's mouth but she continued her investigation of the folders.

"Your soon-to-be-ex co-workers out there, are looking at the poor guy like they've got serious kidnapping and sexual assault plans on their minds," County moved into the room where she undertook her own investigation of the boxes set out across the office.

Mick laughed then, I promise I'm about to head out. Just

wanted to…" she trailed off to take a closer look at a page from one of the files. With a quick shake of her head, she reconsidered the document's importance and set it off to a pile next to a half filled crate.

"Just what?" County inquired somewhat absently as she was then interested in a page she'd come across.

Mick stood, hefted a box. "Just pulling a few note files. Everything I leave behind will be for the garbage or the Contessa House vaults."

"Well hold on, hold on," Slowly County dragged her eyes away from the sheet that had captured her interest, to wave a hand across the sea of packed boxes. "Let's not be so hasty. Is there any book worthy info waiting in all this mess?"

Mick blew at the wayward curl, set down the box and considered. She was opening her mouth to answer when County raised a hand.

"Let me qualify that question by saying that it should be book worthy info that doesn't involve a family of to-die-for men who will have my next author all ga-ga while she comes out of her panties."

"I resent that," Mick crossed her arms over her chest in a pretend huff.

County shrugged. "You *were* that."

It was Mick's turn to shrug. "I didn't deny- I only resented."

The friends shared a laugh. Michaela retrieved the newly packed box and set it to the right of her uncommonly clean desk.

"This is all pretty much just notes from books already done," she looked longingly at a box near the front of the desk. "Like this stuff," she tapped a foot to the box marked 'Shelanon'.

County's smile held a reminiscent flavor. "A lot of notes went into that book," she mused.

"Tell me about it," Mick hooked her index finger inside the invisible pocket along her black Yoga pants and offered her publisher a wry smile. "Got any authors who might be able to get Jacob Shelanon to make a sequel a reality?"

Contessa's full-bodied laughter sent her thick ponytail swinging. "Hell girl, if *you* couldn't get that nutcase to come out of his mountain, no one can."

"Aww…is that a compliment?"

"Hmph," County rolled her eyes, faking a nonchalant air before she grinned. "You bet it is," she opened her arms toward her best friend and laughed when they shared a hug. "Congratulations, Hon," she whispered, pressing a kiss to Michaela's cheek.

***

Michaela waltzed into her house with a playful flourish that was fueled by happiness and excitement for all that lay ahead of her. Following the wedding, she and Quest had decided to make a pit-stop in Chicago before heading off to the sun and fun of their honeymoon. Regardless of Michaela's anticipation of the future however, her steps slowed the further inside she ventured.

Quest moved at a slower pace as well. His entrancing stare was observant yet approvingly so. He loved the way the place practically embodied his wife's persona. The three-story abode shrieked comfort, warmth and was as lovely as it had been when he'd previously visited.

Quest's appraisal of the house was sidelined as he fixed on Michaela strolling on through. His sleek brows drew closer the longer he scrutinized her, taking note of the scant change in her demeanor. He gave her space, watching her move-stopping infrequently to smooth her hand across a piece of furniture or some other object perched on a shelf or table. He waited until she'd journeyed clear out to the gazebo before he inquired.

"Tell me what's wrong," he said after they'd both strode the rather plush construction.

Mick fingered one of the velvety soft artificial vines that snaked round the gazebo's white, wooden planks. It was approaching dusk and time-sensitive lights were just beginning to sparkle sparsely amidst the vines.

"I don't want to be whinny," she said.

Quest leaned close to her against the railing. "From what I understand, it's something wives tend to be," he feigned discomfort when she punched his solid abs.

Her smile held sway, but briefly. "I miss him...Driggers...he was my family-like my father," she sniffled, "it's what I considered him. Except for County, he was my only family.'

"But that's not true anymore, babe," he pushed off the rail, came over to enfold her in his embrace. "I won't pretend to have any insight into Drigger's magic touch when it came to you," he kissed the top of her head, "but I'll spend the rest of my life perfecting my own."

"That sounds very good," she snuggled back into him, sensation jolting through her when he eased his hand down to cup her mound still hidden inside her pants.

"It'll feel even better than it sounds," he touted, his kisses drifting from her head to pamper the shell of her ear and her nape. He was content working her through her pants, but not for long.

Mick cried out into the early evening air when she felt his fingers against her bare flesh. His touch held the sweet deliberation of warm syrup. Eagerly, she allowed it to take her over a sensual incline.

With dusk fully in session there was little need to worry over an onlooker noticing what the newlyweds were up to. While Quest fully intended to have his wife nude and soon, he was then too maddened by desire to have her slake the intense craving she so easily ignited within him.

He pleasured her consistently until Mick felt passion-drugged. When he had what she considered being, an insane idea to relieve her of his touch, Mick gripped his wrist to keep his hand where she wanted it. Lazily, she rolled her head back across his chest and shamelessly freed her gasps and sensation-tortured cries into the wind.

Quest kept her happy with the two finger massage that sent orgasmic pressure steadily building inside her. His thumb launched a wicked play upon her clit, encircling the sensitive nub. He accommodated her by pressing down on it when her hands flexed over his wrist and she awkwardly rode the digits to find her release.

"Please," she urged, hoping to encourage his cooperation when she angled her head back and up to kiss him.

Quest delighted in the gesture, kissing her with mind-melting intensity. Michaela moaned, a wavering moan that gave credence to how thoroughly aroused she was. She was so absorbed by the relentless drives from his tongue plundering her mouth, that she paid no mind to his free hand slowly working the Yoga pants from her hips and over the lush curve of her bottom.

Her next moan held more of a smothering undertone to the previous gurgling intensity. She felt the night air kissing newly bared flesh, below her waist and shivered in response to it and the distinctive sound of his zipper descending.

The kiss broke in tandem with Michaela feeling the unmatched delight of being filled, stretched and ravished when she and Quest became one. She rested her hand over Quest's where his curved over the vine-entwined railing. Her head dipped, shielding her vision as curls tumbled forth.

"Christ Mick…" he groaned, wanting their impromptu love scene to last. He was equal parts frustrated and satisfied by her ability to drive him to the edge so powerfully. An approving smile curved his fantastic mouth seconds before he buried his handsome face in her hair.

He pummeled her with a relentless surge of beautiful thrusts that had them both groaning in shameless abandon. Supreme pleasure had its way and showed no signs of abating. Quest was as much aroused by the way her inner muscles fiercely clenched his cock as he was by the breathy cries she emitted every time he took possession of the haven that was his alone to explore.

Michaela had never felt more alive. Quest's low, affected groans mainlined radiance through her veins as deftly as his powerful frame at her back enveloped her in a cocoon of security.

~~~

"How long will you keep the house?" Quest asked afterwards as they lay on the gazebo floor upon the tangle of clothes and soft vines.

Mick couldn't open her eyes; she was still so very content. "Haven't thought about it," she snuggled her head into a more comfortable position against the broad expanse of his chest. "Not much reason to, I guess," she raised her head, feeling him stiffen beneath her head, following a soft sudden rush of breath.

"Does that make you mad?" she asked.

"No. Just curious," he tugged on one of her curls. "Why do you think you need to keep it? Because of Driggers?"

"Giving it up…" she looked toward the house, golden lit against the night sky. "Makes it too real-the fact that he's gone."

Quest tugged, until she lay flush against him. He pressed a hard kiss to her mouth. "Keep it forever, then," he ordered, kissing her again. "But you should know I plan to try like hell never to give you a reason to want to move back here."

Laughter filtered through Mick and she glided the back of her hand across his smooth jaw, hard jaw. "I plan to try like hell never to give you a reason to want me to."

They sealed the words with low laughter and commitments' kiss.

~~~

The newlyweds returned to the house where they made love again in the shower and ordered take out Chinese made nicer as they dined by candlelight.

"The Shelanon book was my favorite," Quest shared while popping the bottle cap on his second Heineken. He took a swig and then tilted the bottle in Michaela's direction. "Why didn't you put your picture on it?"

She shrugged, smiling as if suddenly shy. "It was about them, not me."

"Understood, but a real let down for the reader, I have to say."

She laughed, catching the playfulness in his uncommon stare. "A let down!"

"Hell yeah," he gave a lazy shrug. "I was already a pretty

big fan when I met you… knowing what you looked like," he shrugged as though he were about to make an obvious point, "knowing what you looked like would've taken my adoration to another place entirely."

She laughed again. "So you're saying I could've been treated to a first-class trip to Seattle long ago?"

"Damn right."

"Mmm…but then that wouldn't have been because of my writing but my picture on the back."

Quest winced teasingly, acknowledging that she'd correctly assumed his motives. "I'd have made time for discussing the book."

"Right!" Her laughter rushed out more abundantly.

"Seriously- it would've been our pillow talk."

The need for more laughter then was fueled by Michaela's own amusement as well as the fact that her husband's sense of humor was nearly as potent as his looks. "It would've been good conversation," she boasted, stabbing a plump broccoli bud from the shrimp lo mein on her plate.

"The Shelanon story got a lot of buzz," she pointed her fork in his direction. "I did a few book shows and interviews- you would've been able to see me then," she reciprocated Quest's actions when he winced again and snapped his fingers as if to signify regret of a lost moment.

Michaela shrugged. "The book was a success, but never rang with total triumph for me."

"Why not?" Quest set his chin to his palm as he watched her.

"Never got the chance to talk to the family's black sheep."

"Hmph, they only had one? I'm impressed."

"He made the other black sheep look gray from what I heard," Mick spoke around the heap of noodles she'd shoveled into her mouth. "Jacob Shelanon- they said he took his share of the family's fortune and just poof! Withdrew from society, carved out some kind of retreat in the base of this mountain."

Quest let out an impressed whistle. "That must've been

somethin' to see," he said while reaching out to snag the last of the Crab Rangoon.

Mick shrugged. "I guess…only no one in the family knew the location. The stories came from folks who'd been on the construction team, but they didn't stick around long. I was told they were paid well to get lost and to keep quiet about it. I did make use of the contact information the family gave me, though."

"Ahh…so he wanted to keep in touch in case there was more money to be collected."

Mick bounced an index finger at Quest to confirm his guess. "Anyway, it didn't do me much good. The guy changed his number after I'd called a few times- the family worked through a lawyer to track any residual earnings his way."

"Sounds like a man who valued his privacy."

"I get that," Mick took a swig from her water bottle. Her amber stare flashed with something intense then. "I was never trying to make light of how important that is, Quest."

"I know," he sighed, understanding that she was speaking of the circumstances that had brought her into his life, "but privacy and distance weren't things I craved as much from the outside as I craved it from my own family."

"The drama element," Mick noted, smiling wanly when he nodded to confirm.

Quest grinned. "Ramsey should be a synonym for drama- it's existed among us for a long time. My uncle West- he's the oldest of us. He wanted to distance himself from the family before me or any of my cousins were even born."

"Hmm…lemme guess…your uncle Marcus had a lot to do with that?"

Chuckling, Quest nodded. "I'm sure he had a lot to do with it- but none of the younger generation ever really got all the story there…" his expression tensed. "He and my aunt Bri went through a lot. Couple stuff…when they had Bill she was like a blessing for them- they had a lot of misfortune in the child department."

Michaela nodded then, thinking of her husband's cousin

SyBilla.

"He didn't want any of the crap this family's capable of, touching his family- his closest family." Quest reached out lightly entwining his fingers with hers. "That's what you are to me Mick- I never want you to regret marrying me."

"Baby no…" Michaela soothed, clutching Quest's hand as she traded her chair at the table for one closer to his. "I'd never want that and I saw your aunt and uncle together at our wedding- they looked as newly-wed as we did."

"Yeah," he smiled, "it's obvious aunt Bri loves my uncle with every part of her only…my guess is there were days when she wished his last name wasn't Ramsey." He drew up Mick's hand, kissed the back of it. "I think that's why I didn't want you around them when you first got to Seattle," he gave another wince. "Didn't want to give you any reason to go too soon and that became even more important to me once I'd decided to convince you to marry me."

"Ah…interesting plan," Mick scrunched her nose and smiled when she saw that the gesture made her husband laugh. "But you do realize that if your last name *wasn't* Ramsey, County wouldn't have thought you were interesting enough for a book."

The couple dissolved into roaring laughter which curbed once their lips met in a sweet kiss.

"Quest?" Mick smoothed the back of her hand down his cheek. "Why me? Why'd you come after me?"

"Because you were cute as hell, why else?"

She laughed and dropped a playful slap to his cheek. "So it was all just superficial?"

"At first," he admitted, sobering. "But by the time you finished that meeting with Quay, it was about more than that."

"And about more than that when you found out you were my first?" she guessed.

He had the nerve to appear accepting of the fact. "I won't lie and say that it wasn't a very nice surprise," he squeezed her hand, tugging until she was snug in his lap.

"Knowing you were mine- all mine that way…it just made

me want to be the one to give you as much of myself as I could and later when I knew even more about you, I wanted to give you all the security you deserved."

She cupped his face, put a soft kiss to his mouth.

"When you left my office that day to go back to Chicago," he set her more snuggly against him, "you took a piece of me with you and I couldn't function without it."

"I could've given it back to you," Mick teased.

He smirked. "Wouldn't have been the same, since it belongs to you now. Won't work properly unless it's in your possession."

She hugged him. "I love you."

"I love you and you're never getting rid of me," he swore.

"Is that a promise Mr. Ramsey?" She countered, laughing when he stood and took her with him.

"For you, Mrs. Ramsey, it's a guarantee," he said.

They branded each other with a searing kiss that was a promise of delights to come that night and all the nights ahead.

***

This Ends Lover's Muse: An Interlude
And Now:
A Lover's Pretense

A

LOVER'S

PRETENSE

The Ramseys Book II

A LOVER'S PRETENSE

~PROLOGUE~

No way. It was impossible. It was simply not possible that this man could be any more magnificent since she last saw him seventeen years ago.

Tykira Lowery pondered what was to her, such a huge improbability as she headed into Damon and Catrina Ramsey's immaculate country estate just outside Seattle, Washington She'd given into her mother's insistent demands that she attend Quest Ramsey's wedding. In truth, she hadn't experienced the urge to back out of the engagement. Besides, she'd been almost afraid to say anything other than 'yes' to the woman. Roberta "Bobbie" Lowery rarely demanded, never yelled and certainly *never* delivered ultimatums.

But she'd done just that and Ty really couldn't hold her mother at fault. After all, she hadn't set foot in Seattle since leaving for college in Hampton, Virginia in the fall of 1990. Bobbie had abided by her daughter's wishes and spent time with her only child anywhere but the state of Washington. Once Ty was financially able, she flew her mother out to one exotic locale after another. Clearly, Bobbie had simply been biding her time, waiting to play on her daughter's emotions and guilt for never visiting home. Ty couldn't blame her and she cursed herself for not being more attentive to her mother's needs.

But now, Ty owned up to the fact that it had been a mistake to give in to her mother's emotional manipulating. As her cream pumps clicked across the gray and black marble checkered foyer in the sunken ballroom and the ruffled hem to the skirt of her rose blush crepe suit flipped flirtatiously with her every step, Ty realized that she had indeed gravely underestimated how powerfully she'd been affected by being there. More specifically, by seeing Quaysar Ramsey again.

It should have come as no surprise. She'd suspected that she'd be more than a little shaken to see him. And shaken she was. She knew he'd attend the wedding, but he was actually the last person she expected to see the moment she arrived.

Tall and muscular, he still had the power to make her feel incredibly small and feminine-something she never admitted to liking. But, being a woman two inches shy of six feet, feeling less dominant was quite often an exquisite luxury. Quay Ramsey had not only the ability to make her feel that way, but when he looked at her, she forgot every and anything else. Those bottomless, pitch eyes were set so deeply beneath the sleek brows that slanted above.

He was still fierce looking and irritatingly arrogant. Confidence personified. He'd had no idea who she was- that was clear. She'd reveled in the power of his confusion as she verbally slammed him for almost hitting her SUV when she arrived a few minutes ago. Of course, during her 'verbal slam' she was constantly trying to hear her own voice above her heart which beat a thousand drums in her ears. Still, she managed to cooly order him to park her car and the look on his face was sheer delight on her part.

The smug smile curving her full mouth diminished slightly. What would happen when she came to return her keys? She hadn't thought that far ahead. *Uh-oh, no time to do so now,* she told

247

herself. A woman who looked like Catrina Ramsey was eyeing her with that *almost* certain look of recognition. Tykira smiled and wiggled her fingers in a tentative wave.

~~~

Quay was strolling back into the foyer then. He jingled the keys against his palm and tried once again to place where he'd seen her. He'd certainly recall having met someone like her- all that rich, black hair; glossy and bouncing to the middle of her back, molasses skin just like his own. Although he was willing to bet his last dime that her skin was supple and satiny with a soft desirable fragrance clinging to it…

Dammit! Who was she? He glanced toward the keys again as if they held some answer. She knew *him* quite well as she'd been so kind to share during their *run in* out in the courtyard.

Then, there was her height and he preferred his women tiny and curvaceous. Of course that was a preference he'd developed in yet another vain attempt to keep his mind off of- Hold it. *No way.*

"Can't be," Quay breathed, his eyes gleaming with a new determination as he bounded toward the ballroom.

He scanned the crowd, knowing she'd stand out. After all, how many Amazons with silky midnight skin, amazing tresses and the most entrancing doe eyes could there be in the world? And suddenly, there she was, swaying to a soft classical tune the quartet performed in the alcove. His steps were halted, just briefly before they resumed and he headed straight for her.

How could he have not known it was her?

They'd been in one another's lives since infancy. Tykira Lowery had taken an immediate and surprisingly intense liking to the overtly sensual and clearly outspoken Quay as opposed to his quieter, more serious twin brother Quest. She'd loved him before he even admitted to liking girls, was Quest's usual tease.

Quay loved her too, but a small voice warned him of the dangers. He couldn't let anything happen to Ty especially when his feelings for her were just as deep and overwhelming. He'd felt the need to protect her no matter the cost. Still, over the years, the man

248

in him had daydreamed of Ty. He wanted just a moment, just one moment to allow himself to pretend they could be a normal couple-loving and living without fear. Quay knew she'd hate him forever afterwards, but he believed he could take that for just another minute in her arms.

~~~

Tykira was laughing and slapped her dance partner's shoulder.

Yohan Ramsey; the groom's cousin, feigned surprise, "Ow," he playfully uttered.

"Ow is right if Mel walks in here and sees us. Stop holding me so tight. I don't want her upset with me," Ty teased, referring to Yohan's wife.

Like someone had pulled a plug, the happiness on Yohan's dark face drained. His eyes pooled with a sadness not to be ignored.

"Han? What is it?" Ty whispered, concerned upon noticing his reaction.

"It's okay," Yohan assured her in his deep voice. "Melina and I are separated. Hmph," he gestured and shook his head as though he were in a state of disbelief. "It's been six years. We should be divorced."

Ty closed her eyes as recollection dawned. Her mother had informed her of the couple's troubles and subsequent separation long ago. "You wanna talk about it?" she searched his eyes with hers.

Yohan's easy expression returned. "Some thing's are best left alone. Besides, I think my cousin wants to cut in."

Ty blinked and turned to find Quay standing right behind her.

"Not quite, Han," Quay curved his hand around Ty's upper arm and lead her from the ballroom.

Ty swallowed, trying to remain unfazed by the feel of his fingers snug around the crisp material of the tailored crepe cutaway jacket.

"What are you doing here?" Quay muttered as they walked.

"It's your brother's wedding day," she reminded him. "Mama threatened to stop visiting me all together if I didn't show up."

At last they were on the balcony. Quay leaned against the doorjamb of one of the French doors and watched her. "Q's wedding? That's the only reason?" He looked completely unconvinced as he settled his hands into the pockets of his black tuxedo trousers.

Tykira's temper flashed and she opened her mouth to retaliate. The sound of approaching guests stifled her remark.

Figuring they would be less bothered if they hid in a crowd, Quay took her arm again and led Ty to the dancefloor. He pulled her into a snug, arousing embrace. Ty tried not to get lost in how fantastic she felt in his arms and fought to recall how much she despised him.

"How long do you plan to stay?" He asked, effectively casting a sour element to the dance.

Ty rolled her eyes. Silently, she warned her hands to remain firmly planted against his chest and not to venture upwards to choke his neck. "I'll be here long enough to visit my mother and your family."

"But not me?" he probed, tugging his bottom lip between his perfect teeth.

"Why you?"

"Tyke..." he almost purred.

When his right dimple flashed, Ty realized that he was taunting her. "You still enjoy hurting me, don't you?" she hated the way her voice wavered on the question.

Something flickered in Quay's dark eyes, but he masked it before it grew too telling. "Hurting you isn't what I had in mind...unless you're into that sort of thing now."

In a flash, Ty jerked out of his arms and laid a cracking slap to the side of his face. Infuriating her more, Quay only grinned while brushing his knuckles across his jaw.

Ty shoved his chest. "You're still the same conceited

jackass you've always been," she sounded as though the discovery really hadn't surprised her. Pressing a hand against her pearl choker, then brushing her fingers across the single button that secured her chic double breasted jacket, she turned and made a regal exit from the dance floor.

The room was alive with laughter over the scene and Quay heard someone remark that he and Ty were like fire and gasoline- a volatile combination. Amidst all the amusement however, Quay's eyes were filled with the darkness of regret.

A LOVER'S PRETENSE

~ONE~

Two Years Later…

The penthouse office of Ramsey Group was alive with conversation and cheer. The executive members of the real estate conglomerate had gathered to discuss final matters concerning one of their largest projects to date. Holtz Enterprises of Vancouver, Canada had commissioned the group to construct a state of the art yet old world style ski resort. The organization had just purchased property in the mountainous regions just outside Banff, in the neighboring province of Alberta. They wanted a mammoth sized, impressive, unequaled, castle-like resort to sit high atop one of those mountains. The organization wanted no expense spared-nothing but the best. Ramsey Group was the perfect choice. It was well equipped to oversee all aspects of the project including contracting and construction. The development division began working diligently two years prior and now the project was nearing completion. Another six to eight months would produce a destination like no other.

While the actual completion of the resort was going smoothly, however, there was one aspect that still needed to be addressed. Transportation. Holtz wanted nonstop service to shuttle passengers from Calgary to the resort by train. The rail would travel up the foreboding mountainside to its peak. Ramsey didn't build trains so the question before them then was who could they entrust with such a gargantuan task?

Quest, who was assigned with finding the rail design company for the project, believed he'd found his choice.

"I'm leaning towards a design firm out of Colorado," he said, standing at the head of the long rectangular conference table, "they're very well known in the rail community in spite of the fact that they've only been incorporated for five years. I want you guys to look over their portfolio," he passed a stack of packets around the table, "I'd like your decisions by Wednesday's meeting."

Everyone at the table nodded their agreement. Some were already tearing into the packets and reviewing the enclosed material.

"If there're no other questions?" Quest prompted, his sleek brows rising as he paused for reactions. "In that case, meeting adjourned," he said when no one spoke up. "Quay? Wait up, man." He called before his brother headed out with the rest of the group.

Quay shook hands with Ross Anderson, one of Ramsey's chief architects. They made plans for drinks later that week. Ross left; closing the meeting room door behind him.

"What's up, Q?"

Quest watched his twin perch on the corner of the long table. Then, bowing his head, he cleared his throat softly. "I'm leaning towards Tyke Designs to build the rail," he announced.

"Tykira?" Quay breathed, his black eyes narrowing as he spoke. Sure he was well aware that she was in the business. Aside from Quest and perhaps Mick, no one knew how closely he'd kept tabs on the woman since seeing her two years prior at his brother's wedding. "Why?" he asked, watching Quest shrug.

"Her company is impressive as hell, innovative and fresh,"

Quest took his place on the opposite corner of the table. "They're a highly sought after group and I don't think we'd be disappointed."

"Cut it. You know that's not what I meant."

"Well that's what *I* meant," Quest's gray stare sharpened as he stared down his mirror image.

Quay uttered a quick, humorless chuckle. "You, better than anyone, know what the situation is here. Why would you suggest this?" he whispered.

"Quay, no one's seen or heard from Wake Robinson in almost three years."

"Is that supposed to reassure me?" Quay threw back with cocky sarcasm. "Because it doesn't."

"Get over it," Quest shook his head and reached for the charcoal brown suitcoat on the chair behind him. "Once I hear from the rest of the team on Wednesday, I'll be putting in a call to Ty."

"And you're so sure they'll go for this?"

"I'm positive."

Quay gnawed the inside of his jaw, his dark eyes following his brother's every move. "And you think the family is going to support this?"

Quest's knowing smile triggered his left dimple. "They all love Tykira, you know that."

Quay waved his hand. "It's not about that," he moved off the table.

Quest studied the invisible pattern his index finger traced on the cherrywood finish. "Well maybe it's about the fact that you've lived like a virtual hermit for the last two years now."

"Dammit Q does it matter that her life is at stake if that fool ever discovers how I feel about her?"

"Ah Quay," Quest sighed, not wanting to tell his brother that he was overreacting. They he felt his worries were unfounded. After all, it had been over fifteen years. For that reason he had no sympathy for his brother. He knew how deeply Quay felt for Tykira. "Have you ever thought of protecting the woman you love by keeping her close instead of shutting her out?"

Quay's hearty, contagious laughter filled the room. "Damn, you're one to talk. Hell Q, I said almost those very words to you back when you were about to lose Mick for good."

Quest smiled. Stepping closer to his twin, he patted Quay's shoulder. "Then I guess you already know what you have to do, right?" he challenged, and then left his brother alone to think.

Quay sank into one of the hunter green arm chairs in the conference room living area and pondered this new upset. Tykira could not come there. While he had no doubts concerning his ability to say enough of the wrong things to keep her at arm's length, he was *full* of doubts about his ability to go through with saying those things.

He smiled, smoothing a hand across the front of the black banded collar shirt he wore. He thought about how incredible she looked two years ago at Quest's wedding-especially when she angrily shoved her hands against his chest. He recalled her storming out of the ballroom. Men's eyes followed her until she was out of view and then sometimes further still. Tykira was viewed by Quay and, he suspected, most every man she met as the epitome of Amazon. Tall, strong, exotic and erotically proportioned, she was a woman who could take care of herself while still being feminine to elicit a need to protect in any man she met.

He thought her height advantage only added to the seductive, intimidating persona. Aside from her mahogany brown doe eyes and glossy mane, her voice was low- shockingly husky and every bit feminine. Quay closed his eyes then. He'd almost kissed her when he took her out on that balcony during the reception. When he pulled her into the dance, every part of him ached to drag her off somewhere and make love to her until she was too weak to leave the bed. She couldn't accept Quest's job offer, he thought. No one would buy that Quay had regarded her as a quick lay, a brief dalliance. Years ago, she'd been a girl who had been kind enough to take the hint and steer clear of him. That had made it impossible to stay away from *her*. Now, she was a full grown woman-*boy was she*, he thought. She would be coming there with a job to do. A job, that would include working with him and he couldn't pretend he'd have strength enough to hide his feelings for her.

Quay shook his head. He couldn't allow her to stay there. She left Seattle once because of him. Surely, he could make her do it again?

***

Denver, Colorado~

"I mean it, lil lady, I'm gonna get you out here if it's the last thing I do! You ain't lived til you take a ride on a private train round the grandest ranch in Texas!"

Tykira wiped a tear from the corner of her eye as she listened to the ravings of Henry Rose. The gregarious petroleum tycoon had commissioned her company to create his specialized rail earlier that year. It went without saying that he was more than pleased with the finished product.

"Henry are you forgetting I've already taken a trip around your ranch?" Ty shook her head as she envisioned the man chugging around his massive El Paso estate/ranch/oilfield. The christening of the car had been a grand society event and now the rail was hard at work traveling from one end of Henry's estate to the other.

"Bah! That was for work. I'm talkin' sheer relaxation, darlin'."

"Mmm hmm," Ty smiled at the man's charm. He'd made no secret how 'interested' he was throughout the time she spent in Texas designing the rail. "I promise to try and get away for a visit soon," she said, chuckling when Henry uttered a 'hot dang' and boasted about how fine a time he'd show her.

Used to such offers, Tykira had perfected the art of accepting them with a cool head. Her light, inviting responses never placed her in a position of being obligated to accept proposals from her adoring clients. While she had no intentions of providing them with anything but the finest in rail design, they each were left feeling that they were unique in her eyes.

Once the call with Henry had ended, Ty closed her eyes, pulled a hand through her hair and swiveled her chair around to take in the view of downtown Denver. Simultaneously calmed and energized by the environment, she thought about her life there which began the year after she'd obtained her graduate degree in engineering from Northwestern. Denver had been her home ever since.

Ty's vibrant brown gaze clouded over momentarily as thoughts surfaced about the reception two years ago. *Lord, why am I thinking of that?!* Because, she admitted with a sigh, *that* involved Quaysar Ramsey and Quaysar Ramsey came to mind whenever she thought of her life in Denver. It was a great life, but it would never include the man she loved.

Oooo! He'd been so arrogant at the reception. Apparently age had no effect on his tact or reason. Perhaps hitting him and storming out in the middle of the celebration had been a tad over the top, but Quay could incite such a reaction by doing little more than stepping on her toe.

He'd actually thought she'd come there to see him. What nerve! She continued to rant. He was right, of course. She could finally admit that. Deep down, she knew he was right. No matter how much her mother had pressured her, she still could have said no.

In spite of the cold way he'd treated her, she still wanted to melt for him. It chilled something inside her to discover after all those years, sex was still the only thing he wanted from her. Of course, she knew had he pressed a little more, she'd have quickly and happily indulged.

***

"Choose quick, Michaela. 'Cause my bags are waiting to be packed. I've had it with you."

"Sweetie, just bear with me a little longer. I know how much you need me, but I have to see this through."

Contessa Warren, Michaela's friend and owner of Contessa House Publishing rolled her eyes and leaned back in the majestic black suede desk chair she occupied. Focusing on one of the three diamonds adorning her right hand, she prayed the sight would calm her as it usually did. Unfortunately, the phone conversations with her top author were growing increasingly annoying. Michaela had decided to continue her work following marriage and she and County had developed a long-distance working relationship between Seattle and Chicago. Of course County wanted Mick hard at work on her next smash family biography, but more importantly, she wanted her to stop wasting time on a dead end.

For Michaela Sellars Ramsey, however, nothing stirred her juices like the subject she'd embarked upon more than two years ago. Although the Sera Black case had virtually come to a stand still, Mick had been like a bloodhound sniffing out every new lead (no matter how minute) on the case of the murdered teen.

"I mean it Mick, I can pack and be there before the end of the day," County warned before a quick laugh escaped her. "I don't know what good *that* would do. Hell, if Quest can't keep you busy enough to take your mind off this damn case, I don't know what makes me think *I* can."

Mick's brows rose as she tapped her fingers against the polished oak arm of the chair she lounged in. "Believe me Count, the man keeps me plenty busy," she shared, thinking of her husband then.

In truth, she'd had very little time to do any real work on the case since becoming Mrs. Quest Ramsey. True, most of their *busy* work resided in the bedroom, but Quest was determined to have his wife be part of every aspect of his life. He sought her opinion on business, family and every other interest he held. Michaela found that she was just as happy doing the same.

"Listen, County, I promise I'll start research on another family soon." Mick tried to assure her publisher in hopes of stifling the woman's weary sighs on the other end of the line.

"Mmm hmm," came the doubtful response.

"County please. Look, I even have my own office space here at home. I've got everything I need to thoroughly research anything and anyone I want," Mick boasted. "Courtesy of my husband," she added adoringly.

"Hmph," County was unimpressed. "Your hubby's just full of great ideas."

"I haven't used this office just to investigate the case, you know?"

"The hell you haven't, Mick. I'm not a fool. You've done an incredible job on this case. Wake Robinson hasn't reared his head in a long time, but still you've given Johnelle Black a peace she's never known. Sera's mother finally has someone she can point a finger at. That's more of a solid lead than she's ever had before."

But what if Wake Robinson is only a part of the story? Mick inquired softly. She had no idea why she felt that way, but the reporter in her had that nagging doubt which rarely led her astray.

"I promise I'll let it go soon," Mick said at last, trying once more to reassure her best friend.

County swung her legs from her desk and stood. "Because I'm damn tired of debating with you and damn sexually frustrated, I'm going to accept your promise."

"Good," Mick said in a laughing tone as she ruffled her black curls. "Go get a massage or something and try to relax," she suggested.

"Hmph, that would depend on the *kind* of massage."

"Goodbye County," Mick retorted, shaking her head over the suggestive reply. Setting aside the white cordless, she returned to her notes. She'd been in the midst of re-reading her interview with Johnelle Black when she scanned something she'd overlooked before. A moment later, she was snatching up the cordless phone and dialing furiously.

***

Quay had taken a drive out to his parents' home instead of heading straight into the office that morning. He'd taken solace in the den where he sat lounging in one of the overstuffed black cushioned sofas. In his lap, was a photo album dated 1979. His mechanical turning of the plastic covered pages halted when he found the photo he'd been searching for- one of him, Quest and

Tykira sharing a 'school's out for summer' party after their second grade year.

Quay and Ty sat closest to one another in the picture. They looked so happy and, even then, everyone thought they'd one day fall in love and live happily ever after. Then, some years later, things began to happen, Quay recalled, his black eyes growing impossibly darker. There were mishaps, disappearances, murder and happily ever after became an impossibility.

Catrina Ramsey waltzed into the den humming a low tune. Her mind was on changing the potting soil in her vases, when she spotted her son- younger by three minutes- on the sofa. Setting aside her gardening basket, she removed her gloves while watching him curiously. Her Reebok Classics padded softly across the fuzzy champagne carpeting until she stood close enough to the sofa where Quay sat. Peering over his shoulder, she saw him with the album.

Quay smiled when his mother's perfume drifted beneath his nose. Turning slightly, he tugged on her wrist and kissed her cheek when she was close enough.

"Reminiscing?" she asked, smoothing her hands across the burgundy shirt he wore.

The melancholy returned to Quay's handsome dark features. "More like regretting," he admitted.

"Yuck," Catrina replied, making a face, "that's no fun."

"Ma how can situations just suddenly fall so far off track?" Quay asked, once again staring intently at the photo.

Catrina perched her slender frame on the arm of the sofa. "It's the nature of life, sweetie. Our job is to ride the waves until they subside and then snatch up as much happiness as possible when they do."

"What if the happiness only leads to more pain?"

Catrina pressed a kiss to the top of Quay's head and then propped her chin there. "Better to have *some* happiness than none at all, right?" she reasoned and then dropped a quick kiss to her son's temple. It was then that she noticed the picture his hand hovered over. "She certainly was beautiful at the wedding."

Catrina smiled down at the young woman who was like a daughter to her. "Not surprising, though, Ty always was such a beautiful child. Bobbie says she's still not married though," Catrina referred to Ty's mother. "I'm sure she has a special man," she added.

"She doesn't."

Quay's brisk reply caused a light to flicker in Catrina's gaze. She moved from the arm of the sofa to take a seat on the cushion near Quay. "That's so hard to believe considering how lovely she is. I can't imagine a man who'd let such a beauty run around unattached," she stared down at the album and pretended to have no clue about how her words were affecting her son.

"Quest plans to offer her a job," he said, needing the conversation to shift from the allure of Tykira Lowery.

"I heard," Catrina responded with a nod. "How do you feel about that?" she asked without looking away from the family photos.

"It's not a good idea," Quay snapped, tension suddenly tightening every muscle he possessed. "Tyke needs to stay where she is, which is as far away from me as possible."

"And how would that solve anything when you two still love each other?" Catrina slyly inquired, setting down the album to the stand beneath the coffee table. Silence met her question and she glanced across her shoulder to find Quay watching her with a stunned expression. "What? What's that look for?"

"We still love each other," Quay repeated in a flat tone of voice.

"Oh Baby," Catrina slapped her hands to her jean clad thighs, "everyone knows how you two feel about each other. Anyone paying close attention to you at the reception could've seen it."

"That might've had to do with another emotion, Ma." Quay spoke pointedly, hoping his mother understood what he meant.

She did and waved off the suggestive reasoning. "It was about more than that. Simple desire has a look you can spot a mile away. Desire mixed with love…well that's seen with more of the heart than the eye."

Quay shook his head. "You're a deep woman Trina Ramsey."

Catrina shrugged. "I know a little somethin' somethin'. You could've had her, you know? Ty loved you so much, but then you went completely crazy and you started to treat her so coldly."

Quay's gaze faltered. He didn't want his thoughts to take him back to that time, but it was unavoidable.

"Anyway," Catrina said with a quick toss of her bouncy silver gray tresses, "I wouldn't blame her for wanting to get as far away from you as possible. Do you think she'll come all the way back here just to take this job?"

Quay's trademark sly grin flashed in an instant. "It's a challenge, it's something most people would expect a man to do and most importantly, she knows I won't like it. Yeah Ma, she'll most definitely take the job."

A LOVER'S PRETENSE

~TWO~

A shiver touched Michaela's spine as she stretched lazily. The sensational kisses showering her back made her want to snuggle in bed forever.

"Quest," she felt his fingers becoming a more pertinent part of the scene. She pressed her face into one of the pillows littering the headboard and began to grind her hips in sync with his thrusting fingers.

A second later, he was turning her to her back and they were kissing madly. Soft moans filled the darkened space of the spacious bi-level bedroom. Mick arched into her husband's sleek, chiseled frame, her nails grazing his neck where his soft hair tapered.

The tiny, yet noticeable ring from the phone on the nightstand chilled the moment. They groaned simultaneously, but the passionate kissing continued.

"Leave it," Quest growled into her mouth when she made a reach for the phone.

Mick was happy to comply and snuggled back into the erotic embrace. Quest broke the kiss to trail his lips down the line of her neck and lower still to the swell of ample cleavage.

"Good morning Michaela, this is Johnelle Black returning your call..."

The sound of the voice rising from the answering machine had Mick's undivided attention. Wrenching away from Quest, she snatched the phone off its hook, before Johnelle could finish her message.

"Good morning!" Mick greeted breathlessly, slapping at her husband's groping hands.

"Michaela? I know it's early. Is this a bad time?"

"No Johnelle," Mick paused to slap at Quest's hands again before flashing him a warning look, "no this is a great time. Thanks for getting back to me so fast."

"Well it sounded urgent," Johnelle noted, a slight twinge of uneasiness colored her words. "Have you had a break in the case?"

Mick winced, pushing herself up in bed. She should have been clearer in her message. The last thing she wanted was for Johnelle to get her hopes up unnecessarily.

"Not exactly, Johnelle. I mean, there could be something. What I really need is the other diary. The one you said Sera may've written. The one you said might be missing," Mick explained.

Johnelle sighed. "I could be mistaken about that. I really never had solid proof that another existed, but from reading the one I did have-"

"You have a strong suspicion there may be another one," Mick finished. "Johnelle it's important that we try and find it."

Johnelle uttered a shuddery sigh on the other end of the line. "I have to tell you that's not something I'm looking forward to going through. Sera's things...it just makes me miss her even more."

"I understand," Mick whispered, pressing her lips together and fearing to say more lest she be responsible for making the woman break down in tears. "I can't even begin to imagine what it really feels like to go through something like this. Take your time on deciding and think about what it could mean if we *do* find the other diary."

"You're right," Johnelle replied, drawing a deep breath and releasing it in a refreshing sigh. "I can't stop searching now. We've uncovered too much."

Mick's amber eyes sparkled with emotion for the woman's strength. "I still want you to take your time with this," she cautioned.

"I know, I know," Johnelle promised, her voice sounding firmer. "But if there *is* another diary, I'll find it. I mean that."

"I'll let you go then," Mick leaned close to the nightstand.

"Alright and thank you Michaela."

Setting the phone back to its cradle, Mick stared at it for a while. A weary smile touched her mouth though when she heard Quest clearing his throat. "I've already heard your upcoming lecture from County," she said, flashing him a knowing glance across her shoulder.

"And it obviously did no good."

"Quest-"

"I'm not going to ask you to stop trying to solve this thing," he promised, folding his arms across his bare chest as he leaned back against the pillows, "I just don't want you so obsessed with it that you forget about everything else."

Mick's smile softened then. She took in the stubborn set to his gorgeous profile before snuggling closer to tease his earlobe with a brush from her lips. "Baby are you trying to say that you think I'll forget about you?"

Quest rolled his eyes. "You could never forget about me."

"Oooo, confidence," she laughingly replied. "I like it," she murmured against his cheek.

"Hmph."

Leaning away, Mick decided to try a different approach. "Honey I know how you feel about this, but it's so important that I find more answers for Johnelle, yes. But, especially for Quay. He needs this and I'm really concerned for him."

Quest shook his head. "Yeah, I'm concerned too. I thought if he at least knew who might be responsible for this it'd be something of a comfort."

Mick grimaced. "Not when that person is running loose and preventing you from going after the woman you love."

"Tykira." Quest guessed.

"Tykira," Mick confirmed.

"You know, everybody except Quay wants her on this project for the rail. I'm calling her as soon as I get to the office."

Mick propped her chin on her husband's shoulder. "You think this'll work?"

Quest's heavy brows rose momentarily in a gesture of uncertainty. "My brother won't be too happy, that's for damn sure."

"But you're hoping he'll be too mesmerized by Tykira to argue?"

"It's happened before," Quest shared, his gray eyes narrowing murderously.

"Mmm," Mick rested back into the crisp, sandalwood linens, "but that was before he felt her life was in danger."

"I have to try," Quest whispered, his hand flexing into a fist. "I want him happy. He's been like a zombie since he saw her at our wedding reception," he turned when he felt his wife's nails grazing his spine. "Besides, it's because of him that I have you," he murmured against her lips when he'd settled next to her again.

The conversation silenced and the moment segued into a sweetly erotic interlude...

***

A group of five men sat stonefaced and silent while they stared at the woman at the head of the table. Their handsome faces were rarely void of grins or full blown smiles. As usual, however, their boss had succeeded in catching them off guard.

Tykira kept a calm smile on her face as she sought to judge the reactions from her crew chiefs. Their expressions gave away nothing. Well- that wasn't exactly true. Ty could clearly see that they weren't a happy bunch. Folding her arms across the front of her V-neck tanned sweater, she waited. Not known for her patience, she cracked a second later.

"Will you guys please say something?!" She demanded.

"You're kidding, right?" Frank Royers finally spoke up.

"She better be," Morton Garner added, his blue eyes snapping with frustration.

"You're just a little tired," Samuel Bloch added.

"Tired or going crazy," Kenny Sutton teased.

Gary Charles ran a hand through his curly blonde hair. "We haven't taken a break in five years," he argued.

"That's why this is the perfect time," Ty pointed out, her brown eyes sparkling with encouragement. "We've been working non-stop and that's not healthy."

"Making money is always healthy, Ty," Kenny challenged.

"What's really going on here, Ty?" Morton asked, his green eyes narrowing as he studied her closely.

Finally, Ty let her façade drop. She stared down at her hands and began to fiddle with the thumb ring she always wore, "I guess I'm bored," she admitted at last, peeking beneath the heavy fringe of her lashes to see her crew frowning out of sheer confusion. "Yes, we've made a great name for ourselves, but now I'm ready for a *real* challenge. Frankly, I think I'll scream if another choo-choo to go 'round somebody's house comes our way," she complained, her low voice still resounding in the room.

The guys exchanged closed looks. "I think you're oversimplifying what we do, love," Samuel chastised quietly.

"I'll say," Gary agreed, "our projects range Ty, you know that."

Closing her eyes, Ty relaxed against the black leather chair she occupied. "I know," she conceded, rubbing her arms through the over-long sleeves of her mohair sweater. "I don't know what's wrong with me," she added in a weary voice.

"Maybe Sam's right," Frank was saying, "maybe you *are* tired. All this on the go work, travelling, up all night, maybe it's starting to wear you down."

"Yeah Ty, maybe you should take a week or three off. Go

home, visit your mom, get some rest," Kenny suggested.

Tykira leaned back in her chair and considered the suggestion. It would be nice to get away and her mother would be quite surprised to see her prodigal daughter arriving home out of the blue. But then, those unwanted warnings of seeing Quaysar Ramsey and anything associated with him resurfaced and she began to silently talk herself out of it.

"Ty?" Morton called. "What do you say?" he prompted.

After another few seconds of silence, Ty graced the men with her most dazzling smile.

"Yeah Jason?" Sam called when the phone buzzed amidst their laughter.

"Hey guys," the intern greeted, "Ty, I got a Quest Ramsey on the phone for you."

Her laughter vanishing, Ty's heart jumped to her throat. Calls from Seattle from anyone besides her mother were about as common as a warm winter in Denver. Immediately, she feared there might be a problem with Bobbie. She was berating herself for not visiting more when she picked up the phone.

"Quest?"

"Hey girl, what's goin' on out there?"

"Is my mother alright?"

Quest hesitated on his end of the line. "Yeah…why wouldn't she be?"

"Dammit, don't scare me like that," she hissed, glancing back to see her crew involved in another conversation. "I already feel guilty enough for not seeing her more."

"Honey I'm sorry, I didn't mean to upset you," Quest said, though laughter still colored his voice. "Maybe we can do something about your not visiting. I have a proposition for you."

Curious then, Ty perched on the edge of the small desk in the conference room. "Continue," she urged.

Quest chuckled. "Afraid I can't. To find out what it is, I'll need you in Seattle before the end of the week."

Shaking her head, Tykira fiddled with a bouncing curl from her ponytail and turned to fix her crew chiefs with a wide grin. "I think that could be arranged," she told Quest.

***

"Are you getting anywhere with this stuff?" Quay eyed the monitor of Michaela's laptop with decided skepticism.

"Wake Robinson is a very educated man," Mick reminded her brother-in-law, her eyes focused as she scrolled the screen. "I never know when an idle search might pay off. It's been close to three years, maybe he's snagged a high level position somewhere. It never hurts to check," she advised.

"I guess it's a good idea when you put it like that," Quay leaned back in the chair he'd pulled behind the desk where Mick was working. "I never realized Wake was so resourceful- making his way through college with no help from family."

"Hmph, it can be done. Trust me," Mick confirmed, a rueful smile curving her mouth. "If you are resourceful, you can slip under the grid by using cash and disposable cell phones."

"I know," Quay said, understanding that his sister-in-law may have done the same and probably had a rougher time of it. Leaning forward, he squeezed her knee. "I'm surprised you never thought to check the net for business ties before," he said after a while.

"Actually I have," Mick confided, with a quick toss of her unruly curls.

Quay slanted a narrow dark glance her way. "What's that tone about?"

"I've been at this for weeks. It's almost become a daily ritual for me. A ritual that produces no results," she groaned.

Quay's handsome features were a picture of concern. "Mick I want you to let go of this."

"What?" she whirled around to face him.

"I don't want you to keep wasting your time on a dead end case," he pointed his index finger towards the laptop.

"Quay-"

"I mean it. Hell, you've already discovered more in less than a year than it's taken a league of detectives."

Mick inched closer to him. "That's because I really want

the truth."

Quay's dark eyes narrowed with suspicion. "You think they didn't?" he asked.

"I think it could've been a show to make people think the Ramseys were after the truth. A pretense," Mick suggested.

Quay leaned back in his chair not bothering to hide his grim expression. A pretense. Yeah, he knew all about pretenses.

"I'm dedicated to you and Johnelle," Mick told him, inching closer still to rest her hand on his forearm. "The truth is out there and I'm like a dog with a bone."

Quay grinned, his right dimple flashing adorably. "Wake better watch it."

"Damn right," Mick confirmed, "especially once Johnelle finds that diary."

Quay blinked. "What diary?"

"That's right," she sighed realizing she'd never told him. "In reading Sera's other diary which was quite short because of her murder, there was no mention of the man she was interested in by name, Johnelle is under the impression that the diary was just a continuation and that there's an earlier one out there somewhere."

Quay scanned the spacious second corner office his twin had constructed onto his home. "You think it could shed more light."

Mick shrugged, her amber gaze as pensive as Quay's. "Did Wake ever say he liked Sera or wanted to get to know her?"

Quay knocked his fist against his knee and reminisced. "If he did, he didn't tell me ad he told *me* everything or so I thought."

Mick massaged his shoulder, a knowing smile tugging at her mouth. She understood his unease. "Honey do you think he could've been responsible for the situations with the other girls?" she asked in the tiniest voice.

Quay shook his head, but he was one hundred percent sure of it. "It'd make perfect sense. You know, after this all came out I started recalling things I never paid any attention to before. Ways he behaved, he'd disappear for days and no one heard from him. I knew he and his mom had it rough but he never wanted any help.

Then he up and disappears when he realizes you're onto him."
Quay looked at Mick and shrugged again. "What other explanation
could there be?"

"Well I'm determined to find out," Mick declared leaning
in to tap her finger to the end of Quay's nose. "We gotta do
something to bring the dazzle back to this handsome face," she
teased, hoping to make him smile. It didn't work. "Hey, why don't
you come out and have dinner with me and Quest tonight. How
does Marone's sound?"

Quay rolled his eyes and grimaced. "I don't know Mick,"
he tried to decline.

"Aw come on, it'll be fun. The three of us haven't been out
in a long time. Please?" She cooed, pouring the begging on extra
thick. "Please?" she blinked her long lashes in rapid succession
that time.

"Enough," Quay ordered with a wave of his hand. "I may
be late for dinner, but I'll definitely be there for dessert."

"Yaay!" Mick sounded every bit the little girl given the
green light to play in her mother's make-up. She threw her arms
around Quay's neck and kissed his cheek. "Eight o'clock,
Marone's," she told him.

"Mmm hmm," Quay tousled Mick's curls before he stood
and left the room.

***

Tykira laughed when she stepped off the elevator and into
Quest Ramsey's waiting embrace. When he pulled away, he
uttered a light whistle.

"You know if I weren't a married man, I'd-"

"Still treat me like I'm your little sister," Ty finished for
him, joining Quest in laughter as they hugged again.

Another whistle sounded in the gorgeous penthouse office,
this time from Ty. "Wow," she blurted, her doe-shaped eyes
growing impossibly wide as she studied the exquisite décor and
overtly masculine aura of the dwelling. "Mommie always told me
this place was somethin' to see," she shared while easing her hands

into the side pockets of her wine-colored pleated hem skirt. "I see business is treating you very well," she complimented with a saucy glance across her shoulder.

Quest threw his hands in the air. "We do alright," he intentionally tried to downplay his pride.

Ty caught on. "I'll say. Mister Fortune Five-Hundred."

"And you're right there beside me. Miss- Only Been In Business Five Years," he challenged.

"Thanks. We do alright," Ty repeated his earlier words with a graceful tip of her head.

Quest waved his hands in the direction of the inner office. "That's why I called you out here," he told her.

Ty folded her arms across the chic, short-waist blazer she sported. "Ah yes, the proposal," she sighed, taking a seat in one of the deep arm chairs before the desk. The easy expression that lightened her lovely features, faded slowly as she cast several nervous glances around the soft-lit room. "Are we alone?" she asked.

"Quay isn't here," Quest assured.

"But he *is* still with the company?"

"He is."

"And I assume your proposal is business related."

"It is."

"And how does he feel about that?"

Quest lowered his gray stare to the pine desk. "I believe you can guess."

Ty fiddled with the lone curl that dangled outside the high chignon she wore. "Unfortunately I can," she replied.

"Honey even my foolish brother can't deny you'd be perfect for this."

"And what exactly is *this*?" Ty crossed her long legs as she became wholly focused on her reason for being there.

"Ramsey was commissioned by a group out of Canada for a ski resort in Banff. A state of the art castle sitting on a mountain was what they wanted," Quest explained.

Ty's dark face brightened with humor. "And I thought I

had some outrageous requests."

"It gets more outrageous," Quest promised, tugging on the cuff of his gray checked shirt, "they want a private rail service to shuttle guests from Calgary to the resort."

Tykira uttered the third whistle of the morning.

"Yeah," Quest acknowledged.

"People work for decades and never get a chance to work on something like this," she testified. "It *is* impressive Quest."

"But?" he sensed her hesitation.

"*But*, the last thing I want to do is bring tension here," she fiddled with the sleeves of her blazer as she stood. "Quay is a very important part of this business and if he isn't on board-"

"Hold it," Quest commanded, raising his hand as though he were about to ask a question. "Follow me," he stood behind his desk and lead the way into the display room on the other side of the office.

Inside the room of maps and boxed models of Ramsey projects, the Banff creation sat in the midst. It was indeed a breathtaking creation and was complete with a replica of the desired rail chugging its way around the mountainside.

"Damn you," Ty muttered to Quest. She was thoroughly mesmerized by the sight. Without a doubt, the real thing would be an even more magnificent accomplishment. The opportunity to take on this assignment was one in a million. Seeing the project this way had truly sealed her fate.

"Is that a yes?" Quest asked when he heard her groan.

"When do we start?" she turned to shake hands before they shared another hug.

~~~

Tykira trailed her fingers along the upturned collar of her blazer as the elevator from the penthouse office made its descent. She was already at work envisioning possible designs in her mind. True, Tyke Designs had undertaken some major projects. Still, she knew they were all preparations for this one. Of course, this particular undertaking would catapult her business to a level of which she hadn't even dreamed of. Life was good, she thought. Business was great. Now, her only question was what to do about the dark cloud that looked above it all?

As if on cue, the elevator doors slid open and said 'dark cloud' stood before her eyes.

"Quay," she breathed, silently cursing herself for the sultry needy overtone clinging to her voice.

Uttering not a word, Quay stepped forward; smoothly urging her back into the car. "Did you accept Q's proposal?" he asked, once the doors had closed behind him.

"I did," she winced when she noticed a smirk tilt the corner of his mouth. *A sensuous pleasure providing mouth- Ty...* she warned herself and cleared her throat as though that would help her to gather her wits. "It's a great opportunity," she managed to say but found it impossible to maintain eye contact when he stood so close.

"Are you sure you can handle it?" he pretended to be concerned with something on the lapel of his hand-tailored black corduroy sport coat.

Ty's lashes fluttered, she was so peeved. "Would you be asking me that if I were a man?"

Suddenly, Quay brought his sinful onyx stare to her face. "If you were a man who'd never done anything like this before- yes."

"Bull."

Quay's smirk deepened.

Tykira took a step closer, dismissing the way his deep set eyes appraised the scooped neckline of her blazer. "I'll admit my team has never designed a train to go up a Canadian mountainside before, but we've taken on some pretty major assignments. I'm sure you know that."

Quay was solely focused on Ty, but he didn't hear a word she said. He was, however, focused on how good she smelled, how beautiful her face and body were... he could scarcely take his mind off what it'd feel like to have her long legs locked around his back as he pressed her against the elevator car and-

"Quay?" Ty called, her heart doing fanatical somersaults inside her chest. The intensity of his look was too intoxicating and she would've given anything to know what he was thinking.

Breaking his stare, Quay ground his teeth and fixed on the short carpeting covering the floor of the car. "Good luck," he whispered and then moved to press a button which re-opened the doors.

Ty tried to utter a response, but the potency of the moment had robbed her of her voice. Taking great care not to brush against any, hard, powerful part of his body, she gingerly eased out of the elevator.

She was in her car before she realized she'd been holding her breath.

A LOVER'S PRETENSE

~THREE~

Tykira, Quest and Michaela had just completed a fantastic Italian meal at Marone's and were waiting on coffee and Biscotti for dessert. Tykira and Michaela had become instant friends the moment Quest had introduced them years prior at the wedding reception. He'd been unable to get barely a word into the conversation as the acquaintances talked non-stop. Of course, Mick was quite intrigued in Tykira's strong interest in what she'd always deemed a male-dominated profession. Likewise, Ty was just as interested in meeting the author whose family saga biographies graced both her living room coffee table and her office bookshelves.

"You've got to tell me what it was like growing up around Quest," Mick urged, knowing Ty must've had some fascinating stories about her husband as a kid.

"Let's see," Ty sighed, leaning back in the cream and leather arm chair she occupied. "if you'd like me to put it in one word, that word would have to be 'crazy'," she joined in when

Mick burst into laughter.

"Hey," a wounded Quest called from his spot at the table.

"Shh," Mick retorted. "Go on, Ty."

"Well, I say that in the most loving way, Quest."

"Mmm," was the low reply.

Ty shook her head. "Anyway, I didn't have any brothers or sisters, so any child that was near was a welcome and needed playmate. My mom lucked out on snagging not only a job at Ramsey Enterprises, but she also snagged the '*guest house*' they owned just a ways from where Quest and Quay lived with their parents."

Mick's light eyes narrowed. "You say guest house like it holds special meaning?"

"Honey guest house is not an accurate description of the place. It was incredible and believe me when I tell you at least fifty guests could've lived comfortably in that place."

"My family believes in treating their employees well. But Ty and her mom were more than that- they were family." Quest explained.

Ty smiled. "Thanks Q. I always felt that way even before my mom actually went to work for Ramsey. My grandparents both worked for Quest's grandparents, then my mom worked for his dad and now *I'm* working for Quest... it's somethin' to wrap your head around," she brushed a tendril of hair behind her ear before propping her chin to her fist. "We've grown up together for generations."

Mick was nodding. "So when the Ramseys moved to Seattle..."

"Oh Mr. D asked my mom to relocate and she didn't hesitate," Ty referred to Damon Ramsey, "It was easy for her to do it since I was on my way to college in the fall. They even constructed a house close to the estate. Aside from us being in Seattle instead of Savannah, not much else changed," she said, although a bit of the light had dimmed in her eyes.

Mick noticed. "Sounds like you had a pretty wonderful childhood," she hoped to improve the mood.

Ty's expression turned mischievous. "Let's just say I'm glad I didn't have to suffer Quest's pranks around the clock. I could escape and go home at the end of the day."

Laughter erupted once more, but quickly silenced when Quest caught sight of his brother across the dining room.

"What the hell...?" he breathed, drawing both Ty and Mick's attention.

Mick shook her head when she saw what caused her husband's outburst. Obviously Quay had decided to join them for dinner. Unfortunately, he didn't come alone.

Ty noticed Quay and his date as well and prayed she'd pull off a convincing job of looking cool and unfazed. Though they were quite a distance from one another, Tykira knew the black, unsettling stare was focused right on her.

"Dammit," Quest muttered, standing when Quay and his companion headed toward the table.

"What's she doing here?" Quay's first words were snarled in his brother's ear once the distance closed between them.

"We invited her to dinner," Quest shared, his usually low voice sounded harsher.

Silence settled then and it was quite uncomfortable. To break the ever thickening ice, Mick stood and extended her hand in a gesture of welcome to the woman at Quay's side.

"I'm Michaela Ramsey, Quay's sister-in-law," she said.

The small voluptuous beauty was completely oblivious to the disconcerting silence at the table. Clearly she was in awe of the devastating dark twins she stood between.

"Oh!" she gave a start before giggling at herself. "Lisa-Lisa Melvin."

"Lisa, so nice to meet you and this is Tykira Lowery," Mick smiled as the women shook hands.

"Have a seat Lisa," Quest urged already pulling out the one vacant chair at the table. "We need to talk," he grated to Quay once Lisa was comfortable.

"What's she doin' here, Q?" Quay demanded to know as the two of them bounded across the golden lit dining room.

Laughter lilted somewhere in the distance and they both glanced back to find that it was Tykira, Mick and Lisa.

"Obviously they hit it off," Quest remarked sourly.

Quay rolled his eyes. "Goody," he remarked in an equally sour manner.

Quest stopped in an area just off from the lobby and folded his hand across the sleeve of his brother's medium-blue wool blazer. "What the hell are you doin' here with a date, Quay? After two years of actin' like a goddamn hermit you pick *tonight* to go out with a woman?"

"Nobody told me she'd be here!" Quay snapped, wrenching his arm from Quest's grip. "I'll be damned if I play third wheel for the fiftieth time and watch you and Mick play touchy feely all night.

Quest uttered a short, humorless laugh. "Right Quay if we'd have told you Ty would be here, you'd have probably shown up with two women instead of one," he predicted.

"That hurts, Q," Quay pressed one hand to the front of his white open-collar shirt.

"Truth always does, Quay."

Quay stopped Quest from turning away by catching the cuff of the tan sport coat he wore. "Q, man do you really think I'd do that to her?"

Quest grinned. "This is a trick question, right?"

Quay released his brother. The spitefully humorous remark sent his infamous temper to simmer. He knew he was merely a few seconds from crashing a fist into his twin's gut. Instead, he shoved that fist deep into his trouser pocket and pressed the other hand to his chest. "Q, I swear I'd never do that to her."

"You did it before."

"I was a stupid kid," Quay excused, his midnight gaze filled with disbelief. "I thought I was protecting her. You know that. Tonight…I just wouldn't have come at all."

Quest looked away, his left dimple flashing as he gnawed the inside of his jaw. Of course he knew that. He could look at Quay and almost feel the honesty radiating from his words and eyes. He could see that his brother was genuinely distressed over what had happened.

"Hey guys," Tykira said when she breezed over.

Their conversation was effectively stifled. Quay was speechless, enjoying the scent of Ty's perfume wafting beneath his nostrils.

"I just wanted to say goodnight. I'm on my way back to the hotel," she told them.

"What about dessert?" Quest hated that his plan to bring his brother and Ty together that evening had unraveled.

Ty lifted the foil duck she carried. "I asked them for a doggie bag. I can't eat another bite," she sighed. "Anyway," she leaned close to hug Quest. "Good night. I'll talk to you tomorrow," She spoke a hushed goodnight to Quay and was about to ease by.

"Tyke wait," Quay urged softly, catching the overlong cuff of her emerald green off shoulder sweater. "I'm sorry for what happened back there," he apologized once Quest had walked away.

"Sorry?" Ty parroted, appearing confused.

Quay blinked. "Walking in here with a date," he clarified, tilting his head as though he didn't quite believe she'd misunderstood him.

Ty shrugged. "She seems very nice."

"But I shouldn't have come up in here with her on my arm. I'm sorry," he went on.

"You don't owe me any apologies, Quay," she was barely able to hear herself over the ringing in her ears. Clearing her throat, she flashed a pointed look toward his hand smothering her wrist.

Slowly, Quay followed the line of her gaze. He winced, stunned by the rush of sensation he felt from the simple touch. Brushing his thumb across the pulse point below her wrist, he finally released her.

Tykira turned and left the restaurant. She ignored her desire to look back, knowing she'd never leave him if she did.

~~~

"We already ordered dessert," Mick was telling Quay when

he returned to the table.

"Thanks Mick, but um, I can't stay," he fixed his date with a soulful remorseful stare. "I'm sorry Lisa, but something came up," he told her kneeling next to her chair as he spoke. "Would you be too upset with me if I took you home now?"

Thoroughly charmed by Quay, Lisa was far from upset. "It's perfectly alright, but I'll expect a rain check and soon," she softly requested.

Quay only nodded, brushing his index finger along the curve of her cheek before he stood. Quest and Mick could only shake their heads at the man's suave demeanor. Clearly living the last two years like a hermit, hadn't affected his way with the ladies.

"Michaela, Quest it was so nice to meet you," Lisa was saying as Quay helped her from her seat.

"Oh, same here," Mick replied, smoothing both hands across her black suede front-split skirt when she stood. She carried on conversation with Lisa, while her husband spoke with his brother.

"Where is she?" Quay asked.

"The Sorenson, room seventeen-thirty," Quest supplied.

***

Ty literally let her hair down when she returned to her suite at the Sorenson. She exchanged the elegant off-shoulder sweater and slacks for more comfortable nighttime apparel of an oversized T-shirt and soft cotton shorts. Settling down in the living area with a bowl of the sinful Italian cookies from Marone's on the coffee table, she started searching the TV listings for a suitable movie. She was about to turn on the impressive plasma screen when the doorbell rang.

Munching on a mouthful of the crunchy cookies, Ty grimaced and reluctantly left the sofa. She helped herself to another bite of the treat and was chewing heartily when she flung open the door.

"Quay!" crumbs sprayed past her lips.

Having worn a fierce scowl for the better part of the

evening, Quay couldn't help but laugh at the picture she made. Her hair was deliciously tousled, eyes wider than usual, her incredible legs bared by the Broncos T-shirt and short athletic shorts she wore. A pang of emotion struck someplace deep in his stomach and he admitted that he didn't think he could let her walk away from him this time.

"What-" she paused to swallow a mouthful of cookie, "what are you doing here?"

Instead of a verbal reply, Quay took her arm, closed the door and led her inside the suite.

"I wanted to apologize," he told her once they'd returned to the living area.

Ty rolled her eyes and shuffled past him. "For the second time Quay, you don't owe me any apologies."

Quay didn't hear her. "Mick and Quest invite me to dinner almost every week. It's sweet and I love 'em for thinking of me," his smirk struck the gorgeous right dimple, "but I spend the better part of the night watching them play the 'newlywed game' at the table. If you know what I mean," he added.

Ty nodded in response to the suggestive remark. "I do," she pressed her lips together.

"I had stopped going, but today Mick made a huge deal about me going out with them and telling me how long it's been. Anyway, that's why I showed up there with Lisa tonight," he smoothed a hand across the back of his wavy close cut hair. "It was a last minute thing. I hardly even know her," he finished and then focused his deep onyx eyes on her face as though waiting for her to utter words of forgiveness.

Instead, Ty was moved to ask a question. It was a question her powerful warning voice demanded she *not* ask. Of course, she didn't listen. "Why are you going to the trouble of telling me all this?"

"I just don't want you to think I'd hurt you that way."

Ty couldn't look at him. "You've done it before," she reminded him. With an edge to her voice, she added, "Not that you have to worry about having done that tonight. As much as you seem to love believing that I spend all my time pining for you, I can assure you that isn't the case."

Hearing the words spoken from her lips instead of his brother's did not fill Quay with anger as they'd done earlier. Instead, he felt sick-sickened by himself and the way he'd treated her all those years ago.

"Listen Quay, all this is in the past, you know? Let's not rehash it okay?" Ty shook her head as if trying to rid her mind of past demons.

Quay watched her take a seat on the sofa and decided to join her. "Why aren't you staying with Ms. Bobbie?" he asked.

"She's on vacation," Ty scanned the TV listings again, "You know how I hate being alone in that big house," she added.

Quay's chuckle caused his deep-set eyes to crinkle adoringly at the corners. "Yeah, I remember. Damn, how many times did you stay at our house when your mom was working late?"

"Lots," Ty replied with a flippant shrug. "Besides, your house was just over the hill. If that wasn't a convenient babysitter, I don't know what was," she didn't want to remember those happier times though. "Anyway, that's why I'm here," she sighed, feeling the way his unwavering gaze focused on her. He made no further comments and his stare never wavered. Ty began to grit her teeth from agitation. Even the delicious cookies she'd been snacking on were starting to leave a sour taste in her mouth.

"Did you just come here to apologize again?" she finally lost her battle at patience.

Quay nodded. "I did."

"Well I'd say you've done that," Ty decided and stood.

Quay tried to keep his hands still, but couldn't. Slowly, his fingers brushed the lush curve of her thigh left bare where the hem of her jersey ended.

Ty could feel her every nerve ending charting a path toward the most sensitized part of her anatomy. Her lashes fluttered and she lingered close to the touch, savoring the fire igniting there. The simple, barely noticeable caress almost forced a moan to her parted lips.

"Goodnight, Quay," she told him suddenly, the danger of remaining close for a second longer had become all too real.

Standing then, Quay blocked her way. "Not yet," he asked, his fingers trailing just a fraction higher.

Ty closed her eyes. "Don't do this," she urged hating the pleading tone of her voice. The soft huskiness of her voice made the simple request sound desire-filled and needy.

Quay lowered his head, his cheek brushing hers as gently as his thumb began to graze the swell of her bottom. "I missed you," he whispered next to her temple.

"Mmm, I figured judging from all the calls I've gotten over the last fifteen years," she celebrated the firm tone of her words even as her nipples tensed against the fabric of the jersey. Finally, uttering a quick sound of frustration, she surprised herself and pushed him away. She smiled when the shove she applied to the unyielding wall of his chest caused him to stumble a little. Capitalizing on his momentary imbalance, she sauntered around him and headed for the front of the suite.

"Get out," she pulled open the door.

Quay was slow to comply. Eventually, he rose from his position against the arm of the sofa and moved forward.

Ty kept her brown gaze averted, knowing he'd never believe she was serious about him leaving if he looked into her eyes. Quay stopped just at the threshold, invading her space once again. He brushed his thumb along the curve of her cheek. The intense dark of his eyes practically smoldered with need. He saw her blink once, twice, three times and knew her feelings were still there; still as powerful as his own and surging just below the surface.

"I did miss you, Tyke," he said and then he was gone.

**

After leaving the Sorenson, Quay drove around for a while trying to clear his mind of Tykira Lowery. God, she was still everything he'd ever wanted. Every woman he'd known since, had barely scratched the surface of coming close to ruling his heart and soul the way she did. He was confident that it would be easy to coax her into bed.

Flexing his hand around the wheel of the Navigator, he gave a smirk. Coaxing her into bed would be more than easy, it would be damn well satiating as hell. But what would it solve besides a hoard of raging male hormones. He barely managed to conceal his reaction to her- semi hard in her presence and rock hard and throbbing when he was alone with thoughts of her rampaging his senses. No matter how many times he took her, it would do nothing to drive her from his mind, he'd simply want more. No matter how many women he had, it would do nothing to forge Tykira from his thoughts. His quest to find *the* woman would never end until he had *her*.

The long thought-provoking drive eventually led Quay back into the city and to Double Q. The upscale jazz and R&B club/restaurant he'd opened with Quest was growing more successful every month. Seattle-ites and tourists alike made a point of visiting the elite dwelling. As usual, the place was packed with even more waiting outside and hoping for an opportunity to party inside.

Quay spoke with the security crew who usually collected in the state of the art surveillance booth just off from the club's entrance. Later, he headed for the bar and took a glass and a bottle of Hennessey to his office nestled far in back. Preparing to dim Tykira's image from his mind with the power of the dark drink, Quay was already breaking the seal on the bottle as he headed for his desk. It wasn't long before he discovered he wasn't the only one who'd sought refuge in the solitude of the paneled office.

A big grin flashed on Quay's face when he saw his cousin Yohan. "As I live and breathe, history is being made this night."

"Don't start, man," a slow, canyon-deep voice rose from the depths of the room.

Quay wouldn't be discouraged. "Now wait a minute, wait a minute. A moment like this calls for recognition. It ain't every day I see the notoriously reclusive, anti-social Yohan Ramsey daring to grace our humble place of biz with his presence."

Yohan couldn't resist his cousin's contagious humor. A smile brightened his unforgettably gorgeous face as he tilted his glass of Jack Daniels in greeting."

"What's up?" Quay inquired, while shrugging out of the cashmere blazer he'd worn that night. "Somethin's gotta be goin' on to bring you out," he knew his cousin's preferred choice for an evening escapade was a night of movies at home, listening to music in his library or; if he was feeling especially claustrophobic, high seas fishing.

Yohan's dazzling gold Herringbone chain sparkled at his neck when he shrugged. "Just wanted to get out, man."

"Mmm hmm, right," Quay threw back rolling the sleeves of his eggplant shirt above his forearms. "We need to mark this one on the calendars," he continued to tease. "What's the date?" he was already heading for the huge wall calendar behind his desk.

Yohan massaged his temple. "Quay-"

"Come on, man. What's the date?"

"My anniversary."

Quay tugged on his bottom lip and winced. Closing his eyes, he uttered a muffled groan. Damn, this was his second screw up of the night. He was rollin' now, he thought.

Glass and bottle in hand, Quay took a seat across from Yohan. "Sorry man," he set his burden to the coffee table.

"Forget it," Yohan's very deep set brown eyes seemed to cloud as they filled with a question. "How long does it take to get over the only woman you ever *really* gave a damn about?"

Quay's long brows rose briefly. Of course, he couldn't answer the question, since the reply would have been 'never'. Somehow, he didn't think that would have done his cousin any good. "Why don't you give Melina a call," he suggested instead.

"And say what, man?" Yohan snapped, the mere mention of his estranged wife's name stirring his frustration. "What do I say to her, Quay? I miss you?" he probed, his syrupy slow voice holding minute traces of humor. "Does it work, Quay?" he asked, the look on his first cousin's face was answer enough. "Thought so," he propped his feet against the coffee table. "Hell Quay what right do I have to say something like that to her after the way I treated her? I got no rights at all after the way I did her."

"You still love her, man," Quay argued in a soft voice. "You still got a right to love her and that gives you the right to change where things stand between y'all."

Yohan's chuckle could chill a spine as quickly as it could incite the need to laugh. "Is that what you tell yourself about Ty, man?"

Quay shook his head, grinning as he swallowed a bit of his drink. "I've never told myself that about Ty, but I think it's damn time I started."

***

"My team should be arriving within the next few days and then we'll be able to get firm ideas down," Ty shared, during a morning meeting with Quest and the top executives at Ramsey Group. Quay wasn't there which; in Ty's opinion made the gathering far more enjoyable.

"Well, unless anyone has more questions?" Quest stood and posed the question, pausing to leave time to voice questions. "In that case, meeting adjourned," he said, when the group remained silent. "Ty? Stay as long as you like, I'm headed out," he called.

"Thanks!" Ty was already sealing her notes in the chic black leather portfolio she carried.

Alone in such spectacular surroundings, Ty took the time to stroll around the fantastic office. She'd never had the opportunity to do so before and was determined to give herself the grand tour. Bobbie had often told her daughter that the office was the inanimate replica of its owners: dark, overpowering and then some. Tykira was studying a painting above the gas fireplace, when the elevator doors opened.

"Quest?" Ty heard someone move about in another part of the office.

~~~

Quay stilled, having retrieved a stack of mail from his desk. After last night, he figured it was best that he not attend the meeting that morning. He hadn't planned on Ty still being there, but no way was he about to complain. Tossing the mail aside, he followed the sound of her voice.

Tykira left the painting and went to say her goodbyes to Quest. Her steps slowed and then drew to a complete halt when she spied the man in the doorway.

It wasn't the olive plaid suit coat he wore over a coordinating gray black shirt and no tie that made him appear such a force, it was his stance. Quay's demeanor always struck her as silk sheathing a sword. It was as though he were ready for confrontation, always on guard in spite of the easy aura that followed him like mist. Unconsciously, she took a step backward.

"Looks like I missed the meeting," he noted.

Ty glanced down at her black suede boots and smiled. "I get the feeling you planned it that way," she challenged softly.

Quay nodded, easing one hand inside his trouser pockets. "Considering the way you high-tailed it out of the Sorenson...I figured my presence here would be the last thing you'd want. I didn't know you'd still be here."

Ty cleared her throat at his mention of her sudden hotel check out and return to her mother's way-too empty house. She tucked the portfolio beneath her arm. "That's about to change, " she said.

"Tyke," he called, smoothly hindering her progress to the door.

Just as smoothly, Ty evaded his grasp. "What do you want, Quay?"

He didn't mean to allow his desire to flash so quickly, but he couldn't help it. She was like a drug he'd only sampled once and was dying to try again. His thoughts were almost totally centered on what it would be like to have her now.

"Incredible," Ty breathed, her lovely doe eyes narrowing with disbelief. "You have no real feelings at all where I'm concerned, do you? It's just like yesterday to you, isn't it? The way you treated me so long ago?"

"Could you accept an apology based on the fact that it *was* so long ago?" he stepped forward, his dark gaze studying her face.

"The things you said at the reception, weren't so long ago."

Quay winced as though she'd slapped him. "I can't believe you remember that," dry humor laced the revelation.

Ty's lashes fluttered. "I remember everything," she refused to break eye contact. By then, Quay was standing right before her. She had dressed for business, stylish and impeccable in the straight, front split skirt and matching button blazer. Still, the familiar feeling of being diminutive and sweetly feminine and powerfully aroused all swirled together.

Quay's piercing black eyes studied hers as though he could read her mind and knew how he affected her.

"You remember everything, hmmm?" he taunted, simultaneously tugging her close and taking her mouth in a throaty kiss.

Ty couldn't think to resist, only to curl her fingers weakly around the lapels of his jacket.

"Quay," she moaned when the kiss broke for a split second. She needed him more in this way- this basic way- that he could ever know. Moaning again, she began to mimic the motions of his tongue. She thrust hers deeply into his mouth and trembled when he groaned in response.

Their bodies were a perfect fit; always had been. The kiss was like heaven. His hands roamed her body, skirting her hips and then traveling upward to mold her torso beneath the snug blazer. He touched her with the patience of a skilled, giving lover who possessed the power to make her swoon, gasp and beg for fulfilment.

This was the man, Ty thought crying out softly when his big hands cupped her breasts. He was the *only* man she'd ever felt even remotely compelled to give herself to. For her there was no other, she admitted feeling his fingers slipping inside the front of her blazer to stroke the lush cleavage bubbling over the top of the lace camisole she wore.

The realization chilled her suddenly. No, for her, there had been no other. Sadly, he didn't feel the same. Worse, he never had.

Quay could sense a change in the way she responded to his touch. Something had chilled and he knew she was having second thoughts about her participation in their encounter. He released her slowly and with great reluctance. As though it were the most important task, he removed the lipstick smudged at the corner of her mouth with the pad of his thumb.

When he walked away, Ty pressed her hand to her heart as though that would still its rampant beating. She prayed her legs would support her until she made it to her car.

A LOVER'S PRETENSE

~FOUR~

Quest's gray stare was fixed on his laptop which was perched on the coffee table. "Maybe we should have a dinner party," he suggested absently while trying to concentrate on his game of online chess.

Mick shook her head, her eyes fixed on a computer screen as well. "Haven't you done enough meddling?" she responded in a tone that held an absent aura similar to her husband's. Seated behind the massive cherry-wood desk in his study, she performed her daily internet scouring for possible leads into the case.

Quest grimaced at his wife's mention of the dinner fiasco earlier that week. "Just bad communication," he excused. "Besides, you should've told Quay not to bring a date when you invited him to be there."

Mick's lips parted and she looked up. "I told him it was just going to be the three of us. How was I supposed to know, he'd bring a date? He hasn't been out with anyone in two years," she argued gently, her gaze narrowing mischievously as she refocused on the desktop screen. "Anyway, *you're* his twin. You should've psychically tapped in and realized he was going to do something stupid." She pointed out in a haughty tone and was promptly hit in the side of the head by the pillow Quest threw.

"Her crew's coming in today," he shared, folding his arms across the Seahawks jersey that emphasized the striking breadth of his biceps and chest. "It might be a nice touch to throw a dinner party for the group. It's sure to be a grueling project and everyone should start off as comfortable as possible."

"Sounds like you've already put a lot of thought into this," Mick was still focused on her screen.

Quest shrugged. "We could have it here, make it very relaxed. We could even cook all the food."

Mick finally looked toward her husband where he sat before the coffee table. "We? You *and* me? Hmph, you're just full of bad ideas today, aren't you?" she teased, leaning back in the chair as she crossed her bare legs. "Do you know what'll happen if we're tied down in a kitchen together?"

Quest blinked, his gray eyes settling on his wife. "Tied down, huh?" he appraised the line of her shapely chocolate form much of which was left bare by the cotton shorts jumper she wore.

Mick shook her head. "Stop Quest."

"Not unless you come over here," he challenged.

Her lashes fluttered and the familiar stirring someplace unmentionable told Mick that was a challenge she would definitely not back away from. "Oh...if you insist," she sighed, leaning close to the PC. "Just let me shut this thing down...can't be," she whispered then and her head tilted just slightly.

Quest's brows drew close. "What?"

Mick was already reaching for the phone and dialing the number to the Police Department in Savannah, Georgia.

Quest left the floor and came to perch his tall frame against the side of his desk.

"Jillian Red, please," Mick was speaking to the person on the other end of the line. She chewed her bottom lip as her nails tapped out a quick tune along the desk.

"Jillian Red."

"Michaela Sellars," Mick hoped her name would sound familiar.

There was a slight pause, and then laughter filtered through the receiver. Mick realized she had indeed connected with her former contact during her reporting days. Of course, Jill refused to part with any information on herself until Mick shared what had been going on in her own life.

"Girl what are you doing down south? Was the windy city too much for you?" Mick was asking.

Jillian was laughing. "That is a very long and dramatic story."

"Well are you still in forensics?"

"Hmph, the powers that be at my *lovely* former precinct didn't seem to appreciate the fact that I was good at my job."

"Uh-oh."

"Mmm, anyway it seemed that I was getting too close to solving my last case and they trumped up some cause to remove me from my team and the force altogether."

"Damn," Mick whispered.

"Story of my life. So now, I'm in charge of the cold cases for the SPD." Jill explained. "It was the only position I could find that was even *remotely* stimulating." She confided.

"So are you working on anything now?" Mick asked.

"Just finishing up reports on a case I just closed."

"Congratulations!"

"Please! I should be congratulating *you*," Jill said, referring to the self-history Mick gave earlier in their conversation. "Successful author *and* happily married woman? Sounds like life is good."

"Oh it is," Mick softly confirmed, tugging on Quest's hand as she spoke, "but even a happily married woman could use a helping hand every now and again."

"Do tell."

"Are we still close enough to exchange professional favors?"

"Of course. Whatcha got?"

Mick smiled. Releasing Quest's hand, she scooted closer to the desk. "Actually it's something I think *you* have- a cold case."

Jill laughed shortly. "Yeah, I've got tons of those."

"Well, if you can crack this one, I'll bet the SPD would create a forensics position for you."

Jill was silent for a few moments as she processed the possibility. "Well don't keep me in suspense girl, what's the case?"

Mick looked up at Quest. "It's who, Jill. Sera Black."

***

Ty stretched, luxuriating in the security of crisp, petal pink cotton sheets and thick quilts. Her eyes opened to thin, doe-shaped slits as though she were uncertain what she might see. The sight of her mother, caused a smile to widen on her face.

"Good morning," she called, seeing her mom brought a rush of warmth to her body.

Roberta 'Bobbie' Lowery looked up from setting out breakfast in the small alcove in the bedroom. Seeing her daughter; nestled in bed, brought laughter lilting into the air. Tykira looked every bit the little girl and Bobbie realized then how much she'd truly missed having her home.

"Good morning, baby. Did you sleep well?" Bobbie asked.

Ty stretched again, curling her fingers around the edge of the pillow cases. "I slept very well. Even though my room doesn't look the same," she added slyly.

Bobbie's head full of coarse tresses bounced merrily when she laughed. "Honey please don't scold an old lady for trying to spice things up."

"Isn't your life spicy enough Miss Jetsetter?" Ty teased.

"You're right," Bobbie sighed. "I'm hardly ever here. Those Ramseys got me flying from one part of the world to another."

Ty threw back her covers. "*Anyway,* you love it."

Bobbie's look was pure cunning. "Sure I do, but they might stop sending me on these all-expense paid things if they knew that."

The room filled with laughter.

"Now, I've got coffee and Danish," Bobbie announced, clasping her hands together as she looked down at the cozy table. "We'll finish the rest of our breakfast downstairs," she decided.

"Mmm coffee and Danish…conversation food," Ty guessed, having left the bed to stroll toward the alcove. Obviously, her mother was in the mood to talk and she had a pretty good idea about the subject. Taking a seat on one of the cushioned cream armchairs she leaned forward and smelled the pot of coffee. "Mmm…Hazelnut. You want to discuss Quay," she surmised.

"Stop being a smart-aleck," Bobbie ordered, with a roll of her eyes as she took a seat. "I know you've seen him."

"I've seen him," Ty's easy expression changed a bit. "And?"

Ty helped herself to coffee. "He's gorgeous."

Bobbie rolled her eyes again. "I know *that*. What else?"

Ty kept her gaze averted. "What do you mean 'what else'?"

"Have you talked?"

Ty eased a stray lock behind her ear. "About what? We haven't seen each other in fifteen years," *more like two years,* she added silently, recalling the wedding reception.

"Exactly," Bobbie said.

Groaning, Ty focused on choosing one of the heavenly Danish from the white floral print china plate. "Mommy have you forgotten the way things ended between us? Sorry, but that's not a conversation I want to replay or memories I want to relive."

Bobbie broke a cinnamon Danish in half. "You're still in love with him."

Ty wouldn't deny it. "What good will it do?" she tucked her long legs beneath her on the chair. "Nothing would change. Quay isn't as outwardly cold to me as he used to be, but there's still a distance. I feel it in myself. I feel it in him too. It's as though he wants to be warm, but then…I don't know," she shook her head and concentrated on adding sugar and cream to the coffee. "Something always changes and that's when I pull away and start to remember. Then I get angry with myself for- for-"

Bobbie reached over to pat her daughter's hand. "I understand. Do you think there's a chance that he's trying to make things right between the two of you?"

Ty frowned over the question. "I don't know why."

"Oh boy," Bobbie shook her head. "So beautiful and successful, but so dense at times." "Mommy?!"

"Is it possible, that he still loves you as much as you love him?"

"After all this time?"

Bobbie waved her hand. "What's so crazy about that? *Your* feelings haven't changed."

"But this is Quay we're talking about," Ty's brown eyes hardened with agitation. "And if he loved me, then why would he have treated me so coldly all those years ago?"

"Honey you two were babies and Quay was just young and stupid. My guess is now he sees what he's missed and he doesn't want to lose you again. Personally, I've wanted to kick his butt for the way things ended between the two of you. But a part of me believes there was more to that entire mess than he ever let on to you or to anyone else."

Ty shook her head, refusing to let her spirits soar over her mother's perception. "I just can't see that," she blew at the surface of her coffee before helping herself to a taste.

"Have you ever just come right out and asked him why he treated you that way?" Bobbie challenged.

Ty's lips parted, but she couldn't respond. She wanted to tell her mother that she already knew why. Unfortunately, telling Bobbie that Quaysar Ramsey had gotten what he wanted from her and was done or that she'd given him her virginity and he'd given her his ass to kiss didn't seem like prime info to be shared in a mother daughter talk.

Thankfully, Bobbie felt that she'd given her daughter enough to think about and decided to leave Tykira be. "Get showered and come down for the rest of your breakfast," she said.

***

Tykira stepped outside the express elevator and into the Ramsey twin's dark, posh penthouse office. She cleared her throat purposefully, hoping one of them- preferably Quest- would appear and they could get the meeting underway. In spite of her dramas with Quay, she had become very involved and inspired by the monumental project.

Ty received her wish, when Quest stepped from the elevator car a short while later.

"Where's your crew?" Quest was asking once they'd finished hugging.

Ty set her black portfolio to the credenza. "They called from the plane to tell me they were just landing," she tossed her thick locks across her shoulders as she secured another larger portfolio beneath her arm.

"Sounds good," Quest nodded as a curious light brightened his gray eyes. "So does the project have your creative juices flowing yet?" he folded his arms across the oatmeal heather polo shirt he sported.

"Does it?" Ty patted the portfolio under her arm. "Ideas started flowing as soon as I left the office after our first meeting."

Quest's sleek brows rose. "Impressive."

"Let me show you," Ty waved Quest toward his desk. The portfolio housed several preliminary sketches, which she spread out on the huge polished surface of the desk. "I'm not sure if the group prefers something more old world style or a more modern look for the rail," she motioned towards the sketches as she spoke. "Maybe they'd like a mix of both styles to show in the finished design."

Quest tugged the long sleeves of his shirt above his forearms. "This is somethin'," he marveled, his gaze intent as he studied the work.

Tykira and Quest were still reviewing the drawings when Quay arrived in the main office.

"Man, you gotta see this. Ty's got some really good sketches for the rail here," Quest glanced at his brother from across his shoulder.

Quay remained silent, unbuttoning the raspberry suitcoat he wore over a jet black shirt. Instead of joining the twosome at the desk, he took a seat at the back of the room and watched from afar.

Almost a week had passed since he and Ty had kissed in that very room. Since that time, his well-known and well-feared temper had begun a slow simmer. Quaysar Ramsey was not a man known for his patience-especially when it came to wooing a woman. He'd never had to be patient when the women came tumbling at his feet. A kiss, a soft-spoken compliment or glance usually did the trick. Many times it had taken far less. As usual, Ty had him stumped. Clearly, she didn't trust him-that was for sure. He knew if he could win that back, she would be his.

Of course, something as precious as winning back trust didn't happen overnight. Therein lay his problem. His thoughts were progressively filled with images of them together so long ago. They were just kids then and still that encounter was the standard by which he'd judged all others. There had been no equal and he knew the only other encounter that could compete would be with her.

Ty tried to keep her mind on Quest and what he was saying, but all she could do was curse herself for wearing the businesslike yet alluringly feminine suit for the meeting. The beige tweed skirt suit, didn't do a damn thing but call attention to her thighs thanks to the high split in the back of the skirt. Not only could she feel Quay's ebony stare on her, she could see it each time she cast a casual glance across her shoulder to see if he'd left the room. No surprise, he hadn't gone anywhere. He just sat there and continued to roam her body with so much familiarity; as though he'd become her lover that morning instead of fifteen years ago.

"These are terrific Ty- just terrific. I can't get over it."

Quest's excitement over the sketches roused Ty's amusement. "I can't wait to see your reaction when you see the real thing," she teased.

"Quay man, you should see this!" Quest once again beckoned his brother. He'd already turned back to scour the sketches further and didn't hear his twin's reply.

"I'm sure it's as good as it looks," Quay's gaze remained unwavering and trained on Ty.

She heard every word.

Quest was shaking his head. "You can really make somethin' that looks like this?" he marveled.

Ty laughed aloud. "I can't believe you're so taken by this when Ramsey creates such phenomenal stuff."

"Mmm hmm, but our stuff is stationary, not moving from place to place," Quest argued.

"Haven't you traveled by train before?" Ty folded her arms over her tailored mocha shirt with its cuffed sleeves.

"I haven't been on a train since me and Quay went to visit our grandparents in Savannah when we were in college. Remember Quay?" Quest recalled the trip they'd taken to visit their mother's folks.

"I remember," Quay responded slowly, more interested in Ty's reaction to Quest's mention of Savannah. He could tell it had definitely affected her. Yes, she was remembering too.

The silence, caught Quest's attention and he tuned into the heaviness of the moment. Clearing his throat, he backed away from the desk and rubbed his hands together.

"I better go check on the refreshments for your crew when they get here," he made his way out of the office.

Ty turned and leaned against the desk, her head bowed. Quay finally relinquished his seat in the back of the office and came to take his place next to her.

"Remember how much fun we used to have at my grandparent's place?" he asked.

Ty let out a deep breath and nodded. "Almost everything fantastic that happened to me, happened in Savannah," she admitted.

Quay inched closer, his shoulder brushing hers. "Remember that week?"

Ty wouldn't pretend to misunderstand. "I remember it. I could never forget it."

Quay's fingers had been aching to touch her since he'd seen her there in the office. Now he gave into his desire and trailed his fingers across the line of her cheek.

Ty leaned into the touch only briefly, before she bristled and moved away. "I'm sure many girls remember the Ramsey estate," she tossed her head back.

Quay winced, the barb causing a flash of hurt to appear in his dark eyes. "I never took other girls there, Tykira."

"Unless they were virgins, right?" she wanted to believe the place had been as special for him as it had been for her and she was failing.

Quay eased away from the desk and moved to stand before her. "You're the *only* one I ever took there," he stared directly into her eyes. "You're the only one I ever wanted to take there."

Ty tilted her head back again, hoping to prevent unexpected tears from spilling. Quay's eyes locked in on the thick, glossy fullness of her hair tumbling down her back.

"You only took me there once," she quietly reminded him.

He cupped both hands around her neck and propped his thumbs beneath her chin. "*That* was the biggest mistake I ever made."

"Quay..." she breathed, her words ending on a moan when he stepped closer.

His hands lowered to her thighs, cupping them gently as his lips trailed the curve of her jaw. The kiss was slow and unhurried and every bit of Quaysar Ramsey being something he never was-the giver instead of the taker. He taunted her mouth with slow lunges that were light and teasing. His hands massaged the firmness of her thighs, loving the feel of strength mixed with feminine allure he felt there. How he wanted to show this woman that his very last intention was to purposely hurt her. Protecting her was what drove him, loving her was almost driving him mad. She was everything to him and; in trying to do the best thing, he'd wound up losing the best thing he'd ever known.

Ty was also intent on being the taker- taking everything Quay had to give. She yearned for him to touch her with demand but he was gentle and that was just as torturously sweet. He caressed her, skirting her breasts, brushing the backs of his massive hands across the nipples straining against her blouse. When his fingers disappeared beneath her skirt, she cried out softly in pleasure. When he simply plied the satiny inner walls of her thighs with his touch and went no further, she arched and rubbed against him hoping to encourage him to move on.

Quay ended the kiss, pressing a soft peck to the corner of her mouth. Not wanting the moment to end, she reflexively tightened her thighs about his waist. Quay only nuzzled the soft flesh below her ear and smoothed his hand across her hip to persuade her to release him. Knowing it wouldn't be long before Quest returned, he wanted to give Ty and himself, for that matter, the chance to catch their breaths and become presentable.

It was a feat almost impossible for Ty to accomplish. Everything shook uncontrollably. Finally, she braced her hands against the edge of the desk and took deep breaths until the feeling passed.

Quay had returned to his seat, just as the elevator doors opened and Quest arrived with Tykira's crew in tow. The not-too-nice side of Quay's temper had subsided to a happy place during his time alone with Ty. It returned then, at a boil that time, as he watched her run to greet the group of men who had arrived with his brother. Of course, they each had to hug, kiss and hold her close for longer than he thought was necessary.

Since Quest had already met the guys, Ty turned to make the introductions to Quay. Quest caught onto his twin's mood when Quay simply waved from his place at the rear of the office. Closing his eyes for a brief prayer, Quest only asked that they make it through the meeting without incident.

But Quay was in no mood for a meeting. He was more interested in surveying Ty with her group of designers. He was especially interested in the one who had been holding her hand since he'd stepped into the office. Quay didn't like it and had no problems admitting that. He disliked it so much, in fact, that he went over to Ty and intruded on the cozy conversation she was holding with Samuel Bloch.

"Why don't we get this meeting started," he suggested keeping his hand at the small of Ty's back while escorting her from Sam's side.

The group took their places in the conference room also nestled within the penthouse office. Ty remained cool and posed while spreading the rail drawings on the table, but inside her mind was racing. She was more than curious about Quay's mood, she was downright dumbfounded. She could barely go for five seconds without him touching her someplace and his unsettling dark eyes practically bored holes through Sam. Thankfully, only she seemed to notice.

"Alright," she cleared her throat while leaning close to the table. "Quest's already taken a look at the prelim sketches I faxed to you guys last week. He seems pleased," she smiled when Quest nodded. "Still, these are only preliminary mock-ups, we've got a long way to go."

Her words, prompted heavy discussion then. Obviously, everyone was stimulated by the demands of the project. Even Quay let go of some of his moodiness to offer his own suggestions regarding the design. In truth, he found it incredible that Tykira had such a flare for the gritty business of railcar design. However, he knew if he were to compliment her on her expertise, she was likely to think he was patronizing her.

"My wife Michaela and I will be having a dinner party to get you all acquainted with the rest of our executive team," Quest was saying. "We'll be in touch with the particulars and if there's nothing else pressing right now…" he paused for last minute comments, "we'll meet back here in the morning," he finished.

"Tyke would you stay?" Quay asked.

Ty flashed a guarded look, but offered no comment. The rest of the guys were preparing to leave and she had no desire to be alone with Quay again. Still, she managed a nod in response to his request. The last thing she needed was to draw attention to what was going on between the two of them.

"Guys, I'm staying with my mom now, but we'll meet later

302

at the hotel, alright?"

"Sounds good," Morton Garner called in response to Ty's question.

"We'll meet you in the hotel lounge," Gary Charles suggested.

"I'll just ask for you at the front desk," Ty added.

The group said their goodbyes and Quest offered to show them out. The instant Ty heard the elevator doors slide shut behind them, she bolted from the chair she occupied next to Quay.

"What are you doing?" she demanded to know.

"What's goin' on with you and Sam?" he appeared unfazed by her words.

"Sam?" Ty rolled her eyes when Quay only stared in response. "He's the head of my crew."

"And what else?"

"He's also my friend."

"And what else?"

"What else, is none of your business," her lovely face had contorted to form a harsh glare.

Quay focused on the silver pen he manipulated between his fingers. "Have you slept with him?"

"What if I have?" Ty challenged, folding her arms across her chest. Her glare lost a bit of its intensity when Quay snapped the pen in half. Dismissing her unease, she stepped closer to the conference table. "What if I sleep with a different one of them every night? It's none of your damn business." She was sick of being sweet and civil.

"I gave you everything Quay and you used it to make me feel lower than dirt," she turned away then lest he see an emotion other than anger fill her eyes. "I doubt you've got any real interest in this side of the project Quay. So why don't you just stay away from it? Otherwise I might feel entitled to inflict a little pain of my own." She turned to face him then. "I think I've damn well earned that right, don't you?" She swiped her belongings into her portfolio and left the room while silently cursing the fact that there was no door for her to slam.

"Small piece of advice, Quay. Our waitress is liable to spit in both our salads if you're more rude to her than you've already been."

Quay slanted his twin a black glare before tossing back what remained of his drink.

"Just a little advice," Quest said, his hazy gaze still focused on his menu.

"You're enjoying this, aren't you?"

"Damn right."

Obviously stunned by his twin's quick, honest response, Quay slammed his glass to the table.

Quest's left-dimpled grin deepened as he used his napkin to wipe away remnants of the brown liquor that had sloshed from his brother's glass. "You deserve exactly what you got and more. I'm surprised Ty waited this long to tell you to go to hell."

Quay's fist slammed to the table in response.

Quest finally ceased his taunts and leaned back in his chair. "You wanna talk about it?"

Quay shrugged. "Why should I when you're right?"

"Give it time, Quay," Quest tossed his napkin to his twin's side of the table. "You hurt her. Bad."

"There were reasons."

"That's right. There were reasons. Maybe it's time to live in the present, hmm?"

"And that would serve what purpose?" Quay queried in his cockiest tone.

Quest rolled his eyes and focused on his menu again. "Tykira's like family. The purpose it would serve is you'd be acting civil toward someone we've known all our lives."

Still brooding, Quay lost a bit of his agitation and considered his brother's words. As soon as his mood began to mellow, he felt his frustration mount once more. His midnight stare narrowed with murderous intensity toward a couple who'd just entered the dining room.

"What are you having? Quay?" Quest glanced up. Seeing the expression his twin wore, sent his mind totally off eating. "Quay?" he sat a bit straighter in his seat. He knew the look well. Any second, Quay would be pounding some poor fool's face. Quickly, Quest glanced around to determine what had gotten the man's jock in a bunch. Then he saw Tykira, beautiful and glowing and laughing at something Sam Bloch had just whispered in her ear.

"Son of a bitch," Quay muttered his hand too weak to even clench a fist.

"Quay..." Quest called in warning, already poised to stop his brother from storming across the restaurant.

Quay however, didn't have the strength to stand let alone *storm* anywhere. A cloud had settled across his brain, rendering him dizzy and completely helpless. His entire body felt weak. His heart was in his throat.

"What's she doing with him?" he whispered.

Quest opened his mouth and then closed it, trying to put his opinion into the most calming terms. "They're business partners, man. I'm sure it's just something to do with the rail." He explained, knowing he probably wouldn't have believed that either.

"I need to get out of here," Quay tugged at the banded collar of his shirt.

Quest was already reaching for his wallet. "You need me to go with you?"

Quay grinned. "Hell yeah, if you expect me to leave without makin' a fool of myself."

Tossing a few bills to the table, Quest stood and kept a firm grip on his brother's upper arm to escort him from the dining room. Of course, the twins never went anywhere unnoticed. Such was the case that day, as every woman who caught sight of them helped herself to an intense study of their heavenly good looks and powerful, lean muscular frames. Not surprisingly, Ty saw them as they walked by.

Quest jerked his brother to a halt, nodding while closing the distance to Ty. "Hey love," he whispered, drawing her into a hug.

"Quest," Ty cursed her fluttering lashes as she fought to keep her eyes off Quay.

"You two got time to join us?" Sam asked while shaking hands with Quest.

"Nah, we gotta run but thanks," Quest winked at Ty when he noticed her relieved expression. Then, catching Quay's arm again, he and his brother left the restaurant.

A LOVER'S PRETENSE

~FIVE~

"You know, we've got food here too?"

Ty smiled at Mick's query and responded with a mock toast of her glass. "This is insurance," she shared.

"Against?" Mick probed.

"Your brother-in-law."

Amused then, Mick leaned next to the bar. "What's going on and is it the reason why he's yet to show up to our little gathering to get your crew acquainted with Ramsey?" unmasked laughter colored her words.

Ty studied a curl dangling from her high ponytail. "You're a smart lady," she tossed away the curled lock.

"Will you give me a few details?" Mick smoothed one hand across her form-fitting ecru trousers as she took a seat on one of the barstools.

Ty helped herself to another sip of her second Martini. "Please Mick, I know Quest has told you the story of my pathetic

307

involvement with his twin."

"I know it didn't work out," Mick took the glass from Ty and placed it on the bar. "I know you were hurt," she said.

"Hmph, hurt," Ty rolled her eyes toward Mick. "And I should get over it, right?"

"Ty-"

"Hell, you're right. It's been, what? Fifteen years? Oh Mick, every day I tell myself the same thing. Do you know what it's like to pine for a man as long as I have and know you probably *never* cross his mind?"

"Oh sweetie," Mick whispered, pulling Ty into a hug. "Honey have you ever wondered if Quay acted the way he did for a reason?"

Ty sighed, and then pulled away. "You sound like my mother," she shook her head, "I guess the man is just damn good at charming his way into the heart of a woman. No one can believe the worst of him."

"Seriously Ty, do you think there could be more going on here than you're aware of?"

"Then, why wouldn't he just tell me what it is and stop playing these games. It's gone on long enough, don't you think?"

Mick agreed and hated she couldn't do more to reassure Tykira. Her amber eyes lit up however, when she looked across the room. "Maybe he'll tell you if you just ask him," she said.

Ty noticed Mick's expression and followed the line of her gaze. Seeing Quay sent her heart jerking ferociously beneath the toffee colored off shoulder blouse she wore. When Mick patted her hand and walked away, Ty finished the last of her Martini. She was accepting her next refill, when she felt him standing behind her.

"I'm sorry," he stood there with his hands pushed into his chestnut colored trousers as he waited for her response.

Tykira tapped her nails along the sides of the glass she held before turning around to face him. "Do you realize you've already apologized to me twice and I still have no idea what's really going on?"

Quay bowed his head, his brows rising briefly as he

acknowledged the truth in her statement. "I guess I'm jealous," he confided finally.

Ty couldn't have appeared more shocked. "Jealous? What could you possibly be jealous of?" her tone was incredulous. It never occurred to her to ask *why* he was jealous when he'd pretty much shunned anything meaningful between them.

Quay hiked his thumb across his shoulder. "Let's try how close you are to your crew for starters."

"Yes, we're close but that's all," Ty swore.

"What about Sam?" Quay's probe was soft.

Ty rolled her eyes. "He wanted it to be more, but I didn't."

Choosing not to show how pleased he was by her words, Quay simply nodded once.

Laughter fluttered past Ty's lips then as she observed him. "You're something else to be jealous of five men," she folded her arms over her chest. "What's five me compared to, what? Two-three hundred women?" she noted.

Quay shook his head, allowing his unease to show. "I guess it would take about that many to drive you out of my head."

"Why would you want to drive *me* from your head?" She demanded, the simply spoken comment affected her more sharply than she realized. "What did I do to make you want me out of your life, Quay? I mean, I know I was a virgin the last time we slept together but was I *that* pathetic in the sack?"

Quay's darkly handsome features tightened with the regret he felt. "You're wrong," he whispered, moving a step closer. "There were reasons why-"

"What reasons?" she cried, frustrated that after all this time he still couldn't just come right out and tell her why he'd treated her with such contempt. Setting an unfeeling mask in place, she fixed him with a level glare. "I can understand you not wanting to be my man Quay," she began, "but after all the years we've known each other, how close we'd become long before sex ever entered the picture, I can't believe you won't even be friend enough to tell me the truth," she hoped her words might penetrate the wall around the explanation she truly felt he wanted to give. Unfortunately, he refused to give in and; rather than beg more than she already had, she moved off the barstool and walked away.

***

Ty's head was bent in concentration the next afternoon as she sketched a quick design that had come to her while she'd picked at her soup and salad. She was practically oblivious to all else around her, but managed to look up in time to thank the waiter when he freshened her tea.

"Everything alright, ma'am?" The waiter asked, having heard has gasp soon after she'd thanked him.

Ty swallowed and managed a nod. "Yes, yes, thank you."

The waiter nodded and moved on as Ty set aside her pad. She'd glimpsed Quay across the room and was momentarily stunned by his presence. Common sense won out after a while and she decided it was too much of a coincidence, him just *happening* to be there. Leaning back in her chair, she used a steady gaze to beckon him to her table. She tilted her head back slightly when he stood and began to head in her direction. Ty's gaze faltered only a few times as she observed the blatant stares of want that followed him. A man with that sort of power over women is a man with no interest-or need- for *one* woman.

Keep things cold, Ty. Get your job done and get the hell out of here, she told herself.

"May I?"

Ty offered no reply when he sat down.

"I only wanted to apologize again," he smiled softly when she fixed him with a confused look. "For dinner," he suddenly appearing uneasy. "And the cocktail party the other night. I'd like to take you out and make up for it."

"Make up?" Ty whispered, then winced. "No Quay."

Quay leaned close, blinking when he noticed her flinch. "Are you afraid of me, Tykira?"

"No Quay…never," she saw the distress filtering his pitch stare, "it's just easier to keep our…whatever this is between us…it's easier to keep it going," she decided while reaching for her portfolio. "Let's not try to go back and make up for anything. I don't think I have the energy," she almost laughed.

"Good afternoon, Mr. Ramsey. Will you be dining with the lady?"

Ty stood before Quay could answer the waiter who'd returned to the table. "The lady is done. Mr. Ramsey will be taking care of the check," she said before walking away.

~~~

Ty cursed and mumbled below her breath as she stomped back to her rented Jeep Cherokee. She'd just thrown her portfolio and tote bag into the back seat, when her arm was caught, stifling any further movement.

"Don't walk away from me, Ty," Quay made her face him.

Thoroughly amused somehow, Tykira's full laughter lilted in the air. "Walk away from *you*? You're one to talk Quay Ramsey, and get your damn hands off me!" she slapped at the hold he had around her arm.

Quay did as he was told, yet stepped closer to invade more of her personal space. "I can't handle this," he confessed, his nose outlining the curve of her jaw as he inhaled her scent. "I can't think straight having you around...and that's dangerous, Tyke."

She allowed herself to lean into his frame, desperate to indulge in a moment of the warmth residing between them. "Then please do as I asked, Quay," she managed. "Distance yourself from the project and-"

"I can't do that," he shook his head even as he remained close to her.

"You mean you won't," Ty forced herself to resist crying out in response to his mouth trailing the line of her neck. She tried to move, but he held her against the side of the Cherokee. "You don't want me, Quay- not really. It's just your guilt...and hormones talking."

The arrogant dimpled smirk appeared. "And I suppose *your* hormones are on vacation?" he unbuttoned the champagne suede blazer that outlined her bosom adoringly.

Ty shoved lightly at his chest. "What is it with you? You think you're so fantastic, that no woman could get over you once you've had her?"

Quay kept his head bowed. His dark eyes fixed on that hand cupping a plump breast. "I don't know about that, Tyke," he studied the mounds, partially exposed where he'd undone her blazer. "I know *you* haven't gotten over me," he applied a proprietary squeeze to her cleavage.

Ty slapped him so hard her palm burned. Yet it was nothing compared to the satisfaction that coursed through her. Her glee was short-lived, though as he caught both her wrists and held them together at the small of her back.

"Can't you just let me do my job and go?" she tried a softer approach. Her doe-like gaze wider and pleading. "Quay? Can't you at least do that for me? At least that?"

Jerking her forward, Quay smothered her mouth beneath his. Tiny whimpers fluttered within Tykira's throat at the sensation of his plundering tongue which rotated and thrust deep. Ty felt her eyes sting with tears as she kissed him back. In spite of it all, he could still reduce her to a pool of nothing with just a kiss.

Quay pulled back, then treated himself to just one more taste of her lips. "No I can't," he wanted to say; *letting you go is something I don't think I can ever do again.* He pressed his forehead to hers and walked away.

***

Tyke Designs began its project with all the gusto they were known for. The railcars would be a dazzling sight everyone was sure. Ty had been working round the clock not only to ensure that the team would meet its deadline, but also in hopes of avoiding Quay and to keep her every waking thought off of him.

She was passing the receptionist's desk one day, when a thought came to mind and she began to sketch right there. Almost five minutes passed before she was interrupted.

"Hey guys," she called to three Ramsey Group V.P.s. She recognized them as easily as everyone else she'd come to know during the last several weeks. "What's up?" she set her pad aside as she observed the strained yet polite expressions each man wore.

Steve Owens, glanced at his colleagues when they nudged him forward. "Tykira we um, we hate to come to you with this."

"What?" Ty shook her head when no explanation was forthcoming.

Bailey Gardner chuckled nervously. "Sorry Tykira, we're just tryin' to be tactful."

"I don't think there is a *tactful* approach here guys," Matthew Clark shared before focusing his brown stare on Ty. "This is about Quay," he said.

Her gaze widened briefly, but she nodded. "Go on."

"Well Ty...we know the two of you were close. *Are* close," he corrected.

"We need you to talk to him," Steve urged.

"If you would," Matthew added.

Ty fidgeted with the hem of the red cardigan she wore over a matching knit top. "Talk to him about what?"

The three men exchanged quick glances. "His temper," Matthew said finally.

Ty, regarded the men with renewed interest. "I know Quay can be a little...difficult... but he's not *that* bad."

"We're glad you've been lucky enough not to see that side of him," Steve said.

"Well what's he upset about?" Ty asked, clasping her hands in her lap while she sat perched on the edge of the desk. "Is it about the project?"

"We um...we think it might be about something going on between the two of you," Bailey guessed.

"A disagreement," Matthew tried.

Ty smiled and waved off the perception. "I haven't even spoken to Quay in a couple of weeks."

Again, the three men exchanged glances.

"We know, Ty, it's pretty obvious the two of you are goin' out of your way to ignore each other." Bailey said.

"He may be willing to try ignoring *you* but the rest of us

haven't been so fortunate."

Ty almost laughed at Matthew's words, but noticed how solemn he appeared. "Well what's he done?" she asked.

"When Quay's on a rampage, he's like a mad man. Quest is the only one who can calm him down."

"Probably 'cause they've both got tempers that can leave grown men quaking in their boots," Steve offered and stepped closer to Ty. "Quay'll come down on you-"

"Hard." Bailey interjected.

"For next to nothing," Steve continued, "leave the office too early, feel his wrath, spend too much time chatting at the water cooler, feel his wrath. Disagree with him-"

"You don't want to know," Matthew added.

"We wouldn't think about working for anyone else- they're awesome guys. But times like this…" Bailey shuddered.

"Everyone's a little on edge wanting to make sure this project goes through without a hitch. Having the twins breathing down your neck- even one of 'em- makes the situation even more stressful." Steve said.

"Guys…I'm sure Quay'll cool off soon," Ty tried to assure them.

The men responded with a round of laughter.

"He sure will," Bailey promised.

"And Heaven help the poor bastard who's in the way when he does!" Matthew added.

Steve moved closer. "We took a chance on calling out our boss, because we think you're the only one who's got the power to do something about it. Would you talk to him Ty? Please?"

Knowing nothing but a promise would soothe their worries, Tykira gave the men a nod. When they'd thanked her heavily and walked off, she closed her eyes and groaned.

"If only I weren't about to leave for the day," she whispered once they were out of earshot. Ignoring the voice calling her a coward, she collected her things and left the building.

***

That evening, Michaela had ordered Ty to take a break and they headed off for a girl's night out. Double Q was set to be their final destination.

The two beauties received tons of nods and even more attention when they entered the club. Thanks to the club staff, it wasn't long before most of the male patrons knew Mick was strictly off limits. Tykira, on the other hand appeared to be fair game. She had loads of fun talking and laughing with the scores of interested men who approached her. Unfortunately, every man Ty met wasn't so gentlemanly as she discovered when one of her dance partners got a little *too* friendly.

"So what will it take to get you to wrap those gorgeous legs around my back tonight?" The twenty something over-confident male whispered against Ty's ear.

Prying her fingers out of the back pocket of her snug fitting boot cut jeans, she fixed him with a knowing look. "It wouldn't take anything at all," humor filtered her smoky brown stare. "You've got about a snowball's chance in hell of that happening."

The remark left a sting that caused momentary surprise to flicker in the young man's eyes. Not about to be bested, he eased his arms about her waist, pulling her close again. "Feel that? Impressive, huh?" he curved his fingers into the small of her back to settle her more snuggly against his aroused state.

Not terrible shocked, but very peeved, Ty easily removed his hands from her waist, "At this moment it's more endangered than impressive," she rolled her eyes as she prepared to turn away.

Sadly, the determined young man wasn't willing to let his partner go so easily. His grip tightened in an attempt to force her compliance. The push Ty applied to his chest sent him stumbling and his confidence wavered when a few people laughed.

"Bitch," he reached for her again.

This time, Tykira curled her fingers into the front pockets of his jeans and tugged him close. "Your prized possession down there is about to be bruised and terribly battered in about the time it'll take me to raise my knee. Then you'll see how powerful these gorgeous legs are."

Swallowing noticeably, the man raised his hands and decided not to tangle another minute with the statuesque beauty. He decided to back off a little too late. A split second after he raised his hands, he was jerked away.

It was a moment or so before Ty realized that it was Quay who had pounced upon her dance partner. Then, watching the crowd part as he dragged the man away, she recalled her earlier conversation with the Ramsey VPs about Quay's temper.

"He'll kill him," she breathed, pushing hair away from her face as she rushed after them. "Quay!" her voice was effectively drowned by the thick crowd. Ty had to fight her way through the mass of bodies that had gathered to witness the scene.

There was Quay, beating the man to a bloody mess. Ty could hear Quay telling his victim to leave her alone and asking why he'd been bothering her in the first place. Of course, every word Quay uttered was followed by a vicious blow to some area of the man's face. Security intervened at last and it almost took the entire group of men to pull Quay off the battered club hopper.

"Call an ambulance!" someone ordered.

"Ty!"

"Mick!"

"What happened?!" Mick shouted over the melee.

Ty ran a shaking hand through her tangled hair. "Quay almost beat some guy to death."

"What?!"

"Mick, I can't talk right now. I gotta find Quay!" Ty was already sprinting in the direction she'd seen security take their boss.

Mick was about to follow, when she felt her cell phone vibrate in the breast pocket of her denim jacket. "Yeah?!"

"Mick? What's goin' on there?"

"Jill?!" Mick heard Jillian Red's voice come in faintly beneath the noise from the crowd.

"Can you talk?!" Jill called.

"Gimme a sec," Mick hurried back inside the nearly empty club to take solace in a quiet corridor. "Alright, what'sup?"

Jill laughed. "First, let me thank you for dropping such a hot pot of a case in my lap. Miss Black's death could've been solved years ago and I damn well intend to do so now."

"Have you been able to turn up anything?" Mick took a seat on one of the royal blue velvet settees lining the hallway.

"Let's just be thankful that the SPD of old hadn't tossed their case files- though dusty and cobweb riddled they were," Jill teased, "there's definitely evidence missing," she added, her tone firming.

Mick nodded, having already told Jill about the Ramseys shady dealings regarding the case. "Will this missing evidence put more of a stump in the investigation?"

"Well," Jill sighed, sounding strangely optimistic, "that's what's strange. Even though actual physical evidence gathered at the scene was missing, the files were still there- *detailed* files."

Mick leaned back against the wall. "*How* detailed?"

"An autopsy was performed as well as crime scene workups."

The beginnings of a frown furrowed Mick's brow. "What are you saying?"

"According to this file, samples were taken from Sera Black's body. There was saliva from her breasts, skin under her nails and semen from the vagina as well as trace amounts on her clothing."

"Who did it belong to?" Mick asked, straightening on the settee.

Jill sighed. "The investigation reached a halt after that. There's no record of the samples ever making it to the lab for analysis."

"Damn," Mick grumbled.

"Obviously there's still more investigating to do."

"You said it."

"At least we know we've got a definite case to solve."

"What's your next move?" Mick wanted to know.

"I'm going to speak with the County medical examiner. He's retired and word is, he's in poor health. It may be a long shot to even *try* to get a face to face with him, but I'm gonna try like hell," Jill vowed.

"Thanks girl," Mick breathed, her lashes fluttering. "I feel a lot more positive about this thing knowing you're on it."

"We're gonna bring down whoever's responsible for this. Look, I'll let you know what happens with the M.E., alright?"

"Sounds good, Jill. Talk to you soon," Mick pressed the phone to her forehead when the connection ended.

~~~

Tykira was approaching Quaysar's upstairs office, when the double doors opened and several men hurried out. She could hear Quay roaring for them to leave.

"You may want to give him a minute, Miss," one of the guards advised.

"*Several* minutes," another stressed.

Ty nodded, waiting for the group of men to disappear around the corner before she turned back to the doors. It was now or never, she realized. Besides, she couldn't handle knowing Quay was lashing out at people because of her. Taking a deep breath, she trailed her fingers along the silver door lever before pushing against it and stepping inside.

The office was dim and mellow of course, but Ty spotted him easily. He leaned against the wall next to the tall windows overlooking the downtown area.

"How's your hand?" she inquired, taking short awkward steps closer.

"Fine," his reply was soft.

"Quay what were you thinking?" she folded her arms across the apricot-colored crop jacket she sported. "I could've handled that."

Quay's smiled triggered his right dimple. "I know you could handle it. I was watching you the whole time."

Something about the admission made her breath catch in her throat. "Then what were you thinking?" She managed.

"He shouldn't have been touching you," Quay smoothed a

hand across the cobalt blue shirt that hung outside his sagging jeans.

Ty bowed her head and smiled. "People touch when they dance, Quay."

"And you shouldn't have been dancing with him."

"Why not?" She couldn't help but ask.

"Mick wasn't dancing," he muttered a curse and pushed away from the wall.

Ty shook her head. "That's because nobody dared to ask her. Apparently Quest set that decree before they were even married."

Quay grinned. "Yeah, I taught Q well," he boasted playfully.

Ty rolled her eyes. "Well, the same doesn't go for me. Men will always approach a woman in a club," she hooked her thumbs through the empty belt loops on her jeans.

Quay's dark stare smoldered, raking her body with unmasked possessiveness. "That's because they don't know you're mine," his voice was low sounding as though he hadn't meant to speak the words aloud.

"Are you serious?" Ty tilted her head as she stepped closer to the desk he stood behind.

Quay shrugged, appearing as though what he'd said was no great revelation.

"I'm yours," her eyes narrowed in suspicion as she rounded the maple desk. "I suppose that's why you've treated me so coldly all this time? Or why you're not being straight with me right now?" she challenged.

"I don't want to do this now, Ty," he groaned and began to massage the back of his neck.

"Oh to hell with you. I'm sick of all this damn beating around the bush. You're attacking and snapping at everyone who gets in your way. Is it all related, Quay?"

"Related to what, Ty?"

She was unruffled, by the growling intensity of the question. "Related to what's happening between us."

"Nothing's happening between us," he countered, rolling his eyes as he massaged his nose. "You've kept that clear," the accusation was soft.

"Please Quay," she tossed up her hands and whirled away from the desk. "Since I've come back you've run hot and cold and I know there's something you're not telling me. I've always felt it," she smoothed her hands over her arms to ward off a sudden chill. "What is it?" she faced him again. "Are you trying to spare my feelings? You never cared about them before. Hurting me, humiliating me seemed to be your preferred activities."

At last, Quay slammed his hand against the window. The thick glass vibrated in response. "Damn Ty, hurting you was never the intention!"

"Then what?!"

"Hell, I was trying to protect you!"

The response stopped her cold. "Protect me?" she headed towards him when he turned away. "From what?"

"Tyke I-"

"No. Not this time. You tell me everything," she stood boldly before him. Again, Quay made a move to retreat and she took hold of the hand he'd bruised during the fight. He winced when she added a bit more pressure. "How painful do you want it?" she asked.

"Don't make me go into this, Ty," he set his other hand into the pocket of his jeans. "It's irrelevant anyway."

She smiled, her eyes narrowing. "Good, then you should have no problem telling me about it, then."

Rolling his eyes, Quay started to turn away once more. "Alright, alright," he conceded when the grip tightened on his injured hand. "When we were kids...you know I always had a lot of girls around me right?" he saw the guarded look that flashed on her face. "You also know that none of those relationships ever worked out."

Ty nodded again, not liking the drawn look beginning to cloud his features.

"A lot of that was my fault," Quay took a seat on the corner of his desk. "But Tyke a lot of it had nothing to do with you."

"What are you saying?" She wasn't altogether certain she wanted to know.

"Things began to happen to them. I always felt there was more to it, like it was more than just coincidence."

"What *things*?" Ty probed.

"Out of the clear blue, they'd move away, their parents jobs would be phased out and they'd relocate, some just up and disappeared." Quay shook his head then. "It was all so smooth, no one really questioned it. I began to think I was cursed with girls or something," he laughed and then sobered the instant his eyes met Tykira's. "I never had a relationship with Sera. We almost kissed before you and I were ever intimate. After she died, I knew somehow it was all connected to me and there was no way in hell I'd let the same thing happen to you."

Ty closed her eyes. "Are you trying to tell me that my life was in danger?"

Quay folded his arms across his chest. "I didn't say anything because I didn't want to upset you but I knew as long as we were together...if Wake ever knew-"

"Wake? *Wake Robinson?*"

Quay nodded. "We think he killed Sera and I think if he knew how I really felt about you, you wouldn't be safe."

Ty felt the pressure in her chest, rising as though she couldn't breathe. It wasn't a disturbing feeling, moreover it was exciting, expectant and slowly she proceeded with her next question. "Quay were you only pretending back then? Were you only pretending not to care about me?"

Before he could tell her, 'yes'. Yes, he'd been pretending and doing a piss-poor job of it since his feelings for her were written all over his face. Before he could tell her he loved her and that it had always been her, the desk phone buzzed. Ty shook her head and turned away when he answered the ring.

"Hey Mick," Quay greeted after Michaela had called his name.

"Are you alright? What was that fight about? Is Ty up there

with you?"

Quay chuckled over his sister-in-law's inquiries. "I'm fine. The fight was my fault- I lost my temper and yes, she's right here."

"Good. Listen, something's come up and I need you to give Ty a ride home. I have to leave right now. You don't mind, do you?" Devilment was clear in Mick's every word.

Quay heard it clearly. "I know what you're up to and you're no good at it," he heard Mick suck her teeth over the line.

"I don't care how good I am at it. I just want it to work," she admitted.

Quay ran a hand over his face and groaned.

"Listen, this might put a smile on your face. I got some very interesting news from my contact in Savannah."

"Talk to me," Quay turned to study Ty as she stared out the window. He listened while Mick rehashed her conversation with Jillian Red. What Quay heard, removed any chance of him telling Ty how he really felt. Wake Robinson had killed Sera like she was nothing and he was still out there somewhere. Wake also knew that his supposed old friend was helping to fuel an investigation that could put him behind bars.

While confessing all to Tykira was right and necessary, Quay couldn't shake the feeling that it could be dangerous. Wake was dangerous, so was he for that matter. Wake Robinson, however, was willing to kill and clearly he didn't care who. Quay did. He cared- loved- who very much. He couldn't risk it. Overprotective and unwarranted, perhaps but he couldn't risk it. He wouldn't chance having Wake turn up and catch him off guard when he least expected it.

His onyx stare narrowed as he watched Ty. Oh yes, his guard would most definitely be way down. He'd have nothing but Tykira Lowery on his mind and in his bed. Hell he'd probably never come into the office and there it would be. Yet another beautiful life for Wake to snuff out and fulfill whatever sickness motivated him.

He tuned into the sound of Mick yelling for him to confirm that he'd give Ty a ride and not to have one of his men do it. They needed to talk, she said.

"I'll take her home myself Mick. I promise. I'll call you…Bye."

"Well Quay?" Ty was saying the instant she saw him set the black cordless phone to the desk stand. "Will you answer me? Were you only pretending not to care?"

"It's late," Quay was saying while he rummaged around in his desk drawer until he found what he was looking for, "we can finish this on the way. Mick asked me to take you home."

***

Ty hated being alone in her mother's too huge house, but she was glad Bobbie wasn't there when she and Quay arrived. He was gentleman enough to see her inside and check around for her, but Ty wasn't about to let him off that easily. She was determined to receive an answer to her question and called herself a fool for wanting to hear his response so desperately after all this time. She tried to dismiss the flutter of her heart which anticipated hearing what she most wanted- that she wasn't just another toss for him. That what happened was as special for him as it had been for her.

"Well Quay?"

Massaging his heart through his shirt, Quay bowed his head. "Ty what the hell do you want to hear?" he sighed.

"The truth!" she didn't care anymore how much her emotions were bared to his gaze. Her heart jerked when he turned and fixed her with an incredible smile and look. *That* look…had the power to make a woman physically ache with expectation of a night in his bed. It held a mix of desire and intensity with just a dash of cocky assurance relaying the notion that once he was done, she'd know what it felt like to experience true pleasure.

In spite of 'the look' however, it took Ty a full thirty seconds to realize an answer to her question would not be forthcoming. She heard herself moan before his arm encircled her waist, before his head lowered, before his incredible mouth melded with hers. Answers be damned, she decided. *This* was what she wanted, to be satisfied by this man and only this man. The low, needy moan ended on a gasp that Quay used to his total advantage. Thrusting hot and deep and thoroughly ravaging, he made love to her mouth and instantly reduced her to a mass of sensitivity.

Feeling her melt against him, Quay knew she was his for the taking and taking was exactly what he intended to do. He lost every coherent thought in his head except one: after that night, she'd want nothing more to do with him, he'd see to that.

The kissing scene continued, growing lustier every moment. Tykira was lost and shameless in expressing how desperately she wanted him. Her fingers sought every exposed area of his molasses skin not covered by his clothes. Breaking the kiss, she let her lips glide across the powerful chords in his neck. Her fingers stroked the back of his head, her nails savoring the feel of his soft, close-cut hair. Wantonly, she rubbed herself across his muscular athletic frame, telling him with every movement how deeply she desired him.

For Quay, it was sheer heaven, the feel of her touching every inch of him in perfect alignment. No other woman came close to feeling the way she did in his arms. Taking a fistful of her thick tresses, he kissed her again. Tortured, helpless moans passed his lips every time he stroked the sweetness of her mouth and felt her suckle his tongue in response. Overcome by a need so powerful, his manhood swelled to the point that his pants felt uncomfortably snug.

"Tell me to leave," he whispered, breaking the kiss to graze her jaw with his perfect teeth.

"I can't," she sobbed, her fingers curled so tightly into the crisp fabric of his shirt that she could have ripped it apart. The next thing she felt was him lifting her and walking in the direction of the spiral stairway.

"Where?" he asked against her cheek, kissing her there.

Softly, Ty delivered the directions. Her hand cupped his jaw as she arched deeper into the embrace. Quay shouldered open the door to her bedroom and the shiver that brushed her body had nothing to do with the temperature of the house. Ty was so affected, so in tune to his every move, she trembled as much from arousal as she did from anticipation.

Quay's magnificent features were sharp and focused. He'd imagined her bared to his gaze since he'd seen her two years ago. He prayed nothing would rob him of the treat now. Dexterous fingers unfastened the button fly of her jeans. He only needed to slightly incline his head to kiss her as his hand disappeared below the lacy waistband of her panties.

Ty felt her legs give when his middle finger curled inside her. The pleasure, so desired and so missed left her gasping his name and shifting her leg to take more of the thrusting caress. Her reaction to him was satisfying yes, but there was more. He drew pleasure from *her* pleasure. His intense dark eyes followed her every reaction to his touch. Smoothly, he added his index finger to the caress and Ty clung to him as her forehead fell upon his shoulder.

"Quay please," she begged in the smallest voice.

"Tell me," he moaned at the flood of moisture he felt against his fingers.

"I need more, please," she responded without shame.

His hormones thundered at her breathless confession and he continued to undress her. The buttons on her crop jacket gave way beneath his manipulations and he shuddered her name at the realization that she wore absolutely nothing else. He weighed her generous breasts, worshipping their firmness and the way they molded to his palm.

Ty's lashes fluttered when he practically ripped the garment from her back and hoisted her against his muscular frame. She felt faint; scarcely able to breathe she was so overwhelmed by the strength and smell of him. Unable to verbally communicate her need, her fingers went to the fastening of his trousers.

Quay stopped her, gripping her bottom that was barely concealed within her jeans. Lowering her to the center of the beautiful midnight blue comforter atop the queen-sized bed, he quickly relieved her of what remained of her clothing. Her breathing was rapid and he was mesmerized by the loveliness of her dark body. How many times over the years had he awakened hard and aroused- his dreams filled of her? He'd mourned the loss of her sharper image from his memory. It had grown fainter as the years passed. Regardless of that, the incomparable pleasure of that experience of making love with her had not faded. It had gone on to both torture and exhilarate him.

"Quay…" Ty wanted total fulfillment.

"Shh…" he breathed against her thighs. "You'll have it," he knew what she yearned for. He yearned for the same.

Ty relaxed upon the coverings which were then a tangled mess thanks to her uncontrollable writhing. Quay held her in place, his tongue plundering her moist sheath with all the devastation he'd used when he treated her mouth to the same pleasure. She couldn't remain still beneath the slow, sultry lunges but had no choice as he kept her hips immovable on the bed. Eventually, he allowed her to arch herself closer to his mouth, his grip tightening in warning when she moved too much. He wanted complete control and Ty had no strength to refuse him anything.

He alternated, nuzzling his nose within the fragrant walls of her core and exploring the treasure inside. Ty raked her fingers across his hair and cried out into the air. Quay carried her to the edge and beyond. He ravaged her senses whispering words of desire, providing the dual caress of seductive strokes to her sex as his fingers rubbed and squeezed her ever firming nipples. He was relentless in his task of pleasuring her and only gave her respite when she climaxed and trembled to no end.

He gave her but a moment to absorb the deep sensations; removing his clothes as he watched her twist and arch upon the bed in the throes of her orgasm. He intended to claim her before she came down from the high. He took one of the condoms he'd pulled from his desk at the club and put protection in place. Then, mercilessly he drove the stunning length of his desire deep. Ty was caught between twin sensations of pleasure and pain. He gave her no time to grow accustomed to his size and her body began to tremble anew as she felt her inner walls stretched relentlessly. Quay didn't want to feel anything except the part of her he'd craved far more than he'd ever craved anything. She was so tight, intimately fisting his shaft in a way that promised swift release. He peeled her hands away from his body and pressed them high above her head. With her legs wrapped high around his back, he penetrated deep; branding her with his touch.

Ty flexed her fingers above his grip and drove herself against him in a wild display of desperation. Quay took intense delight in several filling satisfying lunges, groaning as her moisture built and assisted in deepening his penetration. Then, he was breaking contact and pulling her up. He turned her; bringing her back against his chest and burying his gorgeous face in her hair. Ty turned her head and kissed him, jerking in delight when she felt him take her from behind. One forearm provided a muscular shelf for her breasts while his free hand cupped her hip firmly. He pummeled her body with thrusts that made her want to melt into the covers. Slowly, he began to chant her name. The chanting grew more forceful and rapid as he reached his own peak of fulfillment.

They remained locked in position for the longest time. Ty felt him heaving against her back as he struggled to catch his breath. Her hair was a tousled mass that covered her face when she bowed her head. Slowly, he eased her down to lie on her stomach. He covered her completely and she fell asleep surrounded by him.

~~~

Quay studied the beautiful woman who slept so soundly, so trustingly next to him. His fingers played a tune across the flat plane of her stomach. He then moved to toy with one nipple while his lips nibbled on the other. His intention was to awaken Ty and he took as much pleasure in the task as he did regret.

In her gorgeous eyes that night, he'd seen love and devotion in addition to desire and lust. He wanted everything Ty had to give, but knew if his wants cost her life, everything inside him would shut down.

She woke, stretched and smiled lazily in happiness and the stirrings of arousal. Tugging at Quay's shoulders, Ty snuggled beneath him when he rose to cover her body. Outlining the curve of his mouth with her thumbnail, she leaned close to kiss him lustily.

Reluctantly, Quay acknowledged that the magic would have to end. Breaking the kiss, he looked down at her and smiled. "Must've taken quite a few tumbles for you to be as good as you are now," he said.

Her easy smile wavered, the hint of a furrow beginning to mar her forehead.

"You were so lost in the bedroom back in the day," he stroked her from hip to thigh. "Don't get me wrong, you were still a good hit," a slow smile sharpened his features, "these legs make a brotha hard at first sight."

Ty could feel her heart sinking to her stomach as she listened. His words, so casually hurtful were things no woman should hear after making love to the man she loved.

Quay's heart wasn't sinking, it was breaking. Still, he continued, decided he'd rather have her hate him than to have anything tragic befall her. He could tell his plan was producing the desired effect. The warmth in her enchanting doe eyes, turned cooler with disgust in the wake of every word he uttered.

Tiring of the idle caresses he lavished to her thighs, Quay leaned in for something more substantial. His mouth brushed the smattering of curls shadowing her womanhood. A heavy slap fell across his cheek just then.

"What are you saying?" she whispered, watching him as though he were a stranger. "What are you doing?" she hissed, that time shoving her hands against his shoulders..

"What?" Quay feigned confusion.

Ty shook her head.

"Hey," he prompted, brushing his knuckles across her jaw. "I'm complimenting you here, girl."

"Compliment?" she could hardly pronounce the word.

"Oh, I get it," he nodded slowly, his dark eyes feasting on her breasts which spilled over the sheet she clutched to her chest. "You prefer action to all this talk."

"Stop," she shuddered when he whipped away the sheets to cover her with his body. "Quay don't."

He didn't seem to hear her, appearing far more interested in cupping her breasts as he buried his face in the valley between. His tongue began to stroke the lush curves surrounding his face, his fingers began a dual assault on her nipples.

She wanted to argue, but could manage only one last faint '*stop*'. She felt his powerful body shake when he chuckled and settled himself more snuggly against her. Slowly, the fight drained and she was left with an empty feeling. That is, until sadness rushed in. She lay there feeling his mouth glide across her body and cursing herself for reacting to his touch when he'd succeeded yet again in reducing her to less than nothing.

Quay's long, sleek brows were drawn together in complete concentration as he suckled madly at one nipple. He glanced up in time to see a tear slide from the corner of her eye.

"What the hell's the matter?" he demanded quietly, bracing his weight on his elbows as he looked down at her.

"Just go," she asked, her voice lifeless.

"Tyke-"

"Just go, Quay. I don't want to see you again."

Again, the dimple-triggering smirk appeared. "That's gonna be difficult," he kissed her collarbone and then the swell of her breast, "since you work for me."

"I work for Quest," she stiffened beneath him.

Quay finished his teasing nips at her body. "You work for Ramsey. Don't forget it."

She rolled her eyes. "Get out."

Grinning broadly, he nodded agreeing to the order. He lavished one last, wet kiss to her jaw, neck and breasts before leaving the bed.

From the corner of her eye, Ty saw that he was donning his clothes. She looked away when he cast a glance at her across his shoulder. She waited for him to close the bedroom door behind him and then allowed herself to cry.

Outside the door, Quay slammed a fist to his palm and blinked away his own tears.

~SIX~

"Did she say why?" Quest was asking Samuel Bloch two mornings later when the group met at Ramsey for its weekly meeting.

Sam's light blue eyes reflected concern. "She said something came up and she just couldn't be here. She sounded tired though. *Too* tired. I couldn't get her to tell me there was anything wrong."

Quest grunted in response, stroking his jaw as he listened. He too, was growing concerned.

"Anyway," Sam sighed, glancing back at his crew. "It's been two days, so we're gonna head out to her mom's place and check on her after we're done here.."

"Good idea. Maybe you'll get more out of her with a face to face meeting," Quest figured.

Sam shrugged. "I hope so," he sounded doubtful.

"Listen, keep me posted," Quest slapped the side of Sam's arm before nodding towards the breakfast buffet across the room.

"You better get over there before they clean it out," he teased.

Sam grinned and then shook hands with Quest and went to rejoin his team.

Quest turned and found his twin standing a short distance away. "What did you do?" he knew his brother had been listening in on the conversation with Sam.

Quay didn't bother to play dumb. "I did what had to be done."

"What the hell does that mean?" Quest snapped.

"Dammit Q, don't you ever talk to your wife about this case?"

Squeezing his eyes shut tight, Quest hissed an obscenity. "Not this damn case again...sick of hearing about it." he massaged the bridge of his nose.

"You and me both," Quay folded his arms across the olive wool suitcoat he wore. "It's keeping me away from Ty even after all these years, so how the hell do you think *I* feel?"

"It doesn't have to be like that," Quest argued.

Quay waved his hand. "As long as that fool's runnin' loose, this is exactly how it has to be."

Quest stepped closer to his twin. "I can't believe you of all people runnin' scared."

"Listen Q, the only thing that kept Ty safe back then was that Wake didn't know I cared about her that way."

"I'll buy that," Quest pushed his hands inside the deep pockets of his brown tweed trousers, "but do you really think he's been out there killing all these years? Do you believe he's even got any of us on his mind, let alone doing anything to hurt Ty and how do you explain Sera? You never made a play for her."

Quay cleared his throat while slanting his brother a coy look. "Actually she approached me quite a few times. I told Wake about it."

"You told Wake, but not me?" Quest fixed his spitting image with a wounded look.

Quay couldn't resist smiling at his brother's jealousy and shook his head. "Nothing personal, man. It just wasn't somethin' I

331

wanted the family to know. Especially when Sera and De were such good friends," he referred to their cousin Dena. "Hell Uncle Houston even walked in and almost caught us at their house once. I was this close to kissing her," Quay shared, positioning his index finger above his thumb. "That made me think, Q. I knew if things didn't work out between us- which they probably wouldn't- I'd be in for it from the family since she and De were so close. Besides, I didn't feel that way about her and Sera was a sweet girl. She deserved better than me. So does Tyke."

"There's just one problem," Quest brought a hand to his brother's shoulder. "Ty loves you, fool."

"Hell Q, I love her!" Quay swore in a vicious whisper, his dark eyes sparkling with emotion. "I love her with everything in me, but that doesn't matter now since two nights ago I did everything I could think of to make her hate me," he took a deep breath his gaze faltering. "I'm positive I succeeded."

"Quay-"

"Let's get this meeting started, alright? I'm ready to get the hell out of here," he grumbled and left Quest staring after him.

***

"Just a few moments, Ms. Red. He's very weak," the petite Asian nurse warned as she escorted Jill to Raymond Patillo's room in the stately Savannah mansion he called home.

"I'll be very brief," Jill promised just as the nurse opened the door to the bedroom suite.

Raymond Patillo had served a lengthy term as County Medical Examiner in Savannah. Jill could detect the passion in the man's voice when they'd spoken over the telephone. It was obvious he still missed his former position very much.

"Ms. Red!" A large, imposing man greeted in a surprisingly warm and friendly manner. From his appearance, one would never tell how great a toll the lung cancer had taken on his well-being.

"Mr. Patillo, thank you so much for agreeing to meet with me," Jill reached out to shake hands. "This is about the Sera Black case," she recalled the nurse's instructions to be brief.

The glow in Patillo's eyes dimmed a little. "Sera Black," he recited. "She seemed to have been a lovely girl. At the scene, I remembered thinking that she was a smart young woman," he smiled in spite of himself. "I don't know how I knew that, I just had the feeling there was great potential there."

"You were the C.M.E. when the accident occurred," Jill confirmed, taking a seat in the armchair near the bed.

"It was no *accident*," Patillo confirmed quickly, his warm expression fading completely. "That poor girl was murdered and those people covered it up."

"The Ramseys?" Jill probed, crossing her trouser clad legs. "Did you have any thoughts on who may've been responsible?"

Patillo's smile was sour. "Someone in that family covered this up and I'm still certain that someone in that family was responsible. But not the boys," he added.

Jill's eyes narrowed. "Why?"

Patillo rested his head back against one of the oversized pillows behind him. "I met them, spoke with them at length. They were confident, very sure of their appeal and their capabilities. But murder…I never saw them as murderers," he shrugged. "A haunch Ms. Red, do you know what I mean?"

"I do," Jill nodded, understanding those feelings quite well. "I've been a cop for many years. Forensics was my speciality," she shared.

Patillo nodded slowly, his dark eyes gleaming with a deeper respect for her. Suddenly, the look grew troubled as his cough reasserted itself.

"I'm sorry," Jill whispered, worry clouding her face as she moved from the chair.

Patillo grabbed her hand before she could get too far. "Check the body," he said amidst the roaring cough.

Jill's brows drew close. "Mr. Patillo? The body? I don't-"

"The evidence will be there!" he struggled to smother his coughing. "Please, I'm an old man and I've prayed this girl's killer would be brought to justice. I took the Ramsey's payoff…first there was a phone call from someone saying he represented certain parties of the family. A few days later, a wad of cash was mailed to my office. I let the child's killer get away scot-free. This is an injustice that must be corrected."

Jill moved close to pat his back when the coughs roared to life once again. "Mr. Patillo, I- I don't understand how- she's been dead over fifteen years. Her body's been embalmed how-"

"I'm sorry Ms. Red I'll have to ask you to leave now," Patillo's nurse hurried in issuing the order.

Jill offered no argument. "Thank you both," she patted Raymond Patillo's hand before she moved back from the bed. She returned his wave and nodded at the determination in his eyes.

***

Construction on the rail for Holtz Enterprises began one month after Tykira and her crew finished the designs- a record everyone raved. The people at Holtz had already approved the final layouts via satellite conferencing. Still, valuing the importance of communication, the group decided to meet Ramsey's team about a month and a half into construction.

The group of forty-something businessmen arrived one afternoon and toured the site. Then, it was off to Gabron's for an authentic French meal. During the entire affair, Louie Danoue CEO of Holtz, kept Tykira close to his side. He raved as boldly over her creativity, as he did over her beauty.

Quay had no intentions of attending the lunch, but knew he'd draw Quest's wrath if he tried to back out. Additionally, once he'd discovered Ty would be in attendance he knew he wouldn't want to be anyplace else. A clear wall had been erected between them. While a wall in some form had always existed where they were concerned, this one was different. Ty was openly cordial and responsive to everyone in attendance except Quay. She treated him as though he weren't even there- directing her questions to Quest or any other member of Ramsey.

Still, Quay didn't mind letting his agitation show over Louie Danoue's interest in Ty. She certainly wouldn't notice his mood, neither would any member of her crew. The five men appeared just as agitated by Danoue's adoration as Quay was.

Lunch was a lively affair. The executives of Holtz had the opportunity to review color layouts of the project first hand. They also enjoyed a video presentation featuring a computer animated replica of the finished rail making its way up the majestic mountainside to the towering sky village in Banff.

"Exquisite!" Louie Danoue raved while his colleagues applauded. "We are greatly anticipating your arrival at the resort. It will be quite the celebration." He boasted, and then favored Ty with a meaningful smile. "I look forward to showing you the village firsthand," he said.

"It sounds wonderful," Ty graced Louie with a dazzling smile before she cleared her throat. "If you gentlemen would excuse me for a moment," she pushed her chair away from the table and smiled as every man stood.

Quay's onyx stare followed her until she left the dining room. That stare narrowed with murderous intent when Louie Danoue excused himself less than a minute later.

Tykira and Louie had only been gone a short time. It was far too long for Quay, who went after them without so much as a word to anyone who remained at the table.

Ty was on her way back then; having stopped to speak with one of her mother's church friends. She was inspecting the chic pin-striped skirt she wore and literally slammed right into Quay just outside the main dining room's entrance.

"Sorry," she whispered before realizing who she'd run into. Rolling her eyes, she went to move past him but felt his hand on her forearm.

"What?" She kept her eyes on his hand.

Quay's features were drawn into a closed mask. "Just wanted to see where you and Lou disappeared to," he admitted.

"Why?" her voice was a rasp and she looked up at him.

Quay shrugged. "You've been gone a while."

Ty had the strongest urge to connect the tip of her spike heeled black leather boot to his shin. "What are you getting at?"

His hand flexed on her forearm. "I think you know," he

tugged her just a bit closer.

"What do you want?"

Quay's smile was devilment personified in response to her question. "I think I already got it," he appraised her breasts outlined so prominently against the black turtleneck she wore.

The blow she set against his cheek turned the hearts of the servers who whisked along the corridor. Quay barely felt the sting to his face, but in his heart the blow vibrated a thousand times.

Quest had witnessed the scene, but waited for Ty to storm off before making his presence known. Quay turned when he heard the 'tsking' sound across his shoulder.

"Don't start, Q," Quay prepared to walk away.

"Not so fast," Quest drew his twin towards a quiet corner of the corridor.

"What?" Agitated, Quay tugged at the cuffs of his merlot colored suit coat.

"I can't afford to have her distracted by this drama, Quay."

Quay hissed a foul curse. "There's nothin' goin' on."

Quest hooked his thumbs around the burgundy suspenders he wore over a hunter green shirt. He almost laughed. "Nothin's goin' on? Then why the hell are you always up under her?" Quest walked away when he saw that his brother had no comeback.

***

"I honestly don't have a clue," Mick was telling Jillian who had just told her about the meeting with Raymond Patillo. "None of my research turned up any other evidence, but then I'm not privy to every bit of legal documentation," she noted.

"Check the body, check the body," Jill repeated, hoping it would force some sort of clarification. She heard Mick gasp. "What?" she called.

Mick hesitated only a moment. "Do you think…could he have been telling you to *check* her body- that the evidence was buried *with* her body- actually buried with it?"

"Impossible," Jill breathed. "Are you serious?"

"It's a possibility, Jill."

"But why would Patillo risk his career that way?"

"Jill you have no idea the kind of power the Ramseys wield down there," Mick crossed her legs at the ankles where she relaxed on her bed. "I got a healthy dose of it when I was in Savannah trying to connect pieces to this damned puzzle. Money is a powerful temptation and Patillo pretty much admitted he'd been approached by them right after the murder."

"Murder," Jill massaged her forehead. "So you're certain that's what it was too?"

"That's what I believe and I think after what Mr. Patillo said, it's safe to say it's been confirmed."

Jill sighed, grateful to have someone to bounce ideas off. Almost the entire station had deemed her a pariah for delving into the old case. "We'll have to contact her family to get an order to have the body exhumed. After such a long time, they may not be willing to have her grave disturbed. It could be quite a burden."

"It may not be as big of a burden as you think."

"Care to elaborate?"

"I think it's time to give Johnelle Black another call."

***

At Gabron's restaurant, the meeting was nearing its end. The members of Holtz Enterprises; who had flown down from Canada, were a surprisingly sociable bunch. Ty was very much pleased since she needed something laid back and easy going to keep her mind off Quay who unfortunately had decided to rejoin the meeting following their latest dramatic episode.

"How long do you all plan to stay?" Jeffrey Naven, one of Ramseys chief architects was asking.

"We didn't decide before leaving," Louie Danoue said, "but now I think maybe a longer stay might be a nice idea," he added focusing an appraising look toward Tykira.

Quest slanted his twin a warning look when he heard the heavy sigh Quay uttered.

"We hope to take another tour of the train before its completion," Louie announced.

The Ramsey Group team was delighted and plans were discussed to nail down a date and time.

"This is fantastic," Ty was saying especially pleased by the plans. "We really want to get your input on every phase of the project, but right now at the beginning is the most critical stage. I really want to be sure you get exactly what you're looking for."

"That sounds nice and I'm sure we will," Louie replied.

Quay could tell by the way the man's eyes traveled over Ty's upswept hair and exquisite face that he wasn't just referring to the train. He felt Quest's hand close over his knee and gritted his teeth while praying for an end to the meeting. His prayers were answered when everyone began pushing their chairs away from the table. His cellular chimed and he smiled when he saw the number on the face plate.

"Mick, Mick, Mick," he drawled, chuckling when he heard her voice. He shot Quest a devilish grin when the man heard his wife's name. "For me," he informed his brother in a wicked tone. "Yeah Mick?" he tuned into her voice. "Yeah, he's here…what?... Do I have to?" Quay groaned, rolling his eyes as he looked over at Quest. "She says she loves you and can't wait for you to come to bed."

Quest's hearty rumble of a laugh roared to life. He clapped his brother's shoulder then joined in on a conversation with a few of their people and the Holtz executives.

"Listen, my contact in Savannah just had a meeting with a man named Raymond Patillo. He was County Medical Examiner when Sera was killed," Mick shared.

"Mmm hmm," Quay leaned back in his chair as Mick told him about the call. "What did you say? With her body? Dammit."

"Now calm down," Mick urged, "This is really great news. We may be on our way to catching a murderer."

"Until we hit another brick wall and the bastard continues to enjoy his freedom."

"Sweetie cut yourself some slack, please? You're giving this guy too much power. Try to make things right between you and Ty, okay?"

"Yeah," he said, smirking over the suggestion. "Thanks Mick," he said before their call ended. Remaining seated, he simply watched Ty as she laughed off one of Louie's remarks and gathered her things to leave. She caught Quay staring and, for a few moments, their gazes held. Then, she shook her head and walked away.

Quay clenched his fists, fighting the urge to go after her. He was glad when Quest called him over to speak with one of the Holtz VPs.

~~~

Ty didn't allow the mask she wore to slip until she'd driven out of the Gabron's parking lot and had taken the ramp to the expressway. She cursed herself for being a fool- a weak kneed, emotional woman, swooning for a man's attention.

But Quay wasn't just any man, he was the only man she'd ever loved- her first lover. She cursed herself again and asked why she loved him. She was a smart woman in virtually every other aspect of her life. Why couldn't she pull herself- her heart away from this man- the *only* man who had ever truly hurt her? If anything, the scene a month prior should have changed her opinion of him. But the encounter had only made her want him more. She could admit that to herself. Quaysar Ramsey wasn't simply the only man she'd ever loved, he was the only man she'd ever made love with. Knowing that it was only for gratification on his part was killing something inside her.

She was on a mission then, to work harder than ever to complete the project and get back to Colorado. It would be suicide considering what a large undertaking it was, but she knew that to stay and let herself be wooed into bed again would be just as dangerous.

~~~

"Oh, not tonight," Ty groaned when she finally pulled into her mother's driveway. She spotted Quay's foreboding black SUV parked a few feet away. "What is it, Quay?" she called once she'd

339

left her vehicle and saw him walking towards her.

He smiled, raising his hands defensively. "I only wanted to make sure you got home alright."

"*No*, you wanted to make sure I got home *alone*." She folded her arms across the front of the black turtleneck she wore.

Quay simply nodded, not bothering to argue her accuracy.

Tykira's brown stare narrowed. "What is it with you? One minute hot, the next minute cold. Is this still about Wake? Or do you still just enjoy playing with my head. This isn't high school, Quay. You don't have to play that game anymore, you know?"

"Ty-"

"It's confusing and it's cruel and I don't have time for it. I'm here to work and then leave."

Quay bowed his head, cursing himself. In his desperation to see her, he hadn't stopped to consider how she would perceive his actions. *Nice, Quay. Nice as always.*

"Why don't you use your Casanova skills on one of the many women ready to be wooed by you?" she turned to open the passenger side door of the Cherokee and collect her things.

"And you're not one of those women?" He spoke more to himself than to her. No, she wasn't one of those women- she had never been. She was so much more and she'd never heard him tell her that.

"No, I'm not one of those women, Quay. So stop, alright? Just stop." She rested her head against the side of the SUV. "There's no need. I didn't come here to win a spot in your life. In spite of my…eager participation, I didn't even come here to sleep with you." She ended on a whisper, sighing as exhaustion claimed her.

"Jesus," Quay mistook her sighs for sobs and moved to console her. "Ty please, I'm sorry. Don't cry."

"Snake," she stiffened, "I'm not crying over you Quay. I've done way too much of that."

He nodded, but made no move to back away from her. Instinctively, his hands smoothed across her slender form moving up to fill his palms with the fullness of her breasts.

Ty blinked, her body beginning to tingle with the desire for him that always simmered just below the surface. Helpless to deny its power, she let her head tilt and she arched deeper into his touch.

Keeping one hand curved seductively across her bosom and the other at her hip, Quay trailed his nose across the nape of her neck. The scent of her perfume brought to mind the naughtiest acts of seduction that he ached to subject her to. His perfect teeth found the zipper that secured the turtleneck and he tugged it down, hungry to expose more of her silken dark skin.

How she wanted him, Ty thought as his mouth skimmed her nape. That's all it would ever be, unfortunately- want, desire, sexually satisfying and craved, yes, but nothing more. Dammit, she heard the word echo in her mind. All the years she'd spent feeling fulfilled and successful without him in her life. Now he was there again and torturing her mind and body with his attention. With strength she conjured from someplace deep, Ty slipped out of his embrace and headed toward the front door.

Quay seemed to snap out of his pleasure-driven state of mind as well. Leaning against the SUV, he kept his back turned until Ty had disappeared inside the house.

~SEVEN~

"I love you, Quay, I love you…"

The deep, right dimple appeared as Quay smiled in his sleep. Stretching restlessly against crisp, charcoal gray sheets, he smoothed one hand across the array of taut muscles defining his chiseled abdomen. He was in the midst of a delicious albeit subconscious interlude with Tykira Lowery. Her stunning dark mane flowed wildly as her body rode his. His hands traveled her strong, beautiful form with a lover's possession. On her lips he heard her whisper words of love-

Quay woke with a start, his relaxed expression growing sharp with frustration. He cursed himself then, realizing the incredible scene was an incredible fantasy with no chance of becoming reality. He alone had accomplished that with no help from Wake Robinson. Quay acknowledged that the man was probably on another continent. He had to know that a life behind bars awaited him if he returned.

Quay pressed a pillow across his face and groaned. Tykira. He loved her so much. He had loved her forever and his feelings would never change. All the women he'd used to get her out of his head were only shining examples of everything he *didn't* want.

His temper was reaching that familiar point of no return when the bedside phone rang.

"What?" he practically growled into the receiver once he'd snatched it up. After brief hesitation on the other end, a familiar voice came through the line.

"Wake?" Quay whispered, barely able to find his own voice.

"Been a while," Wake sounded calm yet uncertain.

Slowly, Quay pushed himself up in bed. "Goin on three years. Where you been, man?"

"You knew I had to go."

"Did you do this?"

Wake didn't pretend to be confused. "It's complicated, man."

"What the hell does that mean?" Quay snapped.

"It's *complicated*," Wake stressed.

"Where are you?" Quay asked, ordering himself to tone down his emotions.

"Close."

Quay didn't like it. "Let's meet."

"Not now, but I'll be in touch," Wake said. "We *will* talk man but I have to be sure about the time and place. You got a lot of things mixed up and you don't know the half of it."

"You mean the fact that you killed Sera." Quay pointed out.

Wake muttered a curse. "That's not a fact. It's not even *close* to a fact."

For a moment, Quay believed his old friend. "What's goin on, man?" he asked.

"This isn't a phone conversation and I think you know that. Anyway I already said way too much."

Quay knew Wake was gone before he heard the dial tone signifying the line had gone dead. Leaning back in bed, he closed his eyes and groaned.

***

"I know this is asking a lot considering all you've been through," Mick was saying as she spoke with Johnelle Black by phone.

"Emotions don't control me anymore, Michaela. I need this to come to an end," the grieving mother confided. "If something *is* buried with Sera, something that could bring the answers about her death, I want it done."

Mick nodded. "We'll have to be discreet with the exhumation. The SPD may not approve of us delving into this particular area of the case."

"I understand and I'll do whatever it takes." Johnelle vowed. "Will you be there?"

"Nothing could keep me away," Mick promised.

"You've been a godsend. Thank you Michaela."

"You take care of yourself. We'll talk soon," Mick waited for Johnelle to hang up before she clicked off her phone. She stood from the armchair in the bedroom's tiny alcove.

From their bed, Quest watched his wife massaging her eyes and neck. "Come over here," he issued the soft command.

Mick complied without hesitation, smiling gratefully when he pulled her down to the bed and began to massage her neck and back.

"Are you alright?" he asked.

"Just tired," she admitted, relishing the relief his powerful hands applied to her aching muscles.

Quest let his displeasure show, his gray eyes darkening just slightly. "What leads have you made in the case?" he asked, hoping to mask his frustration.

"We think actual physical evidence may've been buried with Sera- in her...casket."

"What?" Quest hissed, his unsettling stare narrowing dangerously.

Mick turned and scooted forward. "Baby, I told Quay but promise not to say anything to anyone else," she urged, smoothing her hands across his broad, bare shoulders. "The whole situation is

344

a long shot."

"What do you think you'll find?" Quest asked, calming some beneath his wife's touch.

Mick shook her head. "Well, if it runs parallel to the file Jill found, this evidence will lead us to Sera's killer."

"Wake?" Quest probed.

"Wake," Mick sighed, her expression guarded.

"Michaela?" Quest inclined his head to peek into her eyes.

"I think Wake Robinson is a part of the puzzle but as crazy as this sounds, I don't think he did this."

"Why do you think he'd be innocent in all this?"

"I don't know- a haunch? I just really believe this goes deeper than Wake."

"But why?"

"I can't make myself belief he'd have done all this and continued to live around Quay all those years," she shrugged. "I don't know…"

"Have you told Quay?"

"I haven't even told Johnelle," Mick groaned, dragging all ten fingers through her thick curls, "I don't think it'd be wise to tell your brother since he's based *all* his actions on the fact that Wake Robinson is the culprit." She folded her arms across her knees and propped her chin there. "Getting Quay to latch on to the idea of another nameless, faceless perpetrator might push him just a bit too far."

***

For the next two weeks, Tykira maintained her vow to steer clear of Quay. She worked herself to frenzy to the dismay of everyone who knew her. Of course, her crew had seen her that way before but this was even more extreme than usual. She heard nothing but her own voice pushing her to give just a little more to get the job done. Now, that voice was pushing her with another advisement: finish this job and get the hell away from Quaysar Ramsey!

She'd arrived early for the weekly meeting, mostly because

345

she'd worked in the office designated for her and her team. She wound up spending the night. Ty woke, washed her face and brushed her teeth in the office washroom before heading up for the meeting.

~~~

Jasmine Hughes, Ramsey's administrative director, sent Tykira on up to the penthouse office. The moment Ty stepped from the elevator a sofa called to her. Minutes later, she was napping.

Quay arrived early himself that morning. He was in no mood to run into employees and be forced to engage in conversation he had no interest in. He'd been walking a tightrope since Wake's call. He dared not tell anyone about it, not wanting to scare the man away if he was near. Each time the phone rang, Quay jumped thinking it was his old friend.

The reality of that made him experience more than a little self-loathing. He was Quaysar Ramsey and he ran from no one. His facial muscles tightened, drawing his handsome dark features into a fierce mask. He stormed off the elevator, his anger abating when he found Ty asleep on a sofa. He moved closer, taking a seat on the edge of the rich, blackberry suede.

A soft smile curved his mouth when the sound of her snoring touched his ears. Leaning close, he brushed his nose across her temple. Moving back slightly, he took advantage of the moment to watch her slumber. He fondled the tendrils of hair that haphazardly fell from her upswept style and framed her face. He'd heard how hard she'd been driving herself and could see that it was true. He knew it was because of him. Arrogant thinking? Perhaps, but it was accurate. If he were her, he'd want to get as far away from his as possible too. He made a mental note to ask his father how much longer Bobbie Lowery would be on call for her business trips. She'd make sure Ty took better care of herself.

Quay drew a fist at the thought. It should be *him* taking care of Ty. Would he take the opportunity if he had the chance, though? Probably not. After all, he'd already acknowledged that Wake only played a supporting role in the distance he kept from

Ty. She deserved the kind of man who would put her happiness- not his own needs or best intentions- first. He'd already proven time and again that he couldn't be that man.

Ty woke frowning a bit as she sought to get her bearings. Then, she found herself looking right into Quay's disturbingly dark eyes. She realized how close they were and quickly left the sofa. No words were spoken, but the tension was thick and heavy inside the room. Putting distance between them, Ty rubbed her arms across the flare-sleeves of the asymmetrical toffee brown sweater she wore. Her sigh of relief filled the room when the elevator chimed to signal the arrival of their meeting partners.

~~~

The group had chosen that day to visit the project site. Quest announced that the trucks were waiting outside to carry them all to the rail yard once the meeting had drawn to a close. Quay told his brother to count him out of the trip making Ty even happier to attend. That was especially true when she discovered that Michaela would be joining them.

~~~

While everyone convened near the elevator, Mick approached her brother-in-law who sat brooding in his private office.

"Everyone's leaving, Quay," she watched as he glared at papers he held.

"Not goin'," Quay slapped the pages to his desk.

"Why?" Mick stepped inside the office. Quay's pointed look was a clear response to her question. "I can't believe you're still acting so crazy," she scolded, "you already told Ty what's going on."

"I never told her Wake is still out there somewhere."

"So what? What's that got to do with how you feel?"

The flip inquiry brought a hard frown to Quay's face. "I've been asking myself that very question," he admitted.

"Ready babe?" Quest called, finding his wife in the office.

"Yeah," Mick replied idly, smiling when he pulled her back against him.

Quay walked over and planned a kiss to Mick's cheek before quietly excusing himself from the room. Quest held her tight, when she turned to hug him. He relished the gesture but frowned when he felt her leaning deep into the embrace as though she had no strength to stand.

"Hey," he leaned down to search her light eyes with his striking gray ones. "You okay?"

Mick's smile was weak, but she finally began to nod. "I'm just so ready for this case to be solved."

Quest's grimace sparked his left dimple. "Finally, we agree on something," he said and then escorted his wife to the elevator.

***

Savannah, GA~

Jill sat browsing through the Sera Black file for what seemed to be the hundredth time. She could only pray that the pieces of evidence noted in the record would actually be found with the body. She shook her head, silently acknowledging how much of a longshot it all was. However, she also acknowledged that such unorthodox happenings were usually the events that cinched cases.

"Getting fed up?" Greg Youtz teased, seeing his young colleague shaking her head.

Jill blew at her bangs, before massaging her eyes. "I'm wondering if I'll be successful in fitting together all the pieces of this puzzle," she confessed.

Greg tugged at the belt, completely hidden beneath the generous expanse of his belly. "Tell me you're not still working on that Sera Black thing?"

Jill turned to face the man who occupied the desk diagonal from hers. "I have reason to believe it was murder, not suicide," she omitted the information regarding the buried evidence.

Greg lost what little coloring he had in his face. "I was on the force for ten years when she died, you know? My little girl went to school with her."

"Did you know the Ramseys?" Jill folded her arms across her chest.

"Oh I knew the Ramseys," Greg nodded. "You only have to live in Savannah a few days to know the power those folks commanded here."

"Do you believe they could've been involved in what happened?"

"Why would you ask that?" his tone bordered on defensive.

"The twins were suspected," Jill pretended not to notice the man's reaction. "They're very successful now."

"The twins," Greg smirked coldly. "Those boys...let's just say they were the least of Sera Black's problems."

"What do you mean?" Jill leaned forward in her desk chair. "How?"

Greg blinked as though realizing he'd said too much. "Be careful, little girl. The Ramseys are powerful and they claim some nasty members."

"But the case is so old now and-"

"You can best believe someone's watching. Someone's *always* watching," Greg stood and reached for the suit coat to pull over his snug white cotton shirt. "You'll find that out if you dig any deeper into this," with those words, the man took his exit.

***

"Quay? Quay!" Jasmine raced past the opening elevator doors. "Quay," she found her boss reclining on the conference room sofa. "Why aren't you answering your line?"

"Because I don't want to hear any bullshit, bad news, or problems for at least two hours." Quay muttered, recrossing his loafer-shod feet where they rested atop the coffee table.

Jasmine took a deep breath and propped her hands to her hips. "Well then you're not about to like what I'm going to tell you."

"And that is?" Quay left the sofa to fix a drink at the bar.

"There was an accident at the rail yard."

Clamor sounded when Quay's hand weakened. A glass decanter fell, spilling contents of scotch to the pine surface of the bar. "Where's Ty?" his voice was gravel when he turned to Jasmine.

"It was Ty who was involved in the accident." Jasmine winced while relaying the news.

"What happened?"

"I don't-"

"Where is she? Is she alright?"

"All I can give you is the name of the hospital," Jazz was already extending the card she'd scribbled the information on.

Quay hissed a fierce curse and snatched the card on his way out of the room.

Jazz could hear what sounded like a heavy fist being slammed against the elevator's down button and decided it'd be best to take the next car down.

A LOVER'S PRETENSE

~EIGHT~

"She's alright. She's alright," were the first words out of
Quest's mouth when Quay came bounding down the hospital
corridor. "Listen to me, she's *fine*," he stressed, curving both hands
over his brother's shoulders as he tried to allay the man's worst
fears.

Quay's smoldering stare was unwavering. "Who's
responsible?" he asked his twin.

Quest shrugged. "Most likely Ty herself is responsible."

"What?" Quay breathed.

"She hasn't been eating or resting," Quest shared, releasing
Quay's shoulders and pushing both hands into his trouser pockets,"
she lost her bearings while we were taking a side ladder up to the
roof of one of the cars. She slipped and fell crazy on her ankle.
Doctor says she broke it."

"Dammit," Quay cursed, though relief was washing
through him at the same time. "Where is she? Can I see her?"

Quest nodded, pointing down the corridor. "Room five-o-eight."

Quay removed his suitcoat while making his way toward the room. He applied a gentle knock to the partially opened door before stepping inside. His heart slammed fiercely inside his chest when he saw Ty. Lying prone in the bed, she looked beaten, drained like she hadn't slept in weeks. Massaging the bridge of his nose, he cursed himself for being the cause of it.

Mick had been napping in a chair next to the bed, but looked up when she heard someone else in the room.

Quay's dark eyes were fixed on the cast in a sling surrounding Tykira's right foot.

"She broke it in the fall," Mick supplied.

"Was it really an accident?" Quay still eyed the cast.

"Yeah sweetie, it was," Mick knew what he meant. "She hasn't been getting the rest she needs. The doctors say they're more concerned by her fatigue than the ankle."

Quay pushed one hand into his silver gray trousers. "How long does she have to stay here?"

"Not sure," Mick massaged her arms as she yawned. "I know someone should be in soon who can tell you more."

"Thanks Mick," Quay tousled her curls when she walked by him. "I'm glad you were there," he told her, smiling when she rubbed his back before leaving the room.

Settling to the edge of the bed, Quay took Ty's hand and kept it pressed to his chest. He stroked her temple as he'd done earlier that day and thought how easily this could have been something else. When Jasmine told him Ty was hurt, he actually believed he'd lost her. *Really* lost her. Shaking his head to dismiss the thought, he leaned close and kissed her cheek.

Her lashes stirred a bit as she woke. "Quay," she whispered.

He took comfort in the fact that she knew it was him and leaned close to kiss her again.

"What happened?" she grimaced at the scratchy feel of her throat.

"You need to rest, love," he advised, trailing his finger

along the arched line of her brow.

Emotion flickered on Ty's gaze and she looked away. "I have work to do."

"It can wait," he countered, his voice firming then. "If need be, I'll have the whole damn project postponed so you can get the rest you need. Even if you have to go back to Colorado to get it."

Ty shuddered. "When I leave Seattle this time, I won't be back," she vowed weakly.

"Can I do anything? Call your mom?" he offered, not wanting to argue with her.

"No please," she barely raised a hand, "I don't need her worrying over me."

Quay disagreed. Silently, he decided to contact Bobbie Lowery on his own.

Ty tried to push herself up in bed and gasped at the dull ache in the vicinity of her foot. Spotting the cast and sling, her mouth fell open and she couldn't believe she hadn't noticed it before. "What happened?" she cried.

"You fell at the rail yard, honey. During the tour, do you remember?" He stroked her arm when she nodded slowly. "It's your ankle. You broke it."

"Nooo," Ty groaned, falling back against the pillows. Obvious dismay clouded her face over the fact that she'd be bedridden or at the very least quite incapacitated for a time. "Now Mama will *definitely* come home to fuss over me. I won't get a damn thing done," she sighed, eyes narrowing as she contemplated her situation. "Maybe I can get one of the guys to stay with me."

Not a chance in hell, Quay made another silent decision.

"Quay? Are you okay..." she asked, having caught the murderous expression that flashed across his face. Instinctively, she reached out to touch his face and cursed herself for even caring how he was. *Especially when it's my damn foot in a sling!* She chastised.

"I just have a lot going on." He said.

Something in his tone continued to concern her though. "Business?" she watched him shake his head no. Clearly, it was something he didn't want to discuss. Thankfully, there was no time to rack her brain trying to figure out what was going on with him. The nurse had arrived.

"When can I leave?" Were Ty's first words to the woman.

"Now, now Ms. Lowery, the doctors want you to focus on getting more rest. They'll be in to speak with you shortly," the matronly woman announced in soothing tones.

Ty was too unnerved to be soothed. "I can rest at home," she pouted.

"And clearly you haven't been," the nurse challenged, offering Quay an adoring look when he chuckled at her words.

Tykira folded her arms across the front of the awkward hospital gown and remained quiet.

"When you *are* released, you'll definitely need someone to look after you," the nurse was saying as she fussed around the bed making sure the covers were tucked in. She then began to review Ty's vitals on a chart.

"Tyke, I'm gonna head out," Quay was saying then. He moved close to the bed and then leaned down to kiss her forehead. "I'll be back," he whispered.

For a moment, Ty forgot about pouting. The look in her eyes softened as she watched him go.

"Ohhh boy," the nurse sighed, her eyes also following Quay's departure. "I wouldn't mind being looked after if *he* applied for the job."

***

"Detective Red," Jill answered the call absently while rifling through paperwork at her cluttered desk.

"Miss Red, Sawyer Reynolds. Head caretaker and proprietor of Serenity Memorial Gardens."

"Yes, Mr. Reynolds," Jill greeted. Inwardly, she groaned at the sound of the man's heavy southern drawl and the nasal tone of his voice. Clearly Mr. Sawyer Reynolds was accustomed to respect and reverence when he announced his lengthy title. "How are you?" she hoped to set an easy tone to the conversation.

"Not good. Not good one damn bit," Sawyer shared, with no interest in pleasantries. "I got a order here for exhumation. Sera Black."

"Yes Sir."

"This is a scandalous thing you doin' Missy. I don't know how thangs go in Chicago but down here we don't think it's Christian-like to make people relive painful mem'ries."

"I don't' think that way either, Sir," Jill rubbed her tired eyes as she spoke.

"You coulda fooled me, young lady. Reopenin' this case, diggin' up that girl's body. Just gone wound that family all over again."

"And just for my own clarification, Mr. Reynolds would you be referring to Sera's family or the Ramsey family?" Jill didn't bother to hide her disdain.

"Now you listen here-"

"Mr. Reynolds, Sera's mother wants this done. And that's the *only* family *I'm* concerned with."

"You dabblin' with powerful people," Sawyer Reynolds warned. "Don't matter a bit if they colored or not."

Jill rolled her eyes. "Mr. Reynolds this case is far from over and until it's solved, I'm on it," she vowed.

"Be careful young lady," the man advised and then slammed down the phone.

Jill followed suit, looking across her shoulder when she heard Greg Youtz laughing in the distance.

"Told you so," he reared back in his desk chair.

Jill turned, her dark eyes filled with a glare that removed the humor from Youtz's red face. "If it hadn't been for the Ramseys working to cover their asses, no one would've taken a second look at this case, but hiding evidence, payoffs- including one to the girl's own mother have simply caused tensions and regrets to simmer. They're about to boil over, Greg, with Sera Black's murderer coming out in the run off and I'll damn well be there to see it," she swore and then shoved her chair away from her desk and stormed out of the crowded bullpen.

Greg's expression held a trace of foreboding then. "Be careful, young lady," he advised.

***

With the exhumation scheduled for the end of that week, Michaela was preparing for her trip to Georgia. She hoped to finish packing before her husband got home, knowing that her leaving had become a very sore spot between them. Unfortunately, Quest arrived early that evening. He was in time to not only find his wife packing, but also to see her stumble and lean over to brace her hands against the wall as though she were trying to regain her balance.

Mick was taking deep breaths, when she heard the slam of the bedroom door. She whirled around to find Quest shooting his hazy gray stare in her direction.

"Hey baby," Mick greeted in a light breathless manner and cleared her throat to shield the shaky tone of her voice.

Quest didn't buy it. "The trip's out," he tossed a quarter length black leather jacket to the bed.

"Excuse me?" Mick propped both hands to her hips when her husband took a seat on the bed and casually removed his shoes and socks before deigning to give her an answer.

"I've been watching you Mick," he shared in a whimsical tone.

Her expression softened. "You're *always* watching me," she teased.

"Mmm," Quest gestured, flashing her a look of acknowledgement. "Well then, it shouldn't surprise you to hear me say that I've seen all your little stumbles during the last couple of weeks."

Slowly, Mick's teasing expression faded.

"You've been napping all times of day," Quest went on, watching her walk over to the dresser and lean against it. "Thanks to this case, you're not taking care of yourself and I'm sick of it."

Mick shook her head, "Honey I swear that's not it," she hid her hands inside the front pocket on the petal pink hoody he wore, "everything with the case now is at a virtual standstill until Jill gets somewhere with the exhumation."

"Which you won't be attending."

"Quest-"

"That's it."

"Quest, please don't do this. Not now," Mick extended her hands in a pleading gesture while walking towards him. "You know Johnelle needs me to be there."

"And I need you to be *here*," he countered, unbuttoning the black shirt he wore and leaving it to hang open outside his cream trousers. "I need you to be here long after this case is solved."

Mick had no comeback. At last, she succumbed to the weariness she'd been battling. She trudged to the bed and took a seat near the suitcase she'd been packing. Idly, she toyed with the articles that lay inside. Quest closed the space between them and pulled her against his chest. Mick was happy to let herself be held.

***

"She'll never go for it," Bobbie Lowery predicted into the phone as she stood in the middle of her Baton Rouge, Louisiana hotel room.

From his end of the line, Quay smiled. "Considering how badly she wants to be home, I think she'll consider just about any arrangement. But I need to know if you'll be alright with it."

Bobbie sighed. "No baby, I'm afraid I wouldn't be."

"Ms. Bobbie if-"

"Now wait and let me say this," Bobbie sat on the window sill overlooking the busy, rain-slicked street below. "It's not that I don't think you could handle Ty as a patient, though you probably couldn't," she smiled before sobering. "Quaysar the truth is I'm sick of seeing my baby hurt and always upset over you., It's been almost a constant in your lives since forever and now it's so bad my Ty rarely comes home. In fact, aside from this project with the company, she *never* comes home."

Quay heard the softness settling into Bobbie Lowery's

usually firm voice and knew her emotions were weighing in heavily. "Ms. Bobbie, I don't know what to say except I'm sorry. I know what I did to Ty. I know I was wrong, but I had my reasons."

"Which were?"

Quay didn't want the woman any more upset. "I was wrong and I want to make things up to her more than anything. I want her in my life forever," was all he chose to share.

"Quaysar-"

"I love her Ms. Bobbie. I always have and I'll never stop."

Lengthy silence covered the line while Bobbie contemplated on her end. "What do you need?" She finally asked.

Quay uttered a hushed prayer of thanks. "I only need you to take your time on this trip. I need to be alone with her."

"Mmm hmm…don't hurt my baby again Quaysar or you'll be dealing with me and love, you know I'm nowhere near as syrupy sweet as my daughter."

"Yes, ma'am," Quay's tone was reverent, he knew the woman's word were no bluff.

***

Ty woke from another long nap and believed she was still dreaming when she found Quay's face looming so closely to her own. She closed her eyes and opened them to see if the vision remained. It had. "What are you doing here," she groaned.

Quay grinned. Every day the same question. She'd been in the hospital just over a week and he had made an appearance at her bedside each day. He knew she was curious and unnerved, but he had no intentions of letting her out of his sight for long. Ever again.

"Quay?" Ty probed, her doe eyes narrowing when he offered no response.

"How would you like to go home?" he asked.

Ty; who hated being cooped up in bed for any period of time, closed her eyes in a dreamy manner. She smiled, resting her head back against the pillows as though she were envisioning 'home' just then. "That is my greatest wish," she sighed.

Quay chuckled, loving the way contentment added a different glow to her incredible features. "Well I'm here to grant that wish," he announced.

"Huh?" Ty grunted, fixing him with a blank look.

"You'll stay with me until we get the cast off."

"No."

"Yes. Ms. Bobbie already said it was alright."

"What? You talked to her?" Ty watched him nod. "What did she say?" she listened closely as Quay told her. Ty felt her mouth hanging open by the time he was done. Minutes later, she was shaking her head. "Quay...I can't."

"Yes you can."

"No...the guys- the guys can take care of me."

Quay chuckled and leaned back in the chair next to the bed "With you out of commission, they're gonna be swamped with work. They can't focus on that and worry over you at the same time."

Ty settled back. "You're right," she whispered, tapping her fingers to her chin. "I could get a nurse."

"Already taken care of," Quay stood from the chair and moved to sit on the side of the bed "I want to be there too," he said.

"Why would you do this?" Ty dismissed the voice that called her a fool for asking.

"You need someone to look after you," he trailed his fingers along her bare forearm.

Ty grimaced and folded her arms across her chest. "The truth Quay. Just the truth."

"I feel better seeing with my own eyes that you're safe."

Ty blinked. "Does this have something to do with Wake?"

Quay's long lashes shielded his onyx stare from view when he looked down to inspect a button on his caramel-colored suitcoat.

"Quay."

"I don't want you scared Tyke."

"I'm not," her response was firm as genuine courage filtered her gaze. "Besides Wake hardly knew me and thanks to you he never suspected we had anything between us- for the brief time that there was an *us*. Unless…you told him," she subtly inquired, wondering if he'd ever admitted his feelings about her to anyone.

Quay shook his head. "I didn't."

Ty inhaled, refusing to admit how much the confession disappointed her. "Then, there's no need for you to put your life on hold for me," she decided only pretending to be cool just then.

Averting his gaze, Quay forced himself not to admit how much he wanted and needed to be around her. "Humor me, please Tyke," he asked instead.

Ty curved her hands into fists beneath the standard coverings on the bed. She knew that once again Quay Ramsey had her right where he wanted her and she knew that she didn't want to be anywhere else.

"Who's ready to be released?!" Doctor Jonas Orvin asked upon walking into the lamp-lit hospital room.

Ty's expression brightened immediately. "I'm more than ready! Please tell me something good."

Dr. Orvin chuckled. "Well your vitals are far better than when you first came to us," he perused the chart he held before his round olive-toned face. "We still want you to adhere to strict bed rest though. We anticipate the cast being on anywhere from four to six weeks."

Nodding, Ty expelled a deep breath. Thankfully, it appeared that she'd be on her feet before the rail was finished for the trip to Banff.

"Now, about this cast," Dr. Orvin went on, placing his hand across the bulky creation. "I caution you against using a hanger to get to an itch, use a cool blow dryer instead. You should also practice keeping it elevated and use an Emory board instead of scissors to trim any rough edges that may form at the heel or anywhere else. I've got a packet here that'll go into more detail about everything I'm telling you."

Dr. Orvin was still delivering his instructions, when an orderly arrived with a wheelchair. Ty's happy expression dimmed with skepticism.

"I really don't think I need that," she said.

"Tyke…" Quay called in a warning tone from where he stood across the room.

"I'm afraid it's yours until you exit the hospital doors. We've also supplied you with a lovely one to use while you're at home."

"What about crutches?" Ty suggested.

"You'll have those as well.'

"Can't I use them now instead of this wheelchair?"

The doctor was quite amused as he was very accustomed to this final debate by patients who abhorred being wheeled out. "Hospital rules," he said, using the tried and true argument that usually silenced the disagreement. He smiled and then nodded when it appeared to work on the outspoken young woman in the bed. "Now, I'll leave you to freshen up and I'll return within the hour with your release forms." Dr. Orvin patted Ty's cast once more before he shook hands with Quaysar and left the room.

"I'm gonna bounce out of here for a minute too, Tyke," Quay said, following the doctor's departure. "I want to double check and make sure the kitchen's stocked with everything we'll need," he tugged a quarter length gray linen jacket across his white shirt.

Ty couldn't resist smiling. "Don't tell me you're going to cook?" she teased.

"If you'd like me to," he replied, his sensual dark stare focused and intense.

The look caught Ty completely off guard and she couldn't respond.

Thankfully, Quay's expression softened again in humor. "I don't think your stomach would approve of that, though," he pulled keys from his jacket pocket, "see you in a few."

When he was gone, Ty expelled the breath she'd been holding. Leaning back on the pillows with her eyes closed, she questioned the intelligence of releasing herself to the care of Quay Ramsey. Despite the past, she knew she'd always be a fool for the man. But how many more times would she put herself in the line of fire and keep hoping everything would be alright, when again and again she ended up brokenhearted?

Nodding then, she decided she was just going to have to keep things on an even keel. Sure, she was in love with him, attracted to him- thought about them making love more than a few times every day and she couldn't stop the excitement from pulsing through her every minute at the idea of being around him so often during the approaching weeks.

Still, when those truths got in the way of her ability to resist his incredible charm- and that would most certainly happen- she would pull away from him. She would have to. Her very dignity and sanity would depend on it.

~NINE~

"Put that down!" Quay ordered from the driver's seat. His glare was hard and focused on the tall beauty as he watched her through the rear view mirror.

"What?!" Ty fixed Quay with her own glare from her relaxed position along the back seat of the Hum-Vee.

"The doctor said no work," Quay reminded her, moving his gaze from Ty to the traffic.

"I was only reviewing some notes," Ty reasoned already lifting the legal pad she scribbled up during her hospital stay.

"Put it down," he ordered quietly that time.

"Dammit," she tossed the pad to the floor, "will you tell me then what the hell I'm supposed to be doing for the next six weeks?"

Quay cleared his throat, eager to recite the list. "Eat three square meals a day', he began, revealing his right-dimpled smile when she groaned, "snacks are fine, but don't get crazy, no more than four hours of TV a day. So you'll have to decide between soaps in the morning or movies at night. The rest of the time you'll be asleep."

"Mmm hmm and crazy inside of two days," she cast a despairing gaze outside the rear window. "I'll be bored to tears."

"Then sleep will keep your mind off how bored you are."

"Oh please, shut up. *You're* not the one with your foot in a sling."

"No that would be *you*," Quay leaned his head back against the padded rest. "'Course it wouldn't be *you* if you'd been getting enough rest, so you could be more alert. But all that's about to change."

"I don't-"

"No more arguments, Tyke."

Folding her arms across the front of her Colorado Rockies sweatshirt, she pouted.

Once on the freeway, Quay stole infrequent glances at her. He thanked God she'd given in and decided to let him look after her. This accident of hers had put so much into perspective. Sure it was what everyone had been telling him- he was a fool to deny either Ty or himself what they'd both wanted. For so long, he'd pretended she meant little or nothing to him in hopes of keeping her safe. His reasoning had been all wrong. He shuddered, thinking how pushing her away was more dangerous than anything else he'd done. It was a mistake he wouldn't make again. Tykira Lowery was his and it was way past time that everyone knew it.

"Am I allowed to hear music? Or is that against the orders too?" Ty still looked annoyed in the backseat.

Quay offered no response, except to grin at her stubbornness. Dutifully, he hit the button tuned to a classic R&B Soul station. Keith Sweat's "Make It Last Forever" was fading into another slow jam.

When Janet Jackson's "Funny How Time Flies," faded in, Ty gasped and prayed Quay hadn't heard her. Surely, he would never recall what the song meant to her but she would never forget it.

Memories carried her back to one late Savannah summer

when they'd spent a private week at the estate of his late grandparents Quentin and Marcella Ramsey. Of course, no one had any idea that Ty and Quay were secluded in the private cottage across the river that ran through the property. There was hell to pay when the teens finally returned from the trip. Their parents were sick with worry in spite of the fact that Quest had covered for his brother by telling everyone that he and Ty had taken an impromptu road trip with friends.

The cottage was the last slave home left standing on the property that Quentin Ramsey's ancestors dwelled in when their master and his family deserted the plantation following the Civil War. Quentin and Marcella remodeled the three-room dwelling and it was a private oasis for the adults only. Ty was more excited to take part in the adventure Quay had planned. Just the chance to go anywhere with him always sounded like heaven to her.

Their relationship had always been unorthodox. In fact, they'd only gone on a couple of actual dates, nothing serious. Quay always seemed to shut down whenever the chance to venture deeper rose between them. When they stepped inside the tiny cottage, Tykira was stunned. The place was lovely and perfect for a romantic, getaway- music galore, a fully stocked kitchen, mini library/reading area with comfortable throw pillows all about a gorgeous bedroom. They spent the entire day and much of the evening there, before Ty asked when they'd be heading back.

But Quay had no intention of taking her back just then, Ty learned. She smiled then, remembering how uncertain she'd been when he suggested they spend the night.

She wanted to scream the word 'yes' but didn't want to appear fast, smiling she smoothed her hand across the vehicle's champagne suede seating as her memories returned with a vengeance. Quay had continued to encourage her and finally succeeded in drawing that tentative 'yes' past her lips. It was the best day she'd ever had up until that point. One day turned into another and soon almost a week had passed. The Janet Jackson ballad played the first night they made love.

"Why'd you take me there?" she heard herself asking.

Quay shook his head against the rest. The song had triggered his memories too. "You wouldn't believe me if I told you. Remember what you said about me taking other girls- other virgins there?"

"So what's the truth then?" Ty challenged, watching streams of weakened sunlight lay across her sweatpants. "Was it really because you wanted sex and I'd do because I was there?"

Quay thanked God for quick reflexes as he almost rammed the back of another SUV when he heard her question. "You've really believed that all these years?" Incredulous, his dark eyes fixed on her through the rearview mirror.

Ty didn't meet his gaze. "What else could I think? The way you treated me afterwards…" her voice trailed to silence.

Now he'd come full circle in realizing the damage he'd done. What she'd gone through, what she believed he thought of her. The realization was like a knife through his side. He knew she'd be hurt, he'd prepared himself for that and said it was better than having something more hurtful befall her. But somehow he'd foolishly not considered that she would think he thought she was nothing; that she'd only been a convenient source for gratification.

The drive continued with no further discussion and Ty accepted Quay's silence as her answer. Clearly, he didn't want to hurt her feelings by telling her that she was right about him. Her voice of clarity screamed that she hire a nurse and stay at her mother's. But there was more going on- more than Quay refused to say, and she was just too stubborn to let it go. For fifteen years she'd tortured herself with thinking about why Quay refused to let her into his heart. Now she had him right there, taking care of her, no less. Her determination was solid and she could only pray this time would produce the truths she'd waited half her life to hear.

~~~

Quay pulled his Hummer right up to the entrance of the scraper where he kept a penthouse. Ty began looking in the rear compartment for her crutches or the dreaded wheelchair. She found neither.

"How am I supposed to get out of here?" she asked when he came to assist her from the vehicle.

"Your crutches and wheelchair are inside," he informed her as though she should have known.

Ty grimaced while gingerly swinging her casted foot down from the seat. "So how am I supposed to get upstairs."

"I'll carry you."

Ty's mouth fell open and her brown eyes began an immediate search of his black ones. She just knew he'd been teasing. "No thanks," she said upon realizing he was dead serious.

Quay was already easing his arm beneath her knees. "Don't start, Tyke."

"I'm not starting, but this is silly."

"You're right, so please stop with the arguments."

Ty clamped her mouth shut and watched while Quay lifted her like she weighed nothing. *Damn him,* she thought. He was making her feel all soft and deliciously feminine without really doing anything at all.

They approached the tall glass doors leading to The Loft, where scores of wealthy business people resided. At one of the glass doors, Ty braced her hand against the frame and shook her head.

Quay halted his steps. "What?" he asked.

"I can't let you carry me in there?" she hissed softly.

"Why?" he challenged just as softly.

"You can't."

"Why *can't* I?" a smile tugged at his perfect mouth.

"You just can't," she ordered herself to look away from the sensuous curving of his mouth. "It just wouldn't…wouldn't…"

"Yes?" he stood there holding her in his arms as though it were an everyday task.

"It just wouldn't look right," she peeked beneath her long lashes at the people who cast interested looks in their direction.

"Your foot's in a cast," Quay bounced her in his embrace as he delivered the fact. "Are you saying I'm just supposed to let you hobble to the top floor?"

"It's *your* fault for leaving my crutches," she muttered, rolling her eyes at his playful sarcasm. "Besides, I'm sure you're gonna bruise the hearts of many women if they see you carrying me across the threshold, so to speak."

Quay firmed his arm behind her back, forcing her closer. "Right now, I'm only interested in *one* woman. I've bruised her heart more times than I can count and now the only thing I care about is making that up to her."

Ty had to mentally remind herself to shut her mouth. She could scarcely focus on anything until Quay cleared his throat and stared fixedly at her hand on the door. Giving in, Ty let him walk on ahead. Sure enough, they drew stares of almost everyone in the lobby. Her fist clenched at his shoulder when more than a few men complimented Quay on his lovely burden.

"Hey Barker, Jerry," he greeted two security guards upon stopping at the desk. "Anything I need to pick up?"

"No sir," Jerry drawled with a grin.

"Looks like you already have your hands full," Barker nodded politely in Ty's direction.

Quay chuckled. "Definitely, Barker Doyle, Jerry Brown, Tykira Lowery. She'll be my guest while she's recuperating.'

"Nice to meet you ma'am," Barker said.

"Thank you," Ty shook hands with both guards.

Quay moved on. Ty kept her head bowed and her smiles light as they strolled towards the elevator bay. *What is it with these guys and private elevators*, she wondered as Quay selected the car that went only to the penthouse.

Inside the quiet, mahogany paneled car, Ty could almost feel Quay's potent ebony stare focused on her. Suddenly, her comfy sweatshirt and pants felt unbearably hot.

"So is the nurse already here?" she was desperate for conversation.

"You'll meet her in the morning since she'll only be with you during the weekdays," he laughed when he heard Ty gurgle a mournful sound in her throat.

"I wanted to take a bath and I needed her help."

Quay shrugged. "I'll help you."

"Quay-no."

He slanted her an innocent look. "I promise to be a gentleman."

"Mmm hmm, unless I tell you not to be, right?" she knew the words would be the next out of his mouth.

"You need your rest," his sleek brows rose in challenge when he noticed her surprise.

The car stopped and the doors opened into the penthouse living room. Ty forgot her unease and was immediately taken by the décor. She could easily compare it to the office at Ramsey. The twins clearly adored the dark, masculine design. Ty hoped Quay couldn't feel her shiver as she took in the savagely beautiful masks and etchings on the brick walls. There were aquariums in each room and they accounted for much of the light in the place.

Quay didn't set down his burden, until they were inside her bedroom. Ty wondered when the trip would end. After all, she'd be first to tell anyone that she wasn't the lightest woman in the world but Quay seemed quite content though as he carried her through the spacious dwelling.

The room that was to be hers, was mellow and dim- much like the rest of his home. This room, however, was decorated with sweet creams and pastels. In addition to the pillows and linens, other feminine touches gave it another kind of warmth.

"I just had it redone," Quay made a point of telling her while trying to read her reaction. "I hope I got your sizes right," he said while setting her on the bed where her suitcase lay.

When he moved, Ty noticed that the walk-in closet across the room was filled with clothing.

"What did you do?" she breathed, blinking rapidly as she took in the array of pieces.

Quay shrugged and then folded his arms and glanced toward the closet. "I figured you'd have a time getting in and out of your clothes," he cleared his throat softly at the way the words sounded. "Anyway, I had some stuff picked out. You'll find some new PJs that should go on easily over that cast."

Ty had already hobbled across the room and was peering through the clothes, gasping at how lovely they were.

"Tags are still on. I didn't want you to think they belonged to anyone else," he said when she fixed him with a curious look.

Ty shook her head and turned back to the clothes. "This was so sweet and thoughtful," she didn't quite believe he'd done this for her. "Thank you," she added.

"Why don't you get settled in?" Quay wouldn't let himself get sucked in by the moment. "Press six on the cordless when you're ready for your bath," he instructed and turned to leave.

Ty only nodded and watched him go. When the door closed behind him, she left the closet, fell back to the bed and covered her eyes with both hands. If Quay intended to play the charming host for the duration of her stay, she was definitely in trouble. She realized it was far easier to handle- *or conceal*- her needs as long as he remained cool, distant or arrogant. When he switched gears that way, not only was he irresistible, he was downright confusing.

The truth was, she didn't want to believe anything he said- any excuses about why he did what he had to do. She didn't want to even consider that his feelings for her were more than just a desire for another sexual conquest. If he told her something else, something more than she wanted to hear, and then went cold again after letting her have a glimpse into *his* heart, it would kill her.

***

Little over an hour later, Quay returned to check on his houseguest/patient. He found her asleep with her suitcase opened and partially unpacked. Smiling, he crossed the room, pulled her arm from the case and situated her more comfortably. Then, he finished unpacking her clothes and afterwards he pulled a blanket across her sleeping form. He had all intentions of leaving when he heard the bed shift as she stirred.

"Quay?"

"Shh…go back to sleep," he held the door partly open.

"No," she propped up on her elbows. "I need a bath and I'm hungry."

"Alright, well let me bring something up to you but forget the bath until the morning," he bargained and prayed she'd go along. He didn't want to think about having to help her settle into a bath he couldn't enjoy with her.

"Quay please, I just feel so grimy after all those sponge baths at the hospital. I only want to sink into a bubble bath for a while," she closed her eyes and smiled as though she were imagining that very thing.

Averting his gaze, Quay smothered a groan and prayed for strength. Of course, he could understand her desire for a hot bath. "Alright, I'll go get the water run."

"With bubbles," she called before he could walk out the door.

"Get undressed," Quay grit his teeth once the words were spoken.

"Quay?" Ty pointed when he finally turned. "The foam bath is in the overnight case on the dresser," she told him.

He muttered a soft curse and practically snatched the bottle from the bag before he left the room. On his way to the connecting bath, he prayed that he'd be able to remember that she was recovering. She didn't need him coming on to her. That seemed fine as a thought, but in practice it would be murder on the more sensitive parts of his body. *Play it cool, Quay.* She didn't trust him not to hurt her. Winning back that trust had to be his top priority. Again, the words sounded fine in his head. Remembering them when all he wanted was her entwined with him beneath the black satin sheets on his king-sized sleigh bed, would be an almost impossible feat.

"Yeah?!" he heard Ty calling to him from the bedroom.

"Bring me a towel, please!"

Quay massaged the bridge of his nose. "Help me," he groaned.

~~~

He returned to the bedroom in time to watch her maneuver the wide legs of her black sweats across her ankle cast. Leaning

371

against the doorframe, he watched her intently. His seductive black stare slid across the sensuously long length of her legs and he grimaced; actually jealous of her hands where they smoothed along the molasses toned thighs. How he longed to replace her hands with his own.

Ty gave her hair a quick toss and was about to pull the sweatshirt above her head when she realized Quay had returned. She smiled when she heard him clearing his throat and extended her hands for the towel he waved.

"Thanks," she pulled the shirt over her head.

Quay turned his back before he caught a glimpse of…anything. He was about to walk out of the room when she called to him again.

"I'm ready to go to the tub," she said.

He kept his eyes closed for a second or two before turning. Every single one of his hyperactive hormones responded to the sight of her on the bed in nothing but a towel- *and that damned cast*- with her gorgeous hair tumbling to the middle of her back. No way would he let this woman walk out of his life. He would not survive letting her go again.

Tykira's stare was narrowed inquisitively as she focused on the expression tightening his face. "Are you okay?"

"I'm good," he managed the lie. "Let's do this," he smirked and tried again. "Let's get you to the tub."

"Quay?" Ty pressed a hand to his chest when he leaned close. "Are you truly okay with me staying here? I can be a handful," she admitted.

Don't I know it, he took note of how much of a 'handful' she was. Her supple curves, the full breasts, firm ample-sized mounds that a man could lose himself in… "Your water's getting cold," he knew that his thoughts were taking him into dangerous territory.

Ty was only focused on a hot bath and a good meal. She was totally *un*focused on how she was affecting the man she leaned on. The trip to the tub was achingly slow and Quay cursed and savored every minute. Tykira Lowery had the body and face of a goddess yet one could quickly see that she was a force. She was not someone who could literally be pushed aside without very harsh consequences like a black eye or bruised…extremity. But; as overtly as that aspect of her persona was, there was that subtle aura of intense femininity.

As she leaned on him, her hands curled trustingly around his forearm, her temple brushed his shoulder. She pressed her lips together and looked every bit the determined little girl while hobbling her way to the tub.

With gentle words, Quay coaxed her to the bathroom. Once there, Ty stopped, her lips parting as a gasp escaped them.

"What'd you do?" Her eyes widened.

Quay shook his head. "I figured you'd want to enjoy your bathtime."

Ty was speechless after that. The room was already exquisite and spacious, but now it possessed the added effect of sensuality. Candles lit the perimeter of the sunken black and gray marble tub. Their delicious unique aromas swirled throughout the air. Soft music just barely vibrated from the speakers and the huge tub overflowed with white, coconut scented foam.

"You didn't have to go to all this trouble."

"I don't want to hear it," Quay grumbled softly, knowing she appreciated it. "Just don't get too wild in here. You have to keep this cast dry. It's crazy to even think about a bath anyway."

"Thanks anyway for helping me to bend the rules a bit," she said.

With her gaze soft and lingering, Quay knew she had only to ask and he'd have done anything she wanted.

Her mind still on the bath, Ty straightened and let the towel slip to the floor.

"Tyke…" Quay almost lost his hold on her arm.

"Are you okay?" the raw emotion in his striking pitch stare had taken her by complete surprise. "You've seen me naked before," she said.

"You don't have to remind me," he spoke through clenched teeth.

Ty nodded, decided silence was best. Quay finished helping her into the tub of foamy water. He propped her casted foot on the stack of fluffy bath sheets he'd perched on the edge of the tub.

"Do you need anything else?" he came to kneel beside the tub.

"There's a hairpin on the towel," she looked past him. "Could you...thanks," she said when he placed the clamp into her palm.

Quay watched, helplessly fascinated as she wound the magnificent black mass into a loose updo and pinned it tight.

"Mmm...thank you," she sighed, reclining in the sunken tub.

Quay didn't vacate his spot. He longingly studied the bubbles and wanted to delve just one hand beneath the surface and stroke her with his most intimate touch. He wanted to watch her lashes flutter and her lips part as she enjoyed the pleasure he would bring.

"I'll be fine," she felt him watching her, and thought she sensed his concern.

Quay nodded and patted his hand against the tub. "Call me when you're done," he motioned towards a navy cordless phone that was mounted to one side of the black tiled wall above Ty's head. Standing then, he reluctantly left her alone.

A LOVER'S PRETENSE

~TEN~

"I'm sorry," Quest uttered for the fifth time before the weak apology was followed by another round of laughter.

Quay needed something to take his mind off the woman lounging naked in his tub. It was either call and vent to his brother or have a few drinks and build up the nerve to go and take what he wanted. Of course, he realized the latter would probably earn him a busted lip or a shove down the stairs.

"Thanks a lot, Q," he sighed, his dilemma not stopping him from chastising his twin's bouts of chuckling.

"I *am* sorry, man. For real," Quest swore and cleared his throat in hopes of swallowing what remained of his laughter. "I just can't believe you left her up there without making a move on her."

"I'm losin' my edge, Q."

"No, you're not. You're gaining one, if anything."

The perception didn't put Quay at ease. "Gaining what, man? Some punk mentality? Maybe a better word is stupidity."

"Wrong. You're gaining a sense of what it means to love and respect one woman so much that you put what she needs above what you want."

Quay massaged his eyes. "What the hell does that mean, Q? I've always loved and respected Tyke."

"But not enough to keep her close- to be honest with her, right?"

Silence.

"You're in a different place now, my man," Quest pointed out, "this time, you won't be able to just walk away. Not for any of the thousands of reasons you could find to justify it. You're gonna stay and you're gonna fight to keep her."

"What if she doesn't want to stay?" Quay had to ask. "What if she's finally had enough?"

"Dammit man, just tell her how you feel."

"But I already told her about Wake-"

"Not Wake, fool. You. You and how you feel about her. No beating around the bush this time. Tell her. If that doesn't convince her…then you're in trouble."

"Thanks."

"There're no easy answers, here, Quay. You really screwed this up royally. I don't blame Ty for being suspicious."

"Speaking of Ty," Quay said after he was silent for a time. "I asked her to call me when she was ready to get out of the tub. Q, man I need to go," he knew Ty would most likely try getting out of the tub on her own.

After ending the call with his brother, Quay headed back upstairs. He recapped the talk with Quest. It was true- he needed to come completely clean with her. Of course, he knew why he hadn't. It was something he could only admit to himself. He was afraid. Afraid that she really wouldn't believe him and then he honestly wouldn't know *what* to do. Shaking the unsettling thought from his mind, he took the steps two at a time until he was on the wing to the guest bedroom.

He approached the bathroom from the hall entrance and knocked. "Ty? Tyke?"

There was no answer and he guessed she'd gone and gotten out of the tub on her own. He twisted the knob and stepped inside the bathroom. Sensual shock washed over his face when he found her still in the water and asleep. The bubbles were long gone and there was nothing covering her svelte dark frame lying prone beneath the fragrant water.

"I can't do this," he backed away from the tub as he spoke. "Ty?" he called, hoping to rouse her without having to touch her. "Tykira?" he tried again.

She never stirred.

"Dammit," he muttered, kneeling beside the tub then. He bowed his head in a vain attempt to keep his gaze averted. She was in a deep sleep, tiny snores slipped past her throat as she slumbered.

Quay rolled his eyes and faced the obvious; there was no way he could leave her there any longer. He took a bath sheet from one of the unfinished oak cabinets and carried it to the bedroom. Then, he tossed another across his shoulder.

"You're a gentleman, Quay," he chanted. "You're a gentleman," he kept telling himself as he removed his watch and rolled the sleeves of his shirt above his muscular forearms. Effortlessly, he took her from the lukewarm water. His every hormone sizzled in response to what he was viewing- what he was holding.

Ty had obviously washed her hair, for it was damp and hung in wavy, black ribbons. He held her close to his chest and carried her from the bathroom. His grip was firm in order to prevent her slick form from slipping from his grasp. The sound of his own teeth gritting filled his ears as he fought to keep his composure.

Tykira didn't stir once during the brief trip, that seemed to last for an eternity to Quay. He placed her on the bath sheet, he'd spread upon the bed, and would not allow himself the treat of letting his eyes linger over her incredible form. Instead, he focused on the cast she wore and remembered that she was recovering. Dutifully, he began to rub the other bath sheet across her body. He performed the task in a brisk, efficient manner until his baser instincts strengthened. Then, the strokes slowed and became more lingering. Soon, he was smoothing the sheet across spots he'd already dried.

Ty fidgeted in her sleep and mumbled something inaudible before tossing one arm above her head. The movement thrust her breasts more prominently upon her chest.

Quay stopped pretending to still be focused on drying her and simply watched. The bath sheet fell from his hand when he lost patience with sight. One hand clenched into a fist and he hid it inside a deep trouser pocket. The other, he used to trace the curve of one breast with the tip of an index finger. He leaned close, pulling the hand from his pocket and bracing it against the bed while brushing his mouth across her temple. He palmed the plump, chocolate mound of her breast more possessively. His thumb just barely grazed a tender nipple.

"Mmm…" she responded in her sleep.

The sound was like a dash of cold water to Quay. He snatched away his hand, muttering harsh curses to himself. Quickly, he found a cute, but concealing pair of pajamas. He dressed her rapidly, gritting his teeth again as he eased a pair of lacy panties over her hips. Once done dressing her, he almost sprinted from the room.

~~~

Ty woke about two hours later, content yet mildly confused as she studied her surroundings. Then, she remembered she was at Quay's. She remembered something else too: she'd been in a tub of bubbly water. Now, she was deliciously cozy in a new pair of PJs. She couldn't recall making the transformation, so he must've done it for her.

Her groan filled the room then. She experienced her embarrassment post haste as she thought of what a delightful sight she must've been- all seductively nude with a big cast on her foot.

But what about Quay? Had he taken advantage of her submissive state? She didn't think he had, she would've felt certain after affects…she recalled the deliciously bruised state of her sex following their previous…romp Should she ask him? Would she embarrass him? Hmph. It'd serve him right for making her stay with him; knowing all he had to do is look at her long enough and she'd most likely beat him to the bedroom.

Gingerly, Ty pushed herself up and eased her casted foot to the floor before slowly following with her other leg. Switching on a nightstand lamp, she smiled. Her crutches and wheelchair waited across the room. Tossing her hair, that had dried to a wavy tangle down her back, she made her way to the crutches and headed out the door.

~~~

"What are you doin'?!"

Ty was halfway downstairs, when she heard him bellowing to her from the bottom.

"I don't believe you," Quay ranted, curving a hand across the banister as he glared up at her. "Coming down here in a cast, on crutches and by yourself no less? Do you want that damn ankle to heal, Ty?"

"I can't stay up there all night. I have to eat," she was too hungry to be fazed by his voluminous reasoning.

"I was going to bring it to you," he came up the stairs to finish helping her down. "You can relax in the living room while I get everything heated."

Ty's hand tightened around his. "I hope you weren't waiting on me to eat?"

"I wasn't hungry," he led her to a huge, worn black suede armchair. He set a pillow behind her back and made sure she was comfortable before leaving.

Ty dozed in and out completely at peace in the mellow room with Marvin Gaye crooning in the background.

~~~

"It smells great," she complimented when Quay came to collect her from the living room about thirty minutes later. "Did you cook?" she teased.

"I never cook," he eased her curiosity with a haughty look. "That's Quest. But my ordering skills are gourmet."

Ty laughed, allowing him to help her from the chair and out to the kitchen. Quay had set the cozy round table for two and the meal it carried looked as wonderful as it smelled. Quay had ordered Italian and there was a veritable feast. For the next ten minutes, they contented themselves on filling wine glasses and loading their plates with Chicken Parmesan and angel hair pasta tossed with perfectly seasoned steamed vegetables.

"I can't seem to remember getting back into bed after my bath," Ty mentioned after they'd been eating a while.

Quay continued eating and only offered a shrugged shoulder for reply.

"Do you happen to know how I got there?"

The bath was the last thing Quay wanted back at the forefront of his thoughts where it had been for the better part of the evening.

"Quay?"

"Hell Tyke, yes I know how you got there. Who else would've gotten you out, I'm the only other person here."

But Ty was taking great pleasure in torturing him, seeing him so out of sorts. Besides, she had a nagging curiosity to hear him tell her *exactly* how he'd managed.

Quay could feel her staring and gave in. Growling a curse, he slapped his fork to the table. "I took you out of the tub, I dried you off."

Ty smiled when his onyx stare wavered and he coughed.

"I um, I dressed you."

Slowly, she nodded. "Thank you."

Quay bowed his head, slicing off another morsel of the succulent Chicken Parm. "I did what had to be done."

"Mmm…and you always do what has to be done."

"Mistaken again. That's Quest, I'm far more selfish."

"Ha! You get no argument from me there." She took a sip of Riesling.

"It wasn't intentional," he set aside his fork, "not where you were concerned."

Ty kept her eyes trained on her plate.

"Our conversation in the car," he folded his arms across the front of his shirt. "You asked about that weekend- if it meant anything to me? Did I just want sex from you because you were there?"

"Quay stop," she looked up from her plate, "you don't have to-"

"You asked if my taking you there was really about Wake Robinson. You asked if I was trying to protect you then, too."

"Quay I mean it," Ty's warm brown gaze was then fiery with determination. "I don't want you to get into that. I should've never brought it up in the first place. I don't need an explanation. I don't *want* one." She stood and immediately stumbled on her cast. She waved a hand when Quay moved to help her. She shook her head and hobbled over to the hutch where the crutches leaned.

Quay knocked a fist to his forehead, "Fool," he cursed himself when she'd gone from the kitchen. What was he thinking? Hitting her with that her first night out of the hospital? He sat there in silence for a few moments when a thud and then a curse reached his ears.

"Dammit Ty," he found her seated on the stairs where she'd taken another stumble.

"I'm fine," she insisted, tugging on the frosty pink top to her PJs. "Quay no," she whined when he lifted her against his chest.

Ignoring her, Quay carried her back to the guest room. He tucked her in, before taking a seat on the edge of the bed.

"I'm sorry," his dark eyes filled with genuine regret as he voiced the apology. "I was wrong to come at you with that. Especially tonight. I mean that."

She dragged a hand through her hair and yanked a few locks. "I just don't need you feeling like I need you to explain. I was wrong for bringing it up in the first place. It doesn't matter anymore."

Quay brushed his thumb around the curve of her mouth. "That can't be true when it made you so upset just a little while ago."

Ty couldn't look at him and kept her eyes on her lap.

He didn't push. "Get some sleep," he pushed a lock of hair behind her ear when he kissed her cheek. "Goodnight," he moved back. "And don't come downstairs in the morning. I'll bring breakfast to you."

Ty only smiled and waited for him to pull the door closed. Then, she flopped back in bed and pulled the covers above her head.

***

"Hey!"

"Hi, you sound out of breath. I catch you at a bad time?"

Mick switched the phone to her other ear. "Not at all, you caught me on my way out of the study. What's up?"

"I know it's late, but-"

"Are you kidding me? I've been on pins and needles waiting to hear something," Mick cast a quick glance across her shoulder to see if Quest was near. "How'd it go?"

"I tell you, getting this exhumation approved with the top brass almost sounded the end of things. But everything went through incredibly well."

"And?"

"Jackpot."

"You found something."

"Mick *every* piece of physical evidence that was somehow *separated* from the official reports were found with Sera Black's body."

"My God," Mick felt a nauseous rumble float through her stomach in response to the woman's news. "What exactly did you find?"

"Let's see," Jill spoke as though she were looking through the evidence then. "Aside from the clothing from the night of the murder, there were samples- lab samples labeled all nice and neat… whoever wanted this information out of the way, wielded some mighty influence."

"How could Patillo have managed this? To hide evidence this way?" Mick asked.

"From what I understand through conversations with members of the staff when he was C.M.E., the man ruled that lab like it was his own private kingdom. He had free rein to do as he wished- no questions asked. Not to mention the caretaker at the cemetery- Mr. Sawyer Reynolds. He and Patillo were old fishing buddies. It was probably no trouble at all for him to convince the man to… assist him in hiding the evidence. The only question now is, what or who could've persuaded Patillo to put his career on the line this way."

"Yeah…" Mick's thoughts wandered. "How long will it take the get the evidence tested?"

"I'll get to work on it right away and call you ASAP."

"Thanks for everything Jill. We'll talk soon." Mick set the phone aside and thought over what she'd just discovered. She tried to shake off what she was thinking, but it wouldn't go away. Again, the nausea roiled in her stomach and that time it sent her sprinting for the bathroom.

***

Ty dressed in the private guest bathroom the next morning. She'd selected one of the lovely sundresses Quay had supplied her with. She had no idea the lavender chemise-style frock would favor her curves so adoringly, but it was too late to change then.

"Tyke! Breakfast!" Quay called from the bedroom.

Sighing resolutely, she headed down the short corridor which connected the bath and bedroom.

"Will you join me?" she watched as he placed a food laden tray on the bed. "Looks like you've got enough."

"I'd planned on it," he shrugged and gave her a lopsided grin, "but thanks for offering."

Silently, they took their places on the bed, Quay's dark gaze was hooded as he watched Tykira move around in the dress.

He cleared his throat and focused on selecting a muffin when she looked over and found him staring.

"Thanks for making me feel so at home, Quay," Ty hoped to dispel some of the heavy emotion in the room. "You're quite the host," she tucked her uninjured foot beneath her when she sat on the edge of the bed.

"Truth is, I never entertained a houseguest before," Quay shared, adding a few slices of cantaloupe to his plate.

"Bull," Ty sang, selecting a plate and fork then.

"I didn't mean I've never had a guest before, but I've never had one I've asked or even *wanted* to stay longer."

"Thank you," she had to smile over the way he tried to smooth the admission.

For a while the twosome ate in a peaceful silence. Then, Quay hissed a curse when he noticed the time.

"Gotta bounce, Tyke. Another meeting with Holtz Enterprises," he set his plate aside.

"Oh," obvious disappointment reflected in Ty's stare. "Another meeting, huh?"

"Yep," Quay predicted the next question before she spoke another word.

"Quay do you think I-"

"No."

"But-"

"No."

"Dammit," Ty pounded her fist to the bed. "Won't you let me finish?"

"Not if you're about to ask to go to this meeting," Quay moved to leave the bed.

"Please," she folded her hand across his wrist to prevent him from rising. "Please Quay," she scooted closer to him. "I'd just be sitting there. What harm could it do?"

Quay shook his head, while watching her intently. He knew he was seconds away from giving her whatever she wanted.

"Please," she inched as close to him as she could.

Losing all ability to restrain himself then, Quay was

suddenly crushing her mouth beneath his. The surprised gasp she uttered in response, afforded him the opportunity to simultaneously deepen the kiss and position her neatly in his lap. Her casted foot dangled next to his trouser-clad leg while she straddled him. Quay moaned, when he felt her mound cupping and grinding onto the rigid, throbbing part of his anatomy that most wanted her attention. The kiss went on, growing deeper and hotter. Quay's hands applied a penetrating massage to her hips and the small of her back. He settled her closer, groaning when Ty became a more eager participant in the kiss. Her fingers toyed with the open collar of his shirt, teasing the powerful chords in his neck before her hands curved around his broad shoulders.

Quay couldn't resist palming and fondling her breasts; manipulating her nipples to stiff peaks beneath the bodice of the sundress. He played in the heavy darkness of her hair as tirelessly as he splayed wide palms across her thighs. When he would have pulled away, she kept his hands where they were and urged them higher.

"Tyke…" He broke the kiss to rest his forehead against her clavicle. "The nurse will be here soon. She's got a key. I-I'll see you later, okay?" he delivered his words quickly while gently easing her up and off his lap. Returning her to the bed, he dropped a sweet kiss to her forehead and left at a determined pace.

Ty heard the front door close, she grabbed one of the apple walnut muffins from the platter and slathered it with butter. With a hearty bite, she chomped voraciously in a weak attempt to clear the encounter from her thoughts.

~ELEVEN~

"How's it goin'?" Quest asked, when he'd pulled his brother aside following that morning's meeting.

"One night and I'm about to lose it. I have to keep reminding myself that Ty's off limits... that way," he grunted and shook his head. "I have to remind myself all the damn time. I want her Q. Boy, do I want her," his gaze narrowed as visions of Ty lying naked in a tub of bubbles filled his mind. "But if her heart isn't part of the package..."

Quest didn't hide his smile. "This is what I like to hear."

Quay shook his head, allowing his brother to gloat.

"You think you can handle it?" Quest asked.

Quay's expression then was skeptical. "Last night was the first night any woman ever spent the night in my house and woke up the next morning without having been in my bed."

"And it felt like hell?"

Shaking his head at his brother's question, Quay grinned.

"Not hell. Not heaven either, but definitely not hell."

"Damn man, you're growing up. I'm proud," Quest pulled his twin into a bear hug and chuckled while Quay groaned.

***

"Well, this is a treat," Catrina Ramsey pulled her daughter-in-law close for a hug and cheek kiss.

Damon Ramsey was next in line, bestowing his kiss to Mick's cheek and forehead as he escorted her into the living room. "We were so happy to get your call," he told her,

"I know how busy you both are," Mick squeezed her hands as she took a seat on one of the gold loveseats in the living room.

"We're never too busy for you, Sweetie." Catrina said.

Mick nodded. "Thanks, because this is something I couldn't put off any longer."

Damon and Catrina exchanged concerned glances.

"Sweetie is…everything alright between you and Quest?"

"Oh!" Mick started, realizing how confusing her words may've come across to her husband's parents. "No Catrina, no. No everything's fantastic between Quest and me. This is something else," her amber stare clouded again. "It's something that's not very pleasant, I'm afraid."

Damon and Catrina were silent.

"Sera Black," Mick noted the immediate change in the couple's expressions.

"Are there any new leads?" Damon cleared his throat.

Mick told her in-laws everything, holding nothing back. She saved the announcement of the newly discovered evidence for last. When she told them how it'd been uncovered, Damon and Catrina were clearly stunned.

"Obviously someone wanted that evidence out of the picture. I guess they- whoever *they* are, never intended on Raymond Patillo having a crisis of conscience on his deathbed," Mick said.

"And you want to know if we were responsible for the evidence being misplaced?" Catrina asked, her lovely dark face a picture of calm. "If we paid someone off in hopes of protecting our sons in the event one of them- or both of them- were guilty?"

"I'm so sorry to come to you both with this," Mick fiddled with the leather ties on her denim jumper. "And I'm not accusing or standing in judgement of anything," she rambled, "but I have to know. If it helps, I can understand why this was done. I'm not a mother, but I know I'd do anything to protect my child."

"Well then, love I'd say you've already learned the first and most important thing about parenting," Catrina reached out to pat Mick's knee. "But honey, we didn't do this," she said before her expression tightened. "*I* didn't do this," she clarified.

Mick and Catrina looked to Damon who graced them both with his appealing double-dimpled grin.

"Love, I'd be the first to admit that I'd do anything- *anything* to protect my boys," Damon addressed Michaela. "I've already protected them to a great extent," he shrugged. "Perhaps it was wrong, but a parent's love can be a powerful and sometimes misguided thing. Unfortunately, it never occurred to me to do this. When they told me they weren't responsible for that child's death, I believed them."

"Even though Quay was drunk, passed out and couldn't remember a thing?" Mick probed.

"Even then." Damon admitted with a solemn nod. "Guess that makes us a couple of saps, huh?" he glanced at his wife.

Mick smiled. "No, just a couple of loving and trusting parents."

Catrina elbowed her husband's arm. "Uh baby, isn't that loving and trusting stuff equal to saps?"

The threesome burst into laughter, that greatly lightened the mood. Shortly, however, Damon's expression darkened.

"Even though we weren't responsible, I think it's safe to conclude that this was done by someone in the family," he stated. "Only a Ramsey would have had the means and the motivation to pull off a cover-up like this."

"Who?" Mick's gaze narrowed in confusion. "Who else would have reason to? After all, this hidden evidence; whatever it proves, would've protected Quest and Quay. That was *your* job."

Catrina and Damon exchanged glances over their daughter-in-law's naiveté.

"Sweetie in such a large family, it's natural to protect one's own," Catrina said. "What affects one, affects all."

"You're right," Mick sighed, realizing the woman's point. "I still wonder who, though?"

Damon leaned back against the sofa he shared with his wife. "I got a good idea," he said.

***

"How are you?" Quay asked when he knocked upon Tykira's bedroom door that evening.

"Bored," she snapped, without looking his way.

"Nothin' on the tube?" he asked.

Ty shrugged, smoothing her hands across the arms of the thermal knit top of her PJ set. "I really wouldn't know. This is only my first movie."

"Is that right?" Quay took a few steps into the room. "Because I know you watched the soaps earlier today so I'm pretty sure you've gone over your TV limit."

"Quay!" She whined, balling her fists on the bed. "I'm about bored out of my mind. What else do you expect me to do? I begged you to take me with you to the office this morning, remember?"

"Yeah...yeah I remember," his expression tensed as he tried not to envision the sultry scene that followed her request. "You hungry?" he asked, noticing her watching him.

She softened. "I told the nurse, I'd wait for you."

"How's pizza sound?" Quay pulled both hands from his walnut, trouser pockets when she nodded. "I'll go place the order. Be right back," he watched her snuggle down in bed before he headed out of the room.

Out in the hallway, he prayed for more strength to keep his hands off her. He dutifully placed the order, took a quick shower and changed clothes in hopes that the food would be there by the time he was done. Just chatting with Ty could be dangerous. He was beginning to care less and less about the cast she sported.

~~~

Tykira clapped when Quay returned to the room carrying a large square box, paper plates, napkins and a six pack of sofa. He set it to the night table when she made room for him on the bed.

"I'll just eat over here," Quay motioned toward the easy chair across the room.

Ty's lifted a brow. "But you won't be able to see the movie from over there," she argued.

Not wanting to call more attention to his uneasiness, Quay didn't balk. He prepared two plates filled with three slices of the sinful, cheesy vegetarian pizza.

"What is this?" he referred to the movie about to begin.

"I hope you won't be too bored. It's a mystery movie marathon. Tonight they're featuring Agatha Christie."

"I hope they start with a Poirot," Quay was saying as he bit into a gooey slice of the pie.

Ty watched him with an incredulous gaze. "What do *you* know about Poirot?"

Quay leaned against the pillow lined headboard and smirked. "You're surprised?"

"Quite," Ty shrugged. "I wouldn't have pegged you for a mystery lover."

"Why not?"

"I don't know," she took a swig of 7UP. "You don't seem the kind to sit down to read a book much less sit still for a two, two and a half hour movie. Especially one that requires paying attention to more than sex or a series of explosions."

"Damn Tyke, is that what you think of me?"

Ty helped herself to a bite of pizza and let her silence carry for a while. "It's the way you've always been," she had no regard for the stunned expression he wore. "Fast paced, wild, testosterone driven, that's Quaysar Ramsey."

When Quay chuckled and shook his head, her brows rose

inquisitively.

"You're surprised? I'm sure I'm not the only woman who has that perception of you," she ate heartily as she spoke. "You're fun and incredible to be with- but only for a time. You're not exactly a 'long haul' kind of guy."

Quay didn't know why the description bothered him, but it did. Especially when it was Ty who held that perception.

"Tyke-"

"Shh, shh…it's starting," she patted his arm, "looks like you'll get your wish to see Poirot," she said.

Quay settled back and tried to focus on dinner and the movie. *Murder on the Orient Express* was first up for the mystery marathon. Unfortunately, he found that spending an innocent evening next to the leggy, dark goddess was murder on every part of his body. He wanted her every way he could take her. But, of course, she'd be expecting that-just that and nothing more meaningful. After all, he wasn't a 'long haul' kind of guy.

***

Tyke Designs had completed its work. The guys had agreed with Quaysar that it'd be best not to keep Tykira too much in the loop despite her repeated requests for information whenever she called in to the office. The construction crews, architects and interior designers were at peace with the final plans and she would only find new worries to interfere with her recuperation time. As the mechanical building and engineering of the train had already been underway, the group was looking for total completion within a few more months.

Holtz felt that the rail's maiden run, should be something special. They wanted the Ramsey clan on board along with everyone involved with the project. The Holtz Destiny; the name chosen for the train, would reside at the new Banff Tower in Canada. It was Holtz Enterprises' plan to have all parties involved with the creation of the resort, to be on hand to enjoy the resulting vision. Needless to say, everyone was terribly excited and could hardly wait for the event to commence.

~~~

A tiny furrow formed at Michaela's brow as she turned onto her back. She moaned softly, feeling the caress of the sweetest touch. She arched upward, feeling her nipples being suckled and then bathed with lingering strokes. Unfortunately, the feeling that truly caused the furrow in her brow was the subtle roiling in her tummy. The discomfort grew more unbearable even as the sweet caress continued.

"Mick?" Quest pulled away just slightly when he felt her struggling against him.

Mick writhed amidst the covers, only a few seconds more, before she woke. Then, she was bolting from the bed with one hand clamped over her mouth. Quest rested on his elbow, frowning as he watched his wife race to the bathroom. Slowly, he left the bed and followed her.

Leaning against the doorjamb, Quest folded his arms across his bare chest and watched Mick heaving and vomiting into the toilet. The episode lasted at least three minutes.

"Something you ate?" he asked when she was done.

"I-" a totally unladylike burp interrupted her, "I don't think so," she sat on the floor, leaning back against the toilet as she closed her eyes.

Quest pulled a phone from its cradle on the marble counter top. He pressed the button that speed-dialed the family doctor.

When Mick realized who he was speaking with, she waved her hand to get his attention. "Quest no!"

"Just a minute, Doc," Quest held his hand across the mouthpiece and fixed his wife with a slightly humored, slightly ticked-off look. "Hush," he said.

~~~

"When was your last period, Michaela?" Dr. Lucas Sims asked.

Mick blinked and then flashed a quick glance toward her husband. "I don't... I don't remember," she crossed her sneaker shod feet one over the other while wringing her hands in her lap. "But it's usually irregular," she saw fit to share, "especially when I'm stressed or under the pressure of a deadline."

"Is that the situation now?" Dr. Sims inquired.

Mick shook her head and then rolled her eyes toward Quest when he cleared his throat. "Not exactly, but I *am* working on something it...it's been pretty demanding."

"I see," Dr. Sims nodded.

When the doctor reached into his bag; Mick and Quest watched as though he were about to extract a magic antidote. When the man produced a home pregnancy test, Mick backed away as though it were a poisonous snake.

"Doc? What is this?" Even Quest sounded a bit unnerved as he spoke.

Dr. Sims only waved his hand. "I only want to cancel out the obvious first. Michaela, humor me," he held the box in her direction.

Quest was right on his wife's heels once she'd taken the box and was shuffling toward the bathroom.

"Quest, what if-"

"Shh...let's just get the test out of the way first," he suggested even though he was just as rattled as she.

~~~

In the bathroom, Mick handled her business and finished up while Quest placed the test strip on the counter. The only sound in the room was the click of the second hand from the wall clock and Quest's wristwatch, not to mention the methodic tapping from the sole of Mick's shoe as she sat on the toilet cover. She was seconds away from voicing her impatience, when she saw Quest reach for the test box. He read the back and then looked at the test lying on the counter. Then, it appeared as though his legs were about to give and he braced his hands around the rim of the sink.

"What?" Mick called in a frantic whisper. Both her feet tapped as she practically bounced on the porcelain toilet cover.

Quest turned, responding to his wife's query with a brilliant smile.

***

Quay and Ty had already spent three weeks together. It was at times tense-filled and uncertain and other times easy and quiet. Through it all, their emotions strengthened and solidified. The problem? Neither wanted to verbally admit to what those feelings were. Quay had taken to coming home later in the evenings, hoping he'd find Ty sleeping when he went to check on her. Knowing she felt he wasn't a man who could flourish in a meaningful relationship, was like a knife through his heart every time he looked at her. The irony? He'd never given a damn about whether a woman thought he was that sort of man or not. If he wanted a bed warmer, he had one. Now, he wanted more and it was becoming painfully clear that his 'want' would not be fulfilled.

Music touched his ears the moment he left the foyer. He followed the lilting sounds of the violin concerto drifting from the speakers. He found Ty snuggled on what had become her favorite lounge. Quay's dark eyes narrowed as he watched her on the cushioned chair, her fingers toying in her lengthy locks, her toes wriggling where they appeared at the opening of her cast.

She gave a start when she heard him clear his throat. She looked up and greeted him with a lazy wave.

"You and that chair are becoming inseparable," he stepped into the living room.

"Mmm yeah, I'll miss it when I'm gone."

Quay winced, his hand flexing into a fist. His expression turned fierce at the mere mention of her leaving.

"Bad day?" Ty noticed the look darkening his striking features.

"It's not that," he commanded his mood to cool, "things are going pretty smooth actually."

Ty sat up a bit on the lounge. "That's what I've heard. The guys have *sort of* been keeping me in the loop," she smoothed both hands across her arms bared by the thin straps of her black tank top.

"What's that tone for?" he watched her roll her eyes.

"I get the feeling they're trying not to make me feel left out and pitiful because I'm stuck at home with a broken ankle. I got a call from Louie Danoue earlier and he even sounded like he felt sorry for me."

Quay's grin revealed his right dimple and he shrugged. "Come on Tyke, they're just tryin' to look out for ya."

"Well I guess, I'm just not use to it."

Eyes narrowed, he found her words strange. After all, he'd been protecting her for over a decade, hadn't he? The question lodged in his mind and caused him to ponder it for a moment. Maybe he *hadn't* been protecting Tykira at all. With that loaded possibility, he went to fix himself a drink at the pine wall bar and then went to join her at the edge of the lounge.

"Having a man look out for you can't be that extraordinary, can it?" he braced elbows to his knees, while cradling his glass in both hands.

Ty rested back. "Pretty much."

"Bull."

"Why?"

"Ty…look at you."

She followed orders and did just that; looking down at her black tank and comfy white cotton sweats. Then, she shrugged and fixed him with a bewildered expression. "What?" she prompted.

He grimaced, that perturbed by her confusion. "Woman, do you even look in the mirror? A man would do almost anything to have you on his arm. Hell, I swore off tall women when I lost you. You were that deep in my system."

Ty blinked, her cool expression turning to something more inquiring. "When you *lost* me?" her gaze faltered when he set down his glass.

"Yeah, when I lost you," he faced her fully on the lounge.

She was silent for several moments as though debating on whether to speak her mind. "Quay, in losing me, you would've just been making a mistake. You pushed me away and that was a choice."

"By choice or mistake, I was an idiot for letting it happen."

Bracing her hands on the arms of the lounge, Ty angled her legs over the side. "I'm heading up," she said.

Quay looked on helplessly as she stood and prepared to hobble out of the room on her crutches.

"I love you, Tykira. I always have," he said, watching her stop mid-stride. "I know you don't believe me, but I have no intentions of stopping. Ever."

She turned to face him, shaking her head as though in utter disbelief. "You don't know what you- what you're saying."

"Why can't I say it, when you feel the same?" he challenged.

"For all the good it's done me," her sparkling browns appeared more brilliant in the wake of unshed tears. "You say you've always loved me? Do you realize how hard it is for me to believe you felt that way back then? To not be scared out of my mind that..."

"What?" He moved closer, stopping when she backed away.

"I'm going home tomorrow. I won't be here when you get back from work," she said.

Quay commanded himself not to stop her. He'd taken a huge step in telling her how he felt. He watched her until she was gone from view and prayed for the strength he would surely need to make her believe in him.

A LOVER'S PRETENSE

~TWELVE~

The following weeks went by in a blur. Tykira had her cast removed and had made a full recovery. The family was ecstatic to discover that Quest and Michaela would be delivering the newest Ramsey in the summer of the following year. Of course, Quay was already behaving like the proud uncle and everyone loved the show he put on. When he was alone however, his every thought centered on Ty.

He hadn't seen or spoken to her since the emotion-filled discussion so many weeks prior. He'd decided to wait until all the work was completed with the rail and had remained absent from several of the meetings. He kept abreast of things through Quest, and was grateful for his twin's silent support.

Everyone had been looking forward to the party to celebrate the rail's completion. The event would take place aboard the Holtz Destiny. The train would be taking its maiden voyage to Banff, Canada. Arrangements to accommodate the group had been in place for months. Around four p.m. one chilly autumn afternoon, the passengers began to arrive. For a while everyone, simply marveled at the finished result. The majority of the Ramsey clan was in attendance, as were several members of the executive staff and their significant others. County had even made a special trip from Chicago to enjoy the festivities.

Tykira felt like a proud parent as she accepted all the accolades which were bestowed upon her. She almost couldn't believe it herself as she gazed upon the stunning bi-level rail. A luxurious glass-domed gallery overlooked a gracious lounge that could be used as a ballroom. An adjoining dining car would offer passengers fine cuisine in luxurious ambience. Ty couldn't fathom that such a creation had first taken shape in her mind and had developed from simple sketches. Nothing she'd ever done compared to this and it was quite a feeling to be part of such a grand accomplishment.

~~~

Porters rushed to and fro, taking bags and directing passengers. The quarters were all spacious, fully equipped cabins that offered breathtaking views from the widest windows.

Ty decided to head to her own cabin, but stopped just short of taking the steps into the car when she saw Quay. Weeks of not seeing him, were like losing a part of her. She'd missed him terribly, but knew it'd been best to leave when she had. Staying would have been far too costly a price for her emotions. He loved her. He'd said it with no coaxing. For a while, Ty allowed herself to imagine that it was real. That *he* was real and that the things she'd always dreamed they could share together could really happen. Then, the more no-nonsense side of her persona reminded her of the hurt Quay was capable of invoking with his confusing behavior. From that moment, she could only focus on when he'd turn cold again.

She wanted to move on, but her feet seemed to have a mind of their own and refused to budge. Quay caught sight of her, his steps drawing to a halt when he saw her. He dropped his bags where he stood and looked ready to bound toward her.

"Ms. Lowery? Ms. Lowery?"

Ty pulled her gaze from Quay to look down at the young woman calling to her. She could barely hear the girl's voice for the ringing in her ears. "I'm sorry?" she said.

"No, Ms. Lowery, forgive me for stopping you. I'm Corin Forest. I've been hired by Holtz to conduct tours of the train."

"Yes, yes of course, it's a pleasure to meet you," Ty stepped down from the train to shake hands with Corin.

"The pleasure is mine, Ms. Lowery. I can't tell you how proud I feel to be working on this train, a train designed by a woman."

Ty's smile was genuine. "That's so sweet of you. Thanks Corin, I know you'll have your work cut out for you."

Corin's expression seemed to dim with a shade of unease. "Actually, that's what I'd like to speak with you about. The train is so enormous," her brown eyes widened as they scanned the creation. "I only have a few questions if you could spare a few moments?"

Ty was glancing toward Quay again, noting that he was speaking with the conductor of the train.

"Ms. Lowery?"

"I'm sorry," Ty cleared her throat. "Of course you can ask me anything. Why don't we discuss it on the way to my cabin?" she asked, smiling at Corin's delight as the woman began to ramble off questions while they made their way onto the train.

***

Quest and Mick were already squared away in their luxurious cabin suite. They relaxed on the king bed nestled in the far corner. Dressed in burgundy and green plaid linens with green quilting and a matching comforter, the bed released an aura of cozy comfort.

"For the fiftieth time, I'll be fine," Mick snuggled back against her husband while they enjoyed the dazzling view from the window.

Quest pressed his face into his wife's unruly mop of blue-

399

black curls and inhaled. "Just so you know," he said upon exhaling, "if I see you stumble, get nauseous, dizzy or-"

"Sweetie *please*, give it a rest," Mick turned to face him on the bed.

Quest nodded his compliance, before focusing his attentions elsewhere. Easing out from behind her, he moved down to brace his weight on an elbow and smooth a hand across Mick's tummy. "You're having my baby," he leaned down to kiss her stomach.

"That's what they tell me," Mick stroked her fingers through the gorgeous cropped silk of his hair. "Quest?"

"Mmm?"

"I'm scared. Good parenting doesn't exactly run in my family, you know?"

A muscle danced in Quest's jaw at her words. "I won't let you do that to yourself," he fixed her with his extraordinary eyes. "That is precisely why you *will* be the best kind of parent. You know all too well what bad parenting is really like."

Mick gave into the smile begging for release. "Don't you ever get tired of making me feel better?" she curved her fingers around his jaw.

"Just trying to get you where I am," he said, "no one could feel better than I do right now."

"I love you," she leaned close to brush her lips across his.

"I love you," he simply mouthed the words and treated her to the deepest of kisses.

~~~

Ty gasped when she entered her cabin suite. Though she pretty much knew what to expect, she was still awed by the completed product. She hadn't visited the site since before her accident and; after recovering, decided it would be better to be dazzled once the project was finished. Pleased she'd made that decision, she inspected the area.

Unconventional comfort was what Holtz wanted. They didn't want their passengers to feel cramped or lacking any convenience during their voyage aboard the Holtz Destiny. In addition to plush, big beds, all the cabins featured full showers, toilets, storage cabinets, TV, DVD, desks and telephones with beautiful throw rugs and matching pillows on the sofa and desk chairs. The effect was topped off in a rich, cherry-wood finish.

Surrendering to the feel of total contentment, Ty removed her boots and took a seat cross-legged on the bed. With the folds of her beige, suede skirt surrounding her, she indulged in staring out at the view. Of course, at the moment the view from her side of the train mainly consisted of the conductor, engineers, porters and members of her crew seeing to last minute crises before the train departed. Ty looked past them, staring up at the sky and imagined gazing up at the stars over rivers and between mountains as the train chugged along to their destination.

A clicking sound tugged her attention away from the view and she saw a lever turning on one of the doors. When it opened and Quay stepped inside, Ty was stunned. Her legs went immobile and she couldn't have left the bed had she wanted to.

"Quay?" she managed.

"Um," his deep voice seemed to vibrate in the area. "My room…connects…I was just exploring and decided to try the door. I had no idea…"

He trailed off and Ty knew he was just as stunned as she was. "Probably Quest and Mick up to something," she predicted in a wistful manner.

Quay smoothed one hand across the front of his long-sleeved mocha polo shirt. "I fully agree," he muttered.

"I was only teasing."

"I wasn't. I'm pretty sure my twin and his wife are responsible for the…coincidence."

"Sorry," Ty whispered.

Quay waved a hand. "It's not your fault my brother and sister-in-law are such pitiful matchmakers."

The word forced Ty's breath to catch in her throat, but she offered no comment. Quay left it alone as well.

"This place is incredible, Tyke," Quay decided instead to

compliment her work.

"Thank you," the words caught on a breath, his approval pleased her very much.

From the overhead speaker, the announcement was made. The train was set to depart. Ty finally left the bed and joined Quay where he stood at the window to watch the disembarkation.

As they enjoyed the sight, however, Ty could feel Quay's smoldering ebony stare wholly fixed on her. She would have turned and moved away, but he held her upper arm fast. Every part of her then was highly sensitized to his touch and she trembled noticeably in his hand.

Quay gave himself over to the ruthless side of his demeanor and offered no escape where he kept her against the window. He cupped his hand beneath her chin, holding her still for his kiss. His mouth slanted across hers and he took her mouth tenderly at first, then bolder as his tongue plundered deep. He feasted on the sweetness of her mouth as though drinking in the very taste of her. Moans sounded, but it was impossible to tell who was more affected.

The moment was as explosive as ever, but Ty could sense urgency in Quay that she'd never felt before. Tiny sounds of desire passed his lips and she was awed by the helplessness she heard in them. His head angled from right to left as if he couldn't decide which way he enjoyed more. Ty felt as though he were trying to convince her that he was what she needed. Of course, she already knew that and the acknowledgement made her melt against him.

Being in such close proximity to a bed did nothing to quell Quaysar's more insistent hormones. They unnecessarily informed him that she was offering no resistance and that this was the time to take what he'd been obsessed with having. He whispered her name then, burying one hand deep in her thick hair while his other cupped a full breast straining beneath the fabric of the suede blazer that hugged her torso adoringly. When she pushed more of herself against his palm, he almost lost the strength to stand.

Somehow, he managed to resist the irresistible. His hand weakened on her bosom and he broke the kiss to hide his face in the crook of her neck.

"I'll see you tonight," he told her in a voice that was as soft as it was deep.

Ty trailed her lips across his cheek, hoping for just a bit more of his attention. He'd moved his hands, though and stood waiting for her to uncurl her fingers from the collar of his shirt. Reluctantly, she complied.

Quay's dark stare was knowingly intense. He smiled and watched as she focused her gaze to the carpeting beneath their feet.

Ty didn't move until she heard the door close behind him.

***

Mick had been trying to decide between the two outfits she'd laid on the bed when the soft chimes of her cell filled the cabin. Stunned that the thing was even picking up a signal, she retrieved it from her leather tote. "Michaela Ramsey," she greeted.

"Mick? It's Jill."

Michaela laughed, ecstatic to be hearing from her friend.

"Is this a bad time?" Jill asked.

"No, no it's a wonderful time!"

Now, Jill was joining in on the laughter. "I suppose any time is wonderful when you're expecting a baby."

Mick rolled her eyes then. "I can see you haven't heard of morning sickness," she indulged in only a few more seconds of laughter before she sobered. "So tell me, can we get to the dirt now?"

"We can."

"I assume you've had luck?"

"You won't believe how many times I've been stonewalled, Mick," Jill's grimace seemed to come through clearly in her voice. "No one wanted me to test that evidence and I tell you it was quite a chore in light of how dated it was."

Mick perched on the edge of the bed. "But you found something?" nervously, she eased her feet in and out of fuzzy bedroom slippers.

"I did," Jill's voice clouded with disappointment. "Mick I

403

um, honey I don't think you're gonna like it."

Mick felt a roiling in her stomach that had nothing to do with morning sickness. She couldn't even open her mouth to ask Jill to go on.

"There was semen taken from her thigh, skin from her nails and saliva from her chest," Jill continued. "I was able to make a DNA match for two of the specimens- the saliva and the skin. Blood found on one of the pillows was a positive DNA match for the saliva. Thankfully, all the guys who attended the party were tested and that was documented in the file- preventing me from having to chase anyone down."

"Lucky break," Mick murmured, "being that thorough. DNA testing wasn't very common back then."

"Hmph, right you are. That's why Patillo was so revered in his field- he tracked a lot of uncharted territory during his time as M.E. The man was a force and he took great pride in his work."

"Until the Ramsey money came calling," Mick noted sourly.

"Well in addition to the blood on the pillows, there were also trace amounts on the carpeting," Jill said. "I couldn't find a match among the boys at the party and when the murder occurred the two prime suspects were Quest and Quay-being the only ones on the scene when the police arrived. Like everyone else, they were fingerprinted and blood was drawn in light of the fact that a possible rape could have taken place. I even found the actual blood samples in the evidence box."

"I still can't believe they were left behind and not buried with Sera," Mick mentioned.

"Well, there may've been a reason for that."

Mick closed her eyes. "Go on," she said.

"The blood linked to the saliva is a possible match to Quay."

Mick blinked. "Quay," her heart sank.

Jill sighed. "My theory is that the blood samples were left behind-not buried with Sera- as some kind of insurance. Some of the evidence buried with her body would directly link back to

Quay. Keeping his blood sample in open evidence along with all the other boys at the party was smart. To bury Quay's with Sera would've screamed set-up. This way protected the family from scandal but left the door cracked just in case someone had to be sacrificed...or vindicated," she added as though the final possibility had just occurred to her. "It's just a theory," she added.

"But why Quay and not Quest? Identical twins, identical DNA, right?"

"Quay because he was at the scene of the crime at the time of Sera's death. No one could or would put Quest there after about a half hour into the party. Everyone had gone by the time he says he arrived to find his brother passed out and the room trashed-and his story checked out in that regard." Jill explained. "Additionally, there were witnesses that put him at the hotel sportsbar at the time of the murder given the recorded time of death. Unfortunately, due to the Ramseys penchant for...*handling things*, that alibi wasn't given much credibility at the time. Due to the lack of hard evidence..."

"No one was ever taken to trial, so confirming the alibi as truth or manufactured would've just been a formality-one nobody had time for." Mick concluded, understanding then how Quay could've feared Quest may've played a role in what happened to Sera. "And now, thanks to me we've got evidence linking this to someone I really love a lot," she expelled a shaky breath, "Jill are you sure about this?"

"I'm afraid so, honey. I even ran the tests more than once to be sure. That's another reason it took me so long to call with the results."

Mick pressed her hand to her mouth and forced herself to calm. "You said you linked two pieces of the evidence. The skin? Who did that belong to?"

"The skin was a match to Wake Robinson."

"Wake?" Mick breathed, her mind reeling from the revelation. "I was beginning to think he'd been a scapegoat."

"Well I'm not so quick to point the finger at Quay either," Jill cautioned. "Remember there's still one key piece of evidence with no owner."

Mick nodded. "So what happens now?"

"Now, the ball's in your corner. I need you to talk to Quay. See if he can remember *anything*. The answers may be there and he only needs to unlock them. Whatever happened in that room, happened before Quest got there and Quay's the only one who can tell us what that is."

***

Contessa Warren was already working her magic on the room. The myriad of stuffy business conversations mingling around the celebration cocktail party, seemed surprisingly *less* stuffy with County's personal flare for gab.

"Tell me, Ms. Warren, is your publishing company targeting any other wealthy families?" Marcus Ramsey asked when he wangled a private moment with her.

"My company doesn't target wealthy families, Mr. Ramsey," County's easy aura never faded. "In fact the majority of those families come knocking on *my* door looking to tell their stories. The book was my idea," she admitted, her almond shaped eyes sparkling as beautifully as the row of sequins lining the scoop neckline of her curve-adoring crimson gown.

Marcus nodded. "Your idea?"

County smiled. "Mmm. I find your family fascinating, but I too can understand your desire for privacy."

Marcus kept a moderate reign on his tongue. Somehow, he knew his usual overbearing manner wouldn't play well with the no-nonsense young woman he spoke with. "Ms. Warren, *no* family wants *all* their dirty laundry aired before the public."

"I can certainly understand that," she agreed, leaning a bit closer, "especially with regard to your family's situation and all."

"Situation?" Marcus inquired, something dangerous flickering in his dark eyes.

"Sera Black," County specified, her lips curving into a faint smile as she watched the man's dark face turn ashen.

Marcus leaned closer so that he was practically towering

over Contessa. "I would suggest you watch how you throw that name around."

"That name may be thrown around a lot more before long, Mr. Ramsey. I've got a feeling a killer is about to be brought to justice." She stepped back and fixed him with a gleaming albeit phony smile. "Good night Marcus," she strolled on to find more interesting conversation.

"Now there's a young lady who doesn't bite her words."

Marcus bristled when he heard Damon's voice. "She's just like her friend," he told his brother.

"Ah yes, my Mick's somethin' else, isn't she?" Damon championed his daughter-in-law. "She's got drive, spunk, courage," he tirelessly boasted. "I got a feeling you'll have the chance to see lots of that one day," he clapped a hand to his brother's shoulder.

Marcus rolled his eyes and turned. "What the hell are you talking about?"

Damon pretended not to notice the man's agitation. "I think your sons will gravitate toward those sort of women. Mine have."

Marcus smirked. "That's because you never stressed that they marry well. A *lady* who befits having the Ramsey name."

"The Ramsey name?!" Damon bellowed and threw his head back to laugh. "A family who helps its members get away with murder."

"Damn it, if your sons were to blame you would've-"

"What?" Damon inquired, his brother's words having stopped him cold. "What's really goin' on here, Marc?" he breathed.

"I don't know what you're talking about," Marc scanned the semi-crowded lounge.

"Nah," Damon's onyx stare narrowed as he shook his head, "none of that this time, Marc. I know you were the one who covered that evidence."

Slowly then, Marc turned back to his brother.

"You didn't know it still existed, did you?" Damon saw the confusion in his brother's eyes. "Raymond Patillo," he smiled when he saw Marc swallow. "You convinced him to *misplace* that evidence, didn't you?" Damon asked, when Marc opened his mouth to speak and produced no words. "He didn't destroy it, Marc, he just hid it with Sera's body. Too bad for you, he wanted to clear his conscience before he died."

"Bastard," Marcus sneered, "how the hell can you accuse me of somethin' like that?"

"Save it. I'm not buying, Marc." Damon sneered right back. "Which one of your boys did it?"

Marcus seemed to calm then and surveyed his brother with a critical eye. "You always looked the other way, Damon as far away from the family as you could. Especially when one of us was in trouble."

"Now, you can just stifle that shit, Marc," Damon lifted an index finger in warning. "You seem to forget all the times I tried to cut corners to 'help' y'all hide your messes."

"Yeah D, I remember. But in family that's a never ending task but you decided you didn't want it anymore. I never made that choice."

"This is murder we're talkin about, Marc."

"And you wouldn't sacrifice one of your own any more than I would."

Damon searched Marc's dark eyes with his. "Which one? Which one did it?"

"So blind," Marc shook his head. "You haven't been able to see anyone or anything since you had those boys."

"They're my children," Damon reminded his brother in a tone of disbelief. "I want you to stop beating around the bush and talking in riddles. What the hell is going on?"

~~~

"Q?"

Quest smiled, turning to the man who'd taken his arm not long after he and Mick parted ways inside the cocktail party. "What's up, man?" he reached out to shake hands and pull the man into a quick hug.

Fernando Ramsey's translucent stare was fixed across the lively room. "Who's that with Mick?" he asked, inclining his head just slightly.

Quest turned, following the line of his cousin's gaze. He sought out his wife, smiling as a hint of possessiveness crept into his eyes as they raked Michaela's curvy form. Reluctantly, he looked on and nodded. "You mean, County?"

"County?" Fernando parroted.

"Contessa Warren, she's Mick's publisher and best friend."

"Who'd she come here with?" Fernando hadn't taken his eyes away from the woman since she'd sauntered her way into the party wearing a dress that practically had his fingers aching to peel the slinky scrap of material off her body. Having a name to put to the piece of voluptuous eye candy; helped to ease the ache…a little.

Quest frowned a bit, shaking his head. "I'm pretty sure she's here on her own."

"Jesus," Fernando only briefly managed to look away from the woman. She'd stirred his arousal by sight alone and every part of him wanted to uncover the rest of her talents.

Quest smiled, taking keen interest in his cousin's obvious anguish. "Want to meet her?"

Fernando helped himself to another lengthy, heated scan of Contessa, "Don't worry. I plan to."

***

A round of applause filled the room. Tykira had just arrived and the elegant bar lounge was alive with cries commending a job well done. From across the lounge area, Quay maintained his position at the bar and watched her bask in the success. He thought about all he'd put her through and how he'd darkened a relationship that should have been nothing but joy. Now, it was up to him to change things. Ty would be his, she'd believe in him again, he vowed to himself.

"Playing shy tonight, I see."

Mick's voice in his ear, brought a smile to his face. He squeezed her hand when he felt her rub his shoulder.

Quay kept his eyes on Tykira. "Just trying to give her some breathing room."

Mick elbowed his arm. "Why now?" she teased. "Not in the best mood, huh?" she asked when he smiled tightly and offered no comeback to her question.

"Not in the best mood at all," he confessed.

"Then I won't feel so bad about sharing my news," she smoothed both hands across her arms left bare by the wispy straps of her empire-waist gown.

Quay turned, his inquisitive stare turned dark when Mick announced that she'd spoken with Jillian Red. Quay was stunned, but continued to listen as Mick told him everything she'd learned. For so long, he'd tried to believe it was Wake who'd really been solely responsible. Now, there was evidence. His own DNA was at the scene, not to mention the confirmation of a third party.

"Do they suspect Quest?" He had to ask.

"He was tested back then along with you, remember? No one from the party could put him at the scene before they left and then there was the alibi from the hotel restaurant.."

"That was real?"

Michaela shrugged. "My contact is about as thorough as they come. She was able to follow up with some of the witnesses- she thinks they're solid."

"Hmph," Quay closed his eyes as memory resurfaced. "A lot of people thought that was bullshit- even me. I was sure my folks cooked it up to shield him…from something he may've done to protect me," he hid his face in his hands and breathed a relieved sigh.

"Sweetie, do you remember anything, *anything* that happened before you passed out?" Mick's amber eyes intently searched his onyx ones.

"I can't," Quay grimaced then at how helpless he felt.

Mick bowed her head, sending a slew of curls into her face.

"Then, I'm afraid we're all in the dark until Wake comes forward."

Only to himself could Quay admit that he was more than a little terrified to hear the man tell him what part he played in Sera's death.

"Will you tell Ty?" Mick smiled as she looked over at the woman laughing with Holtz executives.

Quay shook his head. "Not tonight."

"Will you pull away from her?" Mick asked.

Quay shook his head. "Not ever again."

~~~

Ty was waving off someone she'd been speaking with, when a pair of steely arms slipped about her waist.

"Congratulations," Quay spoke against her ear, loving the way she felt in the sleeveless black jersey dress. The V-neck bodice emphasized her stunning bosom while the uneven flare hem and open-toed sling back pumps accentuated the lovely length of her legs.

Ty snuggled back against him, deciding to enjoy all the closeness she could.

"I have to say it again Tyke, this train is unbelievable."

She fiddled with his tuxedo sleeve. "I'm glad you're impressed."

"I was impressed before you drew one sketch," he trailed his nose along her nape left bare by the elaborate updo she wore.

Ty turned in his arms then. Instantly, she could see that all wasn't well. "What is it?" she whispered.

Quay shrugged, cursing her perception. "Probably just motion sickness."

"That was your worst lie yet," she tilted her head as she watched him. "Come on, what is it?"

Debating, Quay decided to keep quiet for the time being. "I will tell you everything," he gathered her even closer. "I'm never leaving your side again. You're never getting rid of me," he vowed.

Tentatively, as though she feared he would bolt, Tykira

eased her hands across the crisp material of his jacket. "I never wanted to get rid of you," she linked her fingers behind his neck. "You always seemed intent on leaving, though."

"That's because I was a fool and I wouldn't deserve you if I allowed that to happen twice in a lifetime," he said, smirking when he noticed Louie Danoue trying to get their attention. "I think your public is waiting," he told her.

Ty barely glanced behind her. "What about you? Where are you going?"

"Not far," he curved his thumb around her cheek. "We *are* on a train in the middle of nowhere, remember?"

Ty tugged on her bottom lip and seemed reluctant to leave him alone. She decided not to press and joined the Holtz team on the other side of the room.

Weary and tired of socializing, Quay massaged his eyes and headed back to his cabin. Along the way, his steps slowed and he took time to stare out the glass dome of the corridor leading back to the compartments and main seating area. He could tell they were nearing the upstate toward the mountains. Trickles of snow were tumbling from above. They'd be in the thick of it by morning, he predicted. With a sigh, he reached his quarters. Once inside, he didn't bother with turning on lights, preferring to continue his enjoyment of the passing scenery.

Quay had been relaxing for a while; and obviously far more relaxed than he realized, for he was shocked to his soul when a male voice greeted him in the darkness. Turning in the leather swivel chair before the desk, he saw Wake Robinson emerging from the shadows.

"Don't freak out, man. I only came to talk," Wake cautioned. "I only want to tell my side of things and nothing more."

"Why now?" Quay challenged.

"It's time," Wake said.

"You've had plenty of time," Quay's voice sounded dry, "and I can think of far better places to clear your conscience."

"I doubt that," A half smile appeared on Wake's attractive,

light brown face. "There're certain advantages to meeting on a train."

"Sounds foolish to me, but I thank you for being careless."

"You're right about one thing. I did come to clear my conscience."

"By all means," Quay gave an airy wave. The room was still bathed in darkness but his eyes had already focused in steadily on Wake.

"How long we been friends, Quay?" Wake removed both hands from his jeans pockets as he sat on the leather couch on the other side of the desk.

Quay smiled in the dark, remembering. "Since your mom brought you with her to Ramsey when she interviewed to be my uncle's assistant."

"And have I ever lied to you?"

Quay grunted and straightened to remove his tuxedo jacket. "Considering the circumstances, I'd say that's a yes and this trip down memory lane is getting old. Before you think about sharing the lie you came here with, I should tell you the cops have matched certain pieces of DNA to forensic evidence they uncovered from the murder scene. They've matched me to saliva and you to skin found under Sera's nails." Quay clasped his hands atop the desk and leaned forward. "You understand what I'm saying?"

Wake nodded. "I do. You think I killed her."

"You're here to tell me I'm mistaken?"

"Very mistaken. If anything, I tried to save her life."

"What?"

Wake's gaze narrowed in the moonlight. "You really don't remember, do you?"

"I really don't. And I'd hate it for you if you sit there and tell me-"

"I tried to save her life and that's the truth."

"And a truth like that caused you to disappear for the last two going on three years?"

"No one would've believed it."

"I wonder why?"

413

"There was a fight, Quay," Wake massaged his temples as he leaned forward. "You were drunk out of your head and willin' to take Sera up on her offer."

"Bullshit. Sera wasn't one to give it up like that."

"She was bent on revenge."

"Against who?"

"Against the man she was sleeping with."

In addition to being confused, Quay's anger had reached the boiling point. "I'm not in the mood for riddles," he warned his old friend.

"Look Quay, after you and I fought-it was nothing more than a punch in the mouth which probably explains the blood they found-I got the upper hand and you were out cold, but Sera was determined to wake you up. She kept saying she was going to have a Ramsey-one who was free to have her back. She kicked and scratched at me which is probably how my skin got under her nails. I had scratches for weeks."

Quay smirked. "So I was passed out and you helped yourself?"

"It didn't happen that way."

"Then what way did it happen? Because you obviously know and won't talk," in spite of the dark, Quay could hear the man's voice shaking.

"Just know this, Quay, the man Sera was seeing came to the room soon after we fought. He told me to leave and I did. When I saw Sera again, she was lying on the concrete eleven floors down."

"So you just left her in the room with some guy?" Quay's disbelief was clear.

"Dammit Quay, I was working for that guy. I had been for years."

Quay leaned forward. "Working for him," he could see Wake nodding in the moonlight.

"I was a clean-up man, so to speak. I *never* killed anybody, but I'd...*persuaded* several young women to leave certain Ramseys alone.

"Persuaded..." Quay closed his eyes as so many things began to come together- the disappearances, girls moving away. "This man...the man Sera was seeing, did he have something against me? Since every girl I'd ever shown interest in had conveniently left or been removed from my life?"

"This man hates you and Quest very much."

Quay swallowed past the foreboding lump in his throat.

Wake continued. "What happened with Sera was between the two of them. But when it parlayed into a chance to make trouble for you and your brother, he jumped at it."

"What the hell does he have against us?" Quay demanded, standing so quickly he almost sent the heavy leather chair to the floor.

"It's not so much you and Quest as it is your dad."

Stunned, Quay was already poised to ask his next question when a soft knock sounded against his door.

"Quay? It's me."

Tykira's voice sent Quay's anger fading fast. He forgot about Wake Robinson as he went to answer her knock.

"Hey," he greeted quietly. His dark eyes roamed her face with sweet intensity when he opened the door.

"Are you alright?" Ty curved her fingers just inside the door as she stepped close.

"I was fine, I'm a lot better now seeing you," Quay left his cabin to escort Ty back to hers.

Inside her compartment, Quay turned on a couple of lamps and then prepared to leave. "Don't worry about me," he brushed his mouth across her brow.

She caught his wrist. "Will you please stay?" she wasn't ready for the evening to end and not completely sure that he was okay.

Quay cupped her lovely face in his wide palms and smiled. "You can't know how much your concern means to me, but I'm good. I want you to lock these doors behind me- all the locks Tyke-even the double bolts. And set the door alarms."

"But why-"

He gave her face a bit of a squeeze. "Do this for me, no arguments alright? Let's see if this fancy security system really works. Don't open this door for anyone but me, Tyke. I'll be back, I promise." He had every intention of keeping his word.

Eventually, Ty nodded and accepted that his decision was final.

Again, Quay kissed her forehead and backed out of the cabin suite making sure she had done as he asked before he walked away. Immediately, his thoughts returned to Wake. Unfortunately, he found the man long gone when he returned to his quarters.

Anger returned in the span of a second. Hands clenched, Quay searched for something to slam which would only upset things. Besides, Ty would surely hear him from her cabin and he needed to keep this quiet. Wake couldn't leave the train and would be like a caged animal before too long.

Quay left his compartment, intent on finding the security chief, conductor and Quest. He saw his brother and Mick in the corridor shortly after he'd left the cabin.

Quest took note of his twin's mood the moment they stood face to face. "What?" he asked.

"Wake's here."

"Wake? How?" Mick whispered, stepping closer to the brothers.

Quay gave a brief but accurate recap. Quest made quick work of securing Mick in their cabin and then joined his brother to locate the chief and conductor. They made a pit stop in the lounge to collect their cousin Moses who had coordinated the train security with contacts made through his organization of bounty hunters. Quay and Quest quickly returned to the cabin car where they could brief the men while being in the vicinity of their women. Everyone understood the importance of keeping things quiet. The last thing they needed was panic on a train ascending a snowy mountainside.

"I'm pretty sure Ty is secure in her cabin, but maybe you should join her there, huh?" Quest advised once the briefing had concluded.

"Way ahead of you, Q," Quay moved on down the corridor.

There was no answer from Ty when Quay knocked at her cabin door. He had the chief porter override the security measures to let him in and found that she'd drifted off to sleep while waiting for his return. Silently, he doffed his clothing then slipped into bed with her..

Ty stirred, gasping when she felt his arms encircling her, his lips against her ear. She tried to turn.

"Back to sleep," he urged, his hold tightening.

She tried to turn. "I don't want to."

Quay understood, he was just as starved for her as she was for him. "We've got in the morning," he brushed his mouth across her cheek. "Right now, I only want to sleep with you."

~THIRTEEN~

A steady snow began to fall during the earliest morning hours. It continued on through a hazy dawn and blanketed the environment in a scene of winter white. Ty opened her eyes and focused on the wide window that held her entranced by the passing view. She was filled with a sense of contentment and something else. She was very warm and it had nothing to do with the bed coverings. Moreover, it was the steely embrace surrounding her.

It took some doing, but she managed to turn and gasped when she found herself staring into Quay's striking features. He was awake and watching her with an intense emotion which radiated from his dark eyes.

"Are you alright?" Were her first words. Her nails grazed his jaw as she spoke.

"I'm good," his canyon-deep voice seemed to resonate in the room.

Ty studied every inch of his face. "I want to know what's going on."

"I don't want to talk, Ty."

"But I-"

"Tyke, right now, talking is the last thing I want to do with you."

Tykira's questions faded like mist as his words melted her amidst the luxurious covers. "Quay..." her fingers weakened on his cheek.

Taking both her hands and pressing them close to his chest, Quay lavished her mouth with quick, soft kisses. The innocent pecks grew hotter and wetter in their urgency until he'd kissed a path down the column of her neck and the swell of her breasts.

Ty tugged her bottom lip between her teeth and surrendered to what occupied most of her waking thoughts. Quay paid special attention to the budding nipples that were already firm in anticipation of his touch. It was only then that Ty realized he must've undressed her some time during the night. The man's touch was like mist, she thought warming over the idea of sleeping contentedly while handled her. He tended to one bare nipple with maddening thoroughness. His tongue bathed the rigid peak with languid strokes, before he suckled fiercely. His long brows were drawn close as he focused all his concentration on the task. Persuasive fingers grazed the other nipple. He alternated between squeezing the dark tip and soothing it with this thumb.

Ty arched and moaned, surrounded by a sea of sensation. Quay partially covered her beneath his weight. His hands encircled her waist when she arched. He never ended the maddening assault on her breasts. The glorious mastery of his lips and tongue was wholly centered on her nipples. Tykira's gasps of utter delight in his ear fueled his determination to take her to the cliffs of satisfaction with the simple caress.

Quay settled himself snugly between her thighs and he almost lost all ability to reason when she raised herself against him. The torturously erotic friction forced a moan past his lips. Ty shuddered, feeling his helpless cry against her breast. Her hands gradually gained strength and she stroked the crisp, silkiness of his hair. Unconsciously, she drew his head closer to her chest. Quay switched his attention to the other breast, ravaging it with his tongue and teeth. His hand cupped and fondled the mound as he drew more of her satiny molasses flesh into his mouth.

Ty's breathing was basically a series of shuddery sighs as she struggled to relay her need. Quay knew how affected she was, he felt the same. Her unconsciously sensational grinding against his erection was driving him out of his mind. His head was filled with visions of burying himself deep inside her then. He wanted to plunder the soft creaminess of her sex until she had nothing left to give. More than that however, he wanted to savor the moment and knew that would be a lost fantasy if he gave into his basest urges. He had to see her, smell her, feel her on his mouth.

Tykira cried out her disappointment when he left her chest and showered his kisses across her abdomen. Her hands fell away from his back to lie weakly against the pillows cradling her head.

At the joining of her thighs, Quay simply trailed his nose across the light dusting of tight black curls he found there. He grazed the most sensitive area of her body, the devilish right-dimpled grin appearing when she responded with a delighted shriek. Her hands came to his shoulders, the pleasure he gave her clit was so overwhelming that she didn't know whether to buck or rotate her hips.

Quay was holding her hands to the bed while feasting on the overly sensitive bundle of nerves. Tirelessly, he nibbled and stroked her there without a care for her breathless pleas for mercy. Ty strained against his hold, never had she been so affected. Her hips lifted from the bed and eventually Quay released her wrists to hold her thighs in place.

Ty buried her fingers in her hair and submitted to the sinful pleasure he eagerly provided. She'd climaxed more than twice and knew not whether she could survive the eventual treat of their lovemaking.

Quay offered her a brief respite. Of course, Ty would've been the last one to call it that. He ended the scandalous kiss after plunging his tongue deep inside her for one long, lengthy moment and rotated it slow as he withdrew. Then, he was turning her onto her stomach, tonguing a wet kiss down the length of her spine. He rose to cover her with his body, pushing her thick hair over her head to expose her neck in order to feast upon her nape.

Ty pressed her face into the pillow and arched her bottom against the potent extent of his sex. Quay's hand curved over her hip and disappeared between her thighs. Ty sobbed when his fingers entered her one, two, three at a time. They stroked deep and rotated in an ever increasing wealth of moisture. Quay's kisses to her back grew more ragged as Ty continued to grind her bottom against him.

Completely weakened by desire and the way she sounded while he fondled her, Quay could barely retain his grip on the condom packet he'd taken from his trouser pocket. Ty saw it fall to the pillow in the line of her gaze and she could feel him trembling behind her. Just as overwrought as he, she turned over and managed to remove the condom from its packaging and ease it in place. The simple act took far longer than she'd anticipated. Her eyes widened at the sight of him, his length and girth made her mouth dry with desire.

Quay could waste no more time. His powerful hands curved around her upper thighs; pulling them apart as he thrust forward. He squeezed his eyes shut and clenched a fist that he pounded against a pillow. Never had he experienced such sheer desire for any woman. But Ty wasn't just *any* woman; she was the only woman he had ever truly wanted.

They made love throughout the snowy morning. Quay took his time pleasuring her and allowing himself to be pleasured. Ty felt ravished and welcomed the feeling of being overwhelmed by the powerful dark male she had desired all her life.

~~~

"Quay?" she called when they lay spent and satisfied amidst tangled covers.

Immediately, he raised his head and blinked when he spied the unease in her stare. "What's the matter?" his concern was as evident in his words as it was in his expression.

421

"The night we were together…after the club…"

Quay's eyes darkened, haunted by the memories of that evening.

"I hadn't been with anyone since the night we first made love," she said.

His sleek brows drew close and then his gaze held the look of stunned disbelief. In his wildest dreams, he couldn't fathom the beauty in his arms virtually locking herself away because of him.

"Ty…I'm so sorry for the way that night ended. The way I made you feel," he grimaced as though the words put a sour taste in his mouth.

"I've never been able to imagine myself with another man," her eyes lingered on snowflakes trying to gain purchase along a frosty window, "whenever my platonic relationships took that turn, I'd end them before it happened. I cursed you so many nights. Hmph…I cursed myself for feeling so deeply for you that I couldn't let another man touch me. I was sure you didn't have that problem where other women were concerned."

Quay winced. "Tyke-"

"No, no don't," she shifted to curve her fingers around his jaw, "there's nothing to be sorry for or to regret,. You owned me no loyalty. I only wanted you to know those nights meant so very much to me. I love you. I always have. I fear I always will."

"Fear?" Hurt pooled his gaze.

"When it came to being hurt by you, you never disappointed me. To believe it may really be a thing of the past, scares me. I'm so afraid that I won't be able to handle it if it happened again."

"Ty listen to me-"

"Shh…" she hugged him close when he sprawled across her. "Later. I don't want to talk about this anymore now."

Quay raised his head from her shoulder, not misunderstanding the meaning in her words. He began to love her every bit as passionately as before but with an added urgency. It was laced with tenderness, as though he were trying to tell her that he'd never stop until she was happy and the amount of time that would take would do nothing to discourage him.

Afterwards, they lay staring out the window with Quay's head resting gently against Ty's chest.

"I always wanted to protect you," he said. "I felt that way even when I felt girls were yucky, instead of yummy," he chuckled. "Quest always treated you like you were one of the boys, like you could handle yourself. And you could, but something made me want to keep you safe."

"That's probably why I fell in love with you," she stroked his temple.

"That didn't stop me from being a selfish jackass though," his voice roughened in the wake of his agitation. "I knew I was hurting you by being so cold, but doing what *I* felt was right was my only concern. Truth was, I was only protecting myself and *my* feelings," he turned over and looked down at her. "*I* was the one who'd had girls disappearing and…dying on me. *I* was the one who couldn't handle knowing I was the reason you were in danger or the possibility of losing you. *Really* losing you Tyke, that was something *I* couldn't think about."

Ty braced on her elbows and watched him closely. "And now? Are you saying you don't feel that way anymore?"

"I know you don't believe me," his right dimple appeared when he smiled, "but I can't let you walk out of my life this time. As important as your safety is to me, living without you a minute longer is a reality I don't want to live a second longer." Inching closer, he cupped her cheek. "I know it's going to take you a long time to trust me and I'll wait as long as that takes. You've always meant everything to me and I only ask that you please not shut me out while you make your decision."

Ty felt the slight pressure of tears behind her eyes. She smoothed the back of her hand across his cheek and whispered his name.

***

Catrina Ramsey was adding cream to her Hazelnut coffee when a shadow slanted across her table.

"Houston," she smiled up at her brother-in-law.

"I only stopped to extend my congratulations on your future grandchild. You'll be the most beautiful grandmother I know," he said.

Pleased by the comment and overjoyed by talk of her grandchild, Catrina laughed. "Why Houston, thank you so much. Damon and I can't wait until Michaela has the baby and she's not even showing yet!"

Houston managed to chuckle at the comment. "Yes, it looks like you and Damon are doin' it up as usual- the first grandparents," his tone was mildly biting as he thought of his own children Taurus and Dena.

"Well I'm sure you'll experience the same joy soon enough," Catrina predicted. "Besides, I never thought either of my sons would fall deeply in love with one woman and become content in making a life with her," she shook her head, "it's wonderful to see two ladies men like my boys finally get it together."

Houston appeared confused. "Are you saying Quay has also found someone special?" He asked, sliding into the opposite side of the booth.

"Mmm hmm. Found her *again* would be more accurate. I pray he and Ty will be next."

"Tykira?"

Catrina nodded. Her clipped silver gray locks bouncing around her lovely dark face.

"I had no idea there was anything between them."

"There always has been, since they were kids. Then, Quay started showing his ass and wanting to sow royal oats or whatever. But I think he's finally matured to the point that he realizes that pushing Ty away this time would be the biggest mistake of his life."

"Well my, my don't y'all look cozy!" Damon's playful bellowing drowned out his brother's next question.

"Well *my, my* Damon, still possessive of your toys, huh?" Houston retorted, taking personal offence to his brother's tease.

424

Damon noticed Catrina's hand curve into a fist and he covered it with his own. "You had your chance Hous. Don't blame me because I got the prize," he said.

Houston moved from the booth so quickly, he almost tripped.

Catrina shook her head, watching the man bolt away in a huff. "Children," she chastised.

Damon shrugged and reached for his wife's coffee mug. "He started it," he muttered.

~~~

A few booths away, Quay and Ty sat talking with Quest and Mick. Of course, the topic of discussion was Wake Robinson and his visit. Impossibly, it seemed that the man had disappeared from the train as all searches had turned up no sign of him.

"Do you guys have any idea who this other man Wake mentioned might've been?" Mick asked, watching the twins shake their heads in sync.

"He didn't give me one damn clue," Quay raged softly, "but he did say whoever it was hated me and Q with a passion."

Silence settled as the foursome stared unseeingly at the snow white beauty past the windows.

"Mick?" Quay called, having worked up the nerve to ask the question that had been nagging him since the night before. "How long will Jill hold off on what she discovered about the evidence?"

"Oh honey," Mick reached out to rub his hand. "I understand your concern, but we can trust her. She won't make a move until she hears from me."

Silence settled once more and then Quest nudged his wife's arm. He nodded once toward Quay who sat with his legs extended across the booth while Ty leaned back against him. The couple wore pensive expressions and Mick agreed with her husband that they'd probably want time alone. They quietly excused themselves and left the dining car.

The moment they were alone, Quay expelled the heavy sigh

he'd been holding.

Ty turned, watching as he massaged his eyes. "What is it?" she whispered.

Quay rested his fist to his chin. "I'm scared," he admitted.

She blinked, never believing he could feel such an emotion. She toyed with the comfy material of his black knit turtleneck sweater and realized that he was more than entitled to feel that way. She wanted to reassure him, but decided that he only needed her to be there.

"Isn't this somethin'?" she said, turning to lean back against him. They watched the gorgeous winter white view from the train's huge windows.

***

Banff, Canada~

The Holtz Destiny reached its destination later that afternoon. The view from the mountaintop was a vision that could not be described. Bags were taken from the train and deposited in the specified rooms. All the while, the passengers stood mesmerized by the scenery.

Girard Holtz, Founder and President of Holtz Enterprises, arrived to greet his guests and told everyone he prayed that future visitors would be as taken by the view as they were. The group was treated to hot cocoa topped with marshmallow crème while they breathed in the crisp mountain air. Girard covered his plans for their stay: touring the property via sky lifts, skiing, ice-skating and games. There were also libraries, a movie theatre, and several cafes for their enjoyment. All features would be accessible for the trial visit.

Everyone felt right at home and eventually the group began to disperse. Ty had gotten separated from Quay and found herself tugged aside by her crew chief Samuel Bloch.

"So, is Quaysar Ramsey the one?" Sam asked, once he and Ty had talked briefly about the resort and their grand accomplishment.

Ty rubbed her yellow mittens across the arms of her white ski jacket. "Yeah, it's Quay. It's always been Quay."

Sam nodded. "I can't say I'm not disappointed seeing as how I always thought it'd be me," he feigned despair and joined in when she laughed. "I thank God you aren't doomed to be a beautiful lonely woman for the rest of your life. And don't tell me you were *alone* and not lonely," he ordered when she opened her mouth to argue. "I know what lonely looks like," he tugged on the tassels of her knit cap.

Smiling, Ty nodded. "You're right. I worked and worked to keep myself occupied and even though you guys kept me close, I could never quite escape the feeling."

"I got the feeling there's a lot of hurt there?" Sam probed, his arms folded over his chest as he watched her closely. "You sure about him?"

Ty laughed, "I'm not sure about *anything*, but I know I can't walk away from it. I've wondered for too long what being with him would be like. I can't wonder any longer, you know?"

Sam nodded. "I know," he pulled her close for a hug. "I wish you everything good," he pressed a kiss to her cheek.

***

That afternoon, Mick found her husband seated at the spacious walnut desk in their suite. His laptop was on, but his gray stare was focused beyond the windows. The champagne colored drapes had been drawn and he was staring over the rolling expanse of snow covered land.

"Quest?" She called, already closing the distance between them. She moved behind the chair he occupied and leaned down to link her arms around his neck. "You okay?"

"Are *you* okay?" he countered.

"Uh-uh, Mister. I asked you first. Are you on edge about Quay?"

Quest felt every muscle he possessed, tighten a thousand times. "I know he's innocent, but the reality is the evidence puts him there with Sera. If that evidence surfaces…without Wake to come forward and confirm what he told Quay, Quay will take the fall."

"But Jill-"

"Babe, Jill Red may be a good friend but she's a cop first," Quest warned. "She's not going to sit on that evidence forever. Remember everyone already thinks the Ramseys have been getting away with murder."

Mick didn't want to think about it. "What about the other man Wake mentioned. The one who he said hired him?" She hoped to add a tone of reassurance to the conversation.

"Unfortunately, we still need Wake to resurface and confirm that to someone besides Quay."

"Well, have you been able to think of anyone since breakfast? Anyone who could hate you guys like that- business associates, former friends...or cousins?" She massaged his shoulders beneath the hunter green sweater he wore.

Quest was already shaking his head. "I can think of several business associates, but none who knew us since highschool. As for cousins, in spite of all the drama in the family we've managed to stay close."

When Mick uttered a heavy sigh, Quest turned and had her sit on his lap. "I don't want you worrying over this."

Mick's smile was melancholy. "I'm afraid I will until something presents itself in our favor."

"Hmph, babe..." Quest produced a rueful smile. "I believe the Ramsey luck and double dealing has finally run its course."

Mick's arms tightened around him and they shared the snug embrace for the longest time.

~~~

On the other side of the mammoth sized inn, Tykira found Quaysar in the same pensive mood that his brother was currently battling. He held onto a glass of scotch perched on the arm of the chair he occupied. The sitting room was lit only by the snowy grounds and inside by a fire roaring in a grand stone hearth.

Ty kept a mug of hot tea cradled in her palms as she neared

Quay.

"If you sit anyplace but my lap, I'll be very unhappy," he called out to her.

She smiled at his undying humor and followed instructions. Ty set down her mug and snuggled into his lap, smiling when he grunted his satisfaction.

"You seem unhappy," she noted.

Quay didn't deny it. "Unhappy and unnerved. Not because of what the evidence showed," he said when she turned to look at him, "I was there and I played my part in not conducting myself the way I should have. But it's knowing that there's some fool out there with this old grudge against me and Q."

"Have you thought anymore about who it could be?" Ty folded her arms across the front of her navy blue hoody.

"No one who goes back that far."

"What about jealous cousins? Ones who were outside the closest circle you grew up with?"

Quay gave a slow shrug and then shook his head. "I can't see it. Besides, none of them lived that close. We only saw each other during reunion time- if then."

Ty bit her lip, toying with a lock of her hair as she debated. "What about someone else in the family?" she asked finally.

Quay's sleek brows drew close when he heard the question. Then, his expression cleared as though he were grasping the true meaning of her words. "You think it could've been one of the elders?"

"Have you ever considered that? Wake *did* say this person had something against your dad."

"No," Quay's response was fast. "I mean, we've had our run-ins but they usually got started from basic teenage crap- nothin' to frame a person with murder over."

"Maybe *you* don't think so."

"Uh-uh," Quay denied the possibility by shaking his head. "I can't make myself believe that."

"Alright, it's alright," she feathered kisses across his brow. Snuggling deeper into his embrace, they enjoyed the snowy view for a time.

"I'm not a nice man, Tyke," Quay said after the silence had grown lengthy.

"Hmph, you're tellin' me," Ty didn't lift her head from his shoulder as she uttered the teasing remark.

"I'm serious, Ty. I mean, damn, I've done everything to get you out of my life, out of my mind, out of my heart over some foolish need to protect you."

"All you had to do was be straight with me," she raised her head then to stare at him. "You could've saved us so many years of heartache if you had. But," she replaced her head on his shoulder, "your reasons…I can understand them, but Quay please stop punishing yourself for doing what you felt you had to do." She reached for his hand and planted a kiss in his palm. "I love you. You love me, it's all that matters."

"What about your business?"

Ty shrugged. "What about it?"

"Tyke, your business is gonna be the hottest ticket after word spreads about this project."

Ty snuggled deeper into his embrace. "I'll have time for my business and you too."

"In Colorado?"

"We'll work out something."

"I don't want to work out something," a muscle danced fiercely along in jaw. "That'll get old quick," he foreshadowed.

Tykira blinked, unease finding its way into her thoughts. She feared he was grabbing at excuses to keep them apart then. "Quay what are you saying?" she forced herself to ask.

He waited for her to turn and face him. "I'm asking," he placed a hand over his heart, "I'm asking you to make room for me- for us- to have a life together. Tyke, I'm asking you to be my wife."

Ty was stunned speechless. Seconds- though they seemed closer to minutes- passed before a brilliant smile illuminated her lovely face.

Quay blinked, his magnificent features softened by relief.

"You have no idea how long I've waited to ask you that. I pray you won't wait too long to give me an answer." He sighed, lowering his gaze. "If the answer's 'no', I won't like it, but I'll accept it."

"Yes," Ty searched his dark eyes with her vibrant browns.

Quay closed his eyes as though he were praying. Then, he leaned in quick and provided her with a devastating kiss.

A LOVER'S PRETENSE

~FOURTEEN~

Mick got a late start that morning. She wasn't surprised to find Quest gone, she'd been sleeping later and later; due in no small part to the fact that she was now sleeping for two. When the knock sounded on the door, she celebrated having a reason to motivate herself out of bed.

"Good morning Mrs. Ramsey," the valet greeted in a shy tone from his position on the other side of the door.

"Good morning," Mick returned just as another yawn claimed her. "Sorry," she whispered.

The young man smiled glancing down at his shoes before looking back toward the petite dark beauty that stood before him. "That's quite alright, ma-am. A-a package for you," he announced a bit bashfully.

Mick's amber stare brightened as she watched the short Hispanic man produce a small wrapped package from the valise he carried. She signed the pad he extended, then found a ten dollar bill inside one of Quest's jackets on the coatrack.

"Have a good day," she bid when the young man thanked her for the tip. Sighing then, she closed the door and tore into the package. Finding the name Sera Black scrawled on the front of what looked to be a small book, forced a gasp past her mouth. Her heart began a frantic race when she realized the book must have been the other half of the girl's diary.

"I'd almost forgotten," Mick whispered and immediately opened the book to begin scouring the cream colored pages that were trimmed in a floral print. Closing it then, she decided to call Sera's mother and thank her for never tiring of the search.

Johnelle Black answered her line and Mick relayed her appreciation. Johnelle's reaction however, was not what Mick had expected.

"It's wonderful news, Mick, but for the life of me I don't know how you got it. I've been searching and rechecking places I'd already looked, but I haven't come across it."

Mick's hand went limp around the phone. "Then who?"

"I have no idea…does it shed any more light on the case, though?"

Mick trailed her fingers across the spine of the diary. "I haven't really read it yet, but I'll keep you posted."

"Thanks so much Mick."

"You take care."

The call ended and Mick studied the book. She held onto it reverently as the pensive look deepened upon her face.

***

Tykira was waking, smiling as she burrowed deeper within the covers of the gorgeous king-sized bed with its royal purple dressing and champagne linens which was the basic color scheme of the elaborate suite. Snow trickled past the windows, reminding her of the morning she and Quay spent making love aboard the Holtz Destiny. Delicious smells wafted beneath her nostrils then and she saw Quay arriving with a silver food tray in hand.

"What's this?" she pushed hair out of her eyes as she leaned back against the bed's cushioned headboard.

"Breakfast. I hope you're hungry," he placed the tray upon the covers and took his place on the edge of the bed.

"Well it sure does smell good. What is it?"

"Something I hope you'll love forever."

The strange comment brought a curious smile to Ty's face. She observed the tray. A single red rose lay across two covered platters. A smaller platter sat atop the larger and Ty decided to check it first.

"Quay," she breathed, finding the breathtaking marquis cut diamond ring sitting on a cushion in the middle of the porcelain saucer. "What have you done?" she gasped as he took her hand and eased the silver band onto her finger. "Why didn't you give this to me yesterday?"

"Yesterday was so crazy," he brushed his thumbs across her fingers he stared at his ring adorning her hand. "I wanted us to start today off better. Is this better?" he looked up, smiling when Ty giggled her agreement.

When Quay pulled away, Ty noticed the drawn look clouding his dark face. Tilting her head, she cupped his cheek. "What is it?"

Swallowing, Quay took her hand and kissed the center of her palm. "I need to tell you about Zara."

"No. No you don't," Ty had no desire to discuss the girlfriend he'd flaunted in her face during high school. "Why would you even mention her now?" she gave an uneasy laugh.

Quay took both her hands firmly in his. "You need to hear this."

"Quay, no-"

"Shh…" he urged, pressing a kiss to her mouth. "I need to say this, alright?" he gave her hands a quick shake and smiled when she nodded.

"You remember us together?" he waited for the nod she reluctantly gave. "She went missing the summer after our junior year- do you remember that?"

"Yes, Quay but why-"

"I blamed myself for that."

Ty blinked, confusion marred her features. "But...why?"

"The week I kept you with me, I was so desperate to have you," he stared down at her hands as though the action were giving him strength to continue, "I don't know what I would've done if you'd refused to stay. I knew that I was taking a chance even going there with you, but it was a chance I had to take."

Ty scooted up in bed and focused on him more closely. "Why'd it have to be a- a *chance*?"

Quay squeezed his eyes shut, and then his jaw clenched and he looked up at her. "Because...two other girls I knew had already gone missing during our Christmas break Sophomore year.

"What? B-but how?"

"I don't know," Quay's onyx stare narrowed as though he were concentrating. "At first, I only told Q about what I suspected. Then, we got Ma and Dad in on it. Q was sure the girls- both of whom had fathers working for Ramsey- just moved away or relocated because of something with the company. We checked with Dad and that wasn't it," he swallowed clutching Tykira's hands a bit tighter. "Then there was you. Always there- always caring about me, even when I started treating you cold to make you want to have nothing to do with me. That week with you was about me taking what I wanted- what I'd wanted for a long time and knowing I could never have again."

Ty smoothed the back of her hand across his cheek. "Quay..."

"Anyway...Zara," he massaged the bridge of his nose. "Zara was always there too. She always made it known that she was *available* to us. I don't know how many of us gave in to her, but I knew she'd be the perfect one to show you I was serious about it being over with you and me."

Ty leaned back against the pillows lining the headboard. "The way she used to hang all over you...I figured you guys had something really close."

"Close," Quay grimaced. "Yeah, sexually and that's all it was. Zara wanted it to be more. All of a sudden she wanted to be in love and I was the lucky guy. She was always telling me how she felt and wanting me to say it back, but I couldn't and then…" he shook his head. "One day I was finally honest with her. I blurted out that I loved you- that all this was to make you stay away because it was safer for you. She asked if I cared about *her* safety, but she didn't wait around for me to give an answer. I never saw her again."

"Quay…" Ty soothed, moving to her knees and leaning close to kiss his temple.

"Then, there was Sera, a girl I'd barely known, was barely close to and she wound up dead," he kept Ty close as he spoke the words. "The reason I'm telling you this is because I want you to be sure. I won't lie to you. Having you in my life-letting it be known you're mine- it still scares the living hell out of me." His hold tightened around her slender frame. "I want you to be sure."

Ty inched back to look at him. "I'd rather live a full life with you, no matter how brief it may be," she cupped his face when he winced at her words. "I'll take that *any day* over some half existence without you. I love you, Quay- only you- only you forever."

The unease Quay wore vanished to be replaced by his dimpled grin. "Forever. You mean that."

Tykira settled herself across her fiancé's lap and linked her arms around his neck. "You betcha," she snuggled down within the covers.

Quay followed and they spent the rest of the morning making love.

~~~

Later, Quay had lunch sent up for them to enjoy in bed.

"Quay?" Ty called, once lunch was done and she was arching into the erotic kisses he rained across her thighs.

"Hmm?" His kisses grew wetter as they showered her mound.

"Mmm…do you have any ideas about the wedding?" she managed to ask, talkative despite her present…enjoyment.

Quay was exploring the sensitive folds of her sex with the

tip of his nose. "You can have whatever you want. All I want is you for my wife," he treated her to a lengthy stroke from his tongue and let it linger before subjecting her to a devastating rotation inside her moist heat.

Ty's lashes fluttered as she submitted to the sensual power of the act. Quay's expertise made her orgasmic within minutes and it was quite some time before she spoke another word.

~~~

"Could we have the wedding at your grandparents place in Savannah?" Ty asked once they took a breather to lounge and cuddle.

"Are you sure, Tyke?" Quay's handsome face was then a picture of stunned uncertainty.

She shrugged. "Why not?" she raked a nail across his nipple.

"That's where things started to go wrong for us."

"I don't see that," she pushed herself up a little to look at him. "I see it as the place where my love for you reached a new level and now it's happening again and I can think of no other place I'd want to become your wife."

"I love you," he swore, pulling her close to kiss her again. "You're about to be mine forever," his hands skimmed her dark figure and he reveled in the way their bodies were a perfect fit. "I better start preparing this thing," he said as though he'd suddenly been struck by an idea.

"You're going now?" Ty cried, already anticipating more of his touch.

Quay needed no further persuasion to wait. He pulled Ty out of bed and took her to one of the armchairs set before the frosty windows. Taking his place there and having her straddle his lap, another sensuous scene ensued.

***

Quest's gray stare sharpened when he returned to the suite. He'd assumed Mick had been up and about hours ago and therefore hadn't returned to the room. Finding her sprawled out and asleep sent his concern mounting. He went to kneel next to the bed where he toyed in the dark curls covering her head.

"Michaela?" he waited for her to open her eyes and focused in on them. "Are you okay?"

"Mmm...fine. Just taking a nap. I'm fine," she gave him a lazy smile.

Quest leaned close and kissed the mole at the corner of her mouth. "Dinner's in a couple of hours," he told her.

"Quest..." Mick turned her face into the pillows. The last thing she wanted to do was leave the reading that had proven to be so interesting. "Can't I just eat up here?"

"Why?" her simple request had triggered his suspicion.

Slowly, Mick pushed herself up in bed. "I've been catching up on work I-I just didn't want to break into it," she watched him thumb through the material littering the bed. She snatched away the diary just as he reached for it.

"What's wrong with you?" his unsettling stare narrowed anew.

"Dammit Quest!" She left the bed in a huff then. "I'm pregnant! Does that answer your question!" She raged, faking the hysterical fit and praying he'd buy it. "Jeez, I think I'm entitled to behaving strangely and completely *not alright*," she hissed and folded her arms across the front of the burgundy empire-waist nightie. "Would you please leave me alone now? I promise to be ready for dinner."

Knowing it was completely useless to argue, Quest ordered his own temper to cool. Throwing up his hands, he left the suite muttering below his breath. Closing her eyes in relief, Mick flopped down on the bed and clutched the diary to her chest.

***

Quaysar had sent out special invites to the members of the Ramsey family in attendance. One of the glorious top floor dining rooms of the inn had been specially prepared for the event.

As promised, Mick was ready for dinner and sat looking

lovely yet troubled a fact that didn't go unnoticed by her husband. Quest sat directly across from her. Mick spent the better part of her time fidgeting with the asymmetrical collar of her tanned silk frock and staring blandly around the room. In spite of the fact that she'd barely spoken two words to the woman, Mick was grateful to have County seated next to her and chatting away. County's rambling was perhaps the only thing keeping Quest from grilling her, Mick thought.

County, unfortunately, was far from pleased. Her best friend was barely reacting to a thing she said. If there was one thing Contessa Warren hated was not receiving adequate reactions to her sly outrageous comments.

"I'll bet I'd get your attention if I ripped off this gown and pranced naked up and down this table," she scoffed, folding her arms across the scoop neckline which emphasized more of her ample bosom. A moment later, County felt a soft touch brush the nape of her neck. Turning, quickly, she glanced up and froze.

He has to be a Ramsey, she thought. She swallowed, knowing her words had deserted her when she studied the man whose magnificent caramel-toned face held her in awe.

Fernando Ramsey leaned down a bit, his soothing fingers still brushing Contessa's skin. "You may not have Mick's attention, but you definitely have mine." He said and then walked away as coolly as he'd approached.

Thoroughly embarrassed, County was silent following the brief encounter. Thankfully, the guests of honor arrived. Quaysar and Tykira were the epitome of beautiful chic. Quay wore a gorgeous black tux with a three quarter length jacket that further defined his powerful torso. Ty was undeniably alluring in a figure flattering black gown with flaring long sleeves and thigh high splits on both sides. Open-toed black heels had straps that hugged and accentuated her ankles and toned calves.

Quay helped his fiancée into her chair at one end of the long table and then took the chair opposite her.

"What's this about Quay?" Marcus had to know.

"Patience Marc," Quay urged, getting comfortable at the

table.

"Patience," Marc retorted as though the words pained him to pronounce. "Is that what you told our clients when they asked how long we were going to wait before dining with them?" he leaned forward in his chair to rap his knuckles against the table. "It's ill-mannered and bad for business to exclude our hosts."

"I've already spoken to them. I told them why we wanted time alone with the family."

Feeling foolish for voicing his criticisms, Marc let the subject drop without another word. "Michaela was watching the man so intently; she almost missed her husband's gaze focused with equal intent on her.

"Come on Quay, enough suspense. What's up?" Yohan Ramsey asked his cousin.

Quay's right-dimpled grin flashed and then he was looking at Ty. "I finally wised up and asked the goddess at the end of the table to marry me. She said yes."

At once, the room grew lively as the sounds of best wishes and cheer filled the air. Quest even forgot his mood and bestowed congrats to his brother and future sister-in-law. Conversation and laughter filled the room. A short while later, the servers began to arrive with a hearty meal.

Through it all, Mick was still quite unresponsive. County decided that enough was enough.

"Does this have anything to do with the baby?"

The question effectively pulled Mick from her doldrums. "The baby?"

"Mmm hmm. You *are* pregnant, right?"

"County-"

"I mean, you're sitting over there *not* talking to me, *not* laughing at my jokes. What? Don't you like Tykira?"

Mick rolled her eyes at the absurd question. "I love Ty. She's exactly what Quay needs and the only woman he's ever really loved,."

"Then dammit what the hell is wrong with you?" County practically hissed.

"I know who killed Sera Black."

The hushed statement caused County's hazel eyes to widen. "You know-but-but how? How did you find out? Have you called the cops? Do they have Wake?"

"County Wake Robinson hasn't done a thing except help keep a murderer free."

"Who did it?" County carefully pronounced the words as if Mick were dense.

"I can't say just yet."

"Mick!"

"All I have is circumstantial evidence."

"Which is?"

"The diary," Mick watched County lean back against the chair. "Johnelle Black was right- there were two. But of course Sera couldn't write down her murderer's name in the diary so there's nothing binding that links the murderer to her in that way."

County shook her head to relay confusion.

"She was having an affair with a married man."

"Ah!" County bellowed, glancing across her shoulder. She was happy to find that all the other conversations in the room provided an effective cover for her and Mick's words. "So much for innocent lil Sera. What?!" she cried when Mick slapped her thigh.

"She didn't deserve to die, County."

"Obviously his wifey didn't think so."

Again, Mick looked toward the other end of the table. "It wasn't his wife. In her diary, Sera wrote that she'd threatened to reveal the relationship if he didn't leave her. If we can tie him to that semen evidence taken from her body, maybe..."

County's eyes narrowed almost to the point of closing. "It's someone in the family, isn't it?"

"Everyone could I have your attention please?!"

County's question went unanswered as silence filled the room and everyone looked toward Quay who had spoken.

"During our train trip here, I got a visit from Wake Robinson," Quay allowed voices in the group to rise as a few expressed interest. "We kept it quiet, but we did have Moses and his boys on it," he nodded toward his cousin.

All ears and eyes were riveted on Quay as he divulged every aspect of the conversation he'd had with Wake aboard the Holtz Destiny. The family listened in awe as he spoke on the newly discovered evidence and how he'd remained hidden.

"Dammit boy!" Marcus exploded just as Quay revealed to the group that Sera had been involved with a married man. "Look at the mess you've brought down on this family!"

"Marcus-"

"Don't West," Marc ordered his older brother Westin Ramsey who sat further down the table along with his wife Briselle. "We're gonna be shoveling negative press for the next ten years because of this!"

"Shut up, Marc," Briselle ordered, "if only there were a scrap book big enough to hold all the scandalous news you've been the center of over the years!"

From then on dinner was a nasty, finger-pointing affair. The meal went unfinished as appetites were lost and everyone just wanted out of the dining room. Amidst it all, Quest's entrancing gray eyes were trained on his wife. Michaela had barely noticed when they were virtually alone in the room. When; at last, she pushed back her chair and stood, he was right by her side.

"Bedtime," he announced.

"Quest please don't pull the overbearing husband routine right now, I-"

"Then you're ready to tell me why you're walkin' around here lookin' like you just lost your best friend. You hardly ate a thing."

"Neither did anyone else," Mick pointed out in a meek tone. She swallowed when a muscle ticked wickedly along Quest's jaw.

"I have no more patience left, do you hear me Mick? You say you're not sick because of the baby, but I wonder about that. You won't tell me what's going on and I'm not about to take a chance with your health or our baby's," he sighed, letting her see his unease instead of agitation, "this is all new to me too, you know?"

Bowing her head, Mick sighed acknowledging his right to concern. She said nothing more and let Quest lead her back to their suite. There, he undressed her and selected night clothes which he put her into himself. Then he tucked her in for the evening and seemed content with letting her be.

Mick couldn't stand seeing him so on edge and caught the hem of his tuxedo jacket before he moved away from the bed. "I have the other half of Sera's diary," she confided.

Like his legs were deflating beneath him, Quest settled to the side of the bed. He looked completely drained and Mick scooted close to hug him.

"Sweetie, don't. It's not about Quay. He's not what this is about," she hugged him close.

Quest inclined his head, watching her more closely. "Wake?"

"No…"

"Mick-"

"Shh…" she pressed her fingers to his mouth, "baby please just let it go at that for now. I don't know what to do with what I know and I don't want you anymore upset. Just let me handle this for now, okay?"

Quest thinned his lips, sparking his left dimple while he debated. "I don't like the toll this is taking on you."

Mick agreed. "Do you think it'd look bad if we left a few days early?" she kept her gaze downcast.

"I don't care what it looks like," Quest stood, easing her back beneath the covers. "We'll leave in the morning."

***

Everyone in fact, felt much the same. After the ugly dinner scene the night before, the beauty and luxury of the Banff Majestic had worn thin on them as well. The Ramsey jets arrived by mid-morning the next day. From Canada, it was a non-stop flight to Seattle. Both jets remained void of heavy conversation. Pensive moods struck everyone hard. Even Contessa, who was usually never at a loss for words, had little to say. She stared idly out her window, without really seeing any of the gorgeous blue sky or luminous clouds. With her legs crossed and her hands folded primly in her lap, she had no idea how closely she was being studied.

After a while, however, her senses peaked and she turned towards the muscular caramel-toned male seated diagonally across from her. Surprised to feel a smile tugging at her lips, County cleared her throat softly. She took note of the man's slanting stare which raked her legs in a repetitive and thoroughly erotic manner.

County recrossed her legs and waited.

The man took his time, but eventually his translucent caramel stare rested on her face.

"I hope I meet with your approval?" County said, once their gazes locked.

He smiled, stroking his goatee with a light touch. "I have no complaints."

Obviously, she thought, refusing to let his blatant appreciation excite her. After all, she was Contessa Warren…men always stared at her.

"Who are you?" she believed he was a Ramsey, but didn't know which one.

"Fernando Ramsey," he supplied.

She nodded. "The black sheep."

Fernando's eyes crinkled adorably when he grinned. "That label does little to set one apart in a family like mine."

"Mmm, indeed," County leaned forward to extend her hand. "Contessa Warren," she said and was mildly surprised by her response to his hand enveloping hers.

"Mick's friend. The publisher."

"That's right."

Fernando appeared impressed. His mesmerizing stare was focused like a lion on its prey. "Busy profession."

County toyed with the diamond stud adorning her earlobe. "Busy, but rewarding."

"And draining?"

Thinking of Mick, County's easy mood vanished. "It's *very* draining," she admitted.

"And you don't think Mick should be putting so much of herself into this investigation into Sera Black."

Contessa blinked, stunned by the man's perception. "You're right. I don't. I do pray that Sera's murderer will be caught soon," her gaze faltered when Fernando just continued to study her intently.

"You shouldn't worry," he said finally and rested his big hands on either arm of the chair he occupied. "Mick's strong and one has to keep up a strong front to be part of this family, blah, blah, blah…"

County laughed, surprised that someone who appeared so intimidating could be so animated. "I've noticed that," she told him, her expression sobering. "Kind of sad, don't you think?"

Fernando shrugged. "I never looked at being strong as a sad thing."

County made a tsking sound and stood. "Mr. Ramsey, one should never have to keep up a strong front for family. Excuse me," she whispered leaving Fernando staring after her as she walked away.

***

Seattle, Washington~

"How is she Quest?" Ty asked when she and Quay arrived for dinner one evening.

Quest closed the front door and then turned to hug Ty and shake hands with Quay. "We had to bully her into staying in bed. Doctor's forbid her to do anything more. She's not happy with me for agreeing with him, but the first three months of a pregnancy it can go either way," he shrugged as though that fact settled the argument in his mind.

It had been one week since the group had returned from

Banff. Mick conducted what work she could from the comfort of her bedroom, but finally decided to share what she knew. She arranged a dinner party and asked Quest to make sure Ty, Quay, Catrina and Damon attended. Clearly, Quest was on edge about the gathering in light of her need to rest. Mick knew if she had any chance of her mood improving, she'd have to share the secrets she held.

~~~

Ty sat tapping one of her flat leather riding boots to the carpet. "I'm going to check on her," she stood from the sofa.

"It's okay, girl, I'm here," Mick called, making her way downstairs just then. She walked right over to Tykira and hugged her tight. "Congratulations. I'm so happy for you guys," she whispered, pressing a kiss to Ty's cheek and then doing the same to Quay.

"Alright Mick, enough of the sappy stuff. What's this all about?" Quay kept his arm about his sister-in-law's shoulders.

The bell sounded before Mick could explain and she was glad. Damon and Catrina were just arriving. Hugs, kisses and idle chatter were in order again. When the conversation settled on wedding arrangements, the twins exchanged incredulous gazes.

"Enough!" They bellowed simultaneously.

"Mick, out with the secret, already," Quay urged.

Nodding, Mick agreed this needed to be said *before* dinner. "Everyone sit down," she waved the group into the living room.

"Sweetie, are you feeling well?" Catrina asked once she and Damon were sharing a buttercream leather loveseat near the fireplace.

Mick nodded. "I'm fine," she smoothed both hands across her red silk lounging pants and took a deep breath. "I'd feel a lot better though, if I knew why your brother-in-law hates Quest and Quay so much."

Damon and Catrina watched each other for several moments and seemed to reach their decision in silence. Clearly, Mick had most of her answers and only needed their confirmation.

"I came into the Ramsey family on Houston's arm," Catrina smiled at the surprise on her sons' identical faces. "We'd been seeing each other for two years before he decided to introduce me to his people. Not that he wasn't proud of me, he treated me like a queen. Actually, he seemed less proud of himself. Even with his own family, he was always on edge. Especially around his brothers. He hated Damon. I could see that right away. At first, I thought it was because Damon was the youngest boy, but it went deeper than that."

"I was the laid back one of the group," Damon boasted, winking at his sons when they laughed. "Things always seemed to come easy to me with little or no effort, grades, girls, our parents' love," his expression sobered.

"Damon caught my eye right from the start," Catrina's lovely features brightened with love for her husband. "But I never had any intention of hurting Houston. One day I-I found myself…alone with Damon where he um…made his attraction known," lashes fluttering, Catrina shook her head when Quest and Quaysar whistled and commended their father.

"Anyway," she sighed, "I told Damon I wasn't interested, but he wouldn't back off. After that it was only a matter of time before I'd fallen for him completely."

"What happened to Houston?" Mick asked.

"I refused to leave him in limbo, so I told him about my feelings for Damon."

"Ugly scene," Damon leaned forward as one hand clenched into a fist. "It could've been worse, had I not arrived when I did."

Quest's and Quay's gazes narrowed in unison.

"Did he touch her?" Quest asked.

Damon grimaced. "I walked in just as he knocked her to the floor."

"Son of a bitch," Quest hissed, fists clenched.

"He's dead," Quay muttered matter-of-factly, already out of his chair.

"Damon!" Catrina urged. "Quay!" she called. "Boys please!" she cried.

Damon caught Quay's arm and pulled him close. "Believe me when I say I took great pleasure in handling it," he pushed Quay back to his seat and massaged both his sons shoulders before returning to his own chair.

"We never spoke on it again," Catrina went on, "we've managed to be civil to one another over the years, but I know the hatred is still there and simmering."

"Simmering more than you know," Mick said. "It's why he pushed the book so much. He was determined to see Quay or Quest pay for Sera's death-maybe not with a murder conviction, but a book highlighting the case would've put a definite blemish on their reputations."

"He was pretty much the same when the murder took place," Catrina noted.

"Yeah, for a while he was really pushing the cops to look into it," Damon added. "We knew it was because the room was in the boys' names. But then one day, he just let up and never mentioned another thing about it."

"It was because he knew there was even stronger evidence against him."

The group appeared stunned by Mick's revelation.

"Evidence against Houston?" Quay asked.

"Sera was having an affair with a married man. That man was Houston." Mick said.

"Houston?" Ty cried in disbelief.

Silence settled for a moment and then Damon told everyone about his conversation with Marcus aboard the train. He remembered accusing the man of covering for someone, but had assumed he was trying to protect one of his sons Moses, Yohan or Fernando.

"Not his sons, but his brother," Ty shook her head. "Why'd Houston kill her, Mick?"

"According to Sera's diary, she wanted him to leave his wife. He wouldn't," Mick recalled the words scribbled angrily in the girl's diary. "She said she wouldn't give up until he left Daphne- said she'd go tell her if he didn't."

"Do you really think he killed her, Michaela?" Catrina asked.

"I don't know," Mick trailed her fingers through her curls while leaning back in her chair. "But if the semen matches his, he'll be the prime suspect."

"So what now?" Quay asked.

"*Now*, he'll have to be tested and I doubt that'll happen in Seattle-his lawyers would rally around this quick," Mick warned. "Perhaps we'll have a better chance in Savannah. After all, they'd have jurisdiction, right?

"And how do we get him there?" Catrina asked.

"The wedding," Quest figured.

Damon nodded. "If we could get him down there, he'd be somewhat off kilter and it could be to our advantage."

"Honey this is your brother," Catrina whispered.

Damon kissed the back of her hand. "My brother wanted my sons to pay for a murder *he* committed."

While everyone mulled over the best way to get Houston to Savannah, Quay left his chair to kneel before Tykira's.

"How do you feel about this?" he massaged her knee. "This is your day. Everyone here would understand you not wanting it marred by some sting operation."

"That's right, Ty," Mick overheard Quay's words. "This can be handled in a whole other way."

"Thanks Mick," Ty smiled before turning back to Quay. "It's *our* day and we could've been together so long ago had it not been for all this. That jackass deserves to pay if he's guilty," she bit her lip when the words passed her mouth. "Sorry Mister D," she winced toward Damon who graced her with his striking grin.

"No apologies needed, love," he told her.

Ty nodded and then squeezed her fiancé's hand. "Let's do this."

A LOVER'S PRETENSE

~FIFTEEN~

Savannah, Georgia~

The home of Quentin and Marcella Ramsey had been the meeting place for virtually all the families' happiest gatherings. After the scandal that had rocked them; and with Quentin's and Marcella's deaths, the family had scattered. The beautiful estate was infrequently used.

Tykira Lowery was determined to change that. After all, this was the place where she and her future husband first made love. It was to be the place where they would vow to love each other forever. The property which had been a prosperous plantation was the picture of life. Busy caterers, musicians, florists and valets rushed about seeing to the needs of the arriving guests as well as food and entertainment. The brisk mid-November chill added a cozy feel to the festivities. The event would culminate with the wedding to take place the following evening.

~~~

"You mind?" Damon asked Marc, having found his brother in one of the sitting rooms that had been stocked with a full bar.

"Hmph, father of the year," Marc cajoled with a tired grin. "Can't believe you're about to have two married sons."

Damon knew the remark wasn't meant as a compliment. "Care to elaborate?" he was determined to keep his cool.

Marc shrugged. "Hell, what's there to elaborate on? Those two? Their lifestyles and attitudes... neither is the marrying kind."

"Be that as it may," Damon sighed, pouring a glass of Hennessy, "My boys know how to love."

"And what the hell does that mean? That some dig at my sons?" Marc snapped.

Damon took a swig of the liquor. "Not at your sons, just at their upbringing. You raised them to be suspicious of everyone- even their women," he fixed Marc with a knowing look. "You treated Josie like a possession and taught them to do the same with their women," Damon referred to Marcus' wife Josephine.

"I've watched all three of them lose wonderful ladies because they treated them like possessions- objects for their pleasure," Damon shook his head and turned back to the bar. "Thank God they're finally growing up and seeing the error in their ways."

"Who the devil do you think you are, D?!" Marc left his stool at the bar. "You come in here actin' all big to run down how I raised my boys? Why? Cause yours finally decided to walk down the aisle? Hell, I give both those marriages four years tops! If that!" he gave an indignant sniff.

Damon finished his drink and prepared to leave the bar.

"Hell, I see why Houston hates your ass," Marc rambled. "Possessions? Ha! You wanna talk to me about possessions? That's a laugh considering how you treated Catrina. You took her for your own even when she was on your brother's arm."

"Speaking of Houston," Damon refused to be riled by Marc's words, "did you know how far he was willing to go with Sera before she died?"

Marc appeared to stop breathing. "What are you getting at?"

"There's proof linking Houston to her death."

"You lie."

"Marc please don't waste my time acting like you didn't know that. After all, it's the reason you went to such lengths to protect him all these years, isn't it? Did you know what Houston was planning to do to that child?" Damon whispered when his brother remained silent.

Marc's deep set eyes narrowed with menacing intent toward his younger sibling. "That child was about to rip this family apart," he sneered.

Damon stood. "She was a baby- not even eighteen!"

"She was a conniving woman," Marcus corrected. "Slut, if you will. To let a man use her like that and then threaten to publicly expose him with adultery."

Damon shook his head, trying to will his heart to stop its frantic beating. "So you did know he was going to kill her?"

Marc smirked and turned away. "Your good son routine has no authority here, D. You ain't the police."

"Oh, so you'd prefer speaking with them? They're on their way, you know?"

Marcus turned swiftly. The smug expression he wore vanished.

Damon checked his watch. "They should be coming up the driveway any minute."

"What have you done?" Marc breathed.

"What should've been done long ago to give that girl's family some peace."

"Where's Houston?" Marc demanded.

Damon closed the distance between them. "I suggest you worry about yourself. The law don't look too kindly on accomplices either."

"Son of a bitch!" Marc slammed his beaded whiskey glass against the bar. "This isn't over," he raged.

"It is for our brother," Damon said before Marcus stormed

out of the room.

***

Tykira was going over last minute music selections for the reception when the door to Quentin Ramsey's study closed behind her. "Hey Houston," she greeted with a cool smile. "I'm glad you decided to join us."

The curiosity on Houston's face was a perfect match to the tone of his voice. "I was anxious to see how the place looked. You've done a wonderful job," he commended.

Ty nodded and looked around the study. "Well, truth is, I have to give most of the credit to your nephew. Quay's been more a part of this thing than I have. What?" She noticed the look Houston sent her.

Smoothing one hand across his close shaved head, the man grinned. "It's hard to picture Quay married. Are you certain about him, Tykira?"

"Why Houston, what an odd question," she pretended to be shocked.

"Sweetheart, forgive me, it's just that Quaysar Ramsey isn't exactly known for being a one woman man."

"I'm aware," Ty watched Houston approached her.

"Forgive me," he spread his hands in a defensive gesture, "the last thing I want to do is cloud your day, but you *are* a very beautiful woman," his eyes roamed her body with unmasked appreciation. "You have a lovely personality and I would hate to see a dog like Quay ruin you."

"Dog," Ty repeated, her brows rising. "Well Houston, I've hated Quay a long time. I hated him because all those years ago I loved him and I believed he didn't love me," she turned back to rummage through the pile of CDs and vintage albums cluttering the desk. "It wasn't until I finally went back to Seattle that I discovered he was trying to protect me."

"Protect you?" Houston's gaze narrowed inquisitively.

"Mmm…against a *shameful* bastard who held a vendetta against Quay and Quest because of some old grudge he held

454

against their parents. *Shameful bastard* wreaked havoc," she continued still rifling through music as she spoke, "especially on Quay because he couldn't touch his real enemy- Damon. Quay was so outspoken, so outwardly confident- just like Damon. So in order to drain him of some of that confidence, *shameful bastard*, started targeting the women Quay was interested in. He'd get 'em to leave town or just disappear. Then came Sera Black who wanted a Ramsey and was quite interested in Quay. Then she met *shameful bastard* who proceeded to have an affair with her without a care for his wife and kids. He had a real good time too, until Sera demanded he leave his wife or else," Ty shrugged, "then she, too had to go. You can see how all this would affect Quay. He wanted nothing to do with me because he wanted me to hate him, to leave him alone, to get me as far away as possible before the *shameful bastard* realized he had another victim."

Once Tykira finished her theory, Houston could barely contain himself. His chest heaved beneath the worsted fabric of the three-piece light blue suit he wore. His hands shook noticeably as he tugged upon the white tie around his neck.

"Tykira are you trying to tell me that you -you know someone-someone else was responsible for Se-Sera's murder?" he managed to ask.

"Precisely," Ty confirmed, tossing her hair across her shoulders.

"Based on information Quay got from that Wake Robinson friend of his?" Houston smirked. "Love, I'm afraid without proof-"

"Oh there *is* proof, Houston."

"May I ask what?"

Ty took her selection of CDs to the shelving near the room door. "Oh, proof that was buried. Not destroyed like *shameful bastard* and his equally shameful brother thought. Thankfully, the man who agreed to do away with said evidence had a crisis of conscience on his sick bed," she turned to stroll back to the center of the room. "Then, there's Sera's diary which names *shameful bastard*." She concluded.

Houston shuddered, fighting a losing battle against trying

to maintain his cool. "Shall I guess who, Miss Lowery?"

Ty smiled. "Why no, Mr. Ramsey. You know all too well."

"Houston Ramsey?"

The study door opened and Detective Jillian Red arrived with several uniformed and plainclothes officers.

"Houston Ramsey, I'm Detective Red-Savannah Police. We'd like you to come with us, Sir," Jill requested.

"I'll do no such thing," Houston barked. "What's the meaning of this?"

"Sera Black," Jill nodded to two of the officers who went to stand on either side of Houston. "We have some questions for you regarding her murder."

Houston feigned ignorance. "What would I know about that? Whatever your questions, you can save them for the appropriate party," his voice began to tremble. "Now get out of my parents' home."

"Very well Mr. Ramsey. If you'd just come with us."

"On what evidence?" Houston thundered.

"Based on evidence we have that you and Miss Black were having an affair and semen taken from her body on the night of the murder, we're also requesting a DNA sample. This will hopefully rule you out as a suspect, Mr. Ramsey. It would look far better if you cooperated without being summoned by a court order."

"Preposterous!" Houston raged, knowing he was running out of time. "I'm a married man. How dare you accuse me of-" he stopped himself, watching as Michaela entered the room and handed something to Jill.

"Sera Black's diary," Mick explained to her husband's uncle. "That and a positive match to the semen should help the DA form her case."

"Thanks for your help, Mick," Jill said, "Shall we, Mr. Ramsey?"

"You little bitch!" Houston hissed, charging toward Michaela. The uniformed officer stopped him cold. "How dare you turn this around on me?! I came to *you* with this!"

"Mmm, all a part of your plan to frame the nephews you

hated, right? Mick surmised.

Houston struggled against the officer's restraining hold. "You scheming little- you were never good enough for this family. You-Marc?! Marcus!" he cried, having spotted his brother barging toward the room.

Marc fought his way past the officers filling the doorway. It seemed that much of the family had gotten wind of the uproar, for the entire corridor was filled with people.

"Marcus!" Houston literally cried, tears pooled his eyes and wet his cheeks. "Do you see what they're doing? Help me! Marc!"

"I'll take care of it Houston, calm down!" Marcus urged his younger brother, jostling the officers who kept him from reaching Houston. "Go and answer their questions and I'll be there when you're done," he bartered watching as the officers ushered his brother out of the room. Marc would've left behind them, but he caught sight of Mick. "It was you," he sneered.

"No, it was your brother," Mick folded her arms across the sweatshirt she wore. "I would suggest you get him a lawyer."

"A good one," Ty added.

"You little whoreish bitches," Marcus seethed, turning his full fury on Michaela and Tykira. "Mark my words, you two sluts will pay for what you've done to my family."

Quest and Quay had been virtually silent as they stood side by side and viewed the scene from the study's wide entryway. Hearing their uncle say such vile things to the women they loved, stoked their anger in unison.

"Whoa guys," Damon caught each of his sons by the elbow. It did little good as his children kept moving forward, practically dragging their father behind him.

Just as they twins reached their uncle, they were shoved aside by an even greater force.

The crowd watched in stunned silence as Yohan Ramsey caught his father by the neck and lifted the man from the floor.

"Son of a bitch!" Yohan raged. "I will not listen to you speak to another woman this way! You hear me, Pop?!" Yohan's massive hands encircled Marcus' neck. "I let you run Mel away with this haughty bullshit. Not again!"

No one, not even Yohan's older brothers dared intervene just then. Everyone knew his loss of temper was long overdue. The massive, darkly beautiful young man rarely lost his temper. Those who had seen it happen before, felt a shudder of fear for Marcus. The group watched as Yohan carried away his father. The study cleared as almost everyone followed on their heels.

~~~

The argument spilled into the split-level ballroom. Yohan shoved his father inside none too gently. The caterers and florists who were there preparing for the wedding, needed no coercion to leave the room. Fernando and Moses assured the family that everything would be fine and closed the ballroom's double doors on questioning faces.

"Han please," Josephine Ramsey urged her son, her hands clasped as she prayed frantically.

"Come on, Yo," Fernando urged, using his own considerable strength to restrain his younger brother. "You don't want to do this, man," he whispered,

Moses tried as well. "He's right, Yo. He ain't worth it, man."

Marcus' dark eyes narrowed in surprise. He looked upon his sons with renewed realization and saw no trace of love in their eyes.

"Yohan please," Josephine cried.

"You knew, didn't you?" Yohan grated, his hands still gripping Marcus' neck. "You knew what Houston did to Sera, didn't you? Didn't you?!"

"Afterwards," Marcus gasped, "Later- much later, please-" he sputtered and coughed to catch his breath. "Please believe me, son."

"I don't believe a damn thing you say," Yohan growled, his grip beginning to loosen. "I never would've lost her if I hadn't believed every word that came out of your lying mouth," his thoughts returned to his estranged wife Melina. "But Mo's right," he stepped away letting Marc drop. You ain't worth it," he muttered.

"We have to stick together," Marc cleared his throat while massaging his sore neck. "The family-"

"Aw Pop, save that crap," Moses urged.

"Yeah, Pop, I don't think you got a leg to stand on with that family honor bullshit anymore," Fernando added.

"What will happen to Houston?" Josephine asked her husband in hopes of shifting the conversation and steering male tempers from another flare-up.

"Ma, I think Hous is done for," Fernando answered for his father.

"In light of this evidence, I second that," Moses added, clapping Yohan's shoulder as they stepped away from Marcus.

"You think they'll match him to this semen?" Josephine watched her sons nod.

"It'd be pretty foolish of him to refuse giving the cops a DNA sample," Moses continued, "it'd be almost like admitting his guilt. And then there's Wake Robinson and Sera's diary."

"Where the hell it came from is what I'd like to know," Fernando said.

"Sera's mother probably gave it to Mick," Moses surmised.

Josephine stumbled as though she were losing strength to stand. Her boys rushed to her side.

"Are you alright?" Yohan kissed her temple.

"Mmm," Josephine nodded, managing a faint smile. "Just a bit light headed."

Fernando's gaze was intent as he studied his mother. His hand clenched unconsciously and he was suddenly overcome by the same rage that held his brother moments earlier.

"Fernando?" Josephine called taking note of her middle son's distress. "What is it?"

Fernando leaned down to kiss her hand. "You relax. I'll be back before the wedding, I promise."

"Where you off to, man?" Moses asked.

Fernando slanted a glare toward Marcus who kept his

distance on the other side of the room. "Some things I need to look into," he said.

***

Quaysar and Tykira remained in the study long after everyone took off behind Yohan and Marcus.

Ty stood close to the door, shaking her head as she replayed the earlier scene in her head. Quay shook her ponytail in his hand, before pulling her back against his chest.

"Wanna tell me about it?" he asked.

Ty continued to shake her head. "I don't think I could put it into words," she marveled.

Quay bowed his head to inhale the softness of the perfume that clung to the fuzzy raspberry sweater she wore. "You sure you wanna be part of such a dysfunctional group?" he teased, but realized he was reluctant to hear her response.

"No Quay, I'm not sure," she whispered, missing the helplessness and hurt that flashed in her fiancé's beautiful deep-set eyes. After a moment, she turned in his arms. "But I am sure that I want to be a part of *you*. And since your family comes with the package, I'll have to accept that."

Quay closed his eyes as though he were giving thanks. "I love you," he gathered her close.

"I love you too," Ty giggled when she felt his fingers beneath her sweater. "What are you doing?" she laughed.

"Well if you gotta ask, I guess I need to try harder," his lips brushed her cheek before suckling her earlobe.

Ty arched closer to enjoy the caress. Her nails grazed the back of his head and she shivered when his hands cupped both her breasts. Quay sought her mouth and favored her with a throaty kiss. Their moans rose in unison. Ty was loudest, her cries infrequently muffled as she thrust her tongue eagerly against his.

Quay's brows drew close as a swell of emotion rushed him. Slowly, his fingers slipped beneath the waistband of her jeans. A second later, he'd unsnapped them and was lowering the zipper.

"Quay!" Ty gasped, pulling back at last. "Wait," she shook

her head, swallowed. "We can't. Not now."

The determination on his face offered no clue to whether he heard her or not. His tongue nuzzled within her mouth again, completely taking Ty's mind off her protests. A shuddery sound lilted from her throat when his middle finger slipped inside her panties. He stroked her femininity with deep possessive thrusts that drenched his finger with her need.

"Quay," she called, attempting to triumph over the sensational feelings stemming from the erotic caress. "Sweetie, there's a house full of people."

"And?" he backed her against the study door while his fingers continued to work their magic.

Ty surrendered briefly to the delicious thrusts that were dampening the middle of her panties and forcing her to powerful orgasm.

Quay's sinfully gorgeous face was a picture of satisfaction. "You want me to stop?"

Tykira took several seconds to respond. "I-we should go check on things down there..."

With his free hand, Quay propped up her chin. "I have everything I care about right here."

***

The next morning, Tykira woke to the sound of her mother's humming. Bobbie Lowery flitted around the master suite removing wrappings from her daughter's wedding gown, shoes and other accompaniments. Hearing her daughter's yawn, drew her attention instantly.

"Hey sleepy, you excited about the big day?" Bobbie called, strolling towards the bed. "And just to be clear, I'm talking about your wedding day and not that mess yesterday."

Ty laughed. "I know, Mommie."

"Listen honey," Bobbie took a seat on the edge of the bed. "I have no doubt of your love for Quay and I know he feels the same for you. But you have to know that in marrying him, you'll be claiming *all* the Ramseys and they ain't an easy lot to belong to."

Ty was nodding. "I know Mommie. I had this very talk with Quay yesterday. Don't worry," she patted her mother's hand. "The Ramseys won't be in my door every night."

"Precisely- and there are those in that family who dislike being shut out. Keeping to yourself, having your own life, being content with your husband without their involvement can rattle lots of feathers. You're getting a pretty decent mother and father-in-law, but you watch yourself with the rest of those jackasses and be careful."

Ty laughed louder that time. "Mommie! What would your employees say if they heard you?"

Bobbie waved her hand. "Forget em," she drawled, joining her daughter in laughter as they shared a tight hug.

~~~

A sharp curse sounded in the otherwise silent area of Quest and Mick's guest room just a few doors down from where Ty and Bobbie chatted. Michaela heard her husband's outburst clearly. Her face was a picture of curiosity when she came rushing out of their private bathroom. Quest was on the phone and Mick waited. She listened, not able to gain much from the disturbing cell phone conversation. The moment he ended the call, she raised her hands to prompt his explanation.

"They lost Houston."

"What? How?"

Quest shook his head and tapped his index finger to Mick's chin when he passed her. "This is Savannah, baby. The family's still got a lot of *well-meaning* friends down here."

Sadness clouded Mick's features and she took a seat on an armchair near the bathroom door. "I so wanted to tell Johnelle that we had Sera's murderer behind bars."

"I'm sorry you heard me on the phone," Quest knelt to capture her hands in his. "I didn't want this upsetting you."

Mick smiled, watching him press kisses to the backs of her hands. "I'm fine. I'm fine," she repeated when he looked up at her.

"I worked hard to give Johnelle answers and she knows more today than she did before. Now, the only mother I'm concerned about is me."

Her words were like music to his ears. Quest closed his eyes and rested his head in her lap.

***

Quay had journeyed to his grandfather's smoking room for a drink alone. He'd been there little over fifteen minutes when his father found him.

"You better not be having second thoughts!" Damon teased, joining his son in the intimidating maple paneled room. "Tykira's too beautiful to let get away. Besides, I've been rooting for this since you two were younger," he shared.

"Dad," Quay grinned, surprise tinging his words. "Since way back then?"

"You shouldn't be surprised," Damon poured a bit of burgundy and then waved the canister in Quay's direction.

"I'm good," Quay said.

"Anyway, it was easy to see how you two felt about one another."

Quay's lashes settled over his eyes as a wave of rage pierced through him. "Thank God Houston didn't see it."

"Do you really think he would've hurt her?" Damon leaned against the bar.

"I really do, Dad," Quay replied without hesitation. "Girls I was interested in-we were just foolin' around. Nothing like it was with Ty...it wasn't love with them and they disappeared just the same. He had a hand in that too, I know it."

"I knew he was capable of a lot of things, but never of an evil like that- to murder..." Damon shook his head as he strode over to his son. "I'm proud of you boy," he clapped Quay's shoulder. "You did everything you did to keep the woman you love safe from a monster."

"And I almost lost her in the process."

Damon leaned down, cupping the back of Quay's head.

"The operative word being *almost*. Just don't let it happen again," he landed a playful slap to Quay's jaw.

Father and son shared a close hug for several minutes and then Damon pulled back.

"Let's go get your lady," he said.

***

Quest and Michaela decided to keep Houston's sudden disappearance away from the family until all the festivities had ended. In truth, they hadn't thought much else about it once the wedding events began. The entire group was elated and truly happy for the bride and groom. People mingled, danced and ate from the huge pre-ceremony spread. The gathering was made even lovelier by the fact that Marcus had decided not to attend. Many thought little of it and it seemed that no one really missed him or Houston.

~~~

Tykira and Bobbie arrived in the entryway to the room where the vows would be exchanged. Ty stood mesmerized by the enchanting scene that met her eyes. It was to be a night wedding and the sunroom was a vision of candlelight that flickered and danced all about. The room of glass windows and ceiling offered a captivating view of the starry wintery sky. A cello, flute, violin and oboe quartet completed the fairytale like ambience.

Ty was a vision of classy chic in a creation of chiffon and satin. The gown itself was straight and accentuated her tall, svelte figure. The empire waistline cinched right below her breasts to emphasize their fullness. The sleeves were long and tapered to her wrists while a straight coat of chiffon trailed behind. The coat's upturned collar flattered the graceful line of her neck that was adorned by a thin silver necklace, her only jewelry.

Bobbie barely managed to keep her tears at bay. Tykira looked down at her mother and chuckled at her emotional state. Bobbie uttered a quick 'shhh' in response.

"My big girl," Bobbie cooed, pulling Ty close then. "All

my love and happiness. You've waited so long," she fiddled with the spiral curls that fell from Ty's upswept coiffure to frame her face.

"It was worth the wait, Mommie," Ty sniffled when she and her mother pulled apart.

Bobbie cupped Ty's face and then turned to signal the quartet leader who instructed the group to segue into the wedding march.

Satisfied, Bobbie nodded and winked at her daughter. "Let's go get your man," she said.

Arm in arm, the two strode the aisle. Everyone 'ahhed' or grew misty eyed over the beautiful picture Ty made as well as the fact that her mother was giving her away.

Tykira prayed she wouldn't stumble when she caught sight of Quaysar. He stood between Quest-the best man- and the minister. He was riveting in a gorgeous black satin tux. His gaze was smoldering and intense and he watched Tykira as though there were nothing and no one else in the room.

Side by side, the bride and groom turned to the minister who had married Quay's parents. Sniffles could be heard from the audience as the minister delivered his sage words. The minute snap and crackle of the candles sounded ever so often. Then, the minister announced that the couple had vows to speak. He instructed Tykira to begin. Smiling demurely, she took a deep breath before turning to Quay.

"I loved you the first time I met you Quay. Security and protection always surrounded me whenever you were near and somehow I always knew that no bad thing would ever touch me as long as you existed. My love for you never died or dwindled even through our darkest times." She squeezed his hands tightly. "The only place I will ever want to be is by your side. I'll love you forever."

The minister nodded and then instructed Quaysar to begin.

"Tyke, I believe I loved you before I even knew I liked girls." He cleared his throat and looked adorably nervous while the audience chuckled over his opening statement. "There've been so

465

many ups and downs," he continued, "I've done so many things to make myself forget you when our darkest times seemed they would never end. But I could never stop loving you. Now and forever the *only* place I'll ever want you to be is by my side." He raised both her hands and pressed a kiss to the back of each. "I love you. Always."

The minister cleared his throat to speak his binding words. "Now, by the power vested in me by the state of Georgia, I pronounce you husband and wife. Quaysar you may kiss your bride."

Cheers rose seconds after Quay pulled Ty into a crushing embrace.

"Sisters and Brothers, may I present Mr. and Mrs. Quaysar and Tykira Ramsey!" The minister announced.

Everyone rushed to their feet with more cheers and applause. Quay already had his wife in his arms and was carrying her down the aisle amidst a sea of colorful confetti and best wishes.

~~~

"Quay where are we going?" Ty inquired, breathless from laughing. She saw that her husband hadn't stopped walking. He headed right out of the sunroom, through the house and down the majestic front porch steps to the carriage that waited out front. "I thought we were taking a car to the airport?" she said.

Quay's midnight eyes twinkled gleefully as he settled her into the carriage. "Patience, Mrs. Ramsey."

Thoroughly content, Ty snuggled next to her husband when he joined her inside the cozy carriage. The walkway was lined with brass lamps that shed golden light to mark the path. Eventually, Ty realized they weren't headed for the road, but deeper into the estate. She steeled herself against asking more questions and waited. Her eyes narrowed when she spotted a construction coming into view.

"Quay," she gasped, finally realizing where they were. "I had no idea it was still here. I didn't even want to ask," she clutched his hand while looking upon the quaint cottage where she and Quay first made love so long ago. It had obviously been completely refurbished for it looked newly built and freshly painted where it sat in the middle of the moonlit forest.

Quay left the carriage and walked around to open her side. He cupped her face, holding her still before she could exit. "This place. *Our* place will always be here and *we'll* be here for at least a week," he dropped a kiss to her nose.

"An entire week?" Ty marveled as he pulled her from the carriage and into his arms once more. "Just the two of us?" she smoothed her fingertips across his jaw.

Quay shrugged. "With the exception of the caretakers and security guards who know they'll be taking their lives into their own hands if they even *think* about disturbing us."

Ty looked back toward the cottage. "I never dreamed the next time I saw this place I would be your wife."

Quay stopped walking then. He planted a tender kiss just below her ear. "My wife, my love, my life," he vowed.

Dear Reader,

Thank you for indulging in what; for me, has been, a tremendously, enjoyable, educational and passionate experience. The Ramsey saga has tested my abilities as both an author and reader. In writing it, I have learned and continue to learn the subtle nuances that make the romantic suspense genre such an intensely emotional reading experience. I do hope you've enjoyed the wild ride between two very different couples; Quest and Mick and Quay and Ty, as well as the secondary characters and sub-plots that define the beginnings of this series.

I hope that your reading of these first two novels will encourage you to delve into the remainder of the saga. You will find the titles marking the series listed here following this letter. I always enjoy the thoughts of my readers and ask that you communicate your thoughts to me anytime.
Thank you for supporting the work. I hope you will enjoy the rest of the series.

Blessings,

AlTonya Washington

altonya@lovealtonya.com
altonya@alsreaders.com
https://www.facebook.com/altonyaw
https://twitter.com/Ramseysgirl

~THE RAMSEY (AND TESANO) SAGA~

A Lover's Dream
A Lover's Pretense
A Lover's Mask
A Lover's Regret
A Lover's Worth
A Lover's Beauty
A Lover's Soul
Lover's Allure
A Ramsey Wedding
Lover's Origin
Book of Scandal: The Ramsey Elders
A Lover's Shame
A Lover's Hate
A Lover's Sin
A Lover's Christmas
Vestige
A Lover's Debt

###

An AlTonya Exclusive

www.ingramcontent.com/pod-product-compliance
Lightning Source LLC
Chambersburg PA
CBHW030748030726
47497CB00001B/185